# IN THE HOLLOW OF THE DEEP-SEA WAVE

*By the same author*

Witchwater Country
Spiral Winds

# IN THE HOLLOW OF THE DEEP-SEA WAVE

## A Novel and Seven Stories

GARRY KILWORTH

THE BODLEY HEAD
LONDON

*Feral Moon* was first published in *The Fiction Magazine*, *The Thunder of the Captains* in Isaac Asimov's magazine, and *Filming the Making of the Film of the Making of 'Fitzcarraldo'* in *Omni* magazine

A CIP catalogue record for this book is available from the British Library.

ISBN: 0–370–31265–1



Printed in Great Britain for
The Bodley Head Ltd
31 Bedford Square, London WC1B 3SG
by Mackays of Chatham PLC, Chatham, Kent
Typeset by Gloucester Typesetting Services

*First published in 1989*

# Contents

On Jonson's Atoll, the word *carpenter* is synonymous with *creator*, since there was a time when all artefacts on the islands were made of wood. If you created anything at all, you were a *kapenta*. Thus, in the pidgin (the beauty of which is in its simplicity) just as every living plant, tree or blade of grass is *stick*, and every living animal form, whether bee or elephant, is *beef*, so a Japanese painter, a boatbuilder, a man who carves coral heads, and even the Christian God, are all *kapentas*: those who create pictures, sailing ships, tombstones and waves upon the sea.

To Dennis Potter, whose film option on
my novel *The Night of Kadar*
helped me through lean years.

# One

The girl lay motionless on the white coral dust. Beyond the rainforest, on the beaches, dancing was still in progress, the drums beating out a rhythm conceived in another age. Close by, the waves tore relentlessly at the fringing reef. There was a bright moon, above him.

The teacher wiped away the sweat from his forehead with the back of his hand and noticed that he clutched a rock in his fingers. It was stained with the girl's blood. He let it fall from his grasp. He realised, now, that he was trembling violently, and he steadied himself against a palm tree.

Panic concerning his own safety was held at bay with great difficulty. He knew what he had done: he had raped and killed a young girl, a child of fifteen. If the islanders found him, they would cut him down where he stood. Normally a placid race, they had the Asiatic temperament and would act before their blood cooled. He knew he had to get away, but where could he run to? He was on a coral island, surrounded by thousands of square miles of ocean.

He gathered some dead palm leaves and threw them over the girl's body in an untidy heap. If only she had not started screaming! It was the screaming that had made him panic. Then she had sunk her teeth into him, under his left armpit. The pain had been incredible. He had not been able to make her let go, even when his other hand had found the lump of coral and he had begun beating her with it. Only when he had struck her temple had she finally released him. The torn flap of skin beneath his arm was still excruciatingly painful.

The teacher turned and began running towards the reef. There was an idea in his head that he could take the reef path and cross to Short Island, where the priest lived. He was the only other European on the atoll.

Would Father Maurer help him? Did the Church provide sanctuary in this day and age? Why should it? He was a murderer. Father Maurer would be just as horrified, just as enraged, as the islanders themselves.

The teacher slowed to a walk again as these doubts entered his mind.

On reaching a certain path, he changed his direction, and ran instead towards his house. He avoided going through the centre of the village and entered the dwelling from the rear, without being seen. He changed his clothes and strapped on his money belt. He had remembered the Arab boom, anchored just off the islands. The thing to do, he decided, was to swim out to it and ask them to take him with them on the tide. It was his only chance.

The dhow was anchored between Jorka and Tubb Islands. He waded out towards it, as far as he could, then began swimming. For the first time since he had landed on the islands, he did not consider the sharks as he splashed through the water. There were worse nightmares to consider back there in the rainforest.

Along the reef, the waves clawed to get at him. He allowed himself to be taken by the current, towards the heavy-looking wooden craft, with its big-bellied hull and patched sail. When he reached it, the teacher grabbed the anchor chain and yelled, 'Hey? Anybody there?'

After a minute some of the crew appeared at the side.

'Can I come on board?' cried the teacher.

They stared at him blankly, their dark faces almost black with shadow.

'The captain,' he shouted. 'Fetch me the captain.'

Still no movement amongst them, yet he knew some of them spoke the island pidgin he was using.

A Somali grinned at him.

The teacher struggled with his money belt and eventually unclasped it, waving it over his head while still clinging to the chain with his other hand.

'Money!' he cried.

They threw him a rope and hauled him on board. A few minutes later the boom set sail for the coast of Africa.

# Two

To coral islanders, the sea is a loving mother and a mass murderer in one. We love it, and we hate it. It provides for us, fills our tables and our pockets, yet it snatches victims from amongst us, sometimes by the handful. When I lived in England, I stayed in Brighton. I used to watch visitors go down to the shore and inevitably they would begin throwing stones at the water. At first, I sympathised with this activity. I had often felt like punishing the sea myself.

It was some time before I realised that I had endowed the stone-throwers with the wrong motives. The act was too subconscious to be a deliberate chastisement of the waters. There was a faraway look on the faces of the throwers. They hardly thought about what they were doing. The ocean was there, vast and awesome, and they were drawn to its edge, automatically stooping to find a pebble to toss into its waves.

Then I knew what it was!

They were trying to fill the waters with stones, to bury the sea beneath them. They had, even those who were used to living by it, a deep-rooted fear of the ocean. It was too big, too mighty, too uncontained.

Coral islanders know there is only one way to treat the sea: as an old-fashioned, bountiful god with occasional irrational bouts of savage temper. Once in a while such gods need a sacrifice.

The school teacher was typical of most European and American visitors to the atoll. He came armed with the intention of penetrating our culture as quickly as possible, and of giving us the benefit of his experience and knowledge during the two years he intended staying amongst us. In a way these are quite laudable goals, except that they presuppose areas of ignorance on our part and a rather high opinion of outside values on his.

He arrived by ship from Sri Lanka. I had been waiting for him for several days and had passed the time line-fishing in the lagoon. When the rusty old cargo vessel had appeared over the horizon, I had asked Uncle Letushim if he would ferry the teacher to me in a *dhoni* canoe, before helping to offload the supplies with the other small craft.

I watched the teacher walk down the short quay made of driftwood: slow, unsteady steps after the rolling deck of the ship. He carried two canvas bags and was overdressed. He was a handsome man: tall, lean and athletic-looking. Although he had a blond moustache, he appeared younger than his twenty-six years.

He stopped when he reached the sand and looked at me a little uncertainly. Some of his confidence had no doubt been drained by the voyage in that unstable tub now moored in the lagoon. The fact that there was no welcoming committee had probably shattered another illusion.

I retrieved my line, laid it on the beach and then picked up my golfing umbrella. Under its shade, I went to meet the new man.

'Can I help you with your things?' I asked.

He gave me a sort of pallid, weary smile and said, 'Thanks,' handing one of the bags to me. I had spoken in my own language; a mixture of our own form of English and Divehi spoken in the Maldive Islands, Jonson's Atoll being part of the same archipelago as the better-known Maldives. No language is pure these days, but ours is probably stranger than most. Spoken slowly, it sounds like the pidgin English of nineteenth-century boys' adventure books, but the several Divehi words and phrases injected into it make it a difficult tongue to understand.

'That's very good of you . . . are you alone? I expect all the others are helping to unload the ship?'

His diction and accent were good. The language professor at Cambridge, Millicent Wilson, had obviously taught him well.

'Welcome to Jonson's Atoll. My name is Nathan.'

He stared at me curiously, and he nodded. They would have told him about me, in England, at his interview.

'You're the one they sent to be trained. Didn't you want to take up the teaching post here?'

'No,' I said, then added, 'you look as though you don't approve.'

He frowned. 'It seems a waste – all that time and expense for nothing. Still, I expect you have your reasons. I wouldn't be here if you had decided to take over from Peter Goodwright, so I should be thankful you didn't.'

'I think you'll enjoy it here,' I told him. 'Plenty of sun, sea and sand. It's what most of us want, isn't it? A place in the sun – paradise isle.

This isn't far short of it. I never used to think that way as a boy, but since I've been abroad . . .'

He held up his hand as if my chatter were painful to him. I was showing off, speaking in English, and it was this he wished to call a halt to. He remained with the pidgin as he said, 'You speak English very well. I suppose I shouldn't be surprised.'

'I went to an English School in the Maldives – a school for the children of service families when the Royal Air Force had a base on Gan Island. Then my teacher training, of course. Anyway, most of us speak *some* English. We are the descendants of Englishmen, after all.'

A mutiny on a British ship, similar to that which took place on the *Bounty*, supplemented our meagre population in the early part of the nineteenth century. The mutineers were never caught and exist within us today. Recently, as this fact has become more widely known, we were given the nickname, 'The Other Pitcairn'.

'I'll show you to your house,' I said. 'You're on the leeward side of the island – a little place out of the wind. One of the privileges accorded to the school teacher.'

He stared at the coral-dust path that disappeared into the trees. Then he glanced down the deserted beaches, with their palms bowing to the lagoon. Finally, he turned to me again.

'Isn't anyone else coming to meet me?'

I smiled and said rather cruelly, 'We don't go in for things like that. No garlands or songs of welcome.'

He looked a little piqued.

'But aren't they just a little curious? I would have thought that a new teacher . . .'

'They've already seen you in your predecessor, Peter Goodwright. Any curiosity they had has been satisfied by him. You may look on yourself as a unique individual – but to them you're just the teacher. Not even the *new* teacher. Just the teacher.'

I thought he would question me on the strangeness of my reply, but he must have been weary and probably the whole thing was becoming too much for him to absorb in one day. He shrugged and looked back at the ship, which was now moving away towards the horizon. Ringed by a constantly changing wall of white surf foaming over the reef, he was trapped in our circle of islands. I felt sorry for him. I knew how he felt: a stranger in a strange land. I had once experienced the same feeling, in an exotic place called Brighton – a place which had terrified me at first. At least the islands were not frightening to someone like him:

not on the surface. If he ever cared to look a little deeper he might have cause for some concern, but it seemed he was not going to do that.

'The breakers,' he said, 'they look higher than the island.'

'I know. It bothers me, too.'

'Really?' He regarded me thoughtfully for a few moments. Then he said, 'I suppose I'd better see where I'm going to live,' and started along the coral path, wisely removing his jacket as he walked.

We passed beneath the frangipani trees, some of them over thirty feet high, with their multi-coloured blossoms. He studied them as if he approved of their presence. They were, no doubt, the kind of exotic touch he had been hoping for. When we reached the village the tall, coarse *alang* grass on either side of the path gave way to hard-packed earth.

We crossed the village, the teacher looking curiously into wood-and-thatch houses, presumably for signs of people. Most were down at the shore, helping unload supplies from the small craft.

There was another short path on the far side of the village which led to the teacher's house.

Of course, he was delighted with it, small as it is. It is the only stone-built establishment on the atoll. We had the bricks imported. The design is simple – square and squat – but it has a veranda and a small garden in the front. Waste shower water is channelled through small irrigation ditches between the shrubs, and the white, ancient residue of soap still clings to the banks. The plants do not seem to mind detergents.

I left his bag on the veranda and opened the screen door for him. It was cooler inside, though the ceiling fan was not working. He noticed the switches on the wall and tried one.

'Electricity?'

I explained that while we had a large generator for the island, it was only used during the evening hours, to conserve fuel.

'The supply ship only comes once every six months,' I said.

'What about cooking?'

'Charcoal. We make it ourselves. I'll see you get a good supply of that.'

He nodded, without thanking me, and strolled around the house peering into corners and cupboards. I saw him stare hard at the British Army surplus bedstead, standing like an iron beast with its legs in four cans of water.

'Why the boots?' he asked, pointing at the bedlegs.

'Bugs. The cans stop them crawling up the legs – so the teacher said.

I told him that they drop from the ceiling anyway, but he took no notice. Best to drag the mattress out into the sun once a week. They hate the sunlight.'

His face was blank of expression.

'What do they look like?'

I went to the bed and peeled back the mattress seam. They were there, in a neat red-black row, like flat beads. Taking one, I put it on the floor and stamped on it with my bare heel. It staggered away into a crack in the floorboards.

'Can't do anything to them, while they're empty,' I said, 'but once they're full of blood you can burst them with your nails.'

'Blood?' He stared at the mattress in revulsion. 'Maybe I'll sleep on the veranda until I get rid of those. Anything else?'

'No. One or two snakes, but harmless. All the really dangerous things are in the sea – coral snakes, stone fish, sharks . . .'

'Yes, yes, sting rays, lion fish – I did *some* homework. I was just making sure.'

'Big spiders.' I spread my fingers and scuttled them over a chair arm. 'Hairy too.'

Suddenly he grinned at me. There was a boyish slant to his mouth.

'You're enjoying this, aren't you? Where did you do your training? In England, I mean?'

'Brighton by the sea. They thought it would make me feel less homesick.'

'Others students give you a hard time?'

'No.'

'Oh – I thought maybe you were paying me back for something.'

I realised what he was talking about and said, 'We don't work like that here. At least, not in such a crude fashion. We've refined the art.'

'What art?' It was his turn to look puzzled.

'The art of revenge. What you're saying is that because your countrymen treated me badly, I might be using you as a scapegoat.'

'It's been known.'

I did not reply. I had already said too much. I left him then, to get on with his unpacking, and went back to my fishing. Looking back over my shoulder, just before I left the village on the far side, I saw that he was dragging the mattress out on to the veranda.

The red snappers were biting well and I found the solitude of the beach good for my soul after talking with the Englishman. I made a small bet with myself, as I sat on the hot sands, watching the land crabs build their cones, their stalk eyes forever twitching. I made a bet with myself that the Englishman would be by very soon.

Just before noon he came trotting along, under the palms that formed a half-arch over the beach, wearing running shorts and T-shirt. He had been for a jog, a circuit around the island. They were so predictable, these Europeans. An Arab or an Indian would take weeks to embark upon such a tour, and then it would be a stately walk.

The sweat was pouring from his face and the back of his shirt was soaked. The temperature was in the thirties.

'Two miles long and a mile wide,' I called to him. 'You'll know every inch of it after three weeks.'

'I intend to,' he grunted, walking on. Then he turned. 'When do I get to meet the others?'

'You could meet some of them now – or this evening, after you've rested.'

'I'll wait until this evening.'

I thought he was going to continue his run, but he came back to me then, and waved his arm at the circle of islands.

'Can you give me a quick rundown,' he asked, 'on the atoll? I know this is Tubb Island – and that's Long Island to our left. What's the one on the right?'

He pointed to Jorka Island, where stood the giant coral heads of my ancestors. The white monoliths glinted in the sunlight. My own father was amongst them – and my grandparents – and their grandparents. It was where we were buried after death, the heavy coral heads protecting our souls from *midnight walkers*.

'You would call that Ghost Island. Then comes Pork, and over on the far side of the lagoon is Short Island – that's where the church is . . . and the priest lives there too.'

'Father Maurer, isn't it? Does he come over here, to Tubb?'

'Of course, when he feels it's necessary. He visits all five islands.'

'How does he travel? By canoe?'

'Sometimes, but it's possible to walk around the reef at low tide. It forms a circle, joining all the islands. Just remember to wear something on your feet and to make sure you know the state of the tide, that's all. Otherwise, it's not a dangerous route.'

Jonson's Atoll is on the lip of an extinct, submerged volcano, overgrown with coral. The ring of coral around the wide mouth of the cone pokes above the surface of the sea in five places and these exposed pieces are the islands. They stand about four feet above sea level, although the rainforest makes them seem higher than this. We are like five fragments of a single town, separated by narrow stretches of water.

The teacher left me to my fishing and further contemplation.

I am proud of the islands – more so since I have been away to foreign lands. This is a beautiful part of the earth. At sunset, a sudden event in equatorial regions, the fruit bats glide between the palms and the only sound is that of the waves breaking on the fringing reef. Then, as darkness descends, the chorus of rainforest creatures, the frogs and crickets, fills the night air. They sing until the dawn's rays fall on the frangipanis, which cover the coral paths with blossoms.

There are insects like flowers here, and birds like blown blooms. Nature merges its living things, until it is difficult to tell them apart. The lagoon and waters outside the fringing reef abound with fish that were created by some mad artist with a flair for the grotesque. Colour is everywhere. We eat and drink colour every day of our lives.

The Indian Ocean, a forever of blue water, ensures our isolation from the outside world. I have a circular horizon, beyond which are hundreds of miles of deep ocean. Sri Lanka, to the north, is the nearest country.

We lie at nought degrees latitude. We are the people of the zero. Our only strong fear is that a great wave will someday sweep across the island, drowning us all. At four feet above the level of the sea, we are at the mercy of the ocean. On my living-room wall hangs Hokusai's print of a monstrous deep-sea wave. I purchased it from a shop in England. The Japanese picture – one of several views of Mount Fuji – shows a rigid wave, a wave cast from iron, with a wicked-looking crest bearing claws.

I keep it there to remind me how vulnerable these islands are, even to smaller waves than Hokusai's. We have a fragile homeland, and we must ensure its defences remain adequate, intact. Unfortunately, we are destroying those defences, and consequently are ourselves heading towards destruction.

Shortly before noon, I decided to visit my father's grave on Jorka Island. I waded across the shallows which separate Tubb from Jorka and made my way through the forest of giant coral heads which stare over the lagoon. Their faces are roughly hewn representations of the people buried beneath them. I found my father's face with its high, narrow brow and sensual mouth, and the small hooked nose which was a legacy from his English ancestors. In life my father had always had a kind of urgent expression, as though there were something he had to do immediately, or the world would erupt in chaos. I had asked the *fandita man* to try to capture that look, on carving the head, but the result had been a wistful air of expectancy rather than urgency; almost the opposite of that which should have appeared.

'Pappy,' I told him, 'the English school teacher is here. The poor man has no idea of the situation he has inherited.'

– You call that news? – said pappy. – I'm more interested in what's going to happen to me. When are you going to bring me my grandchild? And what about your mother? Does she miss her husband weaving his limbs through hers? Or has she found a lover? Whose warm body nestles close to hers at night, now that I'm gone? –

Unfortunately, the dead are always preoccupied with the more basic aspects of life and it is difficult to engage their attention when it comes to politics or the fate of an unsuspecting teacher of school children. Pappy will listen for hours on the subject of eating freshly cooked sea turtle, stuffed with sorghum. Pappy will talk for hours about procreation. Getting him away from those two areas takes a great deal of effort on my part.

– Well? – he said. – How many babies have you brought into the world? Ten? Five? One? *None*. That's how many. Not one. Go away from me – he said in a miserable tone – until you have a little replica of myself to gaze upon –

I left him there, grumbling: a sad, old spirit passing on the gloomy news to the long line of my ancestors. No doubt they were as condemning of me as he was, and spent many an eternal hour discussing the weakness of my loins. The dead can be very unreasonable.

However, I did have a plan which I hoped would satisfy all concerned. It wasn't the perfect solution, but it was the only answer I could come up with.

*The school teacher*.

The day turned sultry. This is the doldrums, the region which crews of sailing ships fear and hate. This is the nothing zone, so often empty of winds, where sailors have drifted in their wooden prisons and died of thirst. The Ancient Mariner was here, along our circle, and experienced its madness, its lethargy, its heavy days. We live within the zero, the number that is not a number, the O, the magic ring. I feel this makes us special, though I could not say why.

Towards evening, the fishing boats began drifting across the lagoon.

Islanders were crossing from Long and Jorka, our two immediate neighbours, using the reef as a path. I wound my line around the empty beer can that I use as a reel and made tracks back to my house. On the way I stopped at my mother's home and left her one of the three red snappers I had caught. She was in an irritable mood, so I did not stay long. Since my father had been attacked by a shark and left to bleed to death, she had often slipped into depressions which bore the outward signs of bad temper. It is hard for a woman who waits all day long for someone who will never come home.

When I reached my own home, in the main clearing which holds the cluster of wooden houses raised on short stilts, my wife Ruth greeted me, touching my cheeks with her soft fingertips. I handed her the fish and sat on one of the woven palm mats by the door, so that I could watch the swift descent of darkness.

'The school teacher is here,' I said. 'I met him at the quay.'

'How shall I cook the fish?' she asked.

'On the charcoal.' I hate boiled food.

She began grinding nuts to sprinkle on the white flesh and I took a knife and gutted the fish. The intestinal smell was sharp in my nostrils. I liked the feel of the blade though, slicing keenly through the white underside. It is a satisfying task, cleaning something destined for the plate and the palate. There is a sense of anticipation which one knows will be fulfilled.

I watched my wife at work, preparing the food. She is a delicate woman, with a small face and narrow nose. I like being with her. When we were much younger I used to tease her mercilessly. Then, at about the age of sixteen, on my return from Malé, I found myself leaving small presents – a coconut, or fruit on a broad leaf – on the path where she would walk. I would hide in the undergrowth and watch her pick it up, looking around her with a shy expression on her face. She knew someone was courting her and it pleased her. But I did not dare show myself, because I thought she hated me. I thought if she knew it was me leaving the gifts she would have thrown them away in disgust.

I was in a fever over her, in those days. Everything I did, everywhere I went, I had no thought for anyone but Ruth. I still teased her because I did not know what else to do. I used to push her into the sea when we all went swimming. I would try to duck her, or splash water in her face. She used to get very angry and tell me there was someone who would punish me – someone who thought highly of her.

'Who could think highly of *you*?' I would scorn, my heart in agony over the words. I wanted to blurt out my feelings for her; tell her that it was me who admired her so much; ask her to forgive me.

But I was afraid. I knew she would reject me. I hurt inside, every time I looked at her, but could not stop looking. It was a terrible time. I hope I am never that way again. I was so miserable.

Two years passed, and then one day I came across her alone, as she walked along the sands. She said nothing as we confronted one another and I wanted to run and hide from her. I felt afraid, and guilty.

Then she held out her hand and I saw that she had some spines of a sea anemone in her fingertips. I took the hand and sucked at the spines so that I could pull them out with my teeth. When that was done, she stroked my cheeks, the way she does now.

'I knew all the time,' she said. 'All the time.'

'Knew what?' I demanded, belligerently.

She just smiled and I collapsed inside.

'But you thought I hated you,' I cried.

'If you had started teasing one of the other girls, I would have been very jealous,' she said. 'I would have scratched her face and cried all night. But you never did. It was always me.'

I felt very humble. I wanted to lick the salt away from her eyebrows. I wanted to press her warm hand to my belly. I wanted to kiss her brown knees that I thought were so fine and smooth. She was like a cowrie, fresh from the lagoon. She had all the beauty of the sea and sky in her form.

'Shall I see your father?' I said.

She nodded happily. It was her turn to be shy, but how much was acting, because it was expected of her, and how much genuine feeling I was never to know. She was like that sometimes, in those days. She wanted to please and at the same time satisfy womanly convention.

We held hands and walked back along the shore and I felt as though I had the whole world inside me. Later she told me, 'I did it on purpose. The anemone. I followed you to the beach and put my hand under a rock to get stung. I wanted you to feel sorry for me. Otherwise, it might have gone on forever – until I was twenty or something.'

Now she is my wife, married to me by the priest in the church on Short Island. We get along very well. The three and a half years spent in England only hurt us for the time. There are no children, but that is my fault, not hers. I had devised a plan to change that, which I hoped would fool my father. It involved the teacher. I was going to use the older man to save my family.

# Three

John Trencher woke in his little brick-built house with a sense of delight overwhelming him. He was on a coral island in the middle of the Indian Ocean, far from those heavy and wearing responsibilities of home. Home? He could hear the cocks crowing, the children calling their mothers, the booming surf. Perhaps, in time, he would come to regard the island as his home? That would be a very pleasant situation.

He climbed out from under the mosquito netting and noticed one or two smears of blood on his sheets. The bed bugs! He had been too tired the previous evening to worry about anything but climbing into bed. Oh, well, they had feasted, but he would get his own back. Nothing was going to spoil his first day, he would make sure of that.

He washed and dressed before eating some biscuits he had brought with him for breakfast. It was nice to be able to throw on a pair of shorts and T-shirt, rather than a suit, before going to work. Although it was his first day he still intended teaching school. He had a job to do here, in educating the young, and he wasn't going to neglect that for a moment. He had neglected too many things in his life so far.

Out on the porch, the sun struck him forcibly. He stood for a few moments in thought. He'd intended going for a short run, but changed his mind. Best to become acclimatised first, or he might find himself with heat exhaustion or something. Better to take things a little easy in the beginning.

When he was ready, he picked up his briefcase (a bit incongruous, he realised) and strode off towards the school in sandals, white socks, shorts and a crisp white shirt. He had thrown off the T-shirt at the last minute, thinking he should put up some show of formality, at least for a while. The islanders might not respect too casual an approach, before they knew him to be a good teacher.

Nathan had promised him the previous evening that the parents would be informed of school opening.

'We can get news from one end of the atoll to the other in less than an hour, don't you worry about that, Mr Trencher . . .'

'John – call me John,' he had said.

'OK – John.' And Nathan had given him a broad islander's smile.

Walking along the beach was magical. The lagoon glistened in the sunlight and he watched the frigate birds – large creatures that harassed the gulls into dropping food and then caught it for themselves before it hit the water. Out on the water *dhoni* canoes skipped over the wavelets, probably bringing some of his pupils to the school house. It was all too beautiful, too colourful to take in at once. His heart felt light and easy.

Before he had reached the teak-built school house, standing on stilts and shining with preservative vegetable oil, the shirt that had been laundered and starched on the ship was limp with sweat. He climbed the steps and entered the room.

Inside, it consisted of one large hall-like room with mats on the floor for the pupils. There was a desk for him and a very old-fashioned blackboard complete with chalks and rubber. The windows had been opened and the smell of the rainforest filled every corner. Magical. Everything was magical. And most wonderful of all, a small belltower with a school bell! He fingered the rope, and then on impulse, pulled it several times, charging the air with the sound of the clapper striking the brass.

Before he had finished ringing it, an elderly woman entered and took a mat to a corner of the room. There she sat, cross-legged, and began working on some sewing she had brought with her.

'Hello,' said John, 'are you one of the mothers? I'm going to take class soon.'

She said nothing in reply, not even looking up from her work, so he shrugged, thinking to deal with the matter later. Perhaps she was there to see that all the pupils arrived and that there were no truants? That made some sense. He was as yet unfamiliar with the customs of the islanders and they knew better who should be there and who shouldn't. He decided to ride the waves for a while.

The children began arriving and he greeted them as they came through the door, asking them their names, knowing it would be some time before he was able to hold all of them in his head. The old woman took little notice of proceedings, but John detected something slightly odd about her behaviour. Whenever he moved amongst the children, she would put down her sewing and regard him closely. It was unnerving, to say the least.

By the end of the day his mood had changed.

He wrote in his diary: *I think they hold me in contempt.*

John studied the words for a moment in the dim light of the twenty-five-watt bulb. The statement was not quite accurate. Indifferently? Yes, that was it. They treated him indifferently. Did such a word deserve to go into his official diary, a document that might be read by others, later, when he returned to England? Perhaps that was still the wrong word. I can't write: *They treat me as if I were one of them.* That would sound as if I'm racist or something, he thought.

What he actually wanted to put across was that the islanders showed not the slightest curiosity about him, despite the fact that he was their new school teacher. They spoke to him, if he addressed them first, and some even called a greeting without any prompting, but apart from that he aroused very little visible interest. He was disappointed. He had to admit that to himself. What he had hoped for was warmth and respect, and certainly the former was a long way off mark. He would have received more warmth from a close-knit English country village community.

He was sitting in his small, sparsely furnished living room, with its bamboo chair and table imported from Sri Lanka. It was evening. He could hear the waves grumbling along the reef, and the frogs and cicadas filling the night air with their own particular messages.

Outside, the waxy fronds and vine-covered trees surged forwards, towards the house, in a tidal wave of dark green. Plants grew so fast in these regions, and held all the seasons at once. Some trees were shedding their leaves, while others were producing new shoots. It did strange things with his sense of time. On the one hand it seemed as though time were racing, hurrying through the cycles, encompassing a normal year within a single day. On the other, it was if it were standing still, going nowhere, offering no overall change.

He put down his pen. He was weary. The heat and humidity sapped his energy, and while he was normally very active, he found himself moving quite slowly here.

On the whole, he liked the environment. The islands were certainly very pretty and for the most part the people were a nice-looking race. Their skin was light brown and their features European. Some of them had blue eyes and light-coloured hair, inherited from their mutineer ancestors. A fish and fruit diet kept their bodies slim and attractive.

One or two of them had limbs missing. He had been told these were shark wounds. The only thing that really horrified him was the elephantiasis suffered by a couple of the elderly fishermen. The huge tree-trunk legs and grotesquely swollen testicles revolted and appalled him. There were other diseases on the islands, but the visible disfigurements caused by elephantiasis brought a shock wave with them which rocked him on his heels. He had been worried at first that it might be contagious, but on consulting his dictionary found, to his relief, that it was caused by the multiplication of worms in the body, which once they had died blocked the lymphatic ducts and glands.

The disease was carried by mosquitoes, and while that was alarming, it was not as bad as having a virus on the loose. Presumably not all mosquitoes carried the worms, because so very few of the islanders had the disease, and he intended to make sure he was bitten as infrequently as possible. Mosquitoes were nasty little bastards, he decided. They carried malaria, yellow fever and elephantiasis and he couldn't understand why there hadn't been a concentrated effort to wipe them off the face of the earth altogether. He made a resolution to sleep under a net at all times and to burn tiger coils in his rooms.

He put aside his diary and took out some writing paper. *Dhonis* sailed regularly between the atoll and up the chain of the Maldive Islands, to Malé, the capital of that group. From there his letters would be taken to Sri Lanka and flown home.

So he had no excuse for not writing to Julia.

He wrote:

What I feel I have done by leaving is to give you and our son both space in which to explore each other, thoroughly, without me there as a constant reminder of where the fault lay. I am sure Benjamin will benefit from my absence.

He stared at these words for a long time, willing truth into them, but their falsity screamed at him and eventually he broke down and wept. When it was over, he tried again, having gathered enough strength to put down his real feelings.

The fact is, Julia, I couldn't bear to look at him. I hated him near me. He made me feel revolting to myself. I'm sorry, if you feel abandoned, perhaps even betrayed, but I couldn't help you. I was an unwelcome guest in the house. The two of you are so wrapped up in each other and I couldn't reach either of you. It's better this way, believe me. I would have come to loathe you both and you would have returned that loathing. I wish I could say more than 'sorry', but that's the only word we have. I'll send you money of course. You won't go short, I promise. I just couldn't spend a lifetime with someone crippled in mind and body – someone I had created that way . . .

He finished the letter quickly, before it became a pathetic litany of self-pity. He didn't expect an answer anyway. He didn't want one. This was a new life: he was a different man. If he started to try to justify that other man – the man who used the excuse that Julia no longer loved him, in order to escape from his own retarded child – if he did that he would find himself in a pit of self-hatred which would rob him of his sanity.

After a while he regained his composure and went out on to the veranda to smoke a cigarette. There were still some lights on in the village, about three hundred yards away, but no sounds reached him from the people within. Somehow they had managed to isolate him. People were always doing that to him. Even his own family . . . He thought of his father: rich, powerful, unapproachable. Virtually a stranger, since John had been sent away to school very young, his father not even fulfilling the minimum of visits that most parents felt obliged to make. The old man had rarely been at home, his business interests frequently taking him abroad, so summer holidays had often been spent with friends. Then, university, and Julia. She had persuaded him to reject his father's values and go into teaching. The old man had never forgiven her for that – never forgiven either of them. Damn him.

He looked up into the night sky. The stars were very bright and the Southern Cross, a constellation quite new to him, was visible on the edge of the heavens. Perhaps if he had found some kind of comfort there? But the Church was made up of men – and men had limited understanding. If only one could actually talk to *God*, talk *with* him, explain to him and receive omniscient therapy, but he had tried prayer and it was like speaking to an empty room. The only sound was that of one's own voice; hollow, false and inadequate. Nothing came back. There was no communication. No soothing thoughts, no sudden revelations, no answer to the questions.

Contact was one-way and try as he might, he couldn't imagine anyone listening. He could express little of the agony of his heart and mind.

Language cannot adequately express emotions and thoughts. His words were always rejected by the cold stone of the church, thrown back at him like blunt instruments to further dull his understanding and increase his confusion.

Perhaps there were no answers? Talking to a priest would have been less productive than talking with himself. If he, John Trencher, the man at the centre of the affair, did not understand, why then should a stranger comprehend? When all was said and done, a priest was only a man who formed judgements with inadequate tools: the human heart and mind.

John tossed his cigarette on to the coral path where it glowed for some time. When he had been with Julia, who was a non-smoker and a vegetarian, he had pretended to give up cigarettes. Pretended. In fact he used to sneak downstairs in the middle of the night, or take an evening walk alone, in order to smoke. She knew he still smoked. He knew that she knew. It was a game they maintained as a sort of compromise. Now that he could smoke all he wanted, he had little interest in cigarettes.

There is the sound of the reef and the noises of the jungle, which tend to emphasise tranquillity rather than detract from it. The smell of damp foliage drifts over from the backs of the houses and there is an odour of dried fish wafting from the village. The stars are painfully out of reach. The night has closed down the feeling of horizontal space and opened the vertical.

Suddenly John felt very calm and not the least afraid of anything. The nameless fear that he carried with him much of the time was gone, and an easy strength filled its place. There was a house lizard – a pale and large-eyed gecko – on the veranda rail. John could see its heart pulsing rapidly beneath the taut skin. Was *it* afraid? Or did its heart beat at that pace all the time? He reached out and gently touched the point where its tail met its body. At least, he thought he was being gentle, but the lizard darted forward, leaving its tail beneath John's finger.

'Damn,' said John, annoyed with himself. Why did everything, even living creatures, come to pieces in his hands? The lizard was now on the wall and looked not in the least discomfited. Perhaps the tail was supposed to come away like that? Like a snake, sloughing its skin?

John took one last look at the night sky, with its blaze of white sparks, and then went inside again. He wondered whether he should lock the door, but on inspecting the frame could find no catch or bolt anywhere. He shrugged and made his way to the bed, forgetting about the bugs that were waiting to share his blankets with him.

The following morning he found one or two marks on his skin and knew that the small, disgusting creatures had feasted on his blood again. He dragged the mattress out on to the veranda to give it the full blast of the morning sun.

He heaved the mattress over the rail and left it with the underside exposed, thinking that this was where the main legions of the undesirable insects would be camped.

The morning sun hit him in the chest like the blow from a giant felt hammer. It surprised him. He looked up and had to shade his eyes as he stared into a blue sky that harboured not a wisp of cloud. It was certainly a very fine day. He hoped all days were this good.

As he turned to go back into the house, he almost tripped over some objects lying on the veranda. He hadn't noticed them on the way out, since the mattress had been in his line of sight. There were some coconuts and some fruit. Someone had left him his breakfast. Nathan? He gathered them up and took them inside.

Shortly afterwards, there was a tentative knock on the screen door and an islander stood there. He was a small man, about middle-age, with a slight squint. Heavily favouring his right leg, he stood and regarded John dourly.

'Yes?' John said.

'I come for my money,' said the man.

Immediately, John thought of the fruit and felt very irritated. He had supposed that the goods on his veranda were a gift. This man was taking advantage of him. He did not like that.

'Money? What money?'

'So. Two pounds sterling.' This could be used to purchase goods on Malé. John had already seen, in the film his employers had shown him and in subsequent observations, that the islanders were fond of gaily coloured golfing umbrellas and sunglasses.

He was not going to give in that easily. He could play games too.

'I still don't understand.' He spoke the pidgin slowly and clearly, so there should be no doubt in the other man's mind that he was annoyed at being disturbed. 'I'm just about to begin my breakfast. Can't you come back later, at a more convenient time?'

The islander looked impatient and half turned, gesturing for some reason towards the reef.

'Teacher asked me for some seashells and I brought them to him. That was a long time ago. I still haven't been paid. I want my money. Two pounds sterling, please.'

The use of the word *sterling* rankled for some reason. Why did he have to keep repeating it? John was also more than a little perplexed. Shells? He had seen no shells. Certainly there had been nothing else amongst the fruit. He wondered whether the man might not be a little simple. They struck him as an inbred group.

'Listen – what's your name?'

'John. My name is John,' said the islander. 'I want . . .'

'Yes, yes, I know. Two pounds for the shells.' A man with the same name as himself. Although not an uncommon experience, it seemed so, here on an atoll severed by the equator. You could travel halfway around the earth and meet yourself when you arrived. It wasn't the money – that was little enough – it was the situation that annoyed him. Why should he pay anything at all, when he had received nothing from the man? Perhaps this was a test: one they tried on all visitors from the outside? He didn't want to show weakness, but at the same time he desperately wanted to be liked and accepted. He could rebuff the man, out of hand, but that might be taken as an insult. What the hell was he *supposed* to do?

'Look, I'm sorry but I haven't received any shells from you. I only arrived . . .'

He stopped because the islander was looking indignant and aggrieved. What on earth was the matter with the man? John was feeling out of his depth.

'Look, I brought the shells and now you have to pay for them.' He was shaking with contained rage, gesturing again towards the ocean with his slim hand. 'This is not good – not good at all.' He shook his head and gazed at the ground. 'The teacher asked me for the shells, and I brought them. He said he would pay me later. Two pounds sterling. I waited. I waited for a long time. The teacher has the shells but I don't have the money. All I want is fair payment – two pounds sterling. This is . . .'

'Look here, when was this?' asked John, some light beginning to break through.

'Two months.'

John smiled and ran a hand through his hair. *Now* he understood. Perhaps the islander came from a remote part of the atoll and had only seen Peter Goodwright, the previous school teacher, for the period of the transaction? Maybe – a cliché no doubt – but maybe he had difficulty in telling Europeans apart? He did look just a little bit simple.

John said, 'But that wasn't me. That was the last school teacher. I'm the new man.'

'You are the teacher.' The words were spoken emphatically, as if there could be no argument.

'Yes, but . . .'

'Then you must pay me the money for the shells. I brought the shells, now you pay for them.'

John gave up.

'Oh, for heaven's sake, I'll get the damn two pounds *sterling*. Just don't come round here bothering me again.'

He went inside and searched through his luggage for his wallet. The islander, John, followed him, watching his every move, as if he expected John to abscond once he was out of sight. The whole situation was ludicrous, but it seemed the only way he was going to get rid of the man was if he paid him what he was owed. He found the wallet and handed over a five-pound note. The islander studied it, then opened a pouch on his belt. Incredibly, he had three pounds in change.

'Thank you . . . John,' said John. 'Are you happy now?'

The man smiled. 'Very happy.'

He tucked the note into his money belt and immediately left, banging the screen door behind him.

Later that day, John Trencher had another unpleasant experience. He was sitting, quietly, enjoying a book, when he heard the sound of a soft splash coming from somewhere beneath the house. Although the building was brick-built, it was raised on pillars to allow flood water to run underneath. He knew also, from his research before arriving, that rainwater tanks were situated beneath the houses on the atoll. He got up and went to the corner of the room where the trapdoor to the tank was situated. Lifting this, he peered inside. It was dark. He could see nothing.

He found his torch amongst his luggage and shone it inside the tank. For a minute or two his eyes met only with clear water. Then, a small, silver shape went through the refracted beam. He was revolted. Fish! Fish in his drinking water. How the hell had they got in there?

He became angry. Someone was playing a joke on him. One of the villagers – or perhaps a number of them? He hated being made the butt of local humour.

He searched around in his luggage again and found a string vest. With this he fashioned a crude net and spent the next two hours catching the three fish that cruised nonchalantly through the water he had swallowed without first boiling it. Fortunately the tank was not completely full, or he would have had more difficulty in netting them the way he had caught sticklebacks as a boy. The fish were not as big as he had first thought – about six inches long – and he threw them into the forest at the back of the house.

He decided to say nothing to anyone about it. Let them laugh behind his back. He wasn't going to give them the satisfaction of knowing that he had been annoyed. Better to carry on as though nothing had happened and disappoint the bastards. It was enough to know that he had got the measure of their regard for him.

It was difficult to go back to his book after that and he sat, staring out of the window at the children and the adults moving about the village. Some of the youngsters were playing a war game, with imaginary clubs. He found that delightfully naive: in England they would be shooting guns and throwing bombs.

Shortly after that a football match began on an area of hard-packed earth, just outside the village. The players were barefoot and showed good ball-handling skills, though their team tactics were, in his opinion, quite unsophisticated. They tended to play as individuals and the ball spent a lot of time in the air. Still, it was a welcome touch of home for John, and he allowed himself to be caught up in the general excitement. There were no markings on the pitch, but the players seemed to have a remarkably accurate idea as to the in-play area. There were few arguments when someone picked up the ball for a throw-in or goal kick. John left his veranda to stand behind the two bamboo poles which constituted the goal at the west end.

During the match a tall thin islander, wearing a constant loose smile, ran on to the pitch with a stick, which he waved in the air as he jumped and leaped around players of both sides. Occasionally, this man would kick at the ball, interrupting the play. Once, he missed completely, and fell heavily on his back, having to be assisted to his feet by one of the footballers.

John knew the man was called Hob – short for Rehoboam – and that he was mentally retarded. What was remarkable, in John's eyes, was the fact that instead of chasing Hob away from the game, the players treated him merely as a natural hazard. No one yelled at him in annoyance, or pushed him away from the ball. On the contrary, when he did get a foot to it, onlookers cheered and cried, 'Go on, Hob! Shoot!' The football players remained indulgent throughout the game, played around Hob when they could, and carried on as if nothing had happened when he did get in the way. For his part, Hob looked entirely happy.

John became enthusiastic as the game proceeded and yelled as if he were watching a match back home. One of the players smiled at him, and gestured for him to come on the pitch and join in. He shook his head.

'I'm no good,' he called.

Two of the islanders then grabbed him by his arms and pulled him on to the pitch. An argument then broke out, between a small, dark, stocky man and the rest of the players. Clearly one member did not want him to play.

'It's all right,' said John, not wishing to be the cause of a quarrel. 'I don't mind not playing . . .'

Someone kicked the ball to him at that point, and he returned it, instinctively. Before he realised it, he was racing down the pitch, yelling for a pass.

For a while, he was thoroughly enjoying himself, but then the small man who had not wanted him to play went in hard on a tackle and knocked all the wind out of him.

'Take it easy,' John said, as Hob helped him to his feet. The reply from the little dark man was a savage kick on the shin, which brought tears of anger to John's eyes.

'Hey! What the hell is it with you? What's going on?' cried John, limping towards his assailant.

The man came close to him, said something very quietly, and then walked off the pitch, going towards the huts.

John stood there, bewildered and flustered. Although the man had spoken under his breath, the teacher was quite certain of the words. He sought Nathan out from amongst the onlookers, and limped over to him.

'Who was that?' he asked. 'That small man? Who was he?'

Nathan said, 'That was Numbers.'

'He said he was going to kill me. He said, "I'm going to kill you, teacher," just like that.' John tried to joke. 'Takes his football seriously, doesn't he?'

'Take no notice of Numbers – he gets upset so easily. He's not in his right mind at the moment. I'll speak to him, don't worry.'

John felt unsatisfied by this answer.

'But I *am* worried. I don't know what I've done to offend the man. Why pick on me? Just because I'm the outsider, or what?'

'Yes, it must be that.'

'But to threaten to *kill* me.'

'Just a figure of speech – people use it all the time in England, and don't really mean it. Same here, on the islands. You're just not used to hearing it in another language, that's all. You're taking it all too seriously. I'll speak to Numbers. He won't bother you again.'

'I sincerely hope not.'

This incident seemed to serve to wrap up the game. The players drifted away to their houses. Hob was given a drink and a piece of fruit by someone passing by, and then he crept off to a vegetable patch outside one of the houses. Palm leaves had been spread over a framework in the garden, to protect the young plants from the fierceness of the sun. Hob went to sleep under this shade, again without hindrance from the owner of the vegetable plot.

John went back to his house to bathe his shin, which had been split open, despite the fact that his attacker had been barefoot. He wondered why he had made an enemy so early in his time on the islands.

## Four

When I get up early in the morning, the first thing I do is go outside – passing the Hokusai print – into the sparkling, clear air that these islands have the fortune to possess. Only those like me, who have been to other lands, can appreciate how valuable, how priceless, is that air which so many take for granted. (In England, I could hardly breathe through the stinking fumes that fouled the atmosphere of London.) Yes, the clean air and the ocean all around in its various colours. And the islands themselves, all infinitely precious to me.

There is nothing to compare with that first daily view of my homelands, except perhaps the evenings, after I have spent the day absorbing all my islands have to offer. Some of my fellow islanders are pleased to escape these shores: we have disease and inadequate medical attention; we have poverty; we have the tensions inherent in isolation.

Yet I, for one, would not give up one grain of coral dust for the so-called privileges of a material society. Not one leaf, drop of seawater, puff of wind. These are mine. Let others keep what they have.

I suspect that, had the mutineers never landed on our atoll, we should today belong to the Maldive Islands and come under their authority. However, that runaway band of Englishmen, desperate for a haven, did cross the reef and land on our shores. They brought with them a religion called Christianity, which was eventually merged with the animism and ancestor worship already practised by the islanders at that time. The sailors were happy to accept the islanders' beliefs, for the sake of harmony, and the natives embraced Christ.

The mutual exchange – a mystery for a mystery – seemed to suit both parties, especially since no one had to give anything up, and there was gain all round. The generation which succeeded the mariners, raised on the blended religions, hardly stopped to question it. Where two requirements clashed – as in the burial of the dead – then the one which held the least fearful consequences won. Until now, there have been no burials in the churchyard on Short Island. It is a constant source of grief to the Catholic Church. If they had graves in the churchyard, with little white crosses to mark them, the *midnight walkers* would say thank you very much for the signposts, and duly collect the souls beneath without stopping to pass the time of night. As it is, we keep them out with blocks of coral, under which even the screwpine's roots cannot reach.

With the coming of the mutineers, not only were two or three religions mixed to form a unique stewpot, but ingredients new to both the natives and the sailors were added. This came about as a direct result of the mutiny itself. Fable and legend permeate deeply into our souls, dropping from the conscious mind and seeping into the subconscious. Once the subconscious is soaked in such beliefs, it never completely dries. Stories are passed on to wide-eyed children and natural enemies of foreparents become the supernatural foes of their sons and daughters. The bogeymen of past generations live on.

Not far from my hut is a tree known by Europeans as the screwpine. We call it the *midnight walker*. Its trunk stands well off the ground, supported by a ring of exposed roots, like legs. It looks like a huge spider with a long neck and a tuft at the top. At night, when no human eyes are on it, the screwpine roams its island home looking for the buried souls of my people. When it finds an earthed soul, it plants its roots firmly over the place and sucks the spirit up into its trunk and delivers its cargo to that most terrible of all bogeymen, the Captain.

I explained all this to the teacher, during the funeral of a child. He could not understand why the *fandita man* – a magician we imported into our culture from the Maldives – took charge of the corpse after the Christian priest had completed the rites according to his religion.

'Why has he gone sneaking off into the rainforest with the body?' he asked.

We walked slowly back to my hut and I pointed to the screwpine as we passed by it.

'Because he must hide it from that, until it can be buried beneath its coral head.'

Since it was a child, the *fandita man* was able to carry the corpse on his shoulder. He strolled past us. There was nothing sinister about his movements.

'So you think the screwpine will steal the dead soul, if it can find it?'

'It's more complicated than that,' I replied. 'You see, we believe that certain places are the rightful homes of the souls before life, as well as after death. We can protect souls after death, but before life they are scattered in the forest, under the moss, beneath tree roots. It's the unborn soul that's most vulnerable and at the mercy of the *midnight walkers* . . .'

'How do you reconcile this with Christian beliefs? I mean, it sounds more like a pagan religion to me. What about Christianity?'

We reached the steps of my house and sat on them together.

'We don't try.'

'So, the old ways haven't gone?' He tugged his flimsy blond moustache. 'I must talk to Father Maurer about this. I wonder how he reconciles the two?'

'Half a soul is better than nothing,' I smiled, but he still remained serious.

'You should know better, Nathan . . .'

'Better?' I said. 'You think the *midnight walker* is a fairy tale, a superstition which no educated man or woman would give credibility? How about this? A man is tortured to death. He's hung by his arms from a crosstree in such a way that water and blood in his lungs separate, and eventually he drowns in his own bodily fluids. That's a very real death. People around here know all about drowning. Three days later that man is seen up, walking around and displaying the wounds caused by the nails.

'Or this. There's a Supreme Being that you can't see, hear, touch or smell, but he's there just the same and omnipotent. You're not going to try to apply logic to these things, are you?'

'Yes. No. I don't know. You're an intelligent man, Nathan. You've learned so much in a short time.'

'But I haven't unlearned what I knew before – that's not possible. Not for me.'

He tried a new tack.

'Why an outside influence? The *fandita man*? It doesn't even originate here.'

'And Christianity does? Look, the *fandita man* has a special task and title – that's why he's an outsider. We don't like titles here. Surely you've noticed that we don't have a leader, because he would have to be called something – Head Man – King – Queen – whatever. When we need such people, like magic men and school teachers, we would rather import them. Nobody here likes to use a title. We'll never have an islander for a priest, for example. If we needed a President or something, we would ask for one from the outside. Happily we don't. We manage quite well without.

'The population is small. We can make such decisions as a community. Those with any interest in a situation needing a decision will get together and come to some sort of agreement. Certain personalities are stronger than others, of course, but if you don't feel you can handle something you get a friend with more charisma to argue for you.'

'Jesus, it sounds so muddled.'

'And the outside world isn't? Everything works perfectly in England, doesn't it? Everyone is satisfied with their lot, the judicial system is free of flaws and the government get no complaints.'

He was bridled into a retort.

'It works well enough.'

'So does our system – well enough. It's not perfect, but it works well enough.'

Ruth came out on to the veranda and I smiled at her. The teacher immediately got to his feet and then seemed embarrassed.

'Ruth – we were just talking about the *midnight walker*. The teacher finds it difficult to understand why we believe . . .'

'It seems so silly,' he said.

To his surprise she turned on him abruptly, becoming angry with him. Two red spots appeared on her cheeks and her brow furrowed. She gestured with her hands.

'They robbed us of our child,' she said, and then disappeared into the house again.

He looked at me with a helpless expression on his face.

'I've annoyed her. I didn't mean to do that. What was she talking about, your child?'

'A *midnight walker* must have found the place where our firstborn child lay, and stolen it. We have never had any children.'

His face showed concentration. He desperately wanted to understand, and help us, if he could. I had sensed from the moment he had come to the island – that first day as he walked down the quay – that he was a man looking for a mission. He wanted to help someone, anyone, in order to absolve himself from some past deed.

I knew, from Father Maurer, that John Trencher had left a woman with a retarded child, in England. These things happen – here as well as other places – and they are the fault of no one. But some men and women get it into their heads that they are to blame, and they need to get rid of their guilt. Whether this was the reason for John Trencher's eagerness to find good works or not, I wasn't certain, but I would have been willing to gamble on it.

'You mean,' he said, 'you believe that since your firstborn was taken from you, you can't have *any* children.'

'There's no playing with numbers. A *firstborn* is just that.'

'Perhaps you're just . . .' He paused then, and seemed embarrassed again, studying my brown, dusty feet.

'Sterile? Maybe. A *midnight walker* has stolen the soul that God had marked for my firstborn. Therefore, the child will never see life. Without a firstborn, there can be no second child. Do you see? We are destined to remain childless.'

The teacher stared at the screwpine, as it stood on tip-toe, not far away from us. Perhaps for a moment he had grasped the idea of its function in our lives, but then he ruined this by saying, 'Why not cut the bastards down? Why not chop every one of the bastards down and burn them?'

He hadn't seen it, after all.

'Because that way we would also destroy the souls trapped inside – those in transit. Would you like to be responsible for the death of a child's soul?'

Again there was an expression of helplessness on his face. He wanted to be able to give us back our own, by using the logic he had brought with him from his civilised homeland, but the tight, iron circle that had been forged around us would not allow this. It frustrated him into blurting out, 'But don't you see? You've left no way out for yourselves.'

'Not us. This is how things are. Not how we've made them.'

The breeze was on the rise now, lifting the heads of the palms, and as the tide was coming in, the spume would be flying over the reef. I suggested to the teacher that we might go for a walk along the beach. He agreed.

We left the village and took the short path through the rainforest to the shore. After the darkness of the trees, the blinding sand and sea, glinting in the strong sunlight, hurt our eyes. I put on my sunglasses. The teacher never wore any, and shielded his eyes from the glare as we stared out over the shallow water at the white, kicking waves beyond.

'You like Ruth, don't you?' I said.

He looked down at me, sharply. He was quite a bit taller than I was. I knew he couldn't see my eyes through the glare.

'I like you both,' he said, distinctly.

'I'm glad – but what do you think of her as a woman?'

There was a long pause before he gave the standard cliché.

'You're a very lucky man.'

'Yes. I know. Ruth is the only woman I ever wanted. I would like to be able to give her happiness.'

He said, 'I don't believe in things like that. I mean, you can't make someone happy if they're not already content. You can add to their happiness – complete it – but happiness comes from within. You can't manufacture it from the outside – not for very long, anyway.'

'I'd agree with that to a certain extent, but surely if you give someone something they desperately need . . .'

'If they're basically unhappy, it'll only serve as a balm, not a cure. I thought we were going to walk?' he said, striding off before I could continue the conversation. I noticed that he deliberately stepped over or around the sand piles left by the crabs, though I'm sure they could not have cared less about the waste material from their holes. I suppose it was in his nature, to avoid destroying something that looked as if it had been built carefully, even if that something was useless and unwanted. I realised I would have to take the teacher fishing, to put a little fire in his blood.

'You must come out in the bonito boat sometime,' I said. 'We'll take you with us soon.'

'Why?'

'Because it's very exciting, chasing the shoals of bonito. Not many Europeans have done it – it's very special to us. Our livelihood depends on it.'

That caught him and he took it down. We were honouring him by asking him to join us. Which outsider could resist such flattery? Certainly not a school teacher with an earnest desire to please.

'Well. In that case, thank you. I will.'

As he walked along, he bent down and picked up a shell. It was a strigate auger. Not a very pretty shell, but fairly uncommon. He put it straight in his pocket absently, without looking at it. It seemed an unconscious action, as if he had not realised what he was doing.

'That shell's probably got a hermit crab inside it,' I said. 'It'll be crawling out of your pocket if you don't watch it.'

'What? Oh!' He reached into his shorts and withdrew the auger. Sure enough, two little black eyes on stalks were visible in the opening. He placed the shell back on the sand.

'Habit I got from my grandfather,' he said, 'picking things up. He was a gatherer – of almost everything, when we were out walking. Used to drive grandma wild.'

'Was he mean?'

'No. I don't think so. Quite generous in many ways. He just didn't like to waste anything. He delighted in finding free gifts in the countryside – blackberries, mushrooms – even filled his pockets with horse manure . . .' he chuckled. 'Funny man, I suppose.'

The tide was rushing in now, covering rocks and swilling down the dead coral that showed itself to the sun. Two of the villagers were returning from the reef with a bandsaw and a handcart bearing a large lump of coral. The dark ocean thundered towards their backs, suddenly rearing, tall and terrible, like a giant beast brought up short by an invisible leash. Then it crashed, down on its face, only to rise again and repeat its angry charge. The impulse was to shout a warning to the men: *Look out behind you!*

'We inherit lots of strange ways from our forefathers,' I said.

The teacher was looking at the two men.

'Don't they know what they're doing?'

I presumed he meant stealing from the reef.

'Yes.'

He shook his head.

'I think I'll have a word with Father Maurer about this. Maybe he can do something.'

The teacher had yet to learn that the priest had a clearly defined border to his area of concern for us. He had an iron circle, within which he worked with great zeal, but the outside of which he assiduously ignored.

'By the way,' said the teacher, turning to me, 'some fisherman gave some shells to Peter Goodwright . . .'

'Gave?'

'Sold. But he hadn't been paid. The man asked me to make the debt good.'

'I see.' I waited.

'Well, I thought it would be unfair of me to say no. I felt a little responsible for my countryman's . . . forgetfulness. I paid him.'

I nodded.

'By the way,' he continued, 'have you spoken to that man – the one who threatened me on the football pitch? You haven't mentioned it since. I've seen him around my house – that is, in the rainforest at the back. Is he all right? He looks a bit strange.'

'What do you mean, strange?'

'Sinister. Have you spoken?'

I nodded again. 'Yes – he apologises for being rude . . .'

'Rude? He threatened me with my life.'

'He was overwrought. He's had a recent bereavement – his young daughter.'

'In that case . . .' he began in a flustered voice, embarrassed by someone's loss, but then stopped himself. 'But why threaten *me*?'

'You were there and he boiled over at that moment.'

'Oh.' He wasn't satisfied, I could see, but it was the best I could do. We were holding Numbers in check with great difficulty.

That night when I visited the teacher again, I found him at the eastern end of the island, staring out over the water at the coral heads, visible in the starlight.

The sea laid an arm of white surf all along the shoulder of the coral reef. It was cool. The school teacher stood beside me on the beach.

'Are't you afraid of the dark?' I asked him.

The teacher half turned, away from me, and appeared to be gauging the depths of the black rainforest. Perhaps he thought he could lose the question in there?

'Darkness? No, no I don't think so. Not since I was a child.'

'Every sensible man should be afraid of shadows. If you're not sensitive to hidden forms, then you have no magic in you, no appreciation of mystery . . .'

'Are you accusing me of being shallow?'

'I'm saying if you're not aware of the light behind the darkness – the spirits that we sense, instinctively fear – you're only half conscious of what goes on around you. When you study a painting, a masterpiece, doesn't it move you, emotionally?'

He gave me a haughty look. 'Sometimes.'

'And what causes this feeling?'

'I don't know . . . the craftsmanship of the artwork. Something like that.'

'You aren't moved by a sense of mystery – the light behind the picture? Something behind the colour and form which brushes our souls?'

He seemed annoyed and turned away from me again.

'I don't know what you're talking about. I like paintings because they're skilfully done. No other reason. And darkness is just an absence of light . . .'

'No. You're wrong. Light is an absence of darkness. The darkness was there first. It doesn't matter. It's just that you miss so much, with this practical view on everything. It's a great shame.'

'Don't feel sorry for me.'

'I won't – that would be condescending of me. I'm just glad I'm not you. You live in a world without mystery. I imagine – well, it just seems like such a dull, depressing place.'

'Explain *your* world to me.'

'I can't – the patterns fade when exposed. Mystery and magic defy explanation. That's what makes them so wonderful.'

He stared again over the waters of the lagoon.

'I know you're trying to protect your way of life – or to be more precise your way of death – with these conversations, Nathan, but surely you see that something has to be done about this use of coral from the reef. You're tearing your foundations away. Soon there won't be anything to hold the islands above the sea.'

Oh Lord, he had his mission. He had found a way to help us, whether we wanted it or not.

'It's a problem, but we'll deal with it.'
'I'll try to think of something,' he said.

# Five

The beach is a bright, curved blade abandoned by some careless giant. The tide is out, exposing the coral reef some two hundred yards from shore. Between the reef and the beach is a stretch of shallow water, strewn with boulders. There are several people wading through the lime-coloured shallows, searching for shells and unusual pieces of coral. Mushroom, star and staghorn corals are occasionally lifted from the waters, still bearing their magnificent undersea colours. 'Precious' rose coral, too, though this is uncommon. And the shells: striped volutes, red helmets, sundials, golden-mouthed drupes, venus combs, pontifical mitres – all go into the basket, destined to grow dusty on some shelf in a bungalow in Stockport, England, or apartment in Morristown, USA, or converted Bavarian farmhouse.

It was in these waters that she was searching for cowries and he waded out to see if he could be of any assistance to her. He kept his track shoes on, wary of any coral snakes or moray eels, but removed his shirt because the spray had wet it and it was rubbing against his sore back.

'Good morning!'

Ruth had been intent on her task, for she visibly jumped, and he found himself apologising straightaway. She was wearing a thin sarong, the dampness of which emphasised her figure beneath.

'I'm sorry – I didn't mean to startle you.'

'Oh, it doesn't matter. I was dreaming.' She looked away, shyly, before he had a chance to gauge the reaction to his presence from those deep brown eyes.

'Dreaming? What of?'

She didn't reply. Instead, she clutched a bag fashioned from a fishing net closer to her bosom. He could see the net was full of seashells; the kind tourists will buy. There were a conch, some turbans and a few murexes, but most of them were tiger cowries. The shiny cowries glinted in the sunshine.

'The ocean's bounty,' he said, pointing. 'They're beautiful, aren't they?'

Ruth had a short bamboo cane in one hand, with a loop of wire on the end. This was for searching under stones, without having to endanger herself. Even some of the shellfish were poisonous. The textile cone could kill, with the tiny barbed harpoon which was used to paralyse its small-fish prey, even though the creature was not more than three inches long.

'Can I help?' he asked.

'If you wish. But don't put your fingers under any rocks.' She stared at him frankly, now that the first contact was over. 'There are stone fish in the shallows, and . . .'

'I know – lots of other nasties. I read about them.'

'Turn the rocks over like this, gripping the tops.' She showed him how it was done. He followed suit, gingerly at first, but becoming more confident when he found nothing more dangerous than the odd starfish. It was an exciting game of discovery and he had not felt the same way for a long time – probably not since he was a child, fishing for newts and sticklebacks in the ponds of rural Buckinghamshire. They were looking for treasure. The waters were full of life around them. Coral reefs are teeming with all kinds of creatures, unlike the islands themselves, which have only frigate birds, gulls and herons. He knew that beyond the reef, in the dark, deep waters of the ocean, lurked huge monsters, and this added to his feelings of excitement. It was like being in a fortress surrounded by fabulous beasts.

'This is fun,' he said, coming across a white, spotted tiger cowrie, the staple purchase of tourists. Why *tiger*? he thought. Looks more like a leopard's coat. No fathoming some of the names.

He popped it in her net, carefully avoiding touching her.

Another rock. This time a snake, white with pink rings, flashed its six-inch body through the water. John instinctively stepped back and his neck prickled. His heart was beating fast, but he did not look round at Ruth. He didn't want her to see him in a funk. It took all his effort to turn over the next stone, but he did it, and found a green turban. So that was how it was. Under this rock, death; under that stone, treasure. Like a schoolboy's adventure tale.

By noon the heatwaves were folding the air on the distant horizon, way out to sea, as if intent on wrapping up the morning and putting it away until the next day. Skipjack were dancing on the ocean, outside the reef.

John's back felt sunsore and his eyes were tired with staring down into the water. The tide was surging over the coral and water was moving too fast to make visibility safe for searching. They returned to the beach and sat on the sands.

He kept stealing glances at her. She was one of the most lovely women he had ever encountered, with her slim, lithe body and delicate features. He envied Nathan a great deal.

'Nathan tells me you have no children,' he said. 'This disappoints you?'

She nodded, her dark hair limp from the spray and falling damply around her shoulders.

'I would like a baby.'

'Still – children are not everything. They bring their own problems.'

She looked at him sharply and an emotional pain went through his breast. He thought he knew what she was thinking and so answered the question that had not been asked.

'I have a child.'

'I know. He's in England.'

He sat up. 'You know? Oh, I suppose they told Nathan all about me, did they?' An unreasonable anger was building up inside him.

'Not Nathan – the priest. And all he said was that you had a baby – a boy. Is that so bad? To tell us that? I wish he were my baby.'

'You wouldn't, if you knew him. Besides, he's not a baby. Ben is three years old.'

He picked up a handful of sand and threw it savagely at the water's edge. He was annoyed that his private life was a matter for discussion amongst the islanders. What business was it of theirs if he had a child or not? The priest ought to have kept his mouth shut. That information was supposed to be confidential.

'What about this . . . your priest, Father Maurer?' he asked, changing the subject. 'He seems a difficult man to talk to.'

When John had first heard that he would have European company on the atoll, before he left England, he had been relieved. At least there would be someone with whom he could converse about any problems that arose and about the islanders themselves. Instead, it seemed that he was a blabber-mouth, interfering in other people's private concerns.

When she did not reply, John said, 'How many years has he been here? Father Maurer.'

'He's a Belonger now.'

So, the Father had Belonger status. That meant he had been on the islands over five years and was a full citizen of Jonson's Atoll. The inhabitants were generous with their immigration laws. If you could manage to stay for five years, you were automatically granted full rights as a citizen, just as if you had been born on the islands. You 'belonged'.

'Is he indeed?'

'Yes, indeed he is.'

Her seriousness delighted him and he smiled inwardly. He wondered whether he himself would be allowed to stay long enough to become a Belonger. He hoped so. His contract was for two years, but that could be extended. The previous teacher, Peter Goodwright, had stayed almost long enough – but then he had done something awful (the selection board refused to tell John exactly what) and had left the atoll on an Arab trading dhow.

Suddenly, as he was deep in thought, Ruth did an extraordinary thing. She put her arm around his shoulders and hugged him to her. What was she doing? Trying to comfort him for some reason? Perhaps it had been that conversation about Ben?

What was he to do? His eyes were sore with the salt spray and he wanted to wipe them, but he did not dare move. The situation seemed so unstable. If he moved at all, she might think he wanted her to take her arm away and would be insulted.

Just then, a large wave hit the outer reef and came rolling towards them, as if to engulf them. He jumped up, quickly, but it petered out as it neared the shoreline and merely rippled up the sands to wet their feet.

'I'm sorry,' he said, 'I thought that wave . . . there must be a gap in the reef at that point. Where they've removed some coral I expect.' He sat down again. 'Listen,' he said, without looking at her to see if she had been offended by his abrupt rejection of her arm, 'I've been meaning to talk to you – to someone – about the coral . . .'

# Six

While Ruth was with the teacher on the beach, I went into the rain-forest to get out of their way. I had watched them for a little while, until she put her arm around him, and found myself tearing at a bread-fruit, pulling the white fibrous flesh from within the green football and stuffing it into my mouth. It was then I decided to leave them alone.

As I left the edge of the forest I forced down the hurt feeling, deep, where it would not trouble me. I felt the same way about this as I did when the islands were swarming with frogs – after the long rains – and you could not walk without crushing the poor creatures with every step. There was no way out of these things. Life had to go on. The fishing had to be done and therefore you had to walk to the boats.

I found myself in the dark mangrove swamps at the centre of the island. The flies are more numerous there but the sound of the surf is muted by layers of vegetation. There is a huge bayan tree there, where I played as a boy. I climbed this vertical labyrinth and lay amongst its thick limbs, thinking about my child.

Arrangements had been made with the *fandita man*. The magic had been laid in advance, so that at the moment of conception I would exchange souls with the teacher and it would be my spirit that would send the seed into her womb. The *fandita man* had promised me.

It had to be the teacher. There was a danger, if I used an islander, that the child would eventually be claimed by the surrogate father. I could not go through that kind of heartache: I would rather not have a child at all. The teacher was the safest man to use. It did not trouble me that he had fathered a retarded child. These things happen, but so rarely twice over, and the mother would be a different person. There was nothing the matter with Hob's brothers and sisters.

No. It had to be an outsider. It was good that the teacher was a kind man. He would be gentle with my Ruth . . . A wave of hurt rose within me again, but I forced it down, like a person forces vomit back into the stomach when they do not wish to be sick. I had to banish those pictures, of the couple lying together. They were unnecessary. They were nothing. So much less than the magic of a child.

Jumping from my perch and thence to the ground, I hurried back through the rainforest. The couple were no longer on the beach when I got there. Proof of their interest in one another was evident by the fact that a shell had been left behind and forgotten. I picked it up. It was warm from the sun. I stared at the hollows in the sand, where their buttocks had been. Some of the sandpiles, left by the crabs, had been crushed. They were all on the right side of the teacher's marks. In my mind's eye I could see it happening: the teacher, reaching out unconsciously, grasping at anything within the length of his arm.

I smoothed the indentations of their buttocks from the beach with the palm of my hand. Then I went back, along the path, to the village. Climbing the wooden steps I then entered the coolness of my house.

Ruth was sitting on a mat in the corner, sorting through shells, and she looked up at me. Her eyes told me that nothing had happened.

I kissed her cheek and then hugged her head in the crook of my arm. Afterwards, she gave me a wistful smile and continued lining up the shells. They would be buried in an ants' nest, to clean them of the dead creatures within.

I asked, 'Where is he?'

'Home,' she replied.

There was silence between us for a while, then she said, 'I don't think he has any fire for me. He seems to like me – but there's no passion.'

I marched out of the hut and took the way to the school teacher's house. On reaching the place, I flung open the screen door, entering without being invited. The teacher was lying on his bed beneath the mosquito netting and he jerked upright, looking alarmed.

'Tomorrow,' I stated, 'we go bonito fishing.'

He nodded, dumbly.

I went out again.

I awoke from a jagged sleep. Ruth was lying beside me, snoring softly. I like to hear that sound. It is intimate. It makes me feel special, to be privileged to hear it. She denies she has this affliction.

'Old people snore. I'm not old.'

She had thought I was trying to mock her. She was quite wrong. I like my own. It pleases me that I am the only one who is privy to such secrets. I want no other man to hear that sound.

I rose, carefully, so as not to wake her. Creeping barefoot to the open doorway of our house, I stared out at the morning. The bright zero was just about to appear from below the horizon. Frogs were still calling to one another, discussing their dreams. I wondered what a frog's dream was like. Did they recognise it as a dream, or was it just another part of real life to them?

Not long after I had been in Britain, my own dreams had changed. Finding myself in a strange land, full of machines and devices, my nightmares were of mad inventors who mechanised the dead. Corpses were exhumed and given additional frameworks of steel rods, with joints and springs and connecting wires. They had motorised humps, which controlled their limbs, their jaws, their heads. They would move in a jerky fashion, whirring and clicking. Their heads would switch back and forth and their jaws would clack out words:

'Alive! I'm alive again!'

Nothing travelled fluidly in this nightmare world. All movements were sudden and sharp. Everything was angular. The landscape was covered in automatons, old flesh hanging from their frames. The mechanical dead. They did nothing but jerk clumsily back and forth, knocking into one another and repeating the same hollow words:

'Alive! I'm alive again!'

I still had such dreams, occasionally, but they were not so disturbing here, on the islands. When I woke up I could see that the real world was very different. Recently, I had dreamt I was dead, and while I was dead, I dreamed. But that is an islander's nightmare.

As I was standing there, the wind changed direction and the smell of the rubbish tip assailed my nostrils. It was old fish bones and rotting vegetables. We used always to burn our rubbish, but the new trash – plastic and rubber – carried such an offensive odour when it was burning that we just buried it.

I took the bucket by the door and went down to the pump. A few years previously we had been sent two fan-bladed windpumps by an American diving team which had enjoyed a brief stay, filming the reef and underwater world around our islands. Tubb has one of them, and Long Island the other. Seawater is pumped through a series of coral filters and is drinkable at the head, though still tasting mildly of salt. We had had to pay Sri Lankan engineers to install the pumps, but it was worth it, not to have to rely on the rainwater tanks beneath the houses. The tanks are served by a series of bamboo gutters and pipes, but since the pumps have arrived, we no longer take care to conserve our supply.

There is more than sufficient for our needs. We use the pump water for washing and keep the rainwater for drinking.

A few days previously, I had checked the teacher's tank and found that the fish were missing. I had replaced them. I wondered what he had done with the fish. Eaten them? These outsiders were strange creatures. They did the most unpredictable things.

Ruth was awake when I returned. She was sitting up and combing her hair. I put down the bucket of water and, taking the comb from her hand, continued the task for her. I know she enjoys the sensual feel of another person running the comb through her thick, black locks. She closed her eyes.

I enjoy it too. I like to touch her, to feel the silkiness of her hair. Sometimes this quiet domestic activity ends in love-making.

We ate some clams and fruit for breakfast. By that time the sun was well over the horizon and I went out to meet other members of the crew of the bonito fishing boat. There were Mark and Peter, two men who lived together as man and wife, and John, the shell-gatherer, and Numbers (whose mother had thought that this title was the name of the man who had written that particular book in the Old Testament), and Uncle Letushim, and David, and Achbor, who had only one good eye and liked to be always on the starboard side of the boat, to favour it. In all there would be twelve with fishing rods, four splashers to attract the fish, three on the sail mat, and a steersman. I intended to be one of the splashers, but I wanted the teacher to have a rod in his hands. There is nothing that stirs the blood more than hooking bonito and landing them in the boat. I wanted his blood stirred – well stirred. I wanted it rushing around his arteries like white water.

I met Numbers and Achbor, along with Mark and Peter, on the beach. Numbers had the bait nets and Mark and Peter carried wicker baskets to keep the live fish in. Achbor and I took a net each and we waded out into the shallows, looking for shoals. When we saw one, we shouted, 'Here! Here!'

We whirled the nets above our heads, swirling them on the throw, so that they fanned into a zero on hitting the water, the weights around their edges stretching them into perfect circles. They sank over the shoals. Mark and Peter would come with the wicker baskets and in would go the catch.

An hour was enough to fill the baskets. Then we picked our way, barefoot, over the sharp coral, back to the beach. We inspected the catch. Little slivers of silver crowding the wickerwork in the shallows. Numbers poked around with a finger amongst them.

'Hey, we've got plenty today. No need for a second batch.'

Over the smalt-blue lagoon the birds were wheeling, gathering like a dust storm. The larger frigate birds circled patiently, ready to rob others of their catch. At our backs the rollers thundered along the outer edge of the reef. It was a good day. Achbor looked at me with his one eye. He was squat and square; a strong man. He was also open-hearted and easy to get on with.

'The teacher – is he coming today?'

'Yes. I'll fetch him in a moment, when the boat's ready.'

Achbor grinned.

'So, he's coming to play fishy-fish. Do you think he's up to it? He looks a bit frail to me.'

'Him? He's always doing exercises and running around the island. He's fit enough.'

'You know as well as I do that a few knee-bendings and runs won't prepare someone for bonito fishing. I hope he doesn't get in the way. If he does, I'll have to throw him out and we'll collect him when it's all over.'

Achbor would do no such thing. He was quite shy and overawed by outsiders, but I smiled at him.

'You be careful he doesn't throw you out. I've seen him when he gets annoyed. His blue eyes flash like lightning. Your little brown one is no match for them.'

'My little brown one has always been a match for anything carried by an outsider,' he said, but he was being obscene.

Beach crabs dance sideways, not too far away from their holes in case enemies should make a sudden move towards them. Further along the sands someone is gathering bamboo poles for the rods, selecting the stoutest stems and testing them for their whip. The rods are the most important items on board the bonito boat. It would be terrible to find a large shoal and fail to catch them because the rods were not up to standard.

Today it is Luke, normally a quiet man. His own company is sufficient for his needs most of the time. Except when there is beer to be had. Then he will suddenly become gregarious and talkative. He likes singing at these times and makes himself a nuisance with some of the other men's wives. Sheba, Achbor's wife, once laid him flat on his back with a single punch and Luke apologised the following day, in that sober-soft voice of his, because she had hurt her hand. Today, Luke gathers the rods for us.

I left the others to transfer the live bait to the wells in the bottom of the bonito boat, while I went to fetch the teacher. On the way I stopped at my mother's house. She was sitting in the middle of the floor, staring at the edge of a mat. I put my arm around her shoulders.

'We're off to catch some bonito,' I said. 'I'll bring you one for your supper.'

She nodded, slowly, but said nothing. She once told me that after my father had gone, the worst times were on waking, when there was a tendency to forget he had gone. Then, as realisation filtered into her mind, and she remembered that he was no longer there, it was as if he had died all over again.

I stayed with her a short while, chattering to her without receiving any response. I made her a drink and placed it in front of her, noting with satisfaction that her eyes strayed to it. She would drink it after I was gone. Some of her grief was display, but that was a genuine part of the bereavement rituals. We do not regard such behaviour as false or hypocritical. The soul needs indulgence, to purge itself of the spiritual pain of loss. It needs to be overwatered with tears, in order to fill the hollow left by the loved-one's departure. How this is done is not important, so long as it works.

I left before the sun struck the top step and reached the teacher's house just as a chicken was leaving. The domestic fowl had learned the trick of opening the screen doors with their beaks and stole any scraps of food that were left lying around.

The hen dashed between my legs, clucking softly to itself. I guessed it had been disappointed by the neatness of the teacher's house.

The teacher was awake and moving around in his bedroom.

'Good morning,' I called, slamming the screen door so as to warn him of my presence. 'The bonito boat is ready.'

He came out of the bedroom wearing a pair of running shorts. I could see he had had a little too much sun. His skin looked red and sore.

'Bonito? Oh, yes. The fishing. I'm not sure I want to go.'

I was aghast at this news. All my preparations for nothing?

'But it's Saturday. No school.'

'It's not a matter of whether I have time.' He sounded irritated and began shuffling some cutlery. 'I'm not sure I *want* to go. I have sunburn for one thing.'

I stared hard at him. This was becoming difficult. I had not expected to find him in such an awkward mood and was unprepared for it.

'But we've got the boat ready. I thought you wanted to go. We've been up, gathering live bait, since dawn and the boat's been rigged – people have worked hard.'

He looked me straight in the eyes.

'You mean to say you did all this for me? I don't believe it, I'm sorry. Your economy depends upon the fishing. You'd be going whether I came along or not, wouldn't you?'

'Well, that's true, but we chose a Saturday so that you'd be able to join us, without worrying about lessons.'

He whirled on me suddenly.

'Yes, and about those lessons! What is that woman doing there?'

'Woman?'

'You know what I mean. I'm never left alone with the children. There's always one woman, sitting in the corner of the classroom, watching me.' He picked up a shoe and threw it angrily across the room. 'I feel like I'm in a goldfish bowl. What the hell is she doing there, Nathan?'

I sighed. 'It's for your own protection.'

'What's that supposed to mean?'

'It means that if a child takes a story home, about the teacher, it can either be confirmed or denied by the woman in attendance.'

He looked horror-struck at these words.

'You – you mean – I might be some kind of a *pervert*?'

'It's been known. I told you, for your own protection. Look on her as a kind of helper. Is that why you won't come fishing? Because you're angry about the woman?'

'Yes – no – oh, I don't know,' he shrugged.

A sudden thought occurred to me. Perhaps I was being hasty? Maybe he wanted me out of the way in order to take Ruth somewhere? Was I being stupid by insisting that he come with us? I couldn't ask him what he was doing, of course, because he'd hardly be likely to tell me that he was going to make love to my wife. Most outsiders jump at the chance of such a trip. They are hungry for other people's lives: people with a different culture. They want stories to tell, material for books, inside knowledge, a chance to go native without losing anything of themselves. I *was* being too hasty.

'All right then,' I said. 'Maybe another time? We won't be back until quite later, but I'll look in on you this evening . . .'

'Oh, OK, I'll come then.' He sounded peevish. 'I suppose I could wrap up – in a long-sleeved shirt.'

'No. Don't worry. You stay here and enjoy your day. You should give your sunburn a rest. It's a lot of hard work, anyway, out in the bonito boat. You probably wouldn't like it.'

His chin came out and his head went up. I didn't know what to think.

'Hard work? You think I'm afraid of hard work? I'm as tough as any of you . . .'

I turned to go.

'It's OK. I'll see you later.'

'Well, am I invited or not? One minute you seem anxious for me to go and the next you're telling me I can't. Make up your mind.'

I could have said the same to him. I realised now that he was just being bloody-minded. It didn't matter to him whether he went or not. He just wanted an argument with me. Maybe he was working off some of his guilt on me? I wished he really had something to feel guilty about, but as far as I knew all he had done was hold hands with Ruth. The man was impossible.

'Come on then,' I snapped.

I waited while he dressed. He seemed to take an interminable length of time, fussing with various items of clothing and grumbling when they touched his sore skin. Eventually he was ready. We set out for the boat. On the way, he asked me a question.

'Do you know a girl called Naomi?'

I hesitated a moment before replying.

'Of course. I know all the islanders.'

We passed beneath a fifty-foot breadfruit tree, its male flowers hanging like clubs.

The teacher frowned. 'I can't seem to get anyone to tell me where she is. Her name's still on the class register, but she never attends school. Do you know what's happened to her? Is she ill?'

I thought about lying to him, but it was possible he might talk to someone else and I didn't want him to hear conflicting stories. It was better to tell him the truth.

'She was beaten to death.'

He stopped in his tracks, a shocked expression on his sunburnt face. His moustache twitched at the corners and I bent down and picked a stalk of *alang* grass to chew, simply so that he had time to absorb this information.

'Christ, that's awful,' he said. 'I'm not sure I want to know about things like that.'

'You asked me and I told you. I would prefer not to talk about this. You must cross her name off your register and not mention it again.'

'The register says she's – was fourteen. God, so young!'

A frigate bird wheeled overhead, its shadow crossing the teacher's face. He looked up, startled, and then regarded me again. He still seemed perturbed by my words, as if I had committed some sort of impropriety. I suppose I could have put it differently, but it seemed all the same in the end. And he didn't know her – hadn't known her – so why was he getting so upset?

'Fifteen, I think. We don't keep that close a count.'

'Are you going to tell me any more? I suppose it's none of my business, but I look on all the children in my school as my responsibility. I didn't start taking the register until three days after I began classes – couldn't find the damn book. Did it happen while I was here?'

So that's what was bothering him. He thought that perhaps he had neglected his duties and she had been somewhere else, other than school, without his knowledge. Since he had not known whether she was there, he could hardly have warned the parents that she had not attended school. This man took his responsibilities very seriously.

'You don't need to worry. It was quite a bit before your time. No one thought about the school register, that's all.'

He seemed relieved, but his face indicated that he wanted to hear more. I ignored this and carried on walking. Shortly afterwards he caught up with me. He said nothing more on the subject. I suppose he felt it would be unseemly to question me further. I was glad. His questions made me nervous. I did not want to cheat Naomi's parents of their rights, but I had come to grow fond of the teacher. He seemed a lot like me in many ways. He had that same air of insecurity here, that I had had while in his country. It was not a pleasant experience and I felt he was coping with it well.

We reached the beach. Numbers was holding the prow of the boat, waiting for us. His face was innocent of expression as he helped the teacher aboard. The teacher suddenly recognised Numbers as the man who had threatened him on the football pitch. He pulled his arm away sharply.

Numbers shrugged. I looked at him hard. It was a warning to him, that the matter was being dealt with and not to take the law into his own hands. Numbers was the father of Naomi, the girl we had just been discussing, the girl who had been raped and murdered by the teacher.

'Is he coming with us?' said John Trencher.

'I'm coming with you,' replied Numbers. He stretched out his hand, the way Englishmen do. The teacher seemed to hesitate, then I suppose he realised it was all he was ever going to get in the way of an apology, and he shook the hand.

'Right!' I cried. 'Now let's go fishing!'

## Seven

Long and beamy, the bonito boat resembles a Viking ship. It has similar sleek lines and a snake-like stemhead, except that this craft is built for speed in warmer water; for hunting shoals of fish, not for cutting through icy seas to plunder the gold of coastal churches. The stoutly built hull bobs gently on the waves as fishermen clamber aboard. Decked only at each end, there are extended platforms for some of the rod carriers, who sit out over the water. There is a single, tall mast which carries the mat sail, to be managed by at least three of the crew.

As the islanders climbed aboard, John Trencher studied the longboat and its rigging. It all looked sturdy enough, but one could never be sure. Sailing had never been a favourite pastime of his. It made him feel insecure and as a child he was often seasick.

The crew were full of enthusiasm, chattering in high voices and exchanging mild insults. It might have been the first time any of them had ventured on such an enterprise had he not known differently. It was obvious that they enjoyed the work. There was no sense of order. They jostled each other for the best positions and took no account of the fact that he did not know where to sit, or what to do.

A rod was thrust into his hands. The wicked-looking barbless hook – a piece of metal, hammered flat – swung dangerously from the end. He caught the line and held it close to the bamboo pole.

Finally, some twenty men were in position and the boat was rowed over the shallows towards the fringing reef. The waves of the vast ocean beyond looked frighteningly high. John wondered how they were going to breach those breakers without overturning the craft. He was cursing himself for ever agreeing to go. The plain fact was, he was scared. Did these people really know what they were doing? They seemed about as responsible as ten-year-old children.

The steersman took a course adjacent to the reef, travelling along just a few yards from the crashing surf. John looked up as a breaker curled above them, rearing for a strike at the now exposed coral edge. The sun shone through its translucency, showing light green: a wall of bottle glass with fish trapped inside. Then it came down, booming along the shelf, and rushing, roaring towards them with angry foam.

Amazingly, its run was short and merely caused a ripple under the boat. The sea dragged itself back again, revealing small, worn chasms in the reef, which drained the liquid from its back. A hollow appeared, deeper than the height of a man, below the outer shelf, as the ocean sucked up the water, ready for another onslaught. Wave after wave: a relentless, repetitive action. How had the island withstood it for so long?

Achbor, next to John, tapped his shoulder and shouted above the noise of the breakers. He pointed at the waves.

'There's an interesting wind today. The waves are meeting on the cross. Should be interesting when we try to get out.'

John nodded, gripping his rod more tightly. *Interesting?* What Achbor had meant was that it was more dangerous than usual. Thank you, Achbor, thought John, I really needed to know that.

'Never seen such a strange sea,' cried Achbor, happy, it seemed, to be able to entertain their guest during the boring parts of the voyage. 'They're twisting like ropes, see? All along the reef . . .'

'I see. I see,' replied John, getting a mouthful of spume in the process. 'Well, I'll have something to tell my friends about then.' If I ever see my friends again, he thought miserably.

Suddenly, the steersman swung the craft round and the bow faced the ocean. John's stomach turned over at least twice. Fishermen then began crouching low, gripping the gunwales. John copied them. His heart was racing and a lump of fear had formed in his throat. He had visions of himself later that day: a mangled, torn corpse, shredded by the sharp corals and then thrown up on the beach as food for the crabs and birds.

Suddenly, everyone else gave out a yell, which caused him to shout too, only John's cry was for help. A gap appeared in the reef. As the retreating wave rushed back in a flurry of white water, the craft surged forward, chasing the eddies. The boat dipped once, sharply, into a steep descent. There was the sensation of sliding down a giant slope on a sledge. Then, miraculously, the bows rose again, borne high on the crest of the next wave. John yelled again, this time in exhilaration.

They were through! Water rushed by the gunwales, soaking his shirt in the spray. He glanced towards Nathan, who was smiling at him. Out on the ocean, the boat felt even more fragile than it had in the shallows, but his trust in it had increased. These men knew what they were doing.

'You all right?' asked Nathan.

He nodded, now ashamed of calling out for God's aid when the boat attacked the reef. He hoped no one had heard: hoped that his shout of terror had been lost amongst their own cries.

'Yes. I . . . I got carried away – a little.'

The smaller man acknowledged this with a gesture of his hands. Then both men concentrated on the sea again, as the boat began riding the swell. Up, up, down. Up, down, down. Sometimes it seemed as though they must be engulfed by the sheer height of the wave, but still they came up with streaming, steaming bows, to plough forward, away from the danger of the reef. Then, suddenly, they were in calmer waters and the sail was raised.

The craft slips easily through the cool waters. Behind, there is a low dark line of green foliage, drifting away from the stern. Ahead, emptiness: an unending expanse of blue water, flecked with sunlight. Above, blueness. Below, dark depths into which the mind has difficulty plunging without an accompanying rush of fear. Below is another world, full of mindless giants and the quick, merciless ferocity of killers. A cold world of dim light, through which monstrous shapes glide.

One man stood by the mast, staring out over the sea. The lookout. The vessel skimmed over the surface, running with the wind, in its search for bonito. An hour went by. Then two. No one spoke very much and John began to get bored. It was like being on one of those river cruises, which are all very well at first, but the scenery becomes monotonous after an hour. There is nothing to do but stare out at the water, which soon loses its attraction.

Conditions were cramped and John could hardly find room to stretch his legs. It was surprisingly chilly, too, at times. His lips were chapped. He began to get stiff joints. A manta ray, as large as a dining table, drifted by John's hand. He could have reached out and touched it.

Some of the men were chewing dried fruit, but he could not raise the enthusiasm. Once or twice he looked behind to see that the islands had gone below the horizon and he felt a mild twinge of alarm. He hoped they were good navigators. The man named Numbers was close to him, almost breathing up his nostrils. Like one or two others, he was baling out water.

'How do you find the way home?' asked John. 'Use a compass?'

Numbers paused in his task and shook his head.

'No compass. We watch the sun and take note of the wind – ' he dipped his hand into the water ' – sometimes a thin cold current, like a snake, passes by the boat. That sort of thing. We'll find our way home.'

John nodded. The Polynesians had similar methods of finding their way across the Pacific. They knew the star paths and water temperatures in various regions. They knew which direction to take on the swell and followed lines of underwater volcanoes. He realised he could trust these people. They had been sailing these waters for centuries. To such sailors, there were ancient but clear roads across the surf, which they could follow unerringly.

'Sounds like clever stuff,' he said to Numbers, but the man didn't answer. He seemed intent on his task of baling out water and his eyes had closed to creases, presumably because of spray or sun. John left him to it and turned instead to Achbor.

'Well, this is very pleasant,' he said.

Achbor snorted. 'Boring. Nothing to do at the moment.'

'Well, yes, you're right of course, but all the same I'm quite enjoying it.'

'Wait until you've done it a thousand times. I like the waves and the fishing, but not the looking so much. See, over there? Porpoise.'

John followed the direction of the arm and saw grey shapes sliding humps through the water.

'Boring fish, porpoise,' said Achbor.

'Actually, they're not fish,' replied John, then mentally kicked himself for being such a pedant. He could see the other man looking at him as if he were touched in the head. 'I mean, they breathe air,' he said.

Achbor made a clown's mouth, as if he couldn't care less whether they were archangels. They were still boring, once you had seen them a thousand times. John wondered if he been unlucky enough to choose a seat by the only manic depressive on board. Certainly Achbor was either in sparkling spirits or plunged into gloom.

Round about noon, the wind dropped and they were becalmed. This was the doldrums. They reverted to oars and John took a turn, mainly to relieve the boredom. At one point, he asked who was the captain of the craft and received a horrified look from Achbor.

'We don't have a captain – captains are bad.'

A democratic boat? It seemed an unlikely idea. Who would make the decision to turn round and head back to the islands? Or would they row on forever, a crew without an Odysseus to land them in trouble occasionally with his arrogant tongue? Tedium. Utter boredom. Surely this was the face of Hell, this blank ocean, where nothing stirred that was not caused by the lazy dipping of oarblades on its featureless surface?

The wind came again – a soft touch on the cheek at first, then enough to fill the sail, which swelled into a matron's bosom. The craft slid forwards. Oars were retracted. Men began to chatter, softly. Then, the clear, ringing shout: 'Bonito!'

John followed the line of the lookout's arm. There! Out there! The sea was full of dancing knives. Rods were grasped as the boat tacked sharply, without a warning.

They raced for the bonito.

From the bottom of the boat, where the wells of live bait were situated, fish were tossed in handfuls over the side. Then they were amongst the bonito. More live bait fell like silver rain, splattering on the surface of the water. The sea began to boil with slivers of glass.

They must have fished this way a thousand times, yet every man amongst them was charged with excitement. John could feel it in the air: an electrical storm contained by the boat. It was infectious. Every nerve in his body tingled with anticipation and for the first time he felt at one with these strange people. They were brothers, comrades, spiritual siblings.

Fishermen climbed on to the extended decks, and four men, Nathan being one, began beating the water with long-handled scoops, on either side. These were the 'splashers', and their actions were designed to make the bonito believe that a giant shoal of fish surrounded the boat. The excitement in the water, amongst the bonito, was hysterical. They thrashed and leaped. They snapped instantly at any live bait. They were blind to everything but getting their share.

The lines went over, the islanders shrieking. It was all chrome and chaos. Bonito took anything which hit the water. No need to bait the hooks. The mere flash of the broad, flat pieces of metal were enough to catch the frenzied bonito. The fish swallowed, the men jerked. Bonito streaked through the air and into the boat. Hooks were removed. Lines flew out again. Wild, wild times that fired passions to white heat.

Crewmen bumped into one another, pushed and jostled and yelled. John hooked his first fish: two feet long and darkly striped. It took all his strength to haul it, thrashing, into the boat. He did not have the knack of smaller men. His mind flew open with excitement. The blood throbbed in his temples.

'I got one. I got one,' he shrieked. 'Jesus Christ, I got one!'

He fought with his catch: a creature one and a half times the length of a rainbow trout. Finally, he managed to remove the barbless hook and flicked the line again into the seething mass of bodies around the boat. Instantly, his arms were almost yanked from their sockets. The rod bent into a fine arch. He heaved against the line, now cutting transient, crazy patterns on the surface of the sea.

'I got another!' he screamed.

No one paid him any attention.

The frenzied atmosphere was sustained for the whole of the fishing period. Bonito piled up in the bottom of the boat; a mountain of heaving silver bars. John's arms were aching to the point where he could hardly stand the pain, yet he was hypnotised by those fish. He wanted more. One more. Two more. Just another. And another. He was in a trance of excitement, the fever of the activity taking control of him completely. His lips trembled, his breath came out in short sharp grunts, and his eyes held nothing but the writhing bonito in their retinas. He was obsessed by them. Nothing else mattered – the sun could fall into the sea and go unnoticed – nothing else but the bonito existed.

Lines snapped, but there were more rods. He cut his fingers twice on taut gut, and learned fast.

When it was over there were in the region of seven hundred fish in the boat: a moderate catch. John, who thought he had excelled even the best of the islanders during the catching, realised he had contributed only about a score of them. Still, he was high with the heady activity. He was elated and all his reserve had gone. His inhibitions had evaporated. He slapped Numbers on the back.

'Well done. Jesus, that was *great*. Did you see that third bastard I pulled in? He must have been six feet, I swear. Hey, Nathan! How did you get on? Shit, that was the most exciting thing I've ever done. I remember you said it would be, but I never thought. I can hardly *breathe*. Jesus. Is that it? Do we go home now? They'll be glad to see this lot, won't they? A few meals here, eh? How long . . .'

He could hardly contain himself. He didn't want to. The mat sail was up. The boat cruised effortlessly through gentle seas. It was all so wonderful.

Then he noticed that the islanders were staring at him in a strange manner. There was a hard look on their faces and all tasks had ceased except that of the steersman. John was puzzled. Had he said something wrong?

'What's the matter?' he asked. 'Why are you all looking at me like that?'

What had he done now? Offended them in some way? Crossed some sacred social boundary? He was at a loss to understand their sudden change of mood. He tried to recall what his last few words had been, but failed. He had just been spouting gibberish.

'Look, if I've . . .'

Numbers pinned John's arms by his sides.

Strong hands gripped him by his legs. He was lifted up and cast out, into the sea. The shock of the cold water took his breath away. Green assailed him. The taste of salt was in his parched mouth.

He came to the surface and spluttered, shaking his hair free of water. Orientating himself, he found the boat. It was skimming away, back towards the islands. Panic surged through him.

'Hi!' he screamed. 'Come back.'

He trod water at first and then tried swimming after the rapidly disappearing boat. Fear of sharks had entered his brain. He would be eaten before he drowned.

'Oh Christ!' he wailed. 'What did I say? What did I say?'

Exhausting himself, he stopped and trod water again, trying to gauge his position and the direction of the islands. Could he swim that far? How far *was* it? He had no idea. They had sailed for a long time to reach this place – this featureless stretch of ocean – but they could have gone in circles for all he knew. Perhaps they were only a couple of miles from the atoll? Or maybe ten – or even twenty? He could not swim twenty miles, even if he knew which way was home.

'You bastards!' he shrieked. 'You bloody bastards.'

What was that? Did something break the surface? Oh, God, there were thousands of sharks in this part of the ocean. He waited for a second, anticipating the sharp, numbing pain of a leg being taken clean off. His terror was excruciating. They had left him to die. He was being murdered for breaking some convention.

Just then, he heard a sound from windward. A shape was streaking towards him. It was the boat! Jesus God, it was the boat. He almost sobbed with relief. They had argued it over and forgiven him. They had come back for him.

A line snaked through the air and whipped across his shoulder. He grabbed it and felt himself being drawn through the water. Then he was at the side of the boat and they were pulling him on board, scraping his side. He fell into the bottom. They were laughing, slapping their sides.

Nathan stood over him, smiling.

'What did I say?' groaned John.

'Say? You didn't say anything as far as I remember. It was a joke.'

'A *joke*?'

'Yes. We do it to all the fishermen that come out the first time. It's a well-kept secret from the boys. Thought we'd left you to the sharks, eh?'

Nathan's smile was infuriating.

'I think . . . I think that's the most humiliating . . . it was . . . Jesus . . .'

'Don't worry. The sharks are all back there, with the bonito and live bait. You were safe enough.'

'Safe enough,' John repeated mechanically.

'Yes. And now you have a healthy respect for the sea. You've learned something.'

'I've learned something all right. I've learned what a bunch of idiots you people are.'

They laughed at this. The humour of the situation sufficiently outweighed the insults.

John found his former place by Achbor, who slapped him on the back. He sat and fumed for a few minutes, terribly angry with them. Then, gradually, he saw things in a different light. They had treated him as one of themselves. They had given him the same honour, if it could be called that, which they gave to their own boys. He had been accorded the same initiation rites as their own people. It *was* an honour: one he should accept with dignity. Eventually he found the courage to smile at Nathan.

'You rotten sods,' he said. 'You really took me in that time.'

Much of his former excitement returned to him. He got them all singing on the way back – sea shanties he had learned at school. (He had thought them boring at the time.) He taught them the words and they learned quickly. Surprisingly, they knew some already.

When they reached the reef, he was actually looking forward to the ride over the jaw of coral. It was a more dangerous operation than going out, but he found it difficult to come down from the heights. He felt courageous, devil-may-care. He realised, without embarrassment, that he had an erection. At that moment he might have tried to leap the Grand Canyon, had he been dared.

'Go for it!' he yelled, lapsing into English. He wanted to retain that ecstasy of bold excitement which had transformed his character. Anything to keep it alight. He was not yet satiated. He wanted more. He understood street fights and reckless driving for the first time in his life. If they had turned the boat out to sea again and had gone for a school of sharks, he would have been overjoyed.

The bonito boat is lifted on to the back of the wave and is driven forward, like a surfboard. The bow stands out, clear of the water, air and surf rushing beneath it. It is a battering ram, aimed at the distant beach. It rides over the jagged coral, scraping once, and shoots into the calm, shallow waters beyond. Then it is gliding, all danger past, towards the shore.

The crew jumped out, guiding the boat with their hands. John helped them. Someone had piled empty crates on the sands and the bonito were transferred to these. Most would be smoked and salted, for delivery to Sri Lanka at a later date.

John assisted with the work for a while, but he quickly became exhausted. The salt was crusted on his skin, leaving white charts of unknown territories, and his eyes were red and sore. Though he had worn a hat most of the time, his head was pounding from the fierce attacks of an ignored sun. Nathan led him back to his house and suggested he get a shower and rest. He nodded and expressed his thanks.

However, he did not go in for a while. He sat on the veranda, in the shade, and watched the activities of the children on the village's earth-packed square. Shortly afterwards, he was visited by Ruth.

'Hello . . . I . . . did you want something?'

She sat on the top of the steps, near his feet.

'You liked the fishing?' There were red blotches on her cheeks, as if she had been pinching them. Her face looked childlike and innocent.

'Yes, very exciting. I've never known anything like it.' He sat there, awkward in her presence. Why wasn't she at home with Nathan? He had been away all day, after all. He waited for her to do something more, and she did. She got up from her seat and moved closer to him. Then she brushed the salt from his hairline. The touch of her fingers on his burning skin nearly drove him crazy with desire.

'What . . . what are you doing?' he asked.

'You must learn to relax. I'm helping you.'

The cool hand, with its slightly coarse palm, stroked his brow. He did not know what to do. What did she want from him? Had they been in England, he would have known at once, but he did not trust himself in this culture. He could make a dreadful mistake. It was ironic, considering the arousal he was feeling. What seemed now impossible with Julia might be possible with another woman. But Nathan's wife?

'Where's Nathan?' he asked, fearful again of them being seen from the village.

'In the house. He's asleep. Do you want to go inside?'

He *wanted* to go inside, there was no question of that. He had not wanted something so much for three years now. The thought of taking Ruth into his bedroom made his head spin with excitement. But should he? What a terrible thing, if Nathan ever found out. And would it end in just one . . . or would there be more, until he could not extricate himself?

It was growing dark. He still had not answered her. He could not tell her to go, either. A star became perceptible just above the horizon and a fruit bat drifted between palms.

He wanted her. He wanted her very badly. Why was she doing this? Wasn't she happy with her husband? Perhaps this was normal, natural, on the islands? That a woman could offer herself to whom she wished, without disrupting the harmony of her marriage? He didn't know and suddenly, he didn't care. Thoughts of Nathan were swept aside by that urgent desire he had not felt since God knew when.

He slipped his hand into hers. It seemed natural. And he talked. He avoided looking at her, and he talked. A stream of nonsense to help unblock the feelings that choked his breast. Then he said hoarsely, 'Let's go inside,' just as the generator rumbled to life at the back of the village and lights went on.

John switched on the light as he entered and was aware of a faint buzzing noise. At first he thought it was coming from the lightbulb, but then, when he looked down, he saw a large beetle on the floor. It was on its back, but moving slowly, as if floating, towards the window.

Something was wrong. Then, in the dim light of the lamp, he realised that the floor was moving. It seemed to be swaying. The movement went into the walls, which wavered and rippled. Everywhere was black.

He recoiled in horror, backing into Ruth.

'What's the matter?' she asked, still half in the doorway.

'Ants,' he said. 'The room's covered in ants – Jesus, they're over everything. The place is thick with them.'

It made his flesh crawl. Normally, he did not mind ants – but so many? They swarmed over everything: floor, walls, furniture, window. And they were large ants, some a quarter of an inch long. They were over his feet now, finding their way through the hairs on his legs.

'Shit!' He stamped, trying to shake them off. Then he brushed at them, vigorously. He couldn't believe there were so many. Millions of the creatures. They transformed the room into something live: a surreal piece of architecture that was constantly on the move, yet never changing shape. Some of the ants were carrying white eggs. John felt ill.

'What do I do about them? I can't go in there.'

Ruth said, 'You have to smoke them out. I'll get Uncle Letushim. He has bellows and he'll smoke them out for you.'

She trotted down the steps and towards the village.

John stood outside the screen door, watching the black mass moving on the inside of it, almost blocking out the light. All thoughts of lovemaking had gone from his mind now. He knew, even if she came back and the ants could be banished, that he would not be able to perform. That was now lost – the feeling activated by the day's excitement. The ants had seen to that.

'Bloody ants,' he said, kicking the door. The action made them move around more rapidly, like heated molecules, but they soon resumed their normal speed. John waited for Uncle Letushim to arrive.

# Eight

Equator. This is the land of vertical days, and I am its child. I stand under the sun at its meridian, and know that we are in line, my body a needle pointing at the high zero. And around me, the ocean falls away, gently curving in all directions, down to the rest of the world. Out of the navel of our atoll the sun rose. We gave it birth.

Not so long ago, in years, a new figure entered the mythology of the islands. A dark figure, used to frighten children into good behaviour. The Captain. My ancestors, the mutineers, used to speak of this terrible man with hatred in their voices. The Captain. He had hanged their comrades for infringing his rules. He was a tyrant, a mortal *Wobbly*, insane with power. He had minions, lesser despots, called First Officer and Mate.

It was from the Captain's wrath that the mutineers had fled in their longboat. They told their children, once they were old enough to understand, that the Captain was so powerful his arms could reach across oceans and snatch babies from their beds. The Captain could do this because he was protected by a title, which was eternal. Beware of those who bear a title, said the fathers. Beware of those who attach a universal label to their names, for they continue, even after death. You may kill the Captain, but the Captain still lives. He comes wearing another body, using another name, but he remains the Captain. His power never dies.

In the mythology of the islands there were already shape-changing gods, the worst of whom was *Wobbly*, who swallowed souls, the excreta of which went to fertilise his snares, the screwpine trees, the *midnight walkers*. *Wobbly* was *Wobbly*, whatever his face or form. He was a shadow, a dark area of rain, a cold wind, a bird, a fish, a man. He moved on the surface of the earth, and below it, gluttonous for the souls of men, sucking the roots of *midnight walkers*. *Wobbly* was usurped by the Captain.

'Who is the Captain? He is the Captain. Who is the Mate? He is the

Mate. Who is the Chief? Why, of course, the Chief. Just as the Priest is the Priest. Whatever form he takes, he is still the Priest. He calls himself such. He is his title.'

This, the fathers told their children, was how things were in the outside world. The King is dead! Long live the King! The King never dies. 'I am the King,' he says, 'and therefore you shall, or shall not, as I command.' Thus, it followed, the children told their children, that any responsibility must lie with the bearer, since the bearer has assumed the title to which power is attached. If a man takes on a titled role, inherits power and benefits with that role, then he surely must inherit responsibility for the deeds performed under the banner which protects those privileges, that power? The Captain hanged the comrades of our fathers, they said, therefore the Captain is responsible for their deaths, whatever guise he may assume. The role is more important than the individual.

In 1878, some time after the mutiny, Captain Philip Aldous landed on Short Island and was immediately seized and hanged by the inhabitants. Justice had been done. The Captain, in one of his many guises, had been taught a lesson. Death is a painful business, even for immortals who expect to rise again. From then on, Captains never left their ships to set foot on the islands. Even today, when harboured at the islands, Captains still observe this rule. Mythology is deeply rooted. It takes more than civilisation to dig it out and dispose of it.

From my position in the tree I could see the teacher sitting at his small table, writing, writing, writing. Only the upper half of his body was visible to me: the rest was hidden below the open window. From time to time he looked out, into the darkness, as if he knew he was being observed. He was trying to find the right words. It was as if they were hanging in the night, ready to be plucked from vines, but he could not reach them. Then he snatched, almost angrily, at the piece of paper on the table, screwing it up and throwing it across the room. He began again, on a fresh sheet.

Later, he put down his pen and went to the front of his house. I scrambled down the tree and went after him, creeping through the damp fronds of the rainforest. As expected, he wandered to the middle of the village, where the children were playing in the light coming from the open doorways of the huts.

They stopped and looked up as he passed, a trace of anxiousness in their expressions. He was the teacher and someone, not exactly to be *feared*, but to whom attention must be given. He murmured something to a group of them and they nodded, some of them glancing towards their houses. No doubt he disapproved of the fact that they were up so late in the evening.

He walked on then, and stood outside my home. His position was such that he could be seen from within, though he kept partly to the shadows. It was as if he did not wish to be observed by the rest of the village, but wanted to make his presence known to the occupants of my home. He lit a cigarette and waited. Had I been inside and had come out to greet him, he could have claimed he was out for a stroll, had seen my light and had stopped, wondering whether or not to call on me.

When the cigarette had been half smoked, Ruth came to the doorway. He crushed the butt underfoot and seemed about to walk away when she trotted down the veranda steps and, seemingly ignoring him, took the moonlit path to the beach. After looking around, quickly, he followed her.

By the time I was close enough to see them again, they were walking hand-in-hand along the sands, the hermit crabs scuttling away at their approach. He was talking earnestly to her, though I could not hear what was being said. They looked a strange pair: he, tall and lean, slightly bowed in order to speak down to her; she, small and delicate, like a child in comparison. This meeting had not been planned by me and I tried to crush the feelings it aroused. I kept telling myself that it was necessary. The Englishman was not using us: we were using him. Ruth thought I was visiting a friend on Pork Island. I was not expected until dawn.

She could not get a baby by holding hands, but presumably this would lead to more productive things.

They found a place to sit, under a frangipani tree, where they could watch the sparkling waves tumbling over the reef in the moonlight. From time to time, blossoms from the trees showered them with petals as a gust of wind caught the branches, and these fell on their hair and shoulders. They were talking so earnestly they did not seem to notice the confetti that covered them. I crept up behind them, hidden in the foliage some few yards away.

'I know I'm treading on dangerous ground,' he was saying to her, 'but something must be done. You're destroying yourselves with this foolish practice . . .'

Ruth wrapped her arms around her knees and hugged herself into a ball. This was her *thinking* position.

'Nathan's worried about the same thing. Have you seen the print on our wall? Yes? Well then, you see that if Nathan can't do anything about it, how can you? He knows his own people – we must have our coral heads when we die, otherwise there is no way for the living relatives to talk to us – no protection from the *midnight walkers*, or the Captain.'

She looked him in the eyes.

'I don't want to be the first to go without a head. Even me. No one wants to be the first. I'm sorry, John. I wish I could help.'

He tossed a handful of petals in the air. They floated slowly to earth.

'There's *got* to be a way to convince you all,' he said. 'I'll find it, don't you worry. I intend making these islands my home from now on, so I've got plenty of time.'

She said in a surprised voice, 'You don't want to go back to England?'

'No.'

'But what about your wife and child?'

He stood up and hunched his shoulders like a small boy.

'I've told you before – she's not my wife – and Ben gets on better when I'm not around. I'm much better off here – *they're* better off without me . . .'

'I can't believe that,' said Ruth. 'You're just saying that because you want it that way. Come and sit down . . .' She patted the sand beside her.

He did as he was asked.

She continued. 'Nathan tells me that England is very cold – that even the winds are white there.' She pretended to shiver. 'I don't like being cold.'

Then he whispered something to her and she laughed. I strained to hear, knowing I could not get any closer without being seen. I did not want to be discovered. Ruth would be quite angry if she knew I had been spying on her, and rightly so. We had agreed that she should be allowed to handle the thing in her own way, in her own time, and I was to keep out of the affair.

'It will only upset you, once you know it's happened,' she said. 'The less you know, the better. It's not something I want to do, you understand. He's a nice man, but that's all he is to me. That's all he ever will be . . .'

And here she was, allowing him to murmur into her ear, things I could not catch on the wind. What was he saying that was making her look so happy? Was he offering her another life, somewhere else, away from me? Maybe all that talk about wanting to stay on the islands was deceit? Much more good would have come of it if they had just gone down to the beach, made love, and then returned to their respective houses. There should have been no need for words.

I walked the length of the island, trying to come to terms with my feelings. In the planning stage, this had all seemed so simple, but complications were now arising that I had not given thought to before now. I could probably stop the whole scheme, dead, if I wanted to, but I wondered if I were over-reacting. Perhaps I was misjudging the situation and Ruth had merely tried to be polite? It was a delicate affair to balance.

As my mind pondered these problems, I reached a long shack. There were no cables leading to this area, but a hurricane lamp burned inside the hut and I could hear hammering noises coming from within. I opened one of the large doors and went inside, where the smell of paraffin mingled with that of freshly cut timber. Uncle Letushim was there, working at his bench. He was making a boat and was in the process of fashioning the kingpin. Wood shavings covered the floor and I waded through them to where the grizzled man stood.

Uncle Letushim, at seventy, was one of the oldest inhabitants of the islands. He had seen a great deal in his time, including the short occupation of our atoll by the Japanese in the Second World War. He told the story of how a small garrison had been left – it seemed abandoned – on Long Island, in order to build an airstrip.

He had been a young man then, in his twenties, and was given the job of organising the local labour. There was no difficulty in this, since the islanders quite enjoyed a break from their normal routine and they looked on the exercise as a welcome change. Of course, utilising the men on the clearance of foliage meant that the women had to do the fishing, which they too saw as an opportunity to get away from the rituals of cooking and washing.

At first, everything went well. The Japanese had not hurt any of the islanders and though stiff and reserved seemed reasonable people. Communication presented a difficulty, but sign language and the odd word learned here and there seemed adequate for all involved. Of course, Uncle Letushim and the rest of the islanders were aware that should there be any resistance on their part, the Japanese would use force, but there seemed no need for that. And it wasn't as if the foreigners were staying forever. The islanders are a fairly patient people.

However, it became apparent after a while that there was a major disagreement in the air. The issue was over the width of the runway. The Japanese sergeant wanted it so big – and paced it out, crossing almost from one side of the island to the other. Uncle Letushim shook his head. That was impossible. Such a wide clearance would defoliate the whole island. He told the Japanese that they could have it so big – and paced out about four yards.

The sergeant shook his head furiously. He sat down opposite Uncle Letushim and tried to explain, in sign language, that planes were much larger things than that. They needed to remove all the rainforest from beach to beach.

Sorry, Uncle Letushim indicated. If they wanted a runway that wide, then they would have to put it on Short Island, which was wide enough to accommodate such a clearance without stripping it bare.

The sergeant gnashed his teeth and indicated that Short Island was not long enough. The planes would go into the sea at the far end, and if Letushim and his islanders didn't start work soon, his soldiers would begin shooting them.

Uncle Letushim said that would be very silly, because if the Japanese killed them all they would have no one to do the work and no one to feed them. They would all starve.

When the sergeant finally understood what Uncle Letushim was saying, he replied that perhaps they would only kill half the population.

Uncle Letushim answered that they would need the night to think it over.

By the next morning, all the islanders had gone. They had taken to the boats or walked around the reef to Jorka Island. They stood on the shore and jeered across the three miles that separated them from the Japanese. The sergeant ordered his men, some twenty-five in all, on a trek around the reef to Jorka Island. By the time they had got there, by way of Tubb, the islanders were back on Long Island, their jeers even louder.

The sergeant assessed the situation and began the trek again, leaving five men on each island as he went, until the islanders were crowded on Pork Island, with the remaining five Japanese, the sergeant at their head, crossing from Short by way of the reef path.

When the Japanese were halfway across, Uncle Letushim and some young men set sail in the bonito boat. Crouching low to avoid the rifle fire, which was inaccurate because of the need for the soldiers to keep their balance on the reef, they bore down on the unfortunate outsiders and swept them into the sea. One man was drowned and the others rescued, but without their weapons, which had been lost to the ocean.

The islanders realised there was no going back now. Their defeat of the sergeant and his five soldiers had been witnessed by the Japanese on Short Island, but had been out of sight to those on the other three. The short-wave radio, they knew, was on Long Island, and this had to be destroyed before the soldiers there decided that the situation had got out of hand and tried to obtain assistance.

Uncle Letushim decided to wait until nightfall.

Throughout the atoll there was a network of catwalks joining the tops of coconut palms. These precarious bridges consisted of two ropes, one above the other, which were used by toddy tappers to reach the coconut buds without the need to climb down one tree and up another. The toddy tappers used this aerial system to travel between palm tops twice a day during the season, to bind the buds of the coconuts to prevent them from flowering, and to knock down surplus pods with a bone. At the end of two weeks, the tips of the bound buds were cut to collect the sweet, milky sap of the blossom. This nectar was used in the making of alcohol.

When night came, Uncle Letushim and some strong swimmers crossed the lagoon and made their way up to the toddy-tapping bridges. They passed silently through the canopy above the rainforest, moving from palm top to palm top, until they were above the five Japanese. When the soldiers were asleep, leaving a single, unwary sentry, the islanders fell on them and quickly disarmed them. The radio and weapons were thrown into the sea, the islanders having no use for the rifles and single machine gun.

In this way, Uncle Letushim and his youths gained control of the atoll again, and the sorry contingent of soldiers was rendered defenceless.

The sergeant indicated to Uncle Letushim that if his superiors returned, not only would he be executed, but the islanders would be decimated. Uncle Letushim said they would worry about that when it happened. The population could always take to the boats and fan out, heading for other islands and atolls.

Luckily, the next warship that called was American and the islanders handed over their prisoners, at the same time stating in no uncertain terms that they wanted no more foreign soldiers on their soil.

That, then, was Uncle Letushim's Second World War and he wanted no part in any other, he said.

Uncle Letushim looked up as I entered the hut, and smiled.

'Nathan.'

'Uncle.'

Behind him the half-finished *dhoni* almost filled the interior of the hut. It looked like the majestic skeleton of some huge sea beast, throwing the shadows of its ribcage against the far wall. Once the vessel was complete, the walls would be removed and the craft taken out for launching.

He said, 'Can't you sleep, boy? You should be in bed with your wife.'

He still treated me as if I were ten years old.

'I can't sleep,' I replied. 'My head won't close. It stays open and the thoughts keep whirling around inside. Will the boat be ready soon?'

Uncle Letushim sighed. 'Slowly, slowly, it's coming into shape. I'm growing old, Nathan.' He held out a stringy arm. 'There's not much strength left in me. My eyes grow dim – they're full of shadows these days. Soon I shall join my father. My soul grows weary in my skin – I'm looking forward to going. These bones are as dry as sticks and my mouth plays tricks with taste.' He plucked the withered folds of his stomach. 'This beef will soon be rotting into the ground. I've cut my last *dhoni*.'

He had been saying such things for as long as I could remember. He had always been 'too old, too weary' for yet another boat, but still the craftsman kept on working.

He stared at me in the light of the flaring lamp, the hollows of his face full of concern.

'But you, Nathan. You look full of sorrow. What is it, boy? Why are you crying inside?'

Without meaning to, I blurted out, 'It's Ruth. She's looking at the teacher with soft eyes.' There, it was out, and the shame flooded through me. Not only was my wife giving soft looks to another man, I had admitted such. I was only glad that the words had fallen on an uncle's ears and not someone outside my family.

Uncle Letushim put down the tool he was holding and shook his head, sadly. He knew what my plan was: for Ruth to become pregnant by the teacher. He had warned me of the perils of such a scheme, but I had not listened. I could see nothing but a way to obtain a daughter or son. I so desperately wanted a child, as did Ruth. It had seemed such a simple plan – and safe too. Of course, the priest would not have approved, but then we scorned him for his celibacy anyway. What did he know about the need for children?

Why had it gone wrong? From what I had seen in England, men and women frequently chose to make love and then go their separate ways. This scheme should have been easy.

Uncle Letushim said, 'So Ruth is looking for the eye of the teacher?'

'Yes.'

He was stern with me.

'Nathan, I spoke to you about this. When a man and a woman have made love, they get strong feelings, here.' He tapped his chest, above his heart.

'No, no. They haven't made love. They . . . they talk.'

'*Talk?*' Uncle Letushim's eyes widened.

'Yes, talk. They walk hand-in-hand and they talk. All along the beach.'

Uncle Letushim stared at me and there was a look of bewilderment on his face.

'My soul grows weary in my skin,' he said. He turned back to his bench and began carving the kingpin again. I think it upset him that he did not understand why I was so concerned. Of course, a stranger should not hold the hand of another man's wife, but the fact that he was doing only that, and merely conversing with her, did not seem to Uncle Letushim cause for anguish. I knew what he expected me to do. I was supposed to go home and paddle my wife's bottom. She would be sorry and cry in my arms. Then we would make love and all would be well again. She would have eyes for no one else but me after that.

But these were the old ways and they were not acceptable any longer – not to me, nor my generation – despite the fact that elderly men asserted that they were infallible. I could no more lay a hand on Ruth than I could throw myself to the sharks. I loved my wife and if she no longer loved me, then I should have to step aside. It seemed to me that talk – the kind of talk I had heard this evening – was far more a case for concern than active love-making. Two bodies thrashing around in dark corners can be made to look ridiculous in the light. Limbs can be untangled. Whispered promises, however, can bind people together far more tightly.

I slept on the shavings and sawdust that night, and then made my way home in the dawn. My body tingled with apprehension as I approached my house. Would she be there, or still out on the beach? Or perhaps, with him, in his house? A sudden anger took control of me and I ran towards the teacher's house. As I approached, he was coming out, through the screen doorway. He was dragging his mattress.

He saw me and turned away. Perhaps he realised that such an action was revealing, because he looked back at me quickly, as if just noticing that I was there.

'Bed bugs,' he called. 'Damn things have been eating me all night. Didn't get a wink of sleep.' He lifted his leg, showing me a bare thigh, below the shorts. 'See? Blood smears. I got one or two of them though.'

Bed bugs. How ridiculous the man was. Here was I, worried almost to death about whether he and my wife were binding their spirits together with vows of 'forever' – and he was concerned about bed bugs. Surely such a man could not be taken seriously? Anyway, I reminded myself, his days on the islands might soon come to an end.

I turned and ran back to the house. The hump in the sheet told me she was still sleeping. I woke her gently, touching her shoulder. She smiled up at me, sleepily. We murmured to one another, like two bees, for some time. Then I went back out on to the veranda.

How could I doubt her?

## Nine

It comes every year, from the sky. It can be seen, hours ahead, moving like a wall across the ocean. Small children have been known to turn and run screaming to their mothers, thinking that the Captain, his dark beard filling the space between sea and sky, was sweeping across the water, ready to swallow them whole.

It is the rain.

It comes, preceded by a cool wind which chills the skin, as an onslaught. Alarming in its pace and dense, gloomy aspect, it hits the islands like a wave and takes away the breath of any who may be out of doors. The darkness, within it, is worrying.

It hits the rainforest with such a force that the trees look as though they are being battered to their knees, the heads of the palms going limp and bending under the continual blows. Then they seem to force themselves upright, just a little, as if they have begun to realise that this is a good thing. They start to drink.

Muddy pools form rapidly in any hollow or shallow depression. Water runs from the roofs, gushing down the bamboo gutters and pipes. Palm-leaf thatch becomes sodden and begins to leak within minutes. The noise is deafening. Children now run outside, dancing and yelling, as they play in the rain they had forgotten. The lagoon is grey and dimpled, like hammered iron sheeting, and any small boats race home across its surface.

John Trencher woke with a start as the iron roof began to thunder above him. He looked at his watch. Four o'clock. Day, or night? Afternoon, surely? Yet it was dark outside. No, not dark, but a murky green colour. What the hell was going on? Armageddon? He went to the window and looked through the flyscreen mesh. The island was awash, water running in rivulets, forming pools. The rains. The long rains had come.

Good, he thought, I'm not quite ready for Armageddon. He went back to bed, the sound of the rain comforting for a while. As he tried to sleep, the noise began to worry him again. It was coming down in such torrents. Surely the island could not take hours of this kind of rain? It had nowhere to go. They would all be drowned. There was an irony for you – surrounded by thousands of miles of ocean, and finally drowning in fresh water. He thought, briefly, about getting up and having another look outside, but then there was a flash, and an explosion which rattled the house. Thunder and lightning. It *was* Armageddon. Best try to sleep through it and hope that the forces of Good prevailed.

The rain continued all through the evening. Finally, at about midnight, peace came once more. John drifted in and out of dreams, enjoying the luxury of oversleeping without the usual accompanying guilt.

When he rose next morning, his house was an island. Outside, the water was a foot deep; more in places. Its mirror surface reflected the palms, breadfruits, frangipanis and stilted huts. A looking-glass world.

The man known as Letushim waded past his house, his longi tucked up into his belt like a woman's skirts, and his thin legs causing barely a ripple in the still waters.

'Good morning!' called John, moving out on to the veranda and leaning on the rail.

The white-haired head came up. 'Yes. The rains have come.'

'So I see. I expect you've witnessed many more in your time. Such a lot of rain is quite new to me.'

Letushim nodded. 'Every year.'

It was a silly conversation and John waved to the old man before going inside again. There was a class to take in thirty minutes and he wanted to leave himself plenty of time to walk to the school.

When he arrived there and took the register he found that half his pupils were missing, and those that had come were in an excitable mood. Such a lot of fuss, he thought, about something that merely irritated him when he was in England. But, he granted, it was an event in their otherwise dull lives, and he had to admit that a monsoon downpour was far more dramatic than English drizzle.

When classes were over, he waded back to his house in his flip-flops. The rubber soles acted like suction pads on the mud beneath and he continually had to pause to replace a lost one, having to feel around in the muddy water, now floating with dead wood, leaves and hundreds of small frogs.

Where had all the little amphibians come from? Surely they could not time their change from tadpole to frog so accurately that it met with the coming of the rain? It was uncanny.

Two of his favourite pupils trailed on behind him, watching his reactions to everything that the flood had brought. He was glad they were curious, but he did not exactly enjoy being the object of their amusement. He turned on them.

'Moses. Samuel. What do you want?'

They stared at him. Moses, at twelve, was the elder by two years.

He said, 'Nothing, sir.'

'Well, shouldn't you be going home? Your mothers will be concerned about you.'

They continued to stare at him, not making any move towards the village. He had noticed how much less his authority counted outside the classroom. Had that been the same at home? He could not remember.

John continued his passage to the house and climbed thankfully up the steps to enter. Once inside, he put down his briefcase and sat on his chair. It felt damp. Everything felt damp. *And what the hell was that noise?*

There was a chirruping sound coming from beneath the house. He groaned. With his stomach feeling like bakers' dough, he went to the corner and lifted the lid to the water tank. Sure enough, that was where the noise was coming from. The tank was full of small, green frogs, sitting on the inside lip, or using the water to swim. They seemed to be enjoying themselves.

John went to the doorway and called to the boys. They came running, splashing through the floodwater, obviously thinking they were in for a treat. He showed them his aquarium.

'How do I get rid of them?' he asked. 'You must know. It must happen all the time.'

It certainly did not seem like it. The boys' mouths dropped open and their eyes were wide. Moses went down on his knees and peered into the tank. Then he looked up at his teacher with a searching expression. 'Where did the fish go?'

John experienced a sinking feeling.

'Fish?'

Samuel piped in. 'Yes, sir. Everybody-got-small-fish-in-their-tanks-that-eat-the-frogs'-eggs-and-keep-the-water-clean-for-drinking-' This came out without a pause for breath, as if he wanted to finish before anyone else interrupted and stole his thunder. He beamed at John, having delivered his package of knowledge.

Christ, thought John. That's what the damn fish were doing in the tank! And each time he had found them, he had taken them out and thrown them away. He had thought it a running joke between him and the locals. He had almost begun to enjoy the game.

Now he was exposed. He had robbed the tank of the fish that ate the spawn, algae and mosquito larvae. Oh, he could see what he had done, now. But they must think him soft in the head. What a fool! Why hadn't he just given it that extra bit of thought, instead of immediately jumping to the conclusion that they were out to play tricks on him?

'I don't know where the fish went,' he lied to the boys, and they knew he was not telling the truth. They grinned at each other.

Moses and Samuel went off, to fetch nets, and were soon back. They began to clear his tank of the frogs, taking them outside to join the rest of the multitude. Later they brought him two more fish and put them in the tank. Before they left he made them each a drink, of warm goat's milk, and gave them a precious bar of Cadbury's chocolate (which had turned a strange grey colour, having melted and reset several times) to share between them.

'There's no need to tell this to anyone else, is there?' he said, as they went out on to the veranda.

'Is it a secret?' said Samuel.

'Between just the three of us,' replied John, but he noticed that Moses had adopted a very neutral expression, as if he wanted to be left to make up his own mind as to whether this thing should be kept quiet.

John watched them splash through the flood, carrying their nets, wondering whether he was going to be blackmailed at a later date. He would have to wait and see.

Letushim viewed his nephew Nathan with some concern. Ever since the boy had come to him for advice the other evening in the boat shed, he had felt guilty for turning him away. It wasn't that he did not want to help, because he did. But the world had begun to slip from his grasp. He understood less and less of human relationships and more about death. That was where his current interest lay, naturally. When one was so close to it, one's mortality became an ever-occupying thought. He was morbidly engrossed in the frailty of the flesh.

But today he had shaken that off, determined to help his nephew with his troubles, petty as they might seem to a man who had been dying for nearly twenty years.

'Do you wish me to speak with Ruth?' he asked Nathan.

The boy seemed horrified.

'No, no. I don't want to say anything to her – I think it's best left alone, to work its own way out.'

Letushim shook his head. There, you see? What sort of answer was that from a vigorous young man of Nathan's kind? Do nothing. It was difficult – impossible – to understand what went on in such minds. Letushim would have fought tooth and nail to keep his own wife, when she had been alive . . . no, that wasn't true, he reminded himself. Now that he remembered, he hadn't liked her very much. But if he *had* liked her, no man on earth would take her away without a few scars on his body. Today's youth thought that if you turned your back on something, ignored it, the thing would go away. These were the thoughts of cowards.

'Are you a coward, Nathan?'

'Perhaps.'

There – what could you make of that? You try to sting them into action, provoke some sort of active response by jabbing at their pride, and they agreed with you. Letushim knew very well that all men are afraid, but you didn't go around admitting it to your uncle. He changed tack.

Letushim said, 'I saw the teacher this morning. He seemed to be fascinated by the rain. Don't they have rain in England?'

'Not like ours. There, it's like a cloud of mosquitoes – persistent and irritating. A weak, snivelling kind of rain.'

'Why does he wear that silly hair on his lip?'

'He thinks it looks attractive.'

'Ha. I'm sure the women laugh at him.'

'Ruth doesn't. She thinks his moustache makes him look dignified.'

'What? Dignified? On that lobster face? I can't believe it.'

'Well, it's true. She thinks him handsome. She told me so.'

Letushim was taken aback again. In this day and age the women were hussies. They *told* you when they thought another man handsome? Such things were difficult to accept for an old man who was likely to die at any minute.

Letushim pointed to the can of tea on Nathan's charcoal fire and indicated he would like a refill in his cup.

'Did you punish her for this?'

Nathan poured the tea into the cup, burning his fingers in the process, and sucking them.

He said, 'I can't punish her for telling the truth, can I? Besides, I like it when she's outspoken. It means there are no secrets . . .'

He stopped and looked miserable.

Letushim said, 'There are always secrets locked in a woman's mind – you know that.'

'Well, I can't punish her anyway. I haven't the right and I don't want to. Ruth would be . . . I don't know . . . she'd be astounded and hurt if I ever tried to hit her. I just couldn't do it.'

But that was the idea, wasn't it? To show them you cared for them so much that you would even go against your nature and paddle some sense into them?

Letushim studied the wrinkled fingers that were wrapped around his cup. Were those hands his own? Surely only yesterday they had been thick and strong, with calluses where there were now folds of skin, and bulging sinews where there were now ugly veins and liver spots.

Outside the hut, the village was full of activity. Someone walked past the doorway with the carcass of a goat, slit up the middle, slung over his shoulder. A woman was cleaning her teeth noisily, just a few yards away, with a frayed twig, making grunting sounds. Children were squealing as they played their incomprehensible games amongst the legs of the adults. None of this touched Letushim very deeply. He was too wrapped up in thoughts of himself and how he was fading from life.

He suddenly became aware that Nathan was still talking to him, but he hadn't heard a word. He rose from his haunches, the stiffness in his bones giving him trouble.

'I must get back to my boat,' he said.

He knew that once he started working on the wood, creating new life of a kind, he would forget himself a little and his fears would be blunted, if not disappear. He left the hut with a little wave of his hand and stepped out into the water that surrounded the village.

At four o'clock precisely, the rain returned in bountiful drops the size of pearls. They had the same lustre as those oceanic beads: opaque globules with a hazy white sheen. The difference between this rain, and that which fell on the fields of Europe, was in the space between the drops. On the equator, they followed barely a hair's-breadth apart, forming thick curtains. They fell on to the corrugated iron roof of his house with such noiseful force that it was impossible to concentrate on anything for more than a minute. John gave in to one of his favourite pastimes: sitting and staring into space.

Early next morning, John went for a walk along the ridge at the top of the beach. It was the only continuous strip of sand that was not covered by the flood. The island sparkled in the sunshine and he felt suddenly aware of life in and around him. This was one of those rare occasions when he felt buoyant. He began humming to himself.

It was while out on this stroll that he saw a group of the islanders cutting another block from the reef. The sight worried him. Everywhere in the world people were tearing down the natural walls that protected them, or sustained life in some way. They cut down the forests, defoliated the jungles, overfished the ocean, destroyed the coral reef, and so on, and so on. Where was it going to end? Conservationists were cranks to those with the power to make changes. Their message had begun to bore even the messengers, it had been repeated so often. The expanding dustbowl of the American Great Plains had taught people nothing. The course was set for a dead planet. Unreclaimable. There were no Lazarus miracles left, especially not for whole worlds.

Yet the issues were enormously complex. Demand still ruled the day: supply still ruled the night. What could a school teacher do to influence such mighty powers as these?

He could educate the young, that's what! John made a decision. He would do his bit for conservation by injecting good sense into his pupils.

John watched the coral cutters drag an enormous bolus, dripping with submarine plants, starfish and molluscs, up on to the strand. Its beautiful colours, scarlets and purples, were still buried in its crown. The live creatures, the polyps, would soon die and only the grey-white skeleton – the corallite – would remain.

It wasn't that John was against the destruction of life for reasons which would be regarded as sentimental by the islanders. Not at all. He was against it because it was a fact that a reef took so long to replace, and it was the atoll's only protection against the sea. They were destroying not only themselves, but their future generations. Those that were to come should have a voice in the affair.

That morning he took a large box of Lego blocks into school with him. This was normally his 'keep-them-quiet' kit for rainy days back home in England, but he had another purpose for it today.

Once in the classroom, with the pupils attentive, he built a small house out of the Lego bricks. Then he called Moses to the front of the class. The boy stood before the teacher's desk, looking ill at ease. John soon put his mind at rest.

'There's nothing to get concerned about, Moses. I just want to try you with a puzzle. You see this house? It's a nice house, but too small. I want you to build it higher. Can you take some bricks from the bottom and build the top of the walls higher?'

Moses stared at him as if he were mad. Then a knowing look came into his eyes. He took several blocks from the bottom, leaving stilts, and fitted them round the top of the walls, stepping back so that his classmates could see his handiwork.

'Good,' said John. 'You may sit down. Now Hannah,' he pointed to a girl of thirteen, 'can you take the bricks from the stilts and make the house even taller still?'

Hannah rose from her mat, slowly, and walked majestically to the front of the class. She turned to face her fellow pupils.

'This, what the teacher wishes, is not possible. If I take any more bricks from the bottom of the house, then it will all crash to pieces and the people inside will be dead. Thank you.'

She smiled, and gave a little bow. The rest of the class clapped their hands, delighted at the short performance, and John allowed himself a smile.

'Thank *you*, Hannah. You may sit down again.'

When she had regained her seat, he continued.

'Hannah is, of course, quite correct. If we knock away the foundations – the bricks at the bottom – then the house will indeed fall down.' He demonstrated, for the sake of allowing the little ones to see the subsequent crash. Children enjoy minor catastrophes.

'Now, can you tell me what keeps your own houses from falling down?'

Samuel: 'The sticks?'

He meant the wooden stilts.

'Yes, in a way. But what about the poles themselves. What holds them upright?'

There was silence.

He tried again. 'Could you build a house on water?'

Hannah stood up and stamped her foot.

'No. You must build it on the island.'

'Exactly. The coral island on which we all stand. But what is happening to your island? I'll tell you. People from the villages are cutting it up, to make the heads for Jorka Island. And what they are doing is taking away the bricks from underneath, to build on top. Very soon there will be nothing left underneath – and everything will fall, crash, into the sea.

'Just today I saw men cutting away coral from the reef to make a head. This is not because they are bad men, but because they don't know what harm they are doing. When you grow up, you *will* know, won't you? I want you to promise me now that none of you will take the coral to make heads for your fathers and mothers – otherwise . . .' He swept the whole pile of Lego bricks to the floor dramatically. There was a clatter as they hit the wooden floorboards.

They stared at him. He hoped he had got the message across. He intended to repeat it from time to time, to drum it in. He felt very pleased with himself. Yes, it was indoctrination, but for a very good cause. He wanted them to be fully aware of what was happening to their environment.

The old woman in the corner had looked up from her sewing, startled, when the Lego bricks struck the floor, but John had got used to her presence and had learned to ignore it.

'Now we'll say the Lord's Prayer and class will be dismissed . . .' They put their hands together and the ritual chant from the Pidgin Prayer Book went up to the Great Carpenter, creator of all things:

'*Him, namberwan kapenta, up in sky . . .*'

# Ten

The sky is as soft and as dusty as the wing of a moth; the sea as placid as a turtle. Fishermen are coming home, the children are called from the yards, the women are baking bread. Zero hour for the people of the zero, as darkness sucks up the day.

I see it in the distant fading light of the evening; just a grimace along the horizon. The grimace grows to a black yawn and I know something is coming. It looks like a giant wave, higher than the island's trees. I want to turn and shout 'RUN!' but I know there is nowhere to go, nowhere to hide. So, with frozen heart I stand and watch the wave as it sweeps across the surface of the sea, until it is a towering mass that threatens to fill the sky.

It hits the outer reef with a rushing sound: the noise is deafening. The air is screaming and I fall to the ground, wrapping my arms around my head in a futile protective gesture. Blackness follows, full of the swishing, the creaking of wings, and the cries from thousands of throats. I am buffeted by soft bodies and there are feathers in the air. Then it is gone, passed over.

It was not Hokusai's wave, but a huge flock of seabirds, travelling south.

One day it will come, taller than white-bellied sea eagles. It will gather itself, along a thousand miles, and there will be nothing to stop it: a billion tons of a substance you can't even hold in your hands. There are still giants on the earth.

That evening we stayed indoors, afraid of the open. Once you have been frightened it takes a while to recover. Since we were eating fish with our curds and treacle, our minds turned naturally towards sex and procreation.

Not many outsiders would catch the connection between fish and sex, but to islanders there are many points of contact. For instance, it is a small piece of flat, flexible bone from skipjack that the women use as a contraceptive device. For years the priests had been bewildered by the fact that we managed to limit the size of our families – a necessary restriction on a small atoll – and most had put it down to natural causes.

Ruth said, 'The Bible is the best place to look for these things.'

She was puzzled and affronted at having to go to extraordinary lengths to get a man to make love to her, but she was prepared to make one more effort. I was still fearful of spiritual infidelity and, concerned that it would show in my face, kept my head down.

'What do you suggest?' I asked.

She quoted, '. . . *and he saw the woman washing herself: and the woman was very beautiful.*'

'King David?'

'Yes. If he couldn't resist a woman bathing herself, perhaps the teacher will fall for the same thing? I will be Bathsheba for a day.'

I stared through the window. The sunrise was a flare of crimson, reflected by the ocean. I pictured Ruth, bathing in the waters of the lagoon, the colours of the sea and sky wrapped around her form. It brought a lump to my throat.

'Oh, you will be *very* beautiful.'

'Not for you, Nathan. I don't want you hiding in bushes this time. It just makes you unhappy. If this has got to be done, then I want you out of the way.'

I was stunned. In the first place, how did she know I had been watching her? And in the second place, why shouldn't I? Could I not see my own wife naked? I was about to remonstrate when I noticed that her mouth was set in a firm, hard line. Argument would be useless.

'I shall go and talk with my father,' I said, with dignity.

She nodded. That was good. She was to be left alone. She explained how she would go about the scheme. She would find a quiet spot somewhere along the lagoon. The teacher was always walking or jogging around the island. When he came by, she would remove her sarong and stand in the water, as if she had not seen him. Then she would bathe. The early evening would be the best, so that darkness fell on her form, after it had been caught by the sunset: golden and warm in the swirling scarlets of the dying day.

'Yes, golden and warm,' I said.

'Go and see your father, Nathan.'

Afternoon. A school of skipjack churns the light green water to milk. Yesterday evening's reds are caught below, in the coral, where the clouds dipped themselves. Parrot fish, with pinched mouths, swim through the stagshead, their mean tailfins flicking. The human, wading through their territory, is disregarded.

I waded ashore at Jorka Island – Ghost Island – the warm, fine sand forcing itself between my bare toes. Ruth had mentioned that she would like to travel from the islands one day. I had been to Britain and saw no advantage in going again. I could see how it might attract Ruth, though. To her it was an exotic land (partly my fault, since I tended to colour my experiences there in the telling) and she had never been off the islands. She wanted to see some of the wonders for herself.

I suppose I was frightened that she would become trapped in some way, and be unable to return to the islands. I envisaged all sorts of things happening, from her becoming so captivated with life over there that she had no desire to come home, to being caught in some scheme not of her own making, because she lacked sophistication, and unable to extricate herself. It was not just possessiveness. It was the protective male in me.

The paths on Jorka all led to a central clearing, hidden by a fringe of rainforest from the islands on either side. An artificial slope had been constructed, long ago, which swept down to the lagoon. The coral heads covered this slope, all about waist-high, staring down on to the calm waters.

These were the coral heads of our ancestors, some of them so eroded by the rain that their features had been obliterated; worn to a smooth, blank expression. Around them was a sea of *alang* grass, kept short by the cutters who volunteered their services after each rainy season.

There was a new block of coral in the process of being shaped by two of the relatives of the deceased. (A woman from Tubb Island who had died of natural causes.) I waved to her son and daughter, before making my way to where my own father's head was situated.

I stepped between other heads, murmuring apologies to the people concerned, until I came to my father. Having not long been dead, he was still in good condition, that slight frown he had been given still evident on the high brow. Pappy's coral eyes stared out, over the lagoon and islands within which he had been born and had died, without the slightest desire to see what lay beyond.

I pulled out a vine which threatened to strangle him and cleared some small weeds which were beginning to grow in his hair.

'I came in good time, pappy,' I joked. 'That creeper was about to finish you off.'

He admonished me for being flippant and then added that at least plants procreated. What about his own kin? Where was the grandchild that I'd promised him? Why was I alone? I should have a little boy or girl to show him. He was not asking for a dozen, or even half that number. All he wanted was one. Could I not provide him with a single grandchild?

I showed suitable shame at his words, hanging my head and hoping that his remonstrations would stop, before one of us became too angry at the other and the visit turned into a sulking match.

'I'm trying all the time, pappy, believe me. I can't do any more than that. We'll have a baby to show you soon, don't worry. I shouldn't be surprised if Ruth isn't already pregnant.'

– Ruth – he grumbled – is not the wife I would have chosen for you. She is too small, too skinny. I would have chosen a woman with big hips and huge breasts. Ruth is too delicate for motherhood –

It wasn't Ruth's fault, I almost shouted at him, it was the *midnight walkers*. They had stolen the baby's soul.

– Rubbish – pappy cried. – If it wasn't Ruth's fault, then it must be yours. Now that I am dead I can see how foolish all those stories were, about *midnight walkers* and the Captain. They were just excuses for not wanting to push the hot stalk between a woman's thighs. Personally, I have enjoyed every minute I have spent in that position – he chuckled – many different positions –

'I don't want to hear this,' I interrupted, hotly. 'It's not the kind of things a father should be discussing with his son. You're talking about my *mother*.'

He agreed, reluctantly, that such talk was not for a son's ears. It was a pity, he added, because there wasn't anyone else around with whom to reminisce, except my mother of course, and when she came she didn't want to talk about such things. She seemed more interested in complaining about domestic trivia, which now he was dead no longer interested him. Not that it ever did. He was always more taken with what happened on the mats, after the sun went down . . .

'Pappy!' I warned. 'If you keep this up, I'm going home.'

– All right – he said, huffily – Be a bore. However, the main issue is still unresolved. The grandchild. Don't you make love to your wife, once in a while? –

Yes, yes, I said. Of course I did. That was not the problem. We enjoyed such activity as much as he and mamma had done. But nothing resulted from it. However, I added, I was working on another way.

– Another way? – (He almost raised his coral eyebrows.) So far as he knew there was only *one* way to get babies, but then his generation was relatively ignorant, so far as the modern world was concerned. He supposed there were devices, not heard of in his own time, coming in from the outside world. Personally, he said, he preferred the old-fashioned methods, whatever these new ways were, since he could not imagine any improvements on a good romp over the mats, with both parties getting hot and excited, and touching, here and here, and laughing, and . . .

I let him ramble on, since there seemed no way of stopping him. When he tired of his own talk, I did what I had come to do, which was to supply him with all the news of the family, and others, and describe things in the village – any changes that had been made – and talked about the bonito and skipjack.

He questioned me about the teacher and the fishing expedition, and asked what kind of man he was. I told him he seemed an honourable man, but you never could tell with outsiders. They came from a different culture and had their own concept of honour. I told pappy that the teacher was having difficulty in settling in to our way of life in the village and that he had made several mistakes since he had been with us . . .

'. . . just as I made mistakes, in his country. He tries hard, though.'

Finally, I bade goodbye to my father.

Next time you come, he warned, you had better bring some news of new life in the family.

We left it at that. I went down the slope and with my long knife began hacking at the foliage that threatened to invade the sacred area. We had covered the peritrack with deep sand, but the plants still found root there, especially after the rains. I took my frustration out on the saplings and vines that formed the advance guard of the rainforest, chopping them down with more energy than the task actually required. The sweat ran down my body. It felt good to discharge a certain responsibility towards my father. He had left me other responsibilities not quite so easily carried out, such as the care of my mother and the debts which he had foolishly incurred during his lifetime. I had since managed to clear much of the latter by working for his creditors, but it had already taken two full years of my life.

There was no resentment in me though. He was my father and I his son. We were one. His deeds were my deeds.

In the evening I walked back along the coral ridge, timing it so that

I arrived on Tubb just as it was getting dark. I went straight home, to await Ruth, only to find she was there before me.

'What happened?' I asked.

'I don't really know. It seemed that everything would go fine. He came running along the sands and I stripped off my sarong, without looking behind me, and began washing my thighs in the water. I splashed myself, all over, for a few minutes and then decided to look back at the beach.

'He was gone. Nowhere to be seen.' There were tears in her eyes. 'He must find my body unattractive. He likes to *talk* to me – as often as I want – but nothing more.'

Ruth then went on to say that Luke, a little drunk on toddy juice, had then arrived and attempted to chase her in the shallows, while she was struggling to put on her sarong.

'The silly man.' She started to smile through her tears. 'It's not as if he can do anything when he does catch a woman . . . oh, I can only attract drunk men, these days.'

I held my wife in my arms for a very long while, telling her that she had the most attractive body a man could ever wish for. I told her that the teacher was afraid of beauty – that it dazzled him and made him feel inferior to the task. I told her that he had run away because he felt himself unequal to such a woman as she.

That night my pappy would have been proud of me, though I knew that no child would come of it. It is a great pity that passion is no aid to conceiving, for if it were, Ruth would have been pregnant with triplets.

Bathsheba walks into the shallows of the lagoon, the gentle foam caressing her calves, wetting her knees. A large, red sun touches the distant horizon and, trembling, begins to ripple down into the sea.

Bathsheba removes her sarong and starts to dampen her arms, her shoulders, her breasts. She sings. Out of the rainforest, behind her golden body, comes a coral man – white, all white – with arms and legs that crackle as he walks.

He pauses, blindly tilting his face, as if the warmth from the sun is his only sensual contact with the world. He hears nothing, he sees nothing. He only feels.

*Splash*. One leg. *Splash*. Two legs. He has stepped into the water. A red flush creeps up, past his knees, along his thighs, to his loins. Soon, his whole body is live coral again and his eyes, full of purple polyps, begin to see.

Bathsheba turns, singing . . .

. . . and I sat up in bed, abruptly, staring into the darkness of the hut. I could hear the crickets buzzing and the frogs warbling in the rain-forest. Ruth was beside me, snoring gently. I was glad we were together.

I listened to the noise of the waves, fearful of that roaring, rushing thunder which would be the prelude to the giant which might one day sweep us from our beds.

# Eleven

Short Island lies directly opposite Tubb, across the six miles of lagoon. It is the smallest piece of land in the atoll, being a mile long by half a mile wide, and this was the place chosen by the islanders to build their church. The missionary priest of the time, Father William, objected strongly to the remote position. He believed that while the islanders were prepared to accept a priest, they wanted to keep his trappings at arm's length.

They took little notice of Father William's protests. He was not even a Belonger.

Although the mutineers had brought God and Christ with them in their speech, it had taken Father William some time to convince the islanders that these were Supreme Beings, and not handy expletives for use when one struck one's thumb with a hammer. However, the islanders did eventually embrace Christ and allowed a church to God to be built. It was understood, though, that generous as the natives were with their immigration laws, God had to wait five years, too, before being accepted as a Belonger.

'*Yu tink Him Kapenta klin Bilonger no long wetim? Ples bilong wi namberwans, dan kam Kapenta fifeyer.*'

(Did you think the Great Carpenter could become a Belonger without waiting? The place belongs first to the citizens and *then* the Carpenter – after five years.)

They were liberal with their gifts of citizenship, but the rules were inflexible. even for gods. The minimum period of waiting was five years. How else could you show you were serious about the islands, except by proving to its people that you wanted to live there? So, the Holy Trinity and its entourage had to wait five years to be fully accepted, and by that time the church had been built. Short of dismantling it and rebuilding it on another island, the priest had to put up with its remote location. The present priest rather liked it. Father Maurer said that the journey, across the wide stretches of water, made churchgoers appreciate the service.

'Those that come must really want to be here,' he wrote to his superiors, shortly after his arrival on the islands, 'because it takes many hours out of their day. I watch them walking through the shallows along the reef – just dark shapes in the early morning – or crossing the lagoon in their canoes – and I feel a sense of pride on observing their slow progress. It is not so much a matter of being isolated, as being placed in a special position, where the fishermen heading out and sailing home can see their church, standing proud from the green lawns . . .'

Father Maurer was something of a closet eremite himself. He liked seclusion and would have been happy in a monastery, perched on the pinnacle of a rock somewhere in the Urals. It suited him to have his church, and his house, well away from the rest of the community. It suited the islanders, too, since they liked to get on with their own lives with the minimum of interference from their neighbours, Belongers or not.

Strangely enough, when the islanders referred to the 'Kapenta' they meant God, not Jesus. They were aware of Christ's earthly trade, which enhanced his standing amongst them, but the word 'Kapenta' was synonymous with 'Creator'. Almost everything on the islands was fashioned of wood, especially during the time of Father William, and if you made anything at all, you were a carpenter. God was the 'Namberwan Kapenta' who had made the first people.

Father Maurer knew and accepted all this, just as he accepted that Christianity was only part of their religion. He was aware of the ancestor idols on Jorka Island and saw no reason not to regard these as tombs – figures not dissimilar in function to alabaster angels placed on graves back in Europe.

Father Maurer (unlike Father William, who had returned to Europe with worn teeth through grinding them in frustration) believed in the slow erosion of heathen attitudes and beliefs. Nothing could be done in a hurry, because you were just as likely to fire the resentment of those you wanted to win over that way. You won them over, little by little, until the old ways were safe to discard. There was plenty of time. God was eternal. He might have wished that the mutineers had not been Protestants and had left the remnants of the true faith amongst their children, rather than the residue of blasphemies, but since they had not the challenge had been that much greater. Where was the satisfaction in converting the converted?

Short Island has very few trees and nature has been modified to green lawns with coral paths, all leading to the white wooden church with its simple cross above the entrance. Two ancient gardeners, a husband and wife team, keep the grass short with scythes, and Father Maurer, forever requisitioning white paint, likes to decorate the church himself. He sees it as applying liquid coral to God's house, which is, to him, an appropriate image.

In his more rebellious moments, the priest occasionally thought that if Heaven was not like Jonson's atoll, then it ought to be. Such thoughts were often sharply followed by self-reprimands, but it was difficult to control these wayward speculations.

His only disappointment, to that time, was that the graveyard was empty. Not one of the islanders had allowed themselves to be buried there.

'If I could just get one person to turn away the *fandita man* on his deathbed, then I'm sure others would follow,' he told himself.

He could wait though. There was still time.

Father Maurer was raking the coral path. From early morning he had seen the solitary figure picking its way across the coral reef to Short Island. He knew it was the English school teacher, even before the man was close enough to recognise his light skin, by the careful, almost fussy method of the journey. An islander knew just where to walk. This newcomer had to seek out each foothold.

As the man approached, Father Maurer leaned on his rake and called, 'You're very brave – to come across there alone.'

The tall, slim teacher waved in reply, and when he reached the priest, said, 'I must admit – I was a little worried about stone fish. I can't seem to see the b . . . blighters.'

Father Maurer chuckled.

'I know what you mean.'

They spoke in Jonson, with its archaic English heavily spiced with Divehi, since the priest preferred it to any other language, even his own German. Besides, they had established at an earlier meeting that the teacher's German was only good for shopping or asking the time.

The priest was about to put an arm around John Trencher's shoulders, to invite him into his house, when he noticed that the young man had his shirt in his hand and his back was bare. Father Maurer did not like touching naked skin. He waved his arm in the direction of the house, which stands not far from the church. Unlike the teacher's place, it is a wooden structure more in keeping with the flavour of the villages.

'Drink? How about some fresh coconut milk? It's refreshing and it's good for you – healthy, invigorating.'

'Sounds good,' said Trencher. 'Thanks.'

The rake was placed at the side of the church and they strolled together through the bright sunlight to the house. The priest glanced at the teacher and noticed that his eyes were watering. He guessed it was the glare from the white paths and church. There is no thick foliage to soften the effect of the sun on Short Island.

Once in the house Trencher sat in a bamboo chair which had been placed by the seaward-facing window to catch any breezes from the ocean. The view outside is completely open, and Father Maurer liked to sit and frighten himself with the miles of ocean that rolled towards his small, vulnerable house.

Father Maurer got two drinks and then he pulled up his own seat and faced the teacher.

'So. You decided to visit me at last?'

Trencher shrugged, taking a sip of his drink.

'I thought it was about time. I've neglected you – as a neighbour. I also thought,' Father Maurer knew what was coming next, 'I had better explain why I don't come to the church – to mass . . .'

'Or even to pray,' said Father Maurer. 'Well, I thought at first that maybe you needed a settling-in period. Time to adjust. But it's been two months. So, is it the islanders' attitude? God's out of doors, so why go inside?'

The teacher's fingers were tightly wrapped around one of the priest's precious glasses, twisting it. Those glasses had survived a journey from Bavaria. Father Maurer restrained himself from snatching the object from the young man's hands before it was crushed.

'No, I wish it were that, Father. I'm afraid it's much worse. I've lost my faith. One of the reasons I came to the islands was to escape. I don't want to go to church . . . I don't believe any more.'

Father Maurer felt mildly irritated. What did this young man expect?

That he would be shocked? How many times had he heard such a statement from attention-seeking teenagers, back in München?

'Please.' He reached forward and took the glass, placing it on the table in front of them.

He said, 'You were told at your interview, I think, that had you not been a Catholic you would not have got this post? Well then, young man, you must set an example. If you really don't believe, then it won't hurt you to go through the motions occasionally.'

'Oh, I don't neglect the children. We say our prayers every . . .'

'That's not the point. Not the whole. The fact is, if you, as a member of the society from which this religion came to these people, do not respect it – I can hardly expect them to either.'

Father Maurer did not like this young man. He was too wrapped up in himself – too self-important. The priest was not prepared to pander to affectations.

Trencher had gone pale.

'You mean I should become a hypocrite?'

'How do you know you're not one already?' snapped the priest. 'You've practised deceit by promising to come to the church in order to get the job. Did you tell them at your interview that you'd lost your faith?'

The teacher looked angry.

'They didn't give a damn . . . I'm sorry, they weren't worried, I assure you.'

'They told you it didn't matter?'

'Nothing was said. I gained that impression. Look – they were interested in my ability as a teacher, and whether I would be able to stand it out here – not whether I was a regular churchgoer. I'd better leave.'

He half stood, but the priest waved him down.

'Stop making gestures, for Heaven's sake. Take it easy. Maybe I'll regard you as a challenge. Let's talk about something else. Do you like it here? What do you think of the people?'

'I like them well enough, especially Ruth and Nathan – they're my closest friends here. And the children are very receptive.' He suddenly looked very pleased with himself. 'I've recently structured a few lessons around this business of using blocks of coral from the reef as headstones – on Jorka. I've been trying to get through to them that it's self-destructive. I want to educate them to the fact that if they weaken the reef, they put the whole atoll at risk.'

Father Maurer was a little concerned.

'Have you consulted the elders about this? What does Nathan say?'

'Nathan's not an elder.'

'No, but you say you're close to him. You've surely discussed it with him?'

The teacher shrugged.

'He knows I'm concerned about the reef – says he is too. But I haven't told anyone about the children. Surely they won't approve? I mean, I see their dilemma – it's one of those vicious circles, isn't it? But it's a circle that's *got* to be broken.'

The priest shook his head.

'It's very dangerous to meddle with religions you don't understand. I know – I know – ' He held up his hand. 'I've only just finished telling you how Christian they all are. These heathen practices have to be *eroded*, gently – you can't go crashing in. You'll get yourself into trouble.'

'I thought I *was* being gentle.'

'I think you're being less than delicate, if you don't mind me saying so.'

There was silence between them for a while. Father Maurer studied the young man without being rude about it. He seemed a strange mixture of weakness and strength, which in itself was dangerous. Weak men can be influenced and strong men can be dealt with on their own terms, but those unpredictable types which the priest came across occasionally were much more difficult to manipulate.

'I would be careful, if I were you,' he told the teacher. 'We hardly know these people at all.'

John Trencher looked at him in puzzlement.

'You do, surely. You've been here more than five years. You must have learned something about them in that time?'

'Five years? I'm afraid you've been misinformed. I arrived only a few months before you.'

'But you're a Belonger.'

Ah. Now he understood.

'Yes, you're right. I *am* a Belonger – but that's because of my position here. You see, they regard the post – that of being the priest – as being more important than the individual filling it. I've inherited the years all the other priests spent here. The *priest* is the Belonger, not Father Maurer.'

'But you are the priest.'

Father Maurer nodded. 'True – which means I'm a Belonger – and so will you be, very soon.'

Trencher looked a little taken aback.

'You mean . . . Good Lord, yes. Peter Goodwright. He was here just on four and a half years, wasn't he? I hadn't thought about that. But I'm only the teacher . . .'

'Nevertheless, you have a title. Haven't you noticed they never refer to you by name? It's always *the teacher*. You'll be a Belonger soon.'

'I think I shall like being a Belonger. It means I won't have to go home – not unless I want to.'

The priest sighed, inwardly. All these young people, looking for an escape from the world. They would be better off joining some religious order, where they would get into less trouble.

'Listen, you don't play chess, do you?' asked the Father.

Trencher nodded. 'Not very well, I'm afraid.'

A British understatement, surely? It had been a long time since Father Maurer had had a decent game of chess. He suggested that they might have a quick game now. To his delight, the teacher agreed. He fetched the board and pieces and set them up, giving the teacher white.

'Your move,' he said.

Trencher opened by moving his queen pawn two squares. Father Maurer responded by setting up his usual French Defence. After about five minutes it became clear that the priest's opponent had been telling the truth. The teacher played chess like draughts, taking pieces without any regard to tactics or strategy.

The priest allowed himself another inward sigh. He would have to play badly himself, to stretch the period of the game. It was a pity. A great pity. Still, it was better than no game at all.

To distract himself and thus have a more lengthy and enjoyable game, the priest told the teacher a story.

'You remind me, physically, of another young man,' he said, 'I met in India. He was a German boy of about nineteen. He wasn't doing anything particularly rewarding, a clerk in a store I think, and yet he seemed to me to be a youth of many abilities: very capable, especially with his hands. He loved working with wood and was delighted to find some of the more traditional wood-carving tools, which had gone out of use in Europe, still available in India. He would carve the most beautiful figurines . . . but that is beside the point, really.

'I asked him why he had buried himself on the Indian subcontinent, away from real life. He told me that he considered "real life" to be wherever he himself lived, but he added that there was a reason for being there.

' "My father was in the Gestapo during the war," the youth explained, "and while I was growing up, I was inclined to ignore this fact. However, the time came when I received my call-up papers, for National Service in the German Army, and I confronted my father and told him I was not going to go, even if it meant jail. When my father asked for a reason, I told him it was because of what he had been, what he had done, during the war. I said I found this thought so distasteful, I could not consider military service.

' "My father went very quiet, but after a long time said that he respected my decision and if necessary he would go to court with me, to explain the circumstances of my refusal to do military service. He did this and I was exempted from the duty and put to work in a hospital instead. Afterwards, I left for India."

'But, I said to the boy, if you received exemption why leave?

' "Because, after thinking the matter through, I decided it would be wrong of me to stay. Prior to that time I had considered the Nazi atrocities to be none of my responsibility. I was not even born until after the war. But on further reflection, I realised that Germany had become a rich nation, with many benefits for its citizens. As one of those citizens, I was in a privileged position. If I rejected any responsibility for deeds committed by a society in which I lived, then I also had to reject the benefits that arose from the continuation of that society. My father and his contemporaries had perpetrated those acts, but they had also helped to build the Germany in which I lived. If I accepted what had been established by them, could I then reject responsibility for their history? It would have meant drawing a line and saying, this is where they ended, this is where I began, and the two have no connection with one another.

' "I couldn't do that, because it clearly isn't true. Since I had inherited their Germany – a country full of opportunity and prosperity – I had to inherit responsibility for what happened at Dachau and Auschwitz. So I left."

' "And you feel absolved?" I asked him.

' "No, but I'm able to distance myself from it enough to be able to live a real life," he replied.

'Now, what do you think?'

The teacher looked up from the chessboard, apparently surprised that his opinion on the subject was required. He seemed to consider the matter, then replied, 'I don't agree – with the youth. It seems to me he had no choice but to accept the benefits of the society into which he was born. One might as well say that since the English massacred the Scots, and raped the British Empire, then a baby born today has to bear the responsibility for those actions. That's a ludicrous suggestion.'

'Is it?' the Father said, a little disappointed by the shallowness of the response.

They finished their game of chess and then Trencher said he had to leave. The two men shook hands.

'About that interview,' said the teacher, as he turned to go. 'I think I gave a good account of myself. They seemed impressed with my ability to teach. That's what got me the job and that's what I'm here for.'

'I'm sorry,' replied Father Maurer. 'I'm a bit of a bore.'

The young man smiled and strode away. Father Maurer watched him safely across the first stretch of the reef and then went back inside to put the chess pieces away. Then he had second thoughts. He re-arranged the pieces and began to play himself. He concentrated on the puzzle before him, happy to be faced with problems without serious implications, where the decision to move one of the pieces did not involve life and death, freedom, or loss of liberty.

## Twelve

This is the great circle, the midriff of the earth. On either side, the two hemispheres, where wars take place, where people swarm, where civilisations rise and fall. We have no part in all this. Here it is still, timeless. Perhaps we were once a fragment of the single, great continent, Gondawanaland, but we have slipped away, a mote drifting on a vast ocean. Here is only sun, water and a white coral ring. To the rest of the world, we are lost at sea.

*Ol tink wi los long si. Mi no krai fo dat.*

Underneath the water of the lagoon is another world: the world of coral forests, dark regions and gaudy fish. There, you can swim in colour, with absurd shapes drifting by, or nosing amongst the weed. I used to go there often as a boy, to swim amongst Black and Blue corals, or to search for those seashells which did not find their way up to the beach, like tritons. I robbed the marine world of its treasures, so that conchologists could arrange them, out of context, in neat lines under display-case glass. They had grand names for them: Triumphant Star, Pontifical Mitre, Textile Cone, Glory of the Seas, King Midas, Precious Wentletrap. There are 50,000 different species and some collectors wanted them all.

These jewels of the ocean are the homes of living creatures, and we toss away the life inside in order to keep the pretty exoskeleton. One day a giant is going to dip his hand into the waters of space, to pluck the earth from its bed. He will admire the emerald sphere, with its mother-of-pearl sky, and then winkle out the creatures on its surface so that he can keep this pretty treasure without it stinking of rotten meat. *Mi no krai fo dat, mi fren.*

When Ruth had collected enough seashells to fill several baskets, I joined others in sailing a *dhoni* to Malé, several hundred miles to the north-west.

I enjoyed these journeys, arduous though they were, which brought me into contact with the outside world. I made a trip to Gan Island, in Addu Atoll, when I was seventeen. There was a Royal Air Force base there in those days, which had since been handed back to the Maldives. I was innocent at the time, full of curiosity which had been whetted at the English school on Malé. I had left my father to haggle with the servicemen and had wandered through the buildings and workshops. It was evening and few people were about. Those that were took little notice of me, since I looked like a Maldivian, and the locals were employed as cleaners and permitted to enter most of the offices and workshops.

I came to a room where two young servicemen were working behind a silver dish and I went inside to watch them. The equipment fascinated me. Not because of what it was doing, which was nothing so far as I was concerned, but because of its beautiful coloured wires and shiny projections. Then, one of the men looked up, to see me standing in front of the dish, and he yelled at me.

My presence in the room caused some consternation throughout the

RAF camp, and we were sent away that very evening. One of the Maldivians explained to me that the device, which he said was a radar scanner, had been switched on. By walking in front of the live equipment, I had exposed myself to some rays which might have proved harmful. I have since learned that these metal trees, called scanners, can rob a man of his children as effectively as a *midnight walker*.

We set sail at six o'clock one morning, when the sun was striking the sea from a low position, laying a blade of light across the water. The crew consisted of myself, John (the shell-gatherer), Numbers and Letushim. We followed the direction of the swell in a good wind, taking plenty of food with us, in case we became becalmed and had to row part of the way. A fine spray around the bows of the *dhoni* soon became the home of tangled, transient rainbows, as the sun rose higher in the sky. The journey would take several days.

Uncle Letushim fished as we went. We would eat the catch raw, with breadfruit and ground-rice pancakes. Blue ring angels crowded the bows at the beginning of the journey but these were soon replaced by harmless grey sharks.

'How is our teacher coming along?' asked Uncle Letushim, concentrating on the line that went down into the other world.

'All right,' I said. 'He's worried that we're destroying the reef to make the heads. He thought we made it into houses at first.'

'Some places do – the Maldivians do.'

'But we only take it for the heads. Even so, he may be right. If Hokusai's wave comes, we shall need all the sea defences we have.'

His wizened face wrinkled as he considered my words.

'This – Hokusai – he makes waves?'

I shook my head.

'He's an artist. Was. A Japanese man who lived in the last century. He fashioned carved woodblocks to make prints – pictures. One of these pictures is called "The Hollow Of The Deep-Sea Wave". I have a copy I brought from England – haven't you seen it? Hanging in my home?'

He nodded. '*That* picture. I see.' He paused, then said, 'The Japanese,' as if this explained everything to him. 'A shrewd people.' He smiled. 'Not as shrewd as Letushim, but clever just the same. This Hokusai made the wave-picture, eh? But the Japanese live in the other ocean.'

There were only two oceans, so far as we were concerned. Our navigators never went round the Capes, but we did sail as far as Fiji and the Philippines.

'Yes, the Pacific.'

'And this wave?'

'You've seen it – a terrible wave. It has an iron mouth, with ragged teeth, and can swallow boats, whole. Islands too.'

Letushim nodded gravely.

'I should not like to see a wave like that – but we must honour our ancestors.'

He was afraid that no coral head would be made for him, when he died, and I sympathised with that. Who wants to suffer darkness alone? Jesus promised that our souls would live on, after death, but we knew they did that anyway, because they were there before birth.

'Yes. We must honour our ancestors,' I agreed.

When the stars came out, we followed the paths set by their patterns, passing uninhabited islands, inhaling their aromas. Perhaps while I was away, the teacher would visit my wife and put our child inside her? His child that would be my child. A strange man, the teacher. At a feast one evening we had given him the place of honour, where he could see the dancing, very close. It was a privilege reserved for the teacher. Ruth had danced quite near to him; so near he must have smelled her body odours. She was a good dancer – sinuous – provocative – and she surely must have aroused him. But nothing came of it. We had almost given him up. Perhaps there was another woman? I doubted it. He would have had to have been so very clever for it to have escaped attention. I did not believe he could be that secretive. Not on my island.

When we arrived at Malé, we took the baskets of dried fish and shells to the market. There was a general trader there, Said Achmed, who retailed all our merchandise and gave us a fair price for it. We trusted him. I then went on my own to the hospital and asked to see one of the senior doctors there, a man I knew well. Someone was dispatched to find him and he came out immediately, to shake my hand.

'Nathan – it's good to see you. Shall we have coffee together?'

We spoke in a dialect of Sinhalese: his language.

I nodded in agreement and we made our way to a pavement coffee stall not far from the hospital. Abdulla pulled out a chair and offered it to me, then found one for himself.

The waiter took our order and I relaxed a little, watching the flow of people up and down the street. Malé is a buzzing city, with cars, and buildings of brick – a thriving place when compared with Jonson's Atoll.

He asked, 'How are things, down on the equator?'

'Fine – at the moment. And here?'

He shrugged. 'As you can see, we get along. The tourist trade is booming. They seem to be willing to go further these days. A lot of people despise tourists, but I like them. They're happy most of the time – they spend their joy weeks here. We don't see them miserable and frustrated.'

I got down to business, as the coffee arrived.

'The result of the tests?'

He took a sip of his coffee and I knew the answer before he opened his mouth again. He would have told me any good news instantly.

'I'm afraid it's as you feared. You're sterile – I wish I had better news for you, but I don't.'

'And nothing can be done?'

He shook his head.

'That's that then,' I said, helplessly.

He reached over and touched the back of my hand.

'I know what this means to you, Nathan, and I'm sorry. I could explain it all to you, if it would make you feel any better. The radar scanner . . .'

'No, what's the use? I can't have children – that's the only important thing I want to know.'

We spent about an hour under the pavement palms, chatting together, before I took my leave of him. I said before I left, 'I shall keep trying, you know – to have children. There are more ways than one.'

He looked puzzled, but he nodded.

'As you say on the islands, "*Aion no fit hot if yu no putam fo faia*" '.

The iron will not get hot, if it's not put in the fire. But the fire inside was cold, and though nothing can succeed if it's not tried, there is a point where hopelessness douses even the faintest ember.

I went down to the harbour, to meet the others. When I arrived there I found them asleep in the bottom of the boat, using some packages as pillows. They had been shopping and drinking beer, and had no doubt got a little drunk.

I went out again myself, to buy a few goods. I got Ruth a present; a blue silk sari with gold trimming. She only had cotton saris and sarongs at home, and I knew the extravagance would please her.

When I got back to the boat in the evening, they were still asleep, and would probably remain that way until morning. I trod between the bodies, trying not to disturb them, and found myself a place where

I could curl up and listen to the sounds of the Maldive city. I missed the noise of Ruth's snoring, so it took me a while to get to sleep.

The following morning the harbour was bustling. We sat and ate breakfast, while John and Numbers shouted at people hurrying by on the wharf, both tourists and natives. There was another boat of ours tied up some way down the quay with four men from Pork Island on board. We went to see them, as if making a Sunday visit on relations, and greeted them as if we hadn't seen them for ten years. It was pleasant to be amongst one's own.

Later that day we set off for home, in a convoy of two, making our way down the chain of islands for Addu Atoll in the far south, where we would break for our own islands. The weather turned unusually foul, about halfway home, and we had to beach the boats for several days until calmer seas allowed us to continue. From that time on it was just the swish of water against the bow and the occasional crack of the sail as we altered tack. A timeless occupation. Eventually, we smelled the frangipanis as their blossoms came out to meet us on the wind.

# Thirteen

Ruth was now certain of one thing: she did not want the teacher to make love to her. She liked him too much for that now. If they lay together in the sands, then she might let go, open her heart to him, and then there would be a terrible decision to make. A choice to make between two men.

No, she did not want to have to make that choice. It was better for all of them that they remain friends only, and though Nathan would be devastated by the thought of never having children, she knew he loved her more: more than the loneliness death had to offer.

There was a mystery remaining, though. Why hadn't the teacher made love to her? She had practically *asked* him to, and she knew she was not repulsive to him. She could be angry with the teacher if she did not feel, instinctively, that there was a deeper reason why he remained cold to her sexual advances.

He was a celibate person, like those nuns that had visited the priest once. They had been strange people too. Nathan said they were all virgins, but she had heard one referred to as 'Mother'. How could you be a mother *and* remain a virgin, unless, of course, your child was Jesus?

Still, the teacher would remain her friend for a long time. There was the possibility that he would not go back to England for many years now. Not if he remained on the island past six months. She had even considered telling him, but then she thought of Naomi, the poor, dead girl, and Naomi's parents, and she knew she could not thwart justice for her own selfish ends. To betray her people would be a terrible crime. These thoughts occupied her mind a great deal.

She thought also about the baby that she and Nathan wanted. There was now a strong possibility that she would die without becoming a mother. This did not bother her so much as the fact that, with Nathan, an only son, the line would stop. Her family was safe: she had two brothers with strapping grandchildren on Long Island. But poor Nathan's ancestors . . .

The teacher had visited her twice, since Nathan had been away, but he always sat on the veranda, in full view of the village, never going inside. It made her feel warm when he was around. She liked being a special person to another man, without having to give very much in return, except conversation. Not many men would stay around a woman for that. He seemed to understand her desire to see new places; her curiosity. Yet . . . perhaps she was too old for the teacher? After all, Naomi had been a young girl.

Ruth considered these matters as she walked through the rainforest on her way to the house of Nathan's mother. She did not like visiting Nathan's mother. The old woman, Salome, never stopped complaining. The trouble was, she had put too much of her life in her husband, Nathan's father, and when he had died there was nothing left for her to do. You could not live through a man and not suffer for it later: not if you outlived him, which women normally did. Ruth was determined not to be like that. Some women were chameleons: they took on the colour of their men. Then, when the man left, he took his colours with him, leaving a pale, almost translucent creature behind. That was Nathan's mother.

Ruth wanted to be something other than just a woman. She did not know what it was, but there was something . . . something she would make her own. Something that would make her into more of a person than she was at the moment. Not a wife, nor a mother. Neither of those two things – the only ones that sprang readily to mind – captured her enthusiasm. There was something else, something special for her, which when she tried to reach for it in her mind, slipped away. But it was there.

*I am more than me.*

She recalled that as a young child, she had lifted a large stone and had found a mature toad living in a hollow underneath. She knew that toads lived forty years. That one, unaccustomed to the light, had stared around it blindly, perhaps unable to cope with the realisation of a world so immense, so full of hazy colours and blurred shapes, that it was threatened with drowning in new perspectives, new knowledge, new images. She wanted to experience what she thought that toad had experienced. She wanted life to rear up, like a giant wave, and then flood over her.

*Someone lift my stone.*

She reached Salome's house and went inside. It smelled musty and stale. There were scraps of food on the table which the mice had been gnawing at. Body oil, mixed with sweat, wafted in from a far corner where Salome had thrown an unclean sarong.

'Is that you, Nathan?' said the old woman, not even looking up from the bed where she lay.

'It's me. Ruth. I've come to help you wash. Look at this place, mamma. You'll have the rats in here soon . . .'

'At least it'll be company.'

Ruth ignored this. She scooped up the fragments on the table and tossed them through the open doorway. The frigate birds came.

Then she put some order into the interior.

'Fuss, fuss,' said the old woman. 'I can do it myself, when I get my strength . . .'

'Mamma. You have to get up. Let me take you for a walk.'

Salome sat up, her tired old body covered in folds of wrinkled flesh. Her eyes were dark and hollow, and had sunk deep into her skull. Crisp, untidy hair, only partly grey, hung in wisps around her skeletal features. She was forty years of age.

'What's to get up for?' she snapped, suddenly alert now that she was being bullied by her son's wife. Ruth knew that Nathan was always solicitous, always sympathetic. It only made his mother worse. He was a weak son, in many respects.

'Fresh air for a start,' retorted Ruth, unabashed by Salome's attitude.

'Come on – let's get you up and washed, and then we'll go for a walk.' Ruth took hold of a bucket standing in a corner and advanced towards Salome. As expected, the other woman waved her away.

'I can soap myself. You,' she spat through her gums, 'you're such a rough-handed girl. I hate you washing me. I hate you.'

'You don't hate me, mamma. You don't like me very much, but you don't hate me. I'll wait for you outside. If you don't come out I'll come in and get you.'

'Nasty little sow.' This was almost a whisper as Ruth went through the doorway. She smiled to herself. At least Salome was responding today. On some visits she refused to speak, and sulked all through the day. So she ignored the insult and went and sat on the veranda steps to watch the children at play, in the mud left by the rains. There were shrieks of laughter and a great deal of shouting. Children knew the world was an empty place and tried to fill it with noise.

A little while later, Salome came out, blinking at the day.

'I want to go to my husband,' she said.

Ruth shook her head.

'No, mamma. Not today. You never go anywhere else. All you want to do is complain to him and brood about him afterwards. I'm not taking you to him today. We're going to look for sea turtles' eggs.'

Salome sat down with a thump, on the top steps. It must have hurt her gaunt buttocks, but no expression of pain crossed her face. She was eating a piece of yam and Ruth waited until she had finished.

'Are you ready now?' asked Ruth.

A large blue butterfly fluttered around Salome's head; a piece of sky that had become detached. She waved it away irritably.

'You were always a bully,' she said.

'Perhaps.'

'Where's Nathan?'

'He can't protect you – he's gone to Malé. He won't be back for some time.'

There was a pattering of raindrops on the leaves of the trees in the rainforest nearby, which ceased almost as soon as it had begun. A freak cloud of spray had side-swiped the island. The forest shivered. One of the children ran past, screaming, 'The Captain's coming . . . the Captain's coming . . .'

'The old woman will fetch you a thick ear,' snarled Salome. 'Children. You give your life to raising them and they run off to places like Malé, leaving you to the mercy of bullies.'

'He told you he was going, mamma. Why are you like this?'

Salome turned her ringed, hollow eyes on Ruth. They were like deep caves, full of misery and darkness. For once, Ruth felt a wave of pity swell within her.

Salome said, 'Because there's nothing else to do.' The forest seemed to move away at these words, retreating to safer ground. Ruth began to panic inside. I must get away from here, she thought. I can't, I *won't* be like this woman when I'm her age. I have to find a way out, now, while I've still got the strength and will.

She stretched out her hand and Salome took it. For a moment there was warmth between them. Ruth wanted to hug her mother-in-law, but she was afraid of rejection. Salome's moods could change at a split second and her timing could be devastating. Ruth had been burned more than once, so she simply squeezed the hand and then stood up.

'Let's get on then, mamma.'

The old woman rose reluctantly from the step and padded in her hard, bare feet, covered in thick calluses, to Ruth's side. She was bow-legged, and the prints that she left in the dust were edged inwards, like those of a crab. Perhaps those crooked limbs gave her pain? She never complained about things like that. Her grievances were all directed at people she was supposed to love, or at problems that seemed easy to solve.

The two women made their way through the village towards the beach. Several people called greetings to them. Mostly it was Ruth who answered, but occasionally Salome gave a long, drawn look and a wave of the hand. Many husbandless women of advancing age sat together in wicker chairs, chattering and doing things with their hands while they watched the children for their daughters. The lonely and old were well cared for, as were the mentally ill.

Ruth and Salome came across a party on a remote beach on Pork Island. A dozen or so youngsters were leaping about, improvising a dance to the sounds of a heavy metal rock band. On seeing the two women they scattered, fleeing for the trees, taking their precious contraband transistor with them. Radio and television were banned on the atoll, since it was considered that such devices lured the young away from the islands to places like Sri Lanka and Malaysia. Transistor radios were smuggled in by young fishermen.

When the group had dispersed, one person remained, still dancing away.

Hob was hopping around, using two sticks as if they were a violin and bow. He simulated the sounds of the electric guitars with his deep, husky voice, lost in himself. The white sand sprayed up around his bare feet, as he leapt and twisted, jumped and turned, his eyes closed and his face screwed into a look of utter concentration.

'Hob – what are you doing?' yelled Ruth. 'HOB!'

At last the man stopped, panting hard, and stared around him, his lower lip hanging down. He blinked quickly at the two women. Ruth took the sticks gently from his hands.

'What're these, Hob?'

He snatched them back, defiantly, and retreated a few paces. Then hugged the two sticks to his chest.

'Mine,' he said. He began to hum again, this time softly, while rubbing the two sticks together in the same way as before.

'Leave him,' said Salome.

But Ruth said, 'Hob. You know where to find turtles' eggs. Tell Ruth, Hob?'

Hob took no notice. He began to move his feet again, swaying in time to the music in his head. Ruth smiled at him. Poor Hob. The youngsters were always leading him astray, making him climb palms for coconuts, or putting him up to stealing vegetables from someone's private patch.

Suddenly there was a piercing whistle, which stopped Hob in his tracks. He shook his head, blinking again with watery eyes. The whistle had come from Salome: a trick she had learned, using two fingers from each hand and a lung full of air. The sound was still ringing in Ruth's ears as she heard her mother-in-law say, 'Hob. Where are those eggs? We can't stay around here all day.'

Hob said, slowly, 'Eggs from the turtle. Hob knows. Hob knows. Eggs from the turtle.'

'Can you show us where?' asked Ruth.

Hob nodded and began to walk along the sands, humming again and kicking sand at the crabs. All the while he watched Salome out of the corner of his eye. He led them to the point, where a sand spit went out into the shallows. There he dug down into the hot sand and revealed a clutch of round, leathery eggs. The women gathered some each and offered the remaining seven to Hob. He took them but put them back into the hole, covering it again.

Salome said, 'What's he doing?'

'Leaving some for the turtle,' answered Ruth. 'Come on, mamma. We've got enough. Are you coming with us, Hob?'

Rehoboam looked towards the rainforest, where the youngsters had gone. There was a wistful, lost light in his eyes. He hummed two or three bars of some distorted melody, without moving at all, then he sighed deeply. Ruth took his hand and led him back, with Salome, along the beach. She wondered if she should tell someone about the radio, but decided against it.

That evening, Ruth went to see Sheba, the wife of Achbor. They talked about the follies of men and played a game of backgammon on a tattered board with worn dice and counters. Ruth talked about the emptiness she felt inside sometimes and of her desire to see places outside the islands.

Sheba said, 'I know. Sometimes you stop and think to yourself, *I've got to get away*, but there's nowhere to go – nowhere to run to.'

'Do you ever wish something terrible would happen?' asked Ruth.

'Terrible? How do you mean?'

'Well, like a disaster or something. Isn't that a wicked thing to think? To wish for something like a hurricane, or an earthquake, just for the change?'

Sheba's eyes were wide open.

'Yes, it is. Do you wish for that?'

Ruth stared at the floor.

'Sometimes, when Nathan is talking about how disastrous a tidal wave would be, if one ever hit the islands, and I find myself hoping one will come. Oh . . .' She covered her face with her hands for a moment. '. . . isn't that horrible? There would be drownings and suffering and yet I find myself . . .'

Sheba put a hand on her friend's shoulder and whispered, 'You don't really want that. It's as you said, you just want some change in your life, and you reach out for the only things that could bring change.'

'I know it's wrong, but . . . oh, I don't know. I just *feel* things, which my head tells me are bad. Sometimes the whole of my life seems like one long day, from beginning to end.'

Sheba nodded.

'I know. Things *do* happen. You fall in love, or your husband brings home a rare delicacy, or you find a shell that no one's seen before . . . but these are just small bumps, aren't they? Think what it must have been like when the mutineers landed on the islands! What an event that must have been for the women. Things don't happen like that any more.'

The conversation went on until Achbor came home and flopped on to the rugs, to fall immediately asleep. There was the smell of toddy juice in the room after that and the two women went out again and down to the beach. When they had exhausted themselves of talk, Sheba suggested they play a joke on the school teacher. Once it had been explained, Ruth was a little reticent, but Sheba waived aside any protests.

Sheba stripped naked and Ruth painted the other woman's bottom with berry juices. Then they crept up behind the teacher's house and Sheba threw stones at the wall, to rouse the sleeper within.

A light eventually came on and lit the area outside with its dim luminosity. They saw a figure come to the window and peer out, into the night, moving its head from side to side.

Sheba danced forward, making bird noises with her tongue, and then turned around and bent over, showing her bottom . . .

John was startled. In the light thrown out by his dim bulb he could see a huge primitive face staring at him. Grotesque lidless eyes on bulging cheeks rippled above a dwarfish, malformed body. Two legs topped by a bulbous head! What on earth was going on? He leaned forward, straining to get a better look.

It was someone's backside. A villager had painted his . . . no, *her* backside. What the hell was going on! They were making a fool of him again. Or trying to.

He rapped on the screen.

'Go away!' he shouted.

What kind of joke was this? Had it been one of the children, he might have understood, seen the humour of the thing. But a grown woman. This was too much. To interrupt his sleep with silly games.

The bottom-face danced in front of the window. It looked an evil, mocking figure. Was this some kind of ritual, meant to disturb him spiritually? No one had mentioned anything like this. He felt a little persecuted. More than a little. Damn them. He wasn't going to be intimidated.

He turned off the light.

Sheba rushed back into the foliage, laughing. Ruth, however, had had pangs of conscience when she saw John's face staring out into the night, the expression changing from bewilderment to anger.

'Poor man,' she said. 'He must have thought the jungle devils had come to get him. We shouldn't have done it, Sheba.'

Sheba snorted as she struggled to dress her hefty, muscled body.

'Why not? It didn't hurt him. We brought some change to his life. Did you see his face? I bet he locks his door tonight.'

Despite her misgivings, Ruth giggled.

'Well,' she said, 'it wasn't as exciting as a tidal wave, but it was better than nothing. I hope he didn't recognise you.'

'In that light? Never. Besides, when has he seen my bottom? He'll have to go peeking into all the houses as the women undress, to find one that matches. And anyway,' she smiled, 'I was disguised.'

They said goodnight to one another and then Ruth made her way home. She wondered what Nathan would say when she told him. He would find it funny.

The teacher had looked so *shaken*. It didn't take a lot to frighten men, she thought. Just a woman exhibiting a little bizarre behaviour and he had gone to pieces. Yes, the teacher would lock his door tonight, poor man.

Hob was fast asleep underneath some palms on the beach, nestled in the warm sand like a turtle's egg. Someone shook him awake and he immediately threw his arms about his head. He was always afraid that the stars were going to fall on him.

'Hush,' said the woman, 'it's all right, Hob. Hush there . . .'

Hob whimpered, afraid to move. The bright specks seemed to be raining down on him from above.

The woman lay next to him. He could smell her hair and he recognised her. She snuggled up, warm and close, touching his body. The milky surf churned about their feet. At first he was tense, but gradually, he began to relax. He felt her being kind to him.

'There, Hob. There. That's nice, isn't it? We're going to do something nice, Hob, aren't we? Don't be afraid. I'm here . . .'

He let her do things to him. The surf was in his belly now, washing warmth through him. She was gentle. Her words were soft. They would have sent him to sleep if he had not been excited. The stars were still there. He closed his eyes.

He felt her body move on top of his. She was protecting him from the stars, shielding his body with her own. She was nice. Nice. Nice.

'Whoooooo . . .' said Hob, as she moved up and down.

'That's it. Nathan needs our help, Hob. Nathan needs us . . . oh, *good* Hob. *Good*.'

Hob opened his mouth and tried to swallow the moon. His belly felt warm and milky. He liked her. He liked her very much. He could feel his legs shaking, trembling violently. The stars were rushing around now, frantically. She seemed pleased with him.

'Well done, Hob. Good. You did very well. And this is our secret. Just because you have a silly head, doesn't mean your children will be the same, does it? We know that. Noah was a silly man – as silly as you – but his children were fine. That's good, isn't it . . .?'

'Noah, fine,' said Hob, willing to please.

She stroked his face.

'Yes, of course he was.'

Hob felt stirrings.

'Again?' he said.

The woman stood up and adjusted her sarong.

'Not tonight, Hob. In a day or so's time. Nathan will be gone at least for three weeks. We have some time left . . .'

Hob fell asleep to the sound of her voice. Somewhere, down there, the waves were licking at his toes. He began to drift away into sleep, into warm, milky dreams.

# Fourteen

We came riding in on a breaker, borne high, so that we looked down upon our island home as if from an aircraft coming down to land. It looked small, vulnerable. Yet we were not on an aeroplane, we were on a green-sea wave, taller than the trees on the land.

The wave broke, as if by magic, hissing and steaming towards the beach. By the time we reached the shore it was nothing but a few ripples on the back of the shallows.

Uncle Letushim and the others began to unload the boat and I took the wrapped sari and made my way to my house. The teacher was sitting on his veranda as I entered the village. I called and waved to him. Strangely enough it felt good to see him again.

I received an answering call, not quite as enthusiastic as my own. The teacher looked a little lost, a little out of place, even though he was now as brown as any one of us. It was his height and demeanour that made him stand out: and that funny, wispy moustache. He looked like a long-stay tourist, trying to go native but reluctant to exchange his Adidas shorts and Nike track shoes for the longi and loin cloth. His hair had blonded even more under the sun. He was too clean, as well. He was always too clean. He showered at least three times a day and his hair was always neatly combed, except for the lock that flopped over one eye. He glowed golden, so that you wanted to go up and smell his skin, with its warm, dry cleanliness and fine hair. I have never been interested in men, in a sexual way, but there are some people who are like polished stones, or smooth wooden ornaments: they seem to be made for touching, pressing the cheek against, and inhaling the dry, pleasant warmth of their skins.

I went into my house. Ruth was not there. Going out again, I called to a neighbour.

'Sheba – where's Ruth?'

The big woman looked up and smiled. She was doing something in her vegetable patch and her sarong was tucked into her pants, revealing her huge meaty legs.

'Collecting shells, I think.'

I took the coral path to the beach, and there she was, in her favourite place amongst the rocks. Her sarong, like Sheba's, was tucked up to her bottom and the foam washed around her thighs. She looked beautiful.

'Something for you,' I called. 'A present.'

She looked up, saw it was me, and smiled. She looked radiant and I thought the thing had happened at last. She waded towards me, holding the basket of shells out at arm's length. When she reached me, she said, 'Nathan,' a little shyly.

We hugged each other tightly and I kissed her eyelids and fingertips. She tasted salty. I wanted to lick her all over, but the beach was no place for such things. She had missed me, I think. I know I had missed her. I had saved all the little snippets of news to tell her, of the problems we had encountered on the voyage and of life in Malé. She enjoyed listening to my accounts, just as I wanted to hear all that had gone on in the village while I had been away.

'You're glad to see me,' I said.

'Oh, of course. I always miss you so much. Don't you miss me?'

'A little,' I teased. 'And the teacher . . .?'

Her face clouded over for a moment.

'Nothing . . .'

'Oh.' I was bitterly disappointed, though I knew in my heart what the answer was going to be. I had felt no jolt of the spirit while I had been away.

She hooked an arm around my neck.

'Nathan, listen to me. Have you thought that perhaps we chose the wrong person for this?'

I looked into her eyes, trying to gauge something of what she was saying to me. Was she trying to tell me there was someone else, more suitable? I really did not understand.

'I don't know what you mean.'

Her wet hair stuck to her forehead as she pressed her face to mine. Out of the corner of my eye I could see a frigate bird, wheeling above the waves on the reef. Her arm was strong around me.

'Have you thought,' she said, 'that he might not want to have any more children? There is something he seems to be afraid of – his son was born with something wrong with it. Perhaps he does not want to father any more children because he's afraid they will all have something wrong with them?'

'Wrong?'

'Born silly, like Hob.'

I thought about this and said, 'Hob is one of three. His brother and sister are all right.'

'We don't know anything about his son, Nathan. Maybe the teacher knows that the next child he fathers will be unhealthy in some way. Let's leave him alone now, please, Nathan?'

My mouth was dry of words. I wanted a baby. I *needed* a child. What was I to tell my own father? That he would have to drift into eternal darkness because I had not understood the devices of the outside world? That he and his line were doomed because of ignorance? It seemed so. It seemed so.

Her wide eyes held me and I thought about the wishes of my parents and who would come to talk to *me*, when I was dead. I thought about how nice it would be to have my own to be my own, watching it grow into a walking, talking person; running with me along the beach; helping me with the fishing. There were too many pretty pictures in my head.

'I love you,' I said.

'Yes – I know.'

I have never told her about the radar scanner on Gan Island: how I had walked in front of it and made myself sterile. How could I have known what I was doing? How many men from the *outside* world would have known? I was only seventeen. It was so cruel. It had robbed me of my child, the *midnight walker* that the British had brought with them all the way from England, where such demons are not even natural things, but manufactured, artificial devices. The mechanical dead. In the outside world, they had destroyed all their old, natural mysteries, so they made new ones out of metal and plastic, like their cars and microwave ovens . . . radar scanners that were meant to protect lives, and instead, destroyed them.

They stood on tin legs, but they were *midnight walkers,* just the same.

My responsibility towards my father was to keep his mind fresh, his memories alive. He, in turn, could then do the same for my grandfather, and so on, back along the ancestral chain. Once there was no living motive force at the head of the chain, the dead were lost, their minds doomed to wither, their closed memories sentenced to gradual dimness which would finally extinguish.

And I. Once I was dead, with no child to follow me, I too would stagnate, grow dark, disappear into the murky depths of myself to a place without the quickness of the awake world. A place where there are no fresh breezes, no wild seas, no warm sunlight. I needed a son to tell me about the bonito. A daughter to remind me of the colours of the sunset. I wanted quick voices around me, joy and sadness, gestures, enthusiasm, descriptions of events with the truth pared away and the essence embroidered with fantastical fiction.

The dead are so unimaginative.

They can only remember what was actual: the absolute truth. With death, all fiction drops away, leaving only dry, indigestible facts, which taste like dust. They have no art, no power to embellish the tale in the retelling. The dead cannot lie. The place where there are no lies is foul indeed. It is as boring and rank as a rotten fish. Lies are necessary, in order to inflate the ordinary into what might, should or would happily be. Without the power to lie, there is no poetry, no story, no vision. Lies are as necessary as truths if the mind is to bloom perennially. I am not talking of deceit, or mendacity employed for the purpose of harming others, but the beautiful lie, that builds cities in the mind and gardens in the soul. I would rather see a flower through the eyes of a bee, as told to me by a mystic, than hear its merits from the lips of a scientist, describing its cell structure and the composition of its gases. Lies and truth each have their context, of course, but when I wish to recall the colours of the ocean, or the smell of a frangipani, I want impressions, expressions, that stir the emotion. I want to *feel* the colours, experience the perfume.

The dead have dead minds.

'Ruth? What are we to do?'

'We must carry on. We have to be strong for each other. Perhaps something will happen – who can tell? We don't know all the mysteries of life, Nathan. Perhaps something will happen?'

'Yes, perhaps.'

I looked forward to a death as prosaic and dull as money.

'What's that?' asked Ruth, pointing.

'Oh – the gift.' I showed her the parcel under my arm. She snatched it from me, laughing.

'You brought something for me?'

'You know I always do.'

She tore the wrapping away and the sari tumbled out, unfolding blue and gold, into the sunlight. She gave a little squeal of delight.

'Oh, Nathan. It's lovely.'

She held it to her and twirled, so that the silk wound itself around her body. It pleased me to see her so delighted with it. She took it off and then carefully folded it again. Blue and gold. The colours of the sea and sky. I knew she would like it.

She took my hand and led me back to the house. There we undressed and lay on the mats together, stroking each other. As always, after a parting, our bodies were electric under the touch of each other's fingers. It was as if we were making love for the first time, with a certain amount of shyness on both sides. She murmured words and I drank them down as eagerly as if I had been in a language desert.

I buried my face, first in her hair, and then in her breasts. They burned my cheeks with their soft fire. I could hear her heart beating as her legs wrapped themselves around mine. I began moving to its rhythm – *dubba-dubba-dubba-dubba-dubba* – so good, so very, very good. There were colours in my head, which began to travel down to my loins, as we used our hands and lips, finding ourselves inside each other. Then twisting, turning, slowly at first. The colours flowed. Then faster, until they zig-zagged and crackled, and I trembled, felt her trembling, quickening, hot breath, musty in my nostrils, and then that final gathering of liquid colour beginning at the base of the spine, which surged forward and to which I gave release, allowing it to fountain from me in spasms of white-water exhilaration.

Then, several movements later, her own: flash-flood waves that travelled through her whole frame. I could feel the violence of their force rippling through her body.

And then we were safe once more, in the comfort of each other, drawing in oxygen, relaxed, still enjoying the touch of skin against skin, but without the former urgency of feeling. It was as if I were floating in a pool of warm saltwater, buoyed by calmness, peaceful.

I could hear the distant voices of children, playing, and the muted rumble of the ocean, rolling over the reef. Just as the sea supported our island on its fluid shoulders, I was suspended by my spirit. I had gone outside myself. My spirit had flowed through my pores and now surrounded my body: a wonderful osmosis of the soul. It was not always that way – perhaps once in a hundred times – and when it came like that, it was as if I had been swallowed by one of my own dreams. I trembled on the edge of the real and the beautiful unreal.

'Ruth?'

'Mmmm?' She was almost asleep.

'I'll find a way to get you to England.'

'Oh, Nathan – I don't want to leave you – it's just . . .'

'I know. You'll be back. Maybe you won't even like it there? I didn't.'

'Maybe.'

Soon afterwards she was snoring softly, a kind of soft burr. I hoped when our heads were side-by-side, staring out from Jorka Island over the lagoon, that she still made that sound. It was so intimate. And I did not need to share it with anyone.

Later, when it was dark, I went out to look at the stars, but they had nothing to say to me that I did not know already.

I was beaching my canoe when my mother came from beneath the breadfruit trees, walking in a manner which caused me to stop what I was doing and pay attention to her.

She looked different somehow – more self-assured, even radiant. She stopped when she saw me and seemed to hesitate, as if she did not want to speak to me. I thought perhaps that she was angry, because I had not called on her immediately on my return to the islands. She is a woman who regards a son's duty to his mother as sacred. I began to form excuses, because I knew I was in the wrong.

Yet, when she began walking again, I could see there was no expression of anger on her face. My mother is not a woman who keeps her feelings carefully wrapped: she reveals them in their nakedness. Her expression was calm, serene. In fact, I had not seen her looking so content since the death of my father.

This alarmed me. I could not think of the reason behind it. My first thought was that she had been told some awful secret about herself – that perhaps she had been to the *fandita man* and he had told her that she was going to die soon. I had seen that expression on the faces of others, who had fallen into a state of resignation and a kind of special peace. I did not want to lose my mother, whatever her failings: she was my mother.

Yet, almost as soon as this anxiety was born, it died again. She glowed, visibly, with good news. As she approached me she actually smiled – the way she used to smile at me when I was a small boy, when my father was alive.

'Mamma, I was just coming to see you.'

She pouted. 'Your mother is always the last to see you, after you've been on a trip.'

'That's not true,' I began to protest, 'you . . .'

'Never mind that.'

She sat on the beach and stared out over the lagoon, towards Jorka Island. Her manner was very strange indeed. I didn't know what to make of it.

'Are you all right, mamma?'

She ran a hand through her wispy hair. Then she winked at me. I hadn't seen her wink for a long time and waves of alarm went through me. Was she going mad on me at last?

'I'm pregnant, Nathan.'

She really was mad. I wondered what to do. Pregnant? Should I run for Ruth? What was going on?

'You needn't look so shocked,' she said. 'There are still men who want women like me . . .' She looked down at herself. 'I know what you see. You see a broken-down woman – a sagging old body, with no life in it. Well, my son, it still works.'

'Pregnant?' My mind swam. She was surely crazy. 'Mamma, please . . .'

She looked up at me again.

'Nathan, listen to me. I went to the *fandita man* and he gave me some powder – for fertility – and then I lay with a man. I asked the *fandita man* to make sure your father's spirit was in my . . . my lover, when his seed went into me. This is your father's child. You will have a brother – or a sister. It doesn't matter which.'

'A brother or a sister,' I repeated, dumbfounded. I could not take this in. I was waiting for her to scream or do something totally unreasonable. The whole situation was terrible.

I took her hand in my own.

'But mamma – you're too old . . .'

'I'm forty,' she snapped. 'That's not too old. I may *look* too old, but I'm not. I didn't want any more children – you were enough for me. I kept that damn fishbone stuck up inside me, after you were born. Your father wanted more children, but I didn't like walking around as big as a puffer fish and then all the messy business that followed. Yuk! I hated it. It hurt too. You men – you don't know anything about pain. You cut your fingers and think that's pain . . .'

'But why, mamma?'

'You know *why*. I've seen you – heard you. You think I don't know? Ruth can't have children, can she? Otherwise there would be one here, long ago. How old are you both? Twenty-four? Your father needs his grandchildren. *I* need them. If you can't give them to us, then it'll have to be your brother or sister that does it.'

She stroked my hair.

'I'm sorry, Nathan, but it's true, isn't it? You and Ruth . . .'

'Yes, mamma, it's true.'

'Then you see why I had to do it? It's for your good, too, you know. We need someone to come to the coral heads – you don't want to live in eternal darkness, do you?'

'No, mamma.'

'Well, then.'

I looked out, over the lagoon, to where my father was watching us. It would be a while before he got to see the grandchild he wanted so much, but at least now there was a good chance of it actually appearing.

'Are you *sure*? I mean . . .'

'Yes, I'm sure. Those powders the *fandita man* has . . . did Ruth try them?'

'Yes.'

'Ah. Well, my boy, you can stop worrying now. I know it's been gnawing at you, like a rat inside. You can stop your worrying, can't you?'

What a strange thing. My mother with child, after all this time. It had not even occurred to me. I had thought she was useless; a wretched old woman good for nothing but complaining and moaning about how lonely she was. I had given her up. Perhaps she was not pregnant? No, women knew these things. She would not have come to me if she had not been sure. I was to have a brother, or sister, and the thought filled me with pleasure. It would be like my own child. A child at last.

'Come on, mamma, let's get you home,' I said, pulling her to her feet.

'Yes – you've got to look after me now, haven't you?'

'I always did, mamma.'

'And Ruth will be jealous of me.'

'Now you know that's not true. She'll be a little envious, that a woman twice her age can still have children, while she . . . well, don't you go . . .'

'Oh, I'll be nice to her, don't worry. I won't make her feel bad. I'd rather it was her having the child, anyway, you know that. I'm sure . . .'

She rattled on, as I led her back through the rainforest to her house.

When we got there, I was pleased to hear that she wanted to sit outside. Then I went off to tell Ruth.

## Fifteen

John Trencher had waded out to the reef to remonstrate with two men. He had thought that they were cutting more coral, and had shouted at them from a distance, only to find as he drew nearer to them that they were setting pots for crabs. They looked surprised and a little bewildered by his attitude.

'I'm sorry,' he said, as he reached them. 'I thought you were taking the coral – for more heads – I'm sorry.'

The two men were Peter and Mark.

'What if we were?' said Peter, suddenly becoming belligerent. 'What does it matter to you?'

'It matters to everyone – all of you people on the islands. You mustn't rip the reef apart . . .'

'You mind your own business,' replied Mark. 'We do as we wish. I've heard all about you, teacher, and the things you're telling the children. Oh, yes, Miriam has told us things – how you teach the children that it's bad to honour our ancestors.'

'Miriam? Oh, the old woman at the back of the classroom. Listen, I'm not saying you shouldn't pay due deference to the dead, but you're endangering the whole atoll with that practice. It's time something was done to stop it. Don't you see . . .?'

They waded away from him before he had time to finish and he was left foolishly in the middle of a sentence. He watched them go, anger boiling up inside him.

'Stupid, ignorant people,' he muttered to himself.

He decided to walk off his anger and made his way out to the fringing reef pathway, deciding it was time to do a circuit of the islands. The tide was out and he believed he had plenty of time.

He took off his shirt and draped it protectively around his neck. His skin was now a deep mahogany colour with large dark freckles on his shoulders, where he had previously suffered sunburn blisters.

He had to concentrate on where he trod, which made the exercise worthwhile. It was a test of physical stamina and mind. Having had a fairly easy time of it in the classroom that morning, he needed something to stretch him. Numbers passed him in a boat and beckoned, but John summarily refused the offer of a lift. He wanted to do this thing.

It was amazing to him how many varieties of fish lived on the reef. Mostly they swam, crawled or wriggled around his legs – he was waist-deep on occasions – completely without fear and at ease with this stranger in their territory. He knew only a few of the names. He knew sweetlip, snappers and blue ring angels, and puffers and squids of course, and parrot fish, but there were dozens, hundreds of others which brushed his calves and thighs as if he were merely a walking piece of coral. Some of them even nibbled at the hairs on his legs. Once, he saw a lion fish ducking beneath some horny coral, resplendent in scarlet frills. He kept clear of it, suspecting that something so gaudy as this might prove to have poisonous dorsal spikes. One thing he had learned: to be wary of creatures that made a dressy show of their colours. They were usually the flash guys with deadly tipped knives hidden under their silk cloaks.

At one point, between Jorka and Pork Islands, the water went up to his nipples and he could not see his feet. It worried him, but the stretch of dark sea was narrow – perhaps ten yards – and there was no way he was going to turn around and go back. Nathan had told him that one could walk *all* the way around the reef, and that he was going to do.

He was about to lift his feet and swim the remaining few yards when it happened: an intense, sharp pain in his right foot.

He gasped as the shock went through him. Something had bitten through his track shoe. A shark? Oh, Christ, not a shark, *please*. Half a foot left? But whatever it was, it would not let go. It held him there, its teeth buried in his instep. Waves of pain and nausea went through him.

'Oh God,' he cried, aloud.

He panicked for a moment, thrashing and trying to wrench his foot free from the hold, but it would not come. Then he thought: maybe it isn't a fish? Perhaps it's an iron spike or something?

He felt down his own leg and came to something that turned his stomach inside out, making him gag. It was smooth, slimy and bony. *Disgusting.*

'Help! Help!'

Again he tried to pull his foot free from the creature, but it was as if the extremity had been nailed to the reef. It was immovable. He did not know what to do. Pain still swam through his head, but he was vaguely aware of a greater danger than bleeding to death. The tide was on its way in. If he did not break loose soon, he would surely drown.

He did not know what to do. The situation seemed ludicrous. He couldn't think straight through the pain. What about sharks? There was blood in the water now . . .

He searched the surface anxiously for signs of dorsal fins, but even drawing a blank did not offer much comfort. Sharks often swam below the surface. He realised that he had to keep very still – no thrashing or he would send out vibrations, distress signals, which the sharks in the open sea would pick up. The terror was making him shake and the water was chilling him. After about ten minutes, he saw something moving rapidly through the water, its fin cutting the surface. It was almost as if he had willed the creature to him.

*Oh-God-please-let-it-be-a-dolphin!*

It was a shark, about six feet long. It swam around him, once, and then headed off towards the lagoon, between the islands.

*Don't come back!*

After taking a deep breath the teacher bent double again and tried to push his thumb and forefinger into the eyes of the creature that held his foot, but he couldn't find the right places. The thing below twisted and turned as he tried to grip its slippery head and he had to come up for air, in agony.

The water was rising fast now. It was past his nipples and close to the base of his neck.

He tried once more to find the creature's eyes, but was unsuccessful. Gasping on the surface again, he steeled himself for the pain and attempted to wrench his foot free. Even if he lost a hunk of flesh, he *had* to escape. The pain came, but no release. No matter how hard he pulled, nothing gave way. The track shoe was too tough to tear, being nylon. Everything seemed against him.

Beyond the reef, the water was reasonably calm, but the swell was creating dips and peaks, the latter of which lapped his chin.

The shark returned, swimming casually by, as if it had not noticed him. Probably a harmless reef shark. He watched it turn several times, then it disappeared below the surface. He waited, his heart thudding, for the strike, wondering where it would come, on which part of his body. He tried to protect his abdomen with his arms. Better an arm than his guts spilling out into the water. Oh *please, someone – someone . . .*

He began to feel dizzy and was half-conscious for a while, in a kind of limbo state. The water rose steadily. The sun was now low on the horizon – it burned a path of red light between Long and Short Islands, across the lagoon, and into his eyes. His last sunset? No, impossible. He was not going to die. People didn't die because something held them by the foot. It was too unfair. He could have taken a ride from Numbers. He could have lifted his leg just a second earlier. Too unfair. Too final for such a simple accident. Too slow. Too much time to *think*. There had to be a way.

Now, he felt it was all so unreasonable. Something had to be done, before he started swallowing water and weakening himself and his position even further. This was *stupid*. He wouldn't put up with it. Not the pain. Not the circumstances. 'I *will . . .*'

His head spun and he vomited, fouling the water around him. The pain was a constant, ugly side-affair, that hampered his thoughts. He tried, ineffectually since he was floating now, to twist himself free. The creature held on with iron jaws: immovable.

It was impossible. He was going to drown. *Unfair, unfair, unfair!* This wasn't right. It just wasn't right.

He drifted in his thoughts.

A black silhouette was crossing the lagoon, the sun behind it. A man in a boat. Numbers!

'Help! Help me!' screamed John. 'I'm over here!'

Numbers paused in the act of paddling, seemed to observe John's predicament, then continued on his way.

Unbelievable. It couldn't be happening.

'You . . . come back!' screamed John. 'I'm trapped.'
But the canoeist seemed not to hear.

# Sixteen

Everything has a pulse: the sea, the air, the land – even abstracts have a rhythmic beating, a drum that is sensed, felt, rather than heard. Midnight, for instance, has a pulse of its own, more definite than any other hour of the clock. Midnight beats slowly, as does noon, while the evening hours have a rapid pattering that quickens the world, gives it urgency.

As I rowed back across the lagoon, I could feel the sea's heart pounding beneath – a giant, very slow, very soft, powerful throb, deep down, below. But the air around me was quick with the hour and this duo had me alive to the world about me. I saw a school of manta rays slide under the boat, and a lone frigate bird riding the sunset. Around me, the coral atoll, the ring, was fiery red, burning like a brand in the ocean. I was receptive to the unusual, and it came: a kind of gargled scream, from the gap between Pork and Jorka Islands.

Someone was in trouble.

I turned the *dhoni* towards the shore, dipping the oars deeply and pulling hard. At first I could see nothing. Then came another shout and I noticed what looked like a ball, floating on the water about a hundred yards off, on the outer reef. It was not a ball. It was a head. I could see a wave of the hand.

'Help! For God's sake . . .'

The teacher. He seemed to be struggling with the waves, as if he were wrestling with each one, individually, as they tried to overcome him. They were relentless, like savage creatures, intent on tearing him to pieces before I could rescue him.

When I reached him the swell was passing completely over his face, allowing a short while only for him to breathe in the spaces between the waves. He seemed to be trapped on the reef, his face twisted in terror. I grabbed him by the hair and tried to pull him out of the water, but he screamed.

'No . . . foot . . .' A wave had him gargling, gasping for breath. He coughed, choking in the salt water, then, 'My foot – something's . . .'

I dived into the water and out of my depth, for he was a good deal taller, swam to the bottom. The light was fading above, but I could still make out the submarine shapes of the coral and fish. I found his legs. One of them seemed to be caught in some weeds, which wavered around his calf as if they were caressing it. I pulled at his leg. It was held fast. Not the weed. Something else.

I went up for air, to hear him spluttering, and went down again. I felt along the trapped leg until I came to something narrow and slimy, attached to his instep, through his shoe. I knew then what held him: a moray eel. It had sunk its teeth into his foot and pinned it there, swelling itself in its coral hole so that it was impossible to dislodge.

The teacher had gone limp now. I went up for a quick gulp of air. I needed a knife, but there was no time. The long, muscular body of the eel was as thick as a man's arm and perhaps six or seven feet long. If I had a stick I could possibly prise the jaws apart, but only the oars were available and they were too large.

I dived, gripped the fronds, and pulled myself down close to the creature's head. Its small, wicked eyes stared into mine. I took the top of the head in my mouth and sank my teeth into the rubbery flesh, just where the creature's jaw hinged. I bit hard, applying as much force as my own jaws could muster. After a few seconds I felt something crack – the moray thrashed, its mouth opened, and it released the foot as it squirmed under the pressure of my bite. Then it wriggled free and snaked away on the current.

I shot to the surface, gulping down air. Then I grabbed the teacher by the hair and held his head back against the side of the canoe, so that his neck was straight. I breathed into his mouth, once or twice, then hauled myself into the *dhoni*. I had to let him go to do this, but grabbed him immediately afterwards, before he floated away. Then I pulled him on board, scraping his back against the wood in the process. Laying him out on the bottom of the *dhoni*, face down, I proceeded to pump him until the water trickled from his mouth. He breathed again. Still I pumped, using the fisherman's method to revive the half-drowned man. I had learned other methods in Britain, but in desperate moments, with urgency crackling in our brains, we revert to old, known ways.

After about twenty minutes he was able to talk.

'Nathan? Thank God someone came along. I thought I was going . . .'

He removed his track shoe and winced. The moray's upper and

lower sets of teeth would have met each other through his flesh. It looked painful.

'Damn – that hurts. What was it? Was it poisonous?'

I shook my head.

'A moray. You must have stepped close to its hole – it gripped your foot.'

'Through the shoe? Damn, I thought I was OK with track shoes on. Must have teeth like needles . . . oop . . . groggy . . .'

He lay back down again, staring up into the sky. It was dark now and the star patterns had set above us. I began to row back, to the priest. The teacher would need treatment.

'Those waves,' he said, 'they wouldn't stop. When the thing got me, I didn't know what it was. That's the worst part. Something from the unknown. Did you kill it?'

'No. It swam off.'

His face creased, I thought with anger.

'You should have killed it. Let's go back and get the bastard. It would've killed *me*.'

He rolled over, bursting into tears, and shivering violently.

'We're going to the priest,' I said. 'He's good at doctoring.'

'Thought I was going to drown,' he sobbed.

I left him alone for a while and pulled on the oars, concentrating on the light of the priest's house in the distance. The sound of the blades hitting the surface with a soft plashing noise must have calmed the teacher.

He said, 'Sorry, Nathan.'

'No need. It must have been bad.'

'Those waves – it was as if they were alive.' He wiped his face with his hand; a long pale figure in the bottom of the *dhoni*.

'Good thing you're so tall,' I said. 'You owe your life to your inches. I would have been dead thirty minutes before.'

He laughed, then said in a serious voice, 'I owe my life to you.'

'Because I happened to be passing? It could have been anyone.'

'But it was you. How did you manage to free me – from the eel?'

I thought about how I would tell the story to my father, using the embellishments, the lies that embroidered the ordinary with colourful, imaginative borders – the fictional additions with their fringing designs which made them so much more attractive to the ear.

'I bit its head off. Swallowed it.'

I forced an artificial belch from my belly, wounding the night with the disgusting sound.

The teacher went up on to his elbows. I could see his expression by the light of the stars.

'You bit its *head* off?'

'Swallowed it whole.' Another belch, this time not so powerful. No sense in overdoing it. 'Tasted foul. Like eating a hard rubber ball dipped in oil.'

He stared at me.

'And it still swam away, afterwards?' He grinned.

I'd forgotten that. Still, the story was up now, and it had to stay there. He wouldn't be so impolite as to call me a liar.

'It wriggled away. Probably dead by now.'

'No doubt about that.'

Thankfully we were now by the shore of Short Island. Somehow, telling the teacher stories was not the same as spinning yarns for my father. The difference was that pappy knew of the embroidery and accepted it – it was expected – an essential element in the process of every tale with a core of truth – but the teacher had a different view. He was patronising me.

I shipped the oars and helped him to his feet, putting an arm around him. He leaned on me, heavily, as we stepped out of the *dhoni* and made our way towards the priest's house, the teacher hopping and me trying to keep my feet under his weight.

I called, 'Father! It's Nathan. The teacher's had an accident.'

The door to the house opened and we approached. The priest peered out, into the night, then bustled.

'Bring him in here. What happened?'

He got on the other side of the teacher and together we helped him up the steps.

'A moray eel. Got my foot in its teeth. Wouldn't let go. Almost drowned. Nathan bit its head off.'

The priest's eyebrows shot up.

'Really? That's some bite you have there, Nathan.'

I squirmed. To the priest it was the truth, absolute. That was even worse than being patronised.

Father Maurer said, 'Here – in the chair. I'll get the antiseptic and some warm water.' He inspected the wound. 'Seems – well, it doesn't look too bad. A clean fish bite in salt water is not like being bitten by a dog or rat.'

Half an hour later the injury had been fussed over and the foot was dressed in a clean, neat bandage.

'You'd better stay here,' said the priest, 'at least for tonight. I expect you've had a bit of a shock.'

The teacher nodded, but I said, 'I think I'll go home now. Take care, John. What were you doing on Ghost Island anyway? Outsiders are not permitted.'

'I didn't actually set foot on it. I was trying to get all the way round the reef – to see if it could be done. I was feeling a little miffed and needed an adventure.'

'Why were you angry?'

'I had a fight with Peter and Mark – I thought they were taking coral from the reef, but they were just setting crab pots . . .' He seemed to remember something, because his eyes blazed and he added, '. . . and Numbers passed me in a canoe, when I was trapped. He could *see* I was in trouble. I called to him – he just ignored me. These people . . .'

'I'll see Numbers, it's all right.'

The teacher looked me directly in the eyes.

'You're always saying that, but he still treats me with contempt. What's got into the man? I've done nothing to him.'

I ignored this outburst.

'Goodbye. I'll see you both tomorrow. I'll come in the *dhoni* and collect him, Father.'

The priest nodded and I left them. I made my way to where the *dhoni* was bobbing on the night waves.

Midnight. The slow beat. The pulse at the centre of darkness. A naked man runs through the rainforest; runs and leaps over fallen branches, splashes through the swamp water where the sea has leaked through the coral sand. He is afraid, and his heart beats wildly within him. He runs, but he does not know why he runs. To wake with the terror locked in his breast and run from his house, out into the warm night, is an instinct.

The breakers thunder around him: all around him. The surf forms an ever-changing wall, shaping and reshaping itself under the darkness. It offers tantalising seconds of hissing flatness, too brief to use. It tempts escapees, only to rise like a heavy giant claw a moment later.

The man reaches the beach, runs along it. He runs and runs, until he comes upon footprints. They are his own: full circle. He stops, blinks, and stares. After a while his heart slows its pace, until it is in time with the pulse of midnight. He trudges slowly back to his bed, bewildered by himself.

A woman is taking comfort from the sound of the waves washing over the reef. She turns in her bed, half awake, allowing the irregular rhythm to lull her senses. She hears, without recognising it, the euphony of the womb, the songs of her mother's blood. It is a safe sound, that curls around her body and protects it from the outside world. Safe in the belly of the ocean, nursed by it, succoured by the milk-white surf, she owes her being to the sea. It is part of her: she part of it. It is in her bosom, its currents run through her veins. The rhythms of her body are in tune with the tides, are inseparable from its motion.

The man returns to his bed, takes comfort from the woman. Her peace flows into him: his anxiety into her. The two intermingle: fear of the sea, reverence of the sea. They each move inwards, from extremes. The balance is right and the man and woman fall asleep in one another's arms.

# Seventeen

While John Trencher was recovering from his ordeal, there was a tragedy. The bonito boat had been caught in a sudden, ferocious storm, and had overturned after being swamped by a gigantic wave. Achbor was lost to the sea, though the others clung to the upturned drifting hull. When the accident happened, the boat was only two hundred yards from the reef. As the waves took them towards the islands, the fishermen let go of their craft and rode over the reef on crests.

Numbers failed in the attempt. He was dashed on the sharp coral and his torn body sucked underneath the shelf of the reef, to disappear beneath. His corpse was never found.

Two men lost and the bonito boat shattered by the waves pounding it against the reef.

John was absolutely stunned by the news. *There but for the grace of God* . . . It seemed incredible to him that people could die so easily, and if they could, why it did not happen every day. The deaths of Numbers and Achbor were the first on the islands, barring death by natural causes, since that of a young girl called Naomi.

Nathan, not a member of the crew that day, told his father of the accident. The dead man was sympathetic, but said that the important thing to do was make a new bonito boat. There had been only two on the atoll and the remaining craft was old and untrustworthy.

Nathan agreed with his father for once. Without a large fishing vessel the islanders could not feed themselves adequately. There were chickens, goats and quail, but fish was their staple food. The smaller boats were not fast enough to chase the bonito or skipjack, and the barracuda were only to be found in small numbers that year.

Nathan explained all this to the teacher when he was visiting him one evening.

'Barracuda? You mean there are barracuda in these waters?'

'Of course,' said Nathan.

Ruth was also there. She said, 'The teacher is thinking about when he was trapped on the reef.'

John nodded, stroking his tender but healing wound, which Ruth had rebandaged for him.

'I'm glad I didn't know,' he said.

The smell of bread from a nearby oven filled the room. John's gastric juices began to work. He thought about supper. He was now an islander as far as food went: he liked and ate what they ate. He no longer even picked the dead weevils out of the bread, nor turned up his nose at turtles' eggs.

He said to Ruth, 'You mentioned a picnic?'

Ruth nodded and smiled, undoing some cloth containing hoppers, and watalappan, a spiced jaggery dish that John had come to love. There was also pittu, which was flour and coconut steamed in bamboo, and sliced yam.

They began eating.

John, aware how disastrous was the loss of the bonito boat to the islanders, asked Nathan how long it would take to build a new one.

Nathan told him.

'Can I help?' he offered.

'What about the children?' asked Ruth.

'Well, I only teach in the morning – I have plenty of free time. I suppose you think I'll be more a hindrance than a help,' he added, in a disappointed tone.

'I don't know,' said Nathan. 'We'll have to ask Uncle Letushim – he's the one who will have to organise it all.'

Ruth said, 'I'll ask him for you. He's fond of me. I'm sure he'll say yes.

After all, you'll be a Belonger soon – the initiation ceremony is only two months away.'

John felt excited.

'Yes – that's true. By the way, what about this ceremony? What does it consist of?'

Nathan looked at Ruth and smiled, reinforcing John's feelings of misgiving.

'Oh, you'll find out,' said Nathan.

John said, 'I don't have to kill a shark with my bare hands? Anything like that?'

'Nothing so easy,' replied the islander.

'Fine,' answered John, sarcastically. 'I feel great about the whole affair. Why the secrecy?'

'It's more fun.'

'For whom?'

'For us, of course.'

They ate the food in silence after that. Thoughts buzzed around John's mind like busy flies, but he could come to no definite conclusions. It was a case of wait and see.

A letter from Julia had arrived from Malé recently, brought back by one of the islanders. The tone was quite cold and formal, not surprisingly. She said she was well and had a part-time job at a children's play-school. Ben went with her, of course, and enjoyed the company of the other children. He did not seem to miss his father, and had learned to ask for the toilet, though this was not always a success, since sometimes the function preceded the request. Julia felt it was a big step . . .

She had sounded as if she were coping well without him. It was as John had suspected. Without him there she was far better off. She only had one invalid to worry about – not two. So why the crushing guilt? He knew very well why. You don't abandon a mother and disabled child and get away scot free. You have to pay. You have to pay with sleepless nights and a terrible weight of failure which has to be carried around every day. You have to pay every time you look at another child. You have to pay when you see an invalid trying to cope with his disability. And the payment is never enough. It never will be enough.

'Coconut?' asked Ruth.

He said, 'Oh?' waking from his reverie, and she grated some for him on the yam, without waiting for a definite reply. He actually disliked grated coconut, but ate it anyway.

The evening passed pleasantly enough. John felt he was really getting to know the islanders and their ways now. They accepted him, almost as one of themselves. No more accidents like the fish in the water tanks. No silly cultural errors on his part. They were not so very different from one another, after all, he and the locals.

Letushim agreed to allow John to help with the building of the bonito boat. The old man told him that he expected the work to take sixty days and that meant everyone working full out, nights as well. Letushim explained how the boat was to be made.

The hull would be fashioned of teak imported from India, a stock-pile of which was already on the atoll. No metal would be used in the building, not even for nails, since unpainted metal corroded very quickly. The planks would be sewn together with coconut cord. Coconut husks were left to rot in seawater and then pounded with wooden mallets to weaken the fibre, which was afterwards woven by hand into cord and rope. The boat was to be caulked with resin and covered overall with vegetable oil to preserve the wood. The mast and boom for the lateen-rigged sail would be made of poon trees, also from India.

'What about tools?' said John.

Letushim showed the teacher an adze, honed to an extremely sharp edge.

'Just these?'

The old man nodded and smiled.

'And these,' he added, using two fingers of one hand to point to his own eyes. There would be no plans – at least not on paper – for every part of the boat would be fashioned according to Letushim's judgement. The measurements of the vessel were in his head.

The following day, John was put to work, fashioning timbers for the ribs of the boat, alongside David, Mark and Peter. It was backbreaking work and he was obviously much slower than the other three men, having to pause to have his work inspected, and needing to study the craftsmanship of his colleagues to see that he was proceeding correctly. During his first attempt, it looked like he might ruin a good spar, so one of the others took over, once he had progressed to a point where accuracy became important. This set the pattern for his subsequent assistance. He did rough hacking, someone else completed the job. It was frustrating but he saw the need for caution on their part. Teak was expensive. They could not afford to take the risk of letting him go all the way.

He found the work totally absorbing and even begrudged his

mornings at the school. Evenings were the best. They worked in the open, with the hurricane lamps flaring around them, attracting giant, soft-bodied moths the size of sparrows. These creatures would brush against his back as he cut away at the timber, fluttering over his skin like the eyelashes of the night. Now and then a flying fox would cross the glade where they worked, throwing its shadow on the ground. The size of these creatures still worried him as much as if they had been pterosaurs gliding out of prehistory and into the present.

The smell of woodshavings and sawdust became as opium to him: it burned in his nostrils like exotic snuff. And the chants that were struck, as the men worked at their various tasks, took control of his senses, hypnotising him, so that the aching in his muscles drifted away. He worked to the rhythm of the chant as skilfully as any musician on a percussion instrument, and the sweat rolled from his body as it had never done before.

As the days passed, it was with a new sense of wonder that he witnessed the craft taking shape under the accurate eye of Letushim. The old man, and Nathan, and several others, were responsible for shaping the hull planks and complicated joints. Holes were bored and the planks and beams sewn together as tightly as if the boat were destined to become a coat for some rigid creature, intent on remaining dry in the monsoon season.

It was an exciting experience. At the end of each work session, John would run his hands along the ribs he had helped to fashion, delighting in the feel of the wood, the touch of timber. It was as though it awakened some racial memory in him, which had lain dormant since the coming of machines to the shores of Albion. A great-grandfather rose from a long sleep within his mind and form, and filled him with a sense of well-being.

During the short breaks for meals, tea had never tasted so good before and bread was precious to him. He would sit with the others amid piles of woodchips and shaven timber, staring at the rainforest around him with new eyes, listening with new ears. In daylight, it rolled and swayed, full of murmuring insects. During the night it formed a high, black wall containing the busy throats of a multitude of tree frogs.

After a month he became impatient. He wanted to see the craft out on the ocean, eating the waves. It seemed that, after a certain point had been reached, the boat failed to grow any more. It remained a half-finished piece of work, no matter what effort was put into the building. The hum of passing days began to become an irritant. It was like watching a flower grow. There was no perceptible change, no progress. An eternity of boat-building stretched before him.

'We're not getting anywhere,' he complained to Nathan one day.

The frustration in his voice obviously surprised the islander, who looked up from his seat on the new mast in mild astonishment.

'But we're doing well.'

'Are we? Why isn't it moving then? I can't see where we're going any more.'

An hour later, John pushed Peter violently away from him, and then, when the other man rushed back at him, raised his adze as if to strike the islander. Mark screamed and ran at the teacher, wielding his own adze. Nathan jumped between the three men and was himself in danger of being hit. For a few moments there was a lot of nudging, shouting and waving of hands and tools. Everyone seemed willing to confront somebody.

Finally, Letushim hammered on a log with a four-by-two, until there was silence.

He pointed to the teacher.

'What is the matter?'

John tried to harness his temper before he spoke. His speech came out as a series of choked phrases. He was trembling.

'Not this time . . . I . . . my piece of work. Let me finish it. . . I've worked hard . . . me . . . I can do it now.'

Peter, as usual, had tried to remove a half-finished spar from John, when something inside the teacher had sprung open like a tightly wound spring. He was fed up with being the dogsbody. He wanted to finish the rib himself. Why should Mark and Peter get all the best jobs? It was *his* piece of work. Let them do their own and leave him alone.

Peter waved his hands in the air and spat contemptuously on the ground.

'He hit me in the chest,' he said.

John replied, 'I pushed you. All I did was push you.'

'You threatened him with this,' said Mark, throwing the adze at John's feet. 'You tried to kill him.'

'No. No I didn't. I just . . . I just want to do the job myself.'

Nathan said, 'Let him do it.'

Mark and Peter protested, but the old man waved the arguments away.

'As Nathan says, let him do it. We shall see.'

They all went back to work, with the two lovers whispering

between themselves and casting dark glances towards the teacher.

John felt utterly miserable. He had not wanted to cause trouble: it just bubbled up from somewhere inside him. It was unlike him to lose his temper. It was just frustrating to have his work taken away from him for completion, as if he were a little boy, not to be trusted to get it right.

He worked slowly and carefully at the rib.

As evening approached, he went up to Peter and offered his hand.

'I'm sorry,' he said. 'I didn't mean to offend you. I . . . I just lost my head.'

Peter glared at him at first, and then pumped his hand, grinning.

'Yes. That's all right. You finish it. I expect it'll be better than I could do.'

John was dismayed. 'Oh . . . no. You mustn't say that. I suppose it'll be a very raw job – but I would like to do it by myself.'

'Let him do it,' interposed Mark, as if there were still some question about it.

Peter nodded, a serious expression on his face.

'I think so. I think so.'

'Thank you.'

John went back to his work feeling a lot happier. Nathan winked at him. Letushim nodded gravely. Some of the other men began chattering again, smiling in his direction. He fell in with the rhythm of the work, the sound of metal chunking into wood once more becoming mesmeric. Hurricane lamps were lit. The mosquitoes came in as evening clouds, to feed upon the sweat, to stick and drown there. John began chanting: '. . . hickory-dickory-dock, the mouse ran up the clock, the clock struck one, the mouse ran down, hickory-dickory-dock . . .'

After a few minutes all the islanders had the words and chanted along with him. When they became bored with this one, he introduced another.

'Three blind mice, see how they run . . .'

Later, Letushim asked, 'Are all the boat-building songs of England about mice?'

John blushed.

'No – not all of them.'

The old man nodded thoughtfully and went on with his work.

Days folded into days, and progress still seemed remarkably slow. Then, all of a sudden, the boat seemed to fit together like magic. Just when everyone was becoming lethargic and dispirited, the boat appeared to be complete, except for the rigging and swabbing down with brooms dipped in vegetable oil.

Excitement and pride surged through the school teacher's veins, as he viewed the beautiful new craft. He couldn't believe he had assisted in such a wonderful task. It was surely the best boat that had ever been constructed. In the light of the hurricane lamps it gleamed, and he strode beneath it, inspecting the hewn planks of the hull and inhaling the odour of freshly cut wood. God, he thought, if my father could see me now. He would surely think that I had more in me than just . . . just what? Just a school teacher?

'Does it meet with your approval?'

Nathan had appeared at his side.

'I was just wondering whether *I* met with approval.'

'You did very well. *Very* well. Your help was very much appreciated.' Nathan ran his hand along the hull. 'Nice feel, isn't it?'

John nodded.

'I can't believe Letushim did this all by eye – without the use of instruments. At least, I know he did, but it seems so accurate.'

'Oh, there are mistakes.'

'Not to my sight. Look at the curve of those bows and the proud stance of the kingpin! They're such sensual things, boats. No wonder men fall in love with them. They have such grace . . .'

'Even an appearance of intelligence?'

Nathan was smiling.

'Yes, even that. I want to go fishing in this one. I might not be responsible for the artistry, but that's my sweat on those ribs – these blisters will account for that. I feel this boat is part of me – carries something of myself in its framework. I *know* it. How long will such a boat last?'

'Oh, eighty, ninety, perhaps a hundred years, if it doesn't sink like the last one.'

Again the excitement surged through John's breast.

'By God, that's almost immortality. When I'm in my grave, this part of me will still be slicing through the waves, chasing bonito.'

'You have a child – your immortality is assured.'

John looked up at the mast, shining in the light of the lamp. It reached up, into the night, tall and straight. He could imagine it with the lateen-rigged sail, big-bellied in the wind, and the fibre ropes creaking and stretching. The whole craft was swaddled in leather and fibre and every part of it carved by hand; even the swivel blocks for the tackle. He was intensely proud of being associated with such a vessel.

'I'd rather put my faith in a boat,' he said.

The launching of the bonito boat was an affair which involved all the people of the atoll. They came across the reef in the early evening with flaming torches, to gather around the craft – some five hundred men, women and children. A path of fires, similar to an aircraft flarepath, went down to the shores of the lagoon. Rolling logs were placed in front, beneath the bows of the boat, and a great wave of humanity surged around the sides and stern. At the front, the log movers stood ready and there were people on the ropes attached to the gunwales. The teacher was there, and the priest, and even the resident *fandita man*, without whom no ceremony of any significance could take place.

A cry went up from Uncle Letushim, and as if this were a plug removed from a barrel of sound, the air was filled instantly with noise. Adults yelled, children shrieked and babes cried. The bonito boat began to rumble forwards, over the rolling logs. There were grunts from the rope pullers, as they took up the strain, and moans from those pushing from the rear. Drums began to beat, cymbals clashed.

As soon as a rolling log became free at the back, two men would snatch it up and run with it like rugby scrum halves with a heavy, elongated ball. Down it would go, in the path of the bows, and the boat squeaked and groaned forwards, through the lines of fires which lit the rainforest.

Despite the number of people, John Trencher found the work hard. The rope cut deeply into his right shoulder and at times he felt as if he were the only one pulling. It was probably a fact that only those actually on the ropes, and the people with their shoulders against the craft, were doing anything at all to move the boat. The rest were pushing the pushers, and were probably more hindrance than help. Nevertheless, this was a family affair – the whole atoll – and no one wished to be left out. Certainly no islander would suggest that there were too many cooks and that it should be left to the experts. It was not a case of getting the job done efficiently and quickly – it was a matter for participation and celebration.

Gradually the boat rolled towards the waters which were to be its home for the next hundred years. Uncle Letushim yelled instructions from time to time, but no one took much notice of him. Shadows danced, and for the first time since he had arrived, John could not hear the surf booming along the reef, nor the song of the treefrogs. These were drowned in the wave of noise from the participants in this orgy of ritual tasks. Vegetable oil, smeared over the hull, gleamed in the light from the flares, personifying the boat, investing it with an air of sinister intent. It was not difficult for John to imagine this craft as some sort of legless god of the sea, shining with afterbirth, and now being drawn by its hypnotised, frenzied fanatics to a place where its power would render it invincible. Amid the caterwauling, the feverish excitement, the trance-inducing drums and cymbals, it was comforting to catch the occasional glimpse of the priest walking in front.

The man on the rope to the left of John occasionally swung inwards, when he lost his footing, and twice scraped the teacher's ankle with his heel. The man was barefoot, but the calluses on his feet were so hard and jaggedly sharp they actually tore the European's skin. The ankle became painful as sweat found the open wound.

Finally, they were on the coral beach, crabs scattering in panic as the monster rolled over their bolt holes, crushing their neat marker cones of sand. It was now that the *fandita man*, the jack-of-all-magic – religious scientist, conjurer, herbalist, astrologer, witch and saint, the man who cured sickness, entertained children at parties, ensured the fishing was good and encouraged the crops to grow – it was now that he let out a yell so shrill and blood-chilling that John thought that someone had gone beneath the boat, or at least, at very least, had had a leg severed at the hip.

He dropped his rope, his heart pounding in his throat, wondering which way to turn. Actually, it was merely a blessing, as the boat touched the water for the first time.

Then she was gliding, bobbing gently on the ripples of the lagoon waters. The *fandita man*, having had his say, gave way to the priest, who poured softer, Christian blessings on the craft. Between their extremes, the pagan and the priest, they felt they had provided all possible religious buoyancy aids to keep the vessel afloat in times when disaster threatened.

The craft was moored as it floated serenely on the quiet waters. It looked undressed without its sails and other equipment. John stared at it with pride.

Father Maurer was then by the teacher's side, his moon-white face looking slightly troubled in the light of the torches and fires.

'The initiation ceremony – you're about to become a Belonger,' he said. 'I'll see you tomorrow.'

John was alarmed.

'You're not staying? I'd rather you didn't leave – I mean, they look a bit wild.'

Around the two Europeans, the natives were dancing and yelling, waving torches and bumping into one another. They looked as though they had reverted to a primitive form of themselves, which only emerged during rituals involving outsiders. They looked as though they could roast the teacher on live coals and laugh as he cooked. Their eyes were shining, their mouths were open, and with every moment they seemed to regress to some basic form of humanity.

The priest nodded. 'I have to go. It's not my place . . . well, the ceremony is hardly Christian. I would feel uncomfortable – and so would they. It's best I leave. You'll be all right.'

'But you went through it?'

'Not me – some former priest.'

'Oh, yes. I was forgetting. Who does what? What happens? I don't like the idea . . .'

Father Maurer shrugged.

'The *fandita man* will look after you. Don't worry – you won't come to any harm – any physical harm.'

Then he was gone, into the shadows of the rainforest. John felt terribly abandoned. Dancing had reached a pitch of frenzy, around the fires, and the air was full of heathen cries. *I'm alone*, he thought. *I'm alone with these strange people and their ancient rituals. I'm at their mercy.*

Two women came forward and took his hands. He was led, gently, into the light of one of the fires, where the reptilian, glint-eyed *fandita man*, his hair flailing as he danced with the children, awaited him.

The *fandita man* let out another of his ear-splitting shrieks.

All noise and movement ceased.

John experienced a pressure at the base of his skull, as if someone had placed a great weight on his shoulders. Under the *fandita man*'s intense gaze, he felt submissive and helpless, and his legs began shaking.

'*Kohoma da?*' said the magic man.

Suddenly Nathan appeared by John's side and he translated the Divehi instantly.

'He asks, "How are you?" '

'Very well, thank you,' said John, meekly.

Nathan said, '*Istuti*.'

The *fandita man* smiled, as if he had been won over completely by John's answer. While the two women still held John's hands, the magician began to remove the teacher's shorts, his only item of clothing, so that he stood completely naked before all.

John felt extremely vulnerable and insecure, which he realised was the reason for the disrobing. He was a shy man, and while no one was actually staring at his genitals, he had a schoolboy urge to cover them with his hands. The grips of the two women were firm.

The *fandita man* began chanting, and drummers took up the rhythm. The whole atmosphere – smoky, sinister and thick with the undercurrents of mystery and magic – began to have an effect on John's mind. He found himself slipping into a mesmeric state, in which the figures around him, swaying like shadows from a shadow-world, began to cloy his thoughts with their deep, rich murmuring. He was lost. He was lost. He was sure of only one thing. He would not be the same man tomorrow. They were going to mould his form, manipulate his mind, reshape his soul.

The *fandita man* unrolled a strip of cloth at his feet, and extracted some soft-looking brushes. One of these he dipped into a coconut husk. He then began painting the teacher's body, beginning at his ankles, where the small cuts were, and forming snaky designs up to his loins. It soon became evident that no part of his body was to remain without some symbol or mark.

He stared into the rainforest as the magic man worked his artistry. Amongst the darkness of the trees there was a pulsing; a live beating heart pumping blood to the coral island. John felt a melting, a merging sensation, as if he were becoming part of something much larger than himself. He was aware of Nathan whispering translations of the *fandita man*'s chants into his ear, but he was shocked to realise he could not understand them. He knew the phrases should be comprehensible to him, but some conscious level of thought had deserted him.

Something far deeper was going on, at a subliminal plane, and he was powerless to master it. He did not want to resist. His barriers had dissolved and he had drifted into a state of trust from which there was no retreat. The soft, sensual touch of the brush on his skin made him aware of the sensitivity of certain areas: his nerve-ends tingled, capturing his whole attention. The sensations of his body came into sharp focus.

The final strokes of the *fandita man*'s brush left a red slash on his right side and a small spot in the centre of each palm. A shriek from the artist nailed John's brain to his skull. The dancing had begun again.

He was led to the bonito boat and borne aboard by several hands.

They frapped his arms to the boom with strong cords. Then the boat was cast adrift.

At first he began to panic, thinking that the tide would carry him away to sea. But he remembered he was only in the lagoon. He could not go far. Even if the craft slipped between islands, and floated towards the reef, the waves breaking over the coral would push it back again.

Still, he felt exposed and vulnerable. Overhead, the constellations swam slowly through the firmament. The dark islands, one lit and covered with phrenetic wraiths, swayed around him. Beyond the islands, the ocean rolled ceaselessly. Everywhere there was movement: nothing was still. The whole universe was in a state of gentle flux and he was part of that ebb and flow.

He felt he was close to understanding a great mystery. When he thought about the archipelago, out there in the night; or the mighty ocean, the dimensions of which were as difficult to comprehend as the universe itself; or even the open sky above his head – when he meditated deeply on these entities, it seemed he was near to a great secret. There was a common bond between himself and all these agents which he normally took for granted. It was like an unfelt wind, which flowed through them all, touching them all simultaneously. A magnetic force, which locked them all together. And at the heart of this vague impression, was the idea, the thought, that they understood better than he – that the sea, the sky, the land, were more aware of this bond than were creatures like himself, sentient creatures, beings with intelligence.

'We think too much and *feel* too little,' he murmured to himself. 'If we ignored our brains and just opened ourselves to impressions, we would get closer to it. Busy minds. That's all we are. Little creatures with busy minds . . .'

There was too much outward flow, of spirit, thoughts, expressions, gestures, self. While these moved outwards from his being, they prevented the inward flow from the earth, sea and sky. If he could just stop, sometimes, like this, and open himself, allow a reverse flow, then the impressions from the world around him would give him a greater sense of self than all his efforts – his puny efforts at stamping his mark on space and time – could ever do.

Disappointingly, the mood soon passed and he began to think about other things. This was an all-night vigil. In the morning he would be a Belonger: a full citizen of the islands. He felt he had done little to deserve such an honour. He had continued where another man had left off – that was all. Still, if it was the rule, the law, then he was happy to take advantage of it.

Suddenly, he felt ridiculous. What if Julia (or, worse, his *father*) could see him now? A naked, painted man strapped to the boom of a drifting ship! How foolish either of those two people would think him. The whole scene was bizarre, uncivilised. He was thankful that such people could not view him from afar. They would think he had taken leave of his senses, to allow such a thing to take place.

He thought about his idiot son, Benjamin, and a bolt of guilt went through him. He took it full in his emotional solar plexus. Ben wouldn't think he was mad. Ben would only laugh, or cry, at the strange sight of his father covered in body paint. Benjamin liked to paint his own body. Give him a set of watercolours and he would smother himself in streaks and blotches within minutes. He painted his own face at breakfast, every morning, in the bright hue of a strawberry jam, or the soft tint of honey. Ben was definitely into pagan rites. He was subconsciously aware of the pleasure of abandoning restraint, without needing to understand the reasons behind the requirement.

John's father would want to know *why*, but would at the same time have decided that there was no rational reason for such a fiasco. Richard Trencher's decisions were always the right ones. Just as he always held the correct opinion on any subject. Other people were wrong. He could even tell you the correct method of removing the top of a boiled egg. If Richard Trencher had written *Gulliver's Travels* there would have been no war between Lilliput and Blefuscu. There was only one way to do something – even decapitating an egg – and that was Richard Trencher's way. (Paint one's body? Utterly preposterous! No sensible reason behind that whatsoever.)

Julia, too, would think it silly, but not because she was narrow-minded or bigoted, like his father. She would want to weigh the value of such an act against the time which could have been usefully spent doing something of greater worth. Julia filled her life with useful tasks. She recognised the therapeutic value in allowing Ben to make a mess of himself, but she would not have tolerated it in John. That would be playing games.

John's thoughts drifted towards the islanders and their precarious home. He had decided, at last, that he liked the people. Especially, he liked Ruth, who had made his stay so far . . .

He looked down at his body and realised, to his chagrin, that he had an erection. *Now?* Not *now*. Life was too ironic for even a bitter laugh.

Impotent whenever he was with a woman, he seemed to have no trouble when out on the ocean, miles away from the nearest female. Since the birth of Ben he had remained completely impotent when confronted with the possibility of making love to Julia, or any other woman for that matter. It was so damned unfair. *Useless bloody thing!*

The warm night closed around his body. Gentle breezes caressed his private parts. Bitterness turned to alarm.

*Good God! They'll find me like this!*

He strained at his bonds in panic. It was one thing to appear naked before a group of islanders. It was quite another to be seen nude and sexually aroused. The thought horrified him so much he whimpered out loud. In such a position too! Arms outstretched, body upright, and this thing, like a post, out in front.

I . . . must . . . think. Mundane thoughts. Breakfast . . . what did I have for breakfast? Oh – yes – coconut and yams. And for dinner? Fried breadfruit, that was it . . . Wonderful diet. I'm going to be fit when I leave here. Remarkably fit. I've given up smoking and I take runs around the island. My body will be lean and hard – hell, *not* that. Think of something else. How calm the water looks tonight. I can see the stars drifting on the surface – little silver boats bobbing on the waves.

What's that? Something breaking the surface. Shark? Grey shark? Sand shark, probably. Little harmless sand shark. Looking for blue ring angel fish to eat. Poor buggers. Not much escapes a shark – or barracuda. Barracuda have been known to leap out of the water and snatch low-flying birds. Poor little bug . . . Christ! If they can do that? They can . . .

He looked down again at his stark, white erection and then at the distance between his penis and the water.

No, no. Impossible. Surely the distance . . . I don't believe in those stories. Apocryphal – they *must* be. Barracuda can't possibly leap that far. Nasty bastards . . . razor-sharp teeth. In a book he had read once, the author had put a knife-blade into the mouth of a freshly caught barracuda. The jaws had snapped shut as if worked by strong, steel springs – and all along the metal blade were left the indentations of those savage teeth: a crescent row of impressions.

A piece of blood-filled muscle? Well, you wouldn't even feel it – until afterwards. A single bite. Oh, no. No, no, no. They wouldn't attack a human out of the water. They just wouldn't . . . his penis tingled in anticipation of a saw-blade mouth cleanly severing . . .

'HELP!'

He listened. All he could hear was the harsh sound of merriment from the shores of Tubb. People were enjoying themselves while he was about to lose his manhood to hungry barracuda. Useless manhood, admittedly, but he still wanted to keep it. The thought of blood gushing from the wound, spurting from his groin into the dark waters. Pain. Terrible pain. Helpless to help himself. The humiliation. The indignity of such an ignoble death. He felt faint. He looked down again. He had frightened himself into a limpness which brought relief.

Flaccid. He heaved a sigh. He had saved himself from the sight of the islanders simply by scaring himself sick. Right at that moment he did not care whether he ever got another erection or not.

Calm once again. He drifted in his thoughts.

He was awoken by the boat suddenly dipping at the stern. There was a splashing and it was a few seconds before John realised someone was hauling himself on board.

He looked up. The sky was a pale grey and one or two frigate birds were floating over its face. The boat was somewhere between Short and Pork Islands, to the north-east of Tubb. He could see the white church out of the left corners of his eyes. To the right was Pork, but he could see beyond that, to Jorka, where the great coral heads stood, their eyes upon the surface of the lagoon, watching him . . .

'Who's there?' he called.

'Me. Nathan. You've been out here long enough. Dawn's here.'

John felt his bonds being untied and then he was free. He turned to Nathan, rubbing his wrists.

'That was an interesting exercise.'

He breathed deeply and looked down at himself. Body paint. But he no longer felt ridiculous. He was spiritually refreshed. The vigil in the open had dispelled some of the bad odours of his soul.

Nathan said, 'I suppose it was more for our benefit than yours. Still, I'm glad you took it well. You didn't disappoint them.'

'And now I'm a citizen of the islands.'

Nathan looked away.

'Yes. Yes you are.'

'Is anything wrong?' Nathan seemed embarrassed by something. 'It did go all right?'

'Perfectly. We'd better get you back. I've got a canoe alongside. I'm going to tow the bonito boat back to Tubb.'

'I'll help you row. Did you bring me any clothes?'

Nathan smiled.

'In the canoe. A longi. How did you get on last night?'

'Did a lot of thinking. Didn't reach many satisfactory conclusions, I suppose, but somehow I feel purged. And something else. I felt sexually charged . . .'

Nathan busied himself with the towing ropes.

'Yes. The excitement of the festivities. It happened to Peter Goodwright, at another ceremony . . .' Nathan looked up. 'Things got out of hand for him.'

John was confused, but he thought he understood what Nathan was talking about. There was some scandal attached to Goodwright. The interviewing board had said that Goodwright had left the islands in disgrace. That was virtually all John knew of the matter.

'What was it?' he asked. 'What did he do?'

Nathan had been in the act of climbing down from the bonito boat into the *dhoni* canoe. He looked up into John's face.

'Peter Goodwright murdered Naomi, the young girl. The teacher raped her, then struck her with a piece of coral, over the head, several times. Had we caught him that night – well, he would have been killed. We were very angry . . .'

'Good God, I expect you were . . . Jesus. He raped and . . . Jesus . . .'

Nathan climbed back on to the deck again. He gripped the shocked man by the arm.

'You understand what I'm saying – the teacher did this thing. We have to get you away from here, before the others come.'

John did *not* understand. He was puzzled by the urgency in Nathan's voice. Get *him* away? What on earth for? He hadn't done anything. Why should he want to go? He had only just become a full citizen of the islands. It didn't make sense.

Nathan obviously witnessed the confusion in John's mind by his expression.

'We have old ways still in our blood, John. Certain customs that will be a long time dying. You come under the law now, such as it is. *The teacher killed Naomi . . .*'

Suddenly he realised what was being said.

'And I am the teacher.'

'Exactly. You personally have done nothing – but you are the teacher and are therefore responsible for the teacher's actions. You inherit that responsibility, do you understand?'

Things began to click into place in his mind. He had inherited privileges and gathered time, from Goodwright, and now, also, his crime. He remembered the incident over the shells, with John-the-fisherman, when he had first arrived on the atoll. There were things the priest had told him, which now made some sense. He felt sick.

'Why didn't you tell me, Nathan?'

Nathan was quiet for a long time, before saying softly, 'I'm an islander. I'm one of them.'

'What will they do to me?'

'Tempers have cooled – you might have got away completely had you not stirred up trouble. Numbers – Naomi's father – is dead, and his widow is too torn with grief to be concerned about you. But you've become a nuisance, John, and there are those who want you out of the way. I can take you to the Maldives, now, before the sun gets too high and people are about.'

'What will they do to me?'

Nathan shrugged.

'We don't have the death penalty, for any crime. There are some two thousand islands in this part of the ocean, some of them uninhabited. You'll be sent to one of those for a few years. It's the worst punishment we have – banishment.'

John stared out, over the sea.

'Sounds quaint – old-fashioned. Banishment. Like something out of a medieval tale. *Get thee gone from the kingdom.*'

'It's not a joke, John. You might be sent away for three or four years.'

He was shocked by that. Three years! But what was a life worth? Three years was extremely lenient, considering the crime.

'But I didn't do anything,' he said.

Nathan replied, 'They don't want you here. You've frightened them with your talk about not using the coral to make heads for the dead.'

'It's true though, isn't it? It needs to be said. It needs to be stopped.' John stared at the islander with a bitterness growing within him like an unwelcome flower. Just when he was beginning to get things together, sort himself out, this new development threatened to knock him back again. Back where he was when he first came to the island. Back to that awful indecisive state, where issues were fogged with guilt and despair.

'If I leave with you now,' he said, 'I won't ever be able to come back again, will I?'

'You went about it the wrong way, John. Things have to be eroded from within. You want to chop them off, like rotten wood. You've scared the old men, the elders, and they're the ones who count at the moment.

'You've stated an intention to stay on the islands. You've become a Belonger. They can't get rid of you now – except by invoking the law. Let me take you away from here.'

John almost said *yes*, there and then, but something held him back, some part of his anger. It was a hell of a choice. Stay, and be sent to some godforsaken island for a few years, or leave with Nathan, never to return.

'Why can't people leave me alone?' he said, bleakly. Then, 'Christ, they *liked* me last night. How come they hate me this morning?'

'They don't hate you. You worry them. It's a different thing altogether. Look, we've got to hurry . . .'

'I didn't do anything. I don't have to go, and I don't have to put up with people trying to put me in prison. I'm still a British subject, you know. You can't just push us around when you feel like it.'

Nathan's brown face creased into a look of pain.

'John, listen to me. Are you listening . . .'

'Yes.'

'This is *not* England, and to all intents and purposes, you now have dual nationality. But even that doesn't matter – if you break a law in another country, you have to take the consequences.'

'I didn't break any fucking law!' John shouted. He felt himself going red and hot. 'I never hurt anyone – child, woman or man. I won't do it, do you hear? I'm going to stay and teach my classes. I don't give a damn about you people . . . you can go stuff yourselves, for all I care.'

When he had finished shouting, he stared over the lagoon, at Jorka Island and the enigmatic faces of the dead who were trying to pull the living to early graves: who controlled the future of their descendants with a power that was almost unassailable. But he would find a way to crush the power of the dead, if it took him a lifetime.

'They won't let go,' he said. 'They won't damn well let go . . .'

Nathan took no notice of this further outburst, and John went and sat by the mast. He felt utterly wretched. During the vigil, all the pieces of his life had come together. He had even begun to understand his son. Now it was as if Nathan had thrown a stone and shattered it again. Or had he? There was really nothing lost, except time. In a few years John could be back on the islands, and *nothing* could touch him. *A few years*. It sounded easy, when you said it quickly. But they would be long, empty years. They would pass very, very slowly.

'I really should go with you,' he called to Nathan.

The islander came up to him. Nathan's shadow fell across his shoulders.

'I think you should . . .'

John thought about all the running he had done in his life. He was forever using bolt holes, ducking away from responsibility, not facing up to things. What he *should* do was stay. For once in his life, he should turn and square up to the problem. But it was hard – very hard. Three or four years . . . It wasn't that he was tired of running, either. It was easy to run. He hadn't grown weary of it. It just seemed like a cowardly thing to do, once you had started something. He ought to stay and finish what he'd started. Like the bonito boat. Had it been up to him, he would have given up long before completion. Yet he had gone on, with the others, through that period when nothing seemed to be happening. It was really because he was alone this time. He hated facing things alone. With Ben, he had had Julia for a while. Then she had moved away from him, spiritually, and he found himself in a solitary position. Was that fair? Had she deserted him? Or was he using that as a convenient way out – another bolt hole? Probably.

Well, he was definitely alone, this time, and the decision had to be made. Stay and face the music, or run again. Which? For God's sake, which?

'Now,' said Nathan. 'You have to make up your mind *now*.'

'Don't *bully* me.'

'I just need to know.'

Suddenly a thought occurred to John.

'You've talked this over with Ruth – you must have. You have, haven't you?'

'Yes.'

'And you must have both put forward your ideas, on which course I would take. You must have discussed that.'

'Yes.'

'And what did Ruth say? Did she say I would run? Or stay? Which?'

'I don't think I should . . .'

John stood up, leaning over the smaller man.

'Then I'll tell *you*. You said I would leave and she disagreed, isn't that right? She said I would stay and take what was coming. She did, didn't she? I know I'm right.'

After a few moments of hesitation, Nathan nodded, dumbly.

'Damn,' said John, now that the decision had been taken out of his hands.

# Eighteen

Once I was dressed, I left Ruth and made my way to the teacher's house. He was asleep when I arrived: exhausted by the night's events. I sat on the side of his bed and shook him.

He looked up at me with bleary eyes.

'Nathan?' He stared at his wrist, obviously trying to focus, but there was only a white mark. His watch was on the table. 'What time is it?'

'Almost noon.'

His bed let out a waft of musty odour as he sat up and threw back his sheet. I noticed he did not use the mosquito net any more. It was rolled into a ball in the corner of the room.

He reached for his shorts and pulled them on.

''Scuse me, I'm bursting,' he said, as he ambled out of the bedroom. I followed him outside, to where his open pit lay, some twenty yards behind the house. The birds were noisy in the trees as he performed the function. A large butterfly floated past his nose, distracting him for a moment.

'Nice day,' he said. He looked at the sky. 'It's always a nice day.'

After he had urinated, he added, 'I'll need a new pit soon.' Then he looked me directly in the eyes, and frowned. 'No, I won't, will I? Not for some time.'

'You should have come with me.'

'I *won't* be bullied into leaving. All my life . . . my father . . . they must let me stay. I'm a citizen of the islands. A Belonger . . .'

'They want you out of the way. I'm sorry. I can't help you any longer.'

He shook his head, as if trying to clear it of thoughts. 'I don't understand you people. I keep thinking I know you, Nathan, and at every turn I realise that there are other things going on, under the surface.

The trouble is, we seem so much alike, basically, and I get lulled into thinking we know each other . . . shit. Do what you like with me then. I'll be back, you know. I won't go scuttling off back to England with my tail between my legs. It won't work. I'll serve Goodwright's time for him, and then I'll be back.'

He was silent for a while, then he remonstrated against the former teacher.

'That bastard Goodwright – a *child.* What a swine. If he wanted – well, why not one of the women?'

'Some men are afraid of women.'

The sound of the breakers on the reef seemed to capture his attention. He looked in their direction. He looked lost and alone, and I put my hand on his shoulder.

'Uncle Letushim will be coming for you soon.'

'Letushim?'

'And some of the others.'

'The sins of the fathers,' he said. 'It's very apt in my case.'

I expected him to elaborate, but instead he walked back to the house. Once inside, he poured some water into his plastic bowl and washed his face and hands. Then he cleaned his teeth. I followed him back into his bedroom, where he made his bed, neatly tucking in the corners. Then he put on his track shoes, before packing his bags.

He then sat on the edge of his bed and regarded me thoughtfully, before saying, 'It's funny – you might have had a lot of trouble from *my* father. He's a very powerful man. Lucky for you we despise each other. Lucky for you we hold completely different values.'

'We expect a little pressure from England,' I replied. 'From people like your father. It doesn't matter to us – one way or the other. We – they just want you out of the way. Off the islands.'

He smiled, grimly.

'You won't get rid of me that easily. At last the shoe's on the other foot.'

I admitted I could be wrong about his father, but secretly I thought not. Blood doesn't show its colour until it's exposed to the light. Perhaps he had convinced himself that his father despised him, so that he could renounce any responsibility towards the man. Even supposing his father did feel contempt for him, that did not mean the man would abandon his son. People outside a close relationship can often sense the invisible ties more strongly than those actually involved. Certainly the tones the teacher used indicated a lot more than the words he used.

He desired the older man's approval much more than he realised.

'I can hear them coming,' he said. There were voices, outside. He turned to me again. 'You know, I could serve this three years and call it quits – unload my guilt over Ben – but I'm not going to.' His eyes were intense as he looked directly into mine. 'No, I'm not going to spend three years rotting on some island. The elderly people say I've corrupted the young – or at least, that I'm a bad influence on them. There is *some* truth in that. I do have influence here now, whether good or bad remains to be seen.'

'I don't understand what you're getting at,' I said. 'Are you saying that the young people will demand your release?'

He laughed. 'This *silly* law. You know it's silly, I know it, everyone knows it. When the authorities in England hear what's happened, they'll be movements, tides, that you won't be able to ignore. The young people don't like the traditional ways, the old ways. They like change. They'll come up from underneath and turn it all over. You wait and see. They'll ask for me back. They know I'm on their side. The old people intimidate them, at the moment, but they're getting tired of being told what to do . . . this democracy you have, they'll realise their vote is as good as that of any elder.'

I smiled.

'So you think they'll get you back, to lead the fight against tradition? I think you've got it wrong. All they're interested in is contraband pop music – making it legal. They're not worried about saving the islands from some holocaust way in the future . . .'

'We'll see,' he said, smugly. 'You don't know all the answers, Nathan . . .'

And I must admit, his self-assurance was rather disconcerting – or would have been, had I wished him in the wrong.

I went out, to meet Letushim and the others.

They took him away that evening, in the boat he had helped to build. I saw him wave to Ruth, as he stood by the mast; a tall, solitary figure. There was a genuine fondness between them and I was glad, now, that they had never made love. If he was wrong about arousing rebellion in the young, he had certainly brought something to flower in my wife. She had stated to me an intention to go abroad at some time – not just to Malé, but further, to England or even America.

'I just want to see these places, Nathan. With you, if you'll come too . . .'

And what if I wouldn't? Ah, well, I didn't want to ask that question yet. I might not like the answer.

I walked away from the beach, beneath the palms. Above me, children were playing on the toddy tapper's bridges, swinging on the ropes high above the ground. They were older youngsters, so there was no point in yelling at them to get down. They had, in any case, to get used to working at such heights.

Young Moses came sliding down the trunk of a *midnight walker*, to greet me with a smile. He stood on the tall, stilt-like roots of the tree, an arm hugging the trunk, completely at ease.

'Hello, Moses.'

'The teacher gone?'

'Yes. I expect I'll be teaching you for a while.'

'You the teacher, Nathan?'

'No, but I'll be doing the job until someone else comes. Look, aren't you afraid of that tree?'

He hung out at arm's length.

'This tree?'

'Yes.'

'The Captain's tree? I'm not afraid of *him* – we shout at him all the time. He doesn't fright us. Captain's just a boogeyman for scarin' kids,' said the boy. 'I'd get a lickin' from the others if I was scared of him.'

I nodded.

'Goodnight, Moses.'

'It's still only evenin',' he called, shinning up the smooth trunk again. Once he was at the top, he grappled with a cluster of leaves and swung himself outwards to catch hold of a toddy tapper's rope-bridge. My heart was in my mouth as I watched him. These children were acrobats before they reached the age of ten, but it still worried me to watch them.

That night, as I lay beside Ruth, I thought about a baby. My mother's baby. We had cheated the Captain and his *midnight walkers* after all, though not in the way I would have preferred it to happen. And our youngsters, it seemed, did not believe in the old ways any more. Different viewpoints were flowering amongst us. We were becoming strange to one another. During the boat-building, I had told the teacher and others a joke – just an ordinary joke that had come to me during the evening – and only the teacher laughed. The others looked at me with puzzlement on their faces. It came to me then, that I had changed.

The outside world had changed me. I was not sure whether that was a good thing, or not, but it was a fact.

# Nineteen

Father Maurer sat facing the window that looked out on to the lagoon. He had watched them take the teacher away, just two hours earlier, through the window opposite, but now he studied the *dhoni* crossing from Tubb Island. It was amusing to move his head and so keep the canoe in the position artists call the 'golden section': about two-thirds along from the left of the window frame.

The *dhoni* moved very slowly, as if the man behind the oars wanted to take his time to reach Short Island. In fact there was a fresh breeze blowing, yet the visitor saw fit not to use the sail. That was strange, because evening would be on them soon, and surely the islander would want to be back with his family before dark?

The priest stared at the scene as the brightness began to go out of the light, and thought about John Trencher. Father Maurer had strict instructions not to interfere in the atoll's politics, yet nevertheless he felt justified in speaking out on the teacher's behalf. An innocent man – at least, he modified mentally, a man innocent of that particular crime – was being punished. Not that his protests made any difference. The islanders seemed determined to get rid of John Trencher, one way or the other. Silly young man had insisted on a drama over the use of the coral, and had made enemies.

The canoeist began to draw closer and Father Maurer could see the rower. It was Nathan. The light of the late afternoon sun was on the young islander's muscled shoulders as he pulled the craft through the waters and Father Maurer allowed himself to admire the wiry physique. Nathan had one of those small but deceptively strong bodies which were common amongst the men of this region.

He watched the beaching of the canoe before stirring himself from the creaking wicker chair and going out on to the veranda to welcome his unexpected visitor. Nathan took his time in strolling up to the house. In fact, it almost looked as if the islander were dragging his feet a little, which made the priest wonder if some sort of confession were to follow. There was a definite air of reluctance about the man.

'Nathan? How are you?'

The head came up and dark eyes met those of the priest. The formal reply would seem to be a lie, judging from the disturbance he felt he detected in them.

'Well, thank you, Father.'

The priest thought he noticed a slight hesitation before the word 'Father'. The islanders had only one Father, and that was their paternal ancestor. They recognised no other man by the title, though they made a show for the priest's benefit. It meant nothing. It was all a game to them, this religion called Christianity. They played at it.

They went into the living room and after drinks had been poured, Father Maurer said, 'Bad business, this teacher thing.'

'The crime, or the punishment?'

That was just like Nathan: he baited the priest for the fun of it.

'Both,' said Father Maurer. He tried to change the subject. 'What do you think of my orange trees? Out front. Impressive?'

He received a smile from the dark face: a flash of white teeth.

'Coming along.'

So, Nathan was not there for idle chatter, or he would have launched himself into a torrent of islander's talk. He was there on serious business. The priest began to get worried. Perhaps he, like the young man, had transgressed in some way unknown to him? Or his predecessor?

Nathan's eyes had not left his face and he felt uncomfortable under the steady gaze. He tried to hide the fact that he was disturbed by slurping his drink and then dabbing the corners of his mouth with a handkerchief.

'Have you come to talk to me about something, Nathan? Some aspect of your faith that I can help you with? Or your family? Perhaps you need advice? What is it?'

Nathan's stare was unnerving. It was as if the islander were trying to look into his soul, to find some truth there. In the dim light of the room, as the evening closed in on them, the islander's form took on a sinister aspect. Who could fathom these minds that still reached back to a pagan past?

As if he were reading the priest's thoughts, the dark young man in the loin cloth said, 'My ancestors were Christians.'

It was a flat statement. Nothing more. The priest wondered how he should respond. His mind remained a blank, and when Nathan added with a smile, 'Protestants perhaps, but still Christians,' he was still none the wiser.

Finally he blurted out, 'You know as well as I do that they were more captivated by the pagan practices of the islands than the people here were by their stories of Christ.'

Nathan nodded.

'Don't you find it more attractive? That the memory should live on after death, as well as the spirit?'

'Only the soul will remain after death.' Father Maurer began to feel his feet once more. If it was to be a discussion on theology, he knew he could handle himself. 'It's my job to help you believe in Heaven and Hell.'

'Your job – and others before you. You've inherited resistance, though.'

'That's true.'

Nathan seemed to sink within himself as he said, 'I'm here to make a sacrifice.'

Nathan's expression had suddenly changed to one of deep misery. It was now evident to the priest that the islander was fighting an internal war with himself, which up to that point in their conversation, had been suppressed. Now it came forward, into the surface features of the islander. When islanders confessed, they did not go into a booth – entering a small cupboard unnerved them – and they preferred face-to-face confession. Consequently the priest was used to seeing naked feelings in the eyes of his parishioners. Nathan looked like a man weighed down by some terrible sin.

Father Maurer guessed it was something to do with John Trencher. Perhaps Nathan had been one of those prominently responsible for sentencing John Trencher to three years' imprisonment on another island, and was regretting his part in it? The priest knew that the teacher would be well looked after. Certainly he would not be locked away and would have one or two of his jailors for company. It would not be a pleasant three years, but it did not compare with prisons in the outside world.

'What sort of a sacrifice?' he asked. 'Do you wish to make Confession?'

Nathan clenched his hands into fists.

'No, not that – not now.'

He was silent again and the priest began to get a little irritated. This was becoming a very difficult interview and there were things to do. He had already wasted half a day staring through windows. What did the young man want from him?

'I can't help you, unless you tell me what's troubling you,' he said. 'What's wrong? Is it something to do with . . .'

He was cut short by Nathan blurting out, 'No, I've come to help *you*. I don't need anything – I've come to give.'

'That's very gratifying, but I can't think what – is it a gift? For the Church?'

'In a way – for you and the Church. I know how you feel, you priests, about the way we practise our Christianity on the islands. It's been a great problem for you – all of you . . .' This was indeed something new: an islander recognising them as individuals. But then Nathan was the most Westernised of those islanders, having spent much of his life amongst English people. It was hardly a breakthrough.

'Yes, I suppose you're right, but we're patient people.' He smiled. 'I *hope* we've all been patient.'

'Oh yes,' came the answer, but in a distracted voice, as if Nathan were thinking of something else. 'Yes, patient.' There was a pause, then came the words, 'What if I were to come to you, to the churchyard, after my death? Would that help you? To bury me here? Not so much you of course, but the *priest*?'

Father Maurer was so taken aback that the words took some time to register. His first thought was that Nathan had slipped back again, into viewing them all as one man, all the priests that had been on the islands, that were to come to the islands, but then the meaning filtered through. *Nathan was offering to be buried in the churchyard!*

He said, 'You will stop the practice of making heads for Jorka?'

The young man gave him a grim smile.

'No, I can't do that. The teacher tried that way. What I can do is set an example – others might follow. You see,' he leaned forward, 'it has to be eroded, gradually. You can't just say to them "stop"! They have to see it working.'

The priest glanced out of the window at the empty graveyard. It was a neat patch of white coral dust, still visible in the gloaming. It had been kept bare, carefully weeded, ready for the first islander.

'You'll leave instructions with your next of kin?'

'Yes – don't worry – if I say that it's my wish to be buried here, it will be done.'

'And how will you prove anything?'

Nathan showed the priest his clenched fists.

'You'll bury me with a fig in one hand and a frangipani seed in the other. I'll tell them that if the fig grows, the Captain has my soul, but if his *midnight walkers* fail to suck my spirit into their trunks, then the frangipani will flourish.'

The priest saw certain drawbacks.

'I can't promise that God will intervene on his own behalf. What if the fig . . .'

'It will be up to the priest to water only the right-hand side of the grave. You will bury me with my right fist, containing the frangipani seed, close to the surface. If you want to be absolutely sure, dig down after it gets dark and remove the fig.'

Father Maurer was a little shocked, in spite of his eagerness to obtain a tenant for his little churchyard.

'That seems a little dishonest.'

Nathan shrugged.

'If you feel that way, trust to God – and to the fact that figs need plenty of water.'

'We'll see. I doubt whether I shall be the priest that buries you. You're a young man still. Perhaps he will have fewer scruples than me? I shall leave a transcript of our conversation here today, for whoever has the task – let's hope such an event is many years ahead. In the meantime, I take it I may pass this information on to my superiors?'

'Of course, Father.'

Something occurred to the priest.

'What if both plants grow?'

Nathan smiled again.

'I've seen you doing what you Europeans call *weeding*. You're very zealous.'

It seemed that Nathan's integrity had been thrown out of the window that day. Father Maurer was torn between remonstrating with the young man, and his own desires. Did it really matter that they fooled the islanders? Well, that question could be left to his successor. Unless Nathan were to meet with an accident in the near future, in which case he, Father Maurer, would be interested to see which plant *did* grow. Interested, though one did not test God.

'And what about you, Nathan? Have you completely discarded your beliefs regarding the Captain and his *midnight walkers*?'

'You'll put a cross over my grave. I expect you to make sure that cross protects me. Anyway,' he smiled wryly, 'if my soul's in Heaven – or Hell – the Captain won't be able to get at it, will he?'

Father Maurer's excitement almost bubbled over. Such an example might be all that was needed to thoroughly convert the rest of the islanders. But it was the enormity of the sacrifice that stunned the priest. He knew what Nathan was giving up: an eternal mortality and memories of an earthly life.

In spite of himself, he said, 'I don't really understand why you're doing this, Nathan. To save the islands? There are plenty of coral islands.'

'Not like these,' said the young man, fiercely. 'Anyway, I'm only sacrificing myself, not my line. I learned recently that my presence amongst the heads isn't vital to my ancestors. My mother is pregnant – I'll have a brother or sister who can take my place . . .'

The news that Salome was pregnant was surprising, but not shocking to the priest. He said nothing as Nathan turned away, to look out of the window at the dark ocean.

'My mother has made a sacrifice,' said the young man. 'She's prepared to go through an experience which she found devastating even as a young woman, and she's no longer young. All that will be for nothing, if these islands are engulfed by the ocean.' He turned his hot eyes on the priest again. 'I love these islands, Father. I've seen the world outside and it's nothing, *nothing* compared with our atoll. If a wave were to wash us away, even the dead would suffer. It would be as if we had never existed. We *can't* risk that – it's unthinkable.

'I don't want to be buried in your churchyard – I'm afraid – afraid that the *midnight walkers* will eat my soul.' He reached out and gripped the priest's hand. 'You must teach me to have faith that this will not happen. But I *will* do it. The islanders must stop using the coral – without the reef . . .'

Father Maurer allowed the clutching of his hand, but he was embarrassed.

'I will teach you.'

Nathan withdrew his hand.

The priest said, 'You're a very brave man. Don't think I am insensitive to your courage. The equivalent, I suppose, would be for me to offer myself voluntarily for excommunication, in order to save the lives of others. It's been done – priests have sacrificed their immortal souls for their flock – but the strength to make such a sacrifice . . . I don't think I have that kind of courage. My respect for you goes beyond words.'

Nathan said, 'Just teach me to believe.'

By this time the room was almost dark.

# Twenty

The day after seeing the priest, I visited Jorka Island, to talk to pappy. As I waded ashore, I heard illicit sounds coming from the brush on the far side. Some youngsters had a transistor radio. I wondered what the dead thought of such music. Perhaps they enjoyed it?

A figure came hurrying along the beach towards me. It was Hob. He had been drawn by the music from the radio and no doubt wanted to join the youngsters. He stopped when he saw it was me, and looked around him as if seeking escape.

'It's all right, Hob,' I said.

I passed him and he muttered something about turtles' eggs with a kind of desperation in his tone.

'Go on, Hob. Don't worry.'

He went on, in a hurried shuffle, glancing over his shoulder frequently, and tripping over his own feet. The music makes people like Hob happy. There is not a great deal of the stuff called happiness in his life. Happiness for Hob is a thing carried by the air waves that flood over the oceans. Hokusai's wave is a towering, invisible swell consisting of Western pop music and the voices of sirens. They seduce our young people, taking them away from us. It won't tear our population from its roots, with iron claws, as the wave in the print threatens to do, but it will sweep them away just as effectively. You can't fight an invisible wave, a wave made of air.

I reached the heads and went straight to pappy. He was quiet at first; sulking I think, because I had not been to visit him lately.

Then he spoke. Where is the child? At home with its mother? Why hadn't I brought the child? What was it, a boy or a girl?

'Pappy, it's only two months since I last saw you. You haven't forgotten that much about life.'

– Two months? Well it seems like ten. Are you sure it's only two? Time passes so slowly now that I'm dead. There's nothing to do except watch the frigate birds steal from the gulls. One can count the days, but where's the fun in that? It's a pity I can't get up, occasionally, and go out after bonito. The most lively thing that's happened lately is that a hornets' nest has formed under my chin. I now have a beard –

I ducked down and looked underneath. There was indeed a hornets' nest, tucked in the hollow.

'Shall I remove it?'

– Certainly not. I like the idea of a beard. I could never grow one in life, not a full one. It always came out so wispy and Salome hated it. Is your wife pregnant? –

'No, pappy. Not yet.' It was not up to me to tell him about mamma. That was up to her.

He grunted, noncommittally. The waves looked so good today, he said. Just a touch of white on their peaks. A frisky wind no doubt. He missed the blinding spray of the open ocean, cleansing his magnificent body. He remembered stepping, glistening with saltwater droplets, from the bonito boat, and seeing the desire in Salome's eyes . . .

'Enough of that, pappy,' I said.

Beaded lizards rest on neighbouring heads, or dart after some fantastic flimsy insect struggling in the air against a light breeze, as I tell him all the news. Above, is the hard, blue sky. He listens to the tales of village life. It has all happened before. He has his own tales to tell, if only he could remember them.

We talk until evening. Until the sun is cooling to a deep red disc. It begins to stain the thin clouds: God, mixing his whites and coloureds. Soon, the stains stretch in lanes across the sea – long, dark lanes which look inviting enough to walk along – like plush carpets to another world.

'The night's here,' I said.

– Not afraid are you? –

'Of my own pappy?'

Well, he could have changed, he told me. Death might have turned him into a monster. Maybe he did not recognise me as his son any more? Maybe I was just another living soul, to be haunted by the ghost of his father? Maybe he could torment me?

'Oh, you do that all right, but not in the way you mean.'

I sat on him, using his coral pate as a seat, my legs straddling his face, while I looked out over the sea as the darkness rolled in like a black wave.

–I remember your mother used to do that–he said in a wistful tone.

'Oh, pappy.'

My father was a very coarse man. Death had not cured him of that. If anything, it had made him worse. I left him to his lustful dreams and made my way home, to my wife.

# Filming the Making of the Film of the Making of *Fitzcarraldo*

He told me his name was Cartier and we arranged a meeting at once, in a café on the Boulevard St Augustin. He was a small, thick-set man with dark features and an Eskimo's eyes. He claimed to be a Canadian and spoke a form of French that I had to translate mentally into the purity of my own tongue. His story essentially involved three people – himself, a man called McArthur, and McArthur's niece, a twenty-year-old called Denise. Somehow – this was never fully explained – Cartier got wind of the film-maker Werner Herzog's decision to make the movie *Fitzcarraldo* and the three of them followed Herzog and his crew to the South American jungles, determined, clandestinely, to film the German at work.

I ordered cognacs, before Cartier got too involved with his story, and we waited for a few moments, watching the Parisian passersby, until the drinks were on the table. I then signalled for Cartier to continue.

'We pooled our money – all we had – and set off in pursuit of Herzog's crew. It might seem, now, that taking Denise with us was a bad decision, but she absolutely worshipped McArthur and unfortunately most of the money came from her. Anyway, McArthur had always been strong on family, you know. He wasn't married and his parents were dead. His sister, to whom he had always been close, was working somewhere in Asia. So he felt it was his duty to include his niece, her daughter, in the expedition, if that's what she wanted.'

It was with intense annoyance (a mild word, I should have thought) that Cartier and McArthur realised an official movie of the making of the film was already in progress. In fact it was this second crew that he and McArthur had to shoot, since this party remained a barrier between Herzog's main crew and Cartier's secret camera.

'Denise stayed well behind at this stage, in a second canoe, but McArthur and I disguised ourselves as Indians and followed at a distance as they went up-river. McArthur had the camera in the nose of our canoe, camouflaged with reeds. In any case, we were quite a way behind and we had our Indians, who waved to those in front. We hoped they would just think us curious natives.'

The Cartier-McArthur camp was established a little down-river from the other two crews, and on the opposite bank, their movements hidden by the thick foliage of the rainforest.

'The Indians helped us to make some huts out of the broad-leafed plants. They weren't much, but they provided shelter from the tropical rain. McArthur was like a schoolboy at first. Everything excited him; the jungle life, especially. He had a new single-reflex stills camera – with a close-up lens – and he photographed anything that buzzed, croaked or hissed. The place was teeming with life. It got into all the equipment and our clothes. The only things McArthur wasn't too fond of were the snakes and spiders. His phobias were very suburban.

'Denise, on the other hand, was contemptuous of everything in the rainforest. She showed neither interest in any creature, nor fear. I personally believe she was utterly incapable of being fascinated. That is, she saw no magic in this quite extraordinary world, only squalor. To her there were only two kinds of creature, in myriad shapes – "slimes" and "crawlers". Oh, she knew the names for them all right, but she just wasn't going to waste her time finding the right word. That would have meant giving them a specific identity, acknowledging that they were even of minor importance to her, personally.

'All Denise was interested in was getting the job done. She didn't like me very much either. I think I was a "crawler". And she was forever pestering me. One morning I had the camera in pieces – the spare wasn't working either.

' "Can I help?" she asked, but wearing one of those wooden expressions which I hated. She had several facial masks which were designed to keep me at a distance and in my place.

' "Yeah – you can scratch my insect bites," I told her. "They're killing me." I lifted my shirt to show her three or four large red lumps on my stomach.

'She didn't even say, "You're disgusting," or anything like that. She merely looked at me blankly and remarked, "I mean with the camera."

' "No, I'll have it fixed soon."

' "What about the spare?"

' "I'll work on that next. You're in my light."

'McArthur was busy cooking something and he said, "Get out of his way, Denise. Let him see the light."

'She laughed at that. I didn't think it was very funny, but they did. She went over to one of the Indians then, who was painting his body. He had a cut, which was infected, over the part of his face on which he was applying the ochre. She started remonstrating with him, quietly, though he couldn't understand a word she was saying.

' "Don't mother him," I told her. "He knows what he's doing."

'Sure enough, when she tried to interfere, he slapped her hand away. She went very red, glanced at me as if it were my fault, and looked as though she were going to cry.

'McArthur had seen the incident – a small one you might think, but when all expectations are met with frustrations, and the rainforest is sending its squadrons of insects to harass you day and night, *no* incident is minor or too trivial – everything that happens is of a magnitude which threatens sanity.

'He put his arm around her and she nestled in his shoulder for a moment. I watched them out of the corner of my eye. "All right?" he asked her, and she nodded, still flushed, before getting up and going into her hut.

'The trouble with Denise was she wanted to be doing things, all the time, to help – and there really wasn't that much to do. I didn't see it then, though I do in retrospect. God, she was so eager to help it was stretching her nerves to tight wires. I think if a maniac had run into the camp, waving a gun, she would have looked around eagerly for someone to throw herself in front of, in order to take the bullet. She wanted to make her mark on the project – sacrifice herself – to give it every chance of success, so that afterwards she couldn't be accused of being just a passenger. If I had given her the onions to peel, and said, "You know, Denise, we couldn't have made it without you," she'd have been my friend for life.

'The funny thing was, it was her presence that kept us going, only she didn't realise it. She thought she had to give something physically, or intellectually, or it wasn't worth anything. Her strength of will – the spiritual pressure she applied – was powerful enough to keep us there, working away with almost no material.

'Nothing was stated, you understand. McArthur and I didn't say to each other, "Let's go home," and then, "No, we can't, because Denise will be disappointed in us." The fact that she was there prevented even this much admittance of failure. I just know, in myself, that had she not been with us, we would have gone home after just a few days.

'However, because it was one of those buried truths, *she* didn't know it, and she still sought some way, any way, of proving that her presence was necessary to the project.

'If only I had given her some acknowledgement of the very real part she was playing . . . but I didn't. All I could do was grumble that she was in my way. So we carried on as we were, stumbling around in the dark, and with Denise fluttering around us like some giant moth, ready to throw herself into the candle flame if it would provide us with more light.'

Cartier paused here. There was a tenseness to him which the brandy seemed to exacerbate, rather than relieve. He was gripping the glass as if to crush it.

'It was McArthur who thought of the idea,' he said, placing the glass carefully on the table, 'because nothing, absolutely nothing of interest was happening – not for us. All we could do was shoot that damn boat from a distance and watch the crews working and eating – not the stuff of exciting cinema.

'McArthur had noticed a certain antagonism evident between our own Indians and those in Herzog's camp. Something to do with territorial areas I expect. He said it wouldn't be a bad thing – for us – if something developed.

' "Like what?" I asked him.

' "Well, if one of our Indians should meet, face to face, with one of theirs, we wouldn't be responsible, would we?"

'Denise understood him instantly – they had a strange kind of mental rapport which needed few spoken words. It was only when he said, "I suppose it should be me," did I get the idea. I'm not saying I didn't approve the scheme, because I did. I was as anxious as the other two to go home with something of worth on film. But I was scared. Not only was it unethical, even criminal, it carried a very dangerous undercurrent. We might start something we wouldn't be able to stop.

'So I did endorse the plan, and we made certain preparations. McArthur had volunteered himself because he believed himself to be an archer. He was the obvious choice. I was as dark as he, and my disguise just as convincing, but the man behind the bow had to be good. We didn't want a death on our hands: just a little action for the film, you understand. I could blame the heat, the insects, the rainforest – you know we had to wipe everything, each day, to get rid of the mould that grew on our possessions overnight – the humidity was unbelievable. We had begun to bicker continually amongst ourselves, fighting over silly things that meant nothing – nothing at all – even McArthur, whose initial wonder in the place had since dissipated. There was an indefinable sickness amongst us, that we battled with medication and had a hard time holding down.

'It was another world – a kind of heavy, drug-dream place. A place in which we felt we had a right to make our own rules. We had come a long way from civilisation – used all our resources to get there – and we had to go back with *something*. Oh, I could blame a thousand things – the excuses proliferate, even as I talk to you now.

'So – we did it. The next time we saw a fisherman leave Herzog's camp in his canoe, we followed on foot, keeping pace with it along the bank. McArthur had borrowed bow and arrows from one of our Indians and when the man stepped ashore, he shot him, aiming for his leg.

'Now, I'm not saying that McArthur's expertise with the weapon he normally used was wanting – he was probably very good with a precision-made longbow – but the Indians use much longer arrows and smaller bows. McArthur fired two arrows, I think, or maybe it was three – I can't remember exactly. The idea was to wound the fisherman, have him running back to his people, and provoke some sort of reaction from them. We had a naive vision of flights of arrows whizzing across the river and nobody actually getting hurt – badly, that is – so that some attention would be focused on our side of the water. We wanted a skirmish to film.

'Anyway, it was a disaster. The last of McArthur's arrows caught the fisherman in the throat. There was a kind of gagging sound and the man went down, disappearing into the foliage. I've got it all here, on the film. You'll be able to see exactly what happened when I show it to you. Even now I have difficulty in remembering the details. You know, when you're working, you're too involved with the business of filming to register a conscious blow-by-blow description of the scene in your own mind – the director's supposed to do that, and my director was one of the actors in this particular scene.

'I know I cried, "My God, you've killed him!" when the next thing I realised was that McArthur was on the ground himself. He was staring stupidly at an arrow protruding from his thigh, as if it had just grown there – you know, like a bamboo branch had sprung from his flesh. I'm still not sure where that shaft came from, but I guess the fisherman must have fired back, from a prone position. The angle seemed to indicate something of that nature.'

Cartier must have seen a look of enquiry on my face because he added, 'They fish with bow and arrows, there.

'Anyway, I dragged McArthur away with me and we headed back to camp, he using me as a prop while he limped along. He was as white as fishbelly, I can tell you, and he was vomiting the whole way.'

I interrupted the story here.

'I remember seeing a wounded Indian in the film of the making of *Fitzcarraldo* – was that the same man?'

'I think so. He lived, thank God. Or thanks to the doctor that their crews had taken with them.

'I got McArthur back to our camp and we put him in one of the huts. Denise was absolutely distraught – McArthur was babbling by this time, delirious, and Denise kept shouting about poison on the tip of the arrow. How she got that idea I don't know. I thought it was just shock – there was no obvious discoloration around the wound. No dark red lines going up into his groin.

'She wanted to get the doctor from the other camp, but after what we'd done I thought we'd be in for a nasty reception from the wounded fisherman's tribe. I was absolutely against it. I convinced her that the arrow, which we had left behind, was a fishing arrow and would not be poisoned. Finally, she agreed, and decided to nurse him herself. She went into that hut and . . . well, I have my own ideas about the events which followed, bizarre as they might seem to you now, in the light of a Parisian day. Things were different there. It was all a little surreal. *Our* light, filtered by the roof of the rainforest, was of a sickly, greenish hue, and shadows moved back and forth through it, like phantoms. There were the constant murmur of insects and sudden confrontations with amphibians and reptiles, which seemed to appear on trees, in the grass, as if by magic. The whole place had a sense of the fantastic about it.

'Perhaps the arrowhead *had* been tipped with some kind of substance? Anyway, McArthur went into a state of fever. I heard him yelling occasionally, between bouts of absolute silence. Most of his complaints were concerned with being too hot, or too cold, but I also heard him shouting about the "snake" and the "river" – and following these cries, the low, soft voice of Denise, telling him it was all right, she would protect him. I didn't go into the hut. They had no need of me.

'Of course, fever can bring on hallucinations during bouts of delirium, but I believe it was more than that – something quite extraordinary was happening to McArthur. The mind is a delicate mechanism – if that's the right analogy – and once you tamper with its intricacy, its balance, it can respond in strange ways, playing havoc with reality. As I said before, I have my own ideas – ideas about memories and self-protection.

'The mind is like a camera, recording memories, which are never projected. Short films, locked away and only replayed internally, so there is never any doubt of their unreality. I say *never*, but I think in McArthur's case, there was.

'When McArthur was yelling about the snake, I think he was talking about the anaconda we had seen basking on the river bank a few days earlier. From the canoe we had watched it uncoil its enormous length, as thick as a man's thigh in places, and slip into the river. McArthur had been petrified. He thought the creature might come towards the canoe and he was shaking so much there was a danger of the canoe overturning.

'It didn't. It swam away, up-river – slow, sinuous movements through the brown water, its blunt head showing just above the surface.

'I think that McArthur's mind was replaying this encounter, projecting it and superimposing it on the actual scene – the interior of the hut. A sort of double-exposure effect, which had him believing that the snake was in there with him and as real as everything else around him.'

Cartier paused as a waiter passed our table, as if he did not want any eavesdroppers to hear what he had to say next. Once the man was out of earshot, he continued.

'He was projecting, not just memories of the snake, though, but longer, deeper memories, which he had buried to keep from the light. These too began to emerge, to superimpose themselves on the dim scene within the hut. Memories evoke not only recognition of their familiarity, but emotions. Just as the snake stirred some primal fear within him, those older memories aroused a forbidden desire, a passion indulged during earlier years. McArthur's past was with him in that hut, and he could not separate real from unreal. Combined with this was his need to be protected from that terrible serpent, and Denise was there to provide that protection. She wanted to *help* him, you understand? She saw it as essential to herself to do what she could for him, at the same time, making her contribution to the expedition.'

Cartier took a swallow of his cognac. I sensed that the revelation was about to emerge and tried not to make any movement which might distract him. He seemed on the verge of abandoning the tale altogether. So I sat, quietly, waiting for him to continue.

'They were in that hut three days,' he said. 'I sent in food and drink, of course, but I didn't enter the place myself, not until I heard McArthur talking in more rational tones. I couldn't hear exactly what was being said, there was an intense quality to the speech, but the long periods of silence, punctuated by irregular sessions of screaming, had ceased.

'I went in, then. I'm afraid I interrupted them. I was expecting to see – well, I don't know what I was expecting, but it wasn't two naked bodies locked together. I left immediately, but though Denise hadn't seen me, McArthur had . . .'

I groaned, inwardly, expecting now that I would get a sob story about how much he, Cartier, had been in love with Denise, and that he had never suspected that her uncle would take advantage of her hero-worship.

'So – it was incest,' I said, hoping to ward off his outpourings. 'A fairly mild form though. Both adults – and the relationship not as close as it could have been.'

He stared at me, his dark eyes holding mine, something troubling their depths.

'Yes. That's what I thought – and no doubt Denise. She didn't know either, you see.'

'Know what?'

It was the first time since we had met that I saw anything like real discomfort registering in Cartier's features.

He said, 'She didn't know McArthur was her father.'

My thoughts did a few acrobatics and I said, instinctively, 'But Denise was his sister's daughter . . .' Then I stopped. I had the whole picture. He had fathered his sister's child and had now taken that daughter to bed. What a mess! The whole thing was revolting: incest in layers.

'He told you this?' I asked.

'Shortly afterwards. We pieced together the theory of memory projection from it. You can see how it relates to the film . . .'

'And you want me to distribute this movie?'

I stared out of the café window, waiting for his reply, watching people hurrying along the boulevard. My distaste for this project almost made me jump to my feet and join them, but I decided to see the thing out.

'Yes – we all do. We thought you should have some background to the movie – it might help to create a little publicity, don't you think?'

Cartier's face was devoid of expression. I tried to imagine what was going on in his mind. It wasn't easy.

'Let me take the film away with me. I'll contact you tomorrow.'

He agreed and we went outside and transferred the movie from his car to mine. I did not shake hands with him. I just climbed into my car and said, 'Tomorrow then.'

I had noticed, when we left the café, that he was limping.

As I drove home I thought about my own predicament. The bills were mounting up and I still had not found the successful movie which would get me out of the rut. My recent decisions might have been sound ones, based on my experience in the business, except that no one can predict certain success in the movie world.

That evening I watched the film in my private studio. It was a boring collage of river and forest scenes. The Herzog boat was there, the area around busy with people, but it could have been an amateur movie, taken by a camp follower, or, more likely, it had been put together from stolen discarded cuttings of *Fitzcarraldo* itself, and the film of the film, to form a bastardised child of both. The whole effort folded in on itself, until nothing made sense because it was too internalised. It exposed too much of its inner self, which in the revelation showed nothing but a confusion of scenes and snatches of close-ups. It revealed everything, yet it revealed nothing, because at any core, whether it is human emotion or something more substantial, there is no truth which can be grasped and understood. Everything becomes a cluttered wash of incomprehensible colour tones, weakened further by the continual rinsing of the thing in itself, until all you have is a faded copy of a copy, recurring.

When the film reached the scene where the arrows were exchanged, I paid particular attention, but even here I was disappointed. The light was all wrong, either too weak or too strong. There were figures in the gloom of the forest, and action certainly took place, but, bright and dark, what came out of it was a flurry of furtive movements, glimpsed through curtains of leaves and fences of treetrunks. There was a close-up of the wound in McArthur's leg, which looked genuine enough, as did the agony on his face, but it had been done better, by Charlton Heston in *El Cid*. McArthur, on film, was of course the spitting image of the man I met in the restaurant, calling himself Cartier.

There was also a single scene of the niece, or daughter, or both, half hidden behind smoke from a campfire. Either the shot was over-exposed or she was thin and pale, almost translucent, with red-rimmed eyelids. The sort of will-o'-the-wisp female that gets cast as a fairy extra in *A Midsummer Night's Dream*.

What it amounted to was an unholy tangle. Of course, if the story were true, there were enough vultures in the world to make the film a success in terms of sales at the box office. Artistically, it stank, but some cinema-goers would be curious about this trio and their incestuous goings-on in the South American jungle. If it was released to the media, the gutter press would provide all the publicity needed.

However, I doubted very much that the story *was* true and I had my integrity to consider.

I met Cartier, or McArthur, at the same café the next day.

I gave him the standard rejection.

'It's not good cinema,' I said.

He seemed very disappointed, leaving me his card and saying I was to call him if I changed my mind. I replied that there was little chance of that. Once I had made a decision, I told him, I usually stuck with it.

His eyes went to a corner of the café, where there was a door with a small window set in it. I thought I caught a flash of something behind the glass of that window and turned back to him. He had a dejected expression on his face.

'Who's behind the door?' I said.

He seemed about to argue, then must have changed his mind. I suppose that, since I had rejected his offer, he saw nothing to gain by denial.

'A friend of mine – cameraman. He's filming us. I thought it would make a good postscript to the movie – you and I meeting, discussing the project . . .'

I looked him straight in the eyes.

'*You're* McArthur, aren't you? Who's that behind the door? Cartier?'

Before he could reply, I saw his eyes widen as he looked up, over my left shoulder. Then a tremendous explosion filled my head. I felt the heat of a blast on my cheek, and smelt the acrid odour of cordite. My head rang with the noise and for a few seconds I could not see, let alone hear anything. If any sensible thought at all crossed my mind, it was that the café had been bombed by some terrorist organisation.

When I was able to register a conscious understanding of what was happening, I realised that McArthur was sprawled on the floor, where he had gone flying backwards. There was blood in his hair, on his collar. What I had heard was the sound of a revolver being fired close to my ear.

As I turned around, still groggy and shocked, she was just putting the barrel of the gun beneath her chin. There was another explosion, not so loud as the first, since it was muffled by soft flesh. The body struck my shoulder as it fell and I think I screamed.

The next thing I knew I was being helped to my feet and led away towards the bar. My legs were shaking violently and someone forced a brandy down my throat. I couldn't even hold the glass, my hands were trembling so much. There was a lot of shouting, which I could hear above the ringing in my ears. I remember glancing back at the woman's corpse, once. But it was impossible to tell whether the face – now covered in gore – belonged to the girl I had seen in the movie the previous evening. It crossed my mind that it might even be McArthur's sister; the mother of their daughter.

An unholy tangle. The police came and took me into another room at the back. I can't recall what I told them, but I must have just recounted what had passed over the last two days, between the man on the floor and myself. I found out later that they had secretly videoed my statement. Finally, I remembered about the cameraman, behind the window in the door, and started to tell them when one of them pointed towards the corner of the room. There was another man there, talking to more policemen. He glanced across at me and I recognised him.

There was a movie camera, on the table, between him and his interviewers. He gave me a look, as he nodded at his recording device. It was difficult not to interpret that gesture into a language I knew well, that said:

'I've got it all here, on film, if you want to use it.'

That was just before the TV crews arrived, and I believe you saw what followed, for yourselves, on the six o'clock news.

*Alain d'Ivry, the talk-show compère, offers me a glass of water, and with the cameras still working, I take a long drink.*

*'Are we still on?' I say.*

*He nods. 'But don't worry – we'll edit this out later. Let's get back to the café scene. You say you didn't recognise the woman's face after she turned the gun on herself, but now of course . . .'*

# The River-Sailor's Wife

Actually, you do know all there is to know about life at seventeen – or at least, all you're ever going to know. You just don't believe most of it until you experience it, or witness the experience in others. Certainly, I seem less aware of the world at forty-seven than I was at seventeen. This is not nostalgia for a lost golden age: it was youth that was golden, not the time. I was vital then, to the whole scheme of things. Without me, the world would have squealed to a halt, seized and rusted. Everything was internal, to me, and I was not just an observer, as I am now. I was an enthusiastic participant.

Oh yes, the ego was so important then.

There is another important aspect about being seventeen. It is an age when you are at your most vulnerable, emotionally, yet ambiguously, at your strongest. You fall in love – love to the point of death – yet you recover amazingly swiftly. One day you are suicidal over a rejection, the next you have found someone else and the hurt disappears overnight. These days the wounds are not so deep, but they are slow to heal.

At seventeen I was in Singapore: a young British airman on my first posting abroad. Changi RAF Station. I was dazzled by the tinselled atmosphere of the new (to me) culture into which I had been tossed. Changi was not a closed station. There was an entire native village in the middle of it, with a double row of open-fronted shops and stalls lining the main street. There were also surrounding kampongs.

Singapore city was just twenty minutes away in a Mercedes 'flying taxi' – one that stopped for passengers, as would a bus. Sometimes we found ourselves sharing them with pigs and chickens on their way to market. In 1958 the journey cost just two dollars one way – about four shillings and sixpence. We would often pay an extra dollar, getting into separate taxis, for them to race. If a fare hailed down the car you were in, that was all in the game. Around Chinese New Year, we would throw firecrackers out of the window at the mah-jong players by wayside stalls. If they could have caught us, they would probably have killed us: the game was sacred to them.

I spent as little time at work, in the communications centre, as possible. We did shifts – two days on, three days off – so we had a lot of leisure time. Mostly, I walked the streets or rural paths around the city, looking at temples with their roofs covered in fantastical figures of men and beasts; strolling through Tiger Balm Gardens where an alien hell was depicted with three-dimensional models; walking along the wharves packed with overcrowded sampans; taking in the sights and smells of the food stalls along Bugis Street or at the bazaars which seemed to spring out of the ground with their colourful displays of textiles, brass and wood. God, it was all so wonderful. I loved it. The waves of Asiatic people with their waxpaper umbrellas, the heavy, damp heat like a constant sauna, the exotic lizards, birds, snakes, monkeys, that ran wild, the sudden wall of water that would descend at four o'clock on the dot during the monsoon season, the choruses of bullfrogs, chit-chats and cicadas. I loved it all. Even the mosquitoes that helped to feed my pet mantis which remained uncaged on my bedside locker, as faithful as a Labrador dog.

I suppose part of my sentimental feelings for Singapore, now, stem from the fact that I lost my virginity in a brothel somewhere amongst the seething backstreets of Chinatown.

It was Christmas Eve. I had plenty of money and we – Bill and I – had been to a swimming-pool party. There were girls at the party, but untouchables: daughters of elder servicemen. They could be 'fondled but not fucked'. In any case, at that age, I was too shy of girls of my own race, creed and age. I needed the distancing factors that bargirls provided. Bill, my closest friend at that time, suggested that the two of us go downtown to a brothel. With a stomach full of electric butterflies, I agreed.

Bill had already been to a whorehouse. It was one of the first things he did on arrival in Singapore. I had been much too frightened of catching something during those first three months, but Bill had got away with it, so I saw no reason to hold back any longer. I was prepared to risk my physical health to satisfy a psychological need. As a virgin, I felt spiritually incomplete and was positive that what I lacked was the experience of a sexual encounter; that once I had been with a woman, the secrets of the universe would all be revealed to me and I should never feel inadequate/bashful/unhappy/empty again. The whole, broad canvas of the complete man would be mine to possess, simply by fusing my flesh with that of another human being. Such were the misunderstandings of a seventeen-year-old. I had heard so much about the ecstasy of an orgasm that I was convinced that at the point of complete unification I would see everything clearly and become one of the wise, with positive opinions on every subject. People would realise, just by my face, that I was a man who *knew*.

We took a flying taxi from Changi village. There were several ways of obtaining a woman in Singapore. You could go to one of the twenty-five-cent dance halls and pay for a string of dances with one of the hostesses on the understanding that you could spend the rest of the night with them. You could go to a bar and pick up a bargirl. Or you could get in a taxi and say, 'Jig-jig John,' and be taken to a brothel. It sounds sordid, doesn't it? It sounds crass. But it didn't seem like that then, to youth overwhelmed, drugged, by a way of life that captured our souls, our impressionable imaginations, with its atmosphere perfumed by the scent of camphorwood, by the fragrance of blossoms that only the Orient can produce. It seemed right. In our adolescent ignorance, we believed that the women did what they did because they wanted to.

The brothel was clean, if not wholesome. It smelled of joss sticks and perfume and was not in the least bit as intimidating as I had expected. I was shown to a room by an elderly, quietly spoken Chinese, who left me there on my own for a few minutes.

The room was whitewashed, with a large overhead fan turning slowly and clicking rhythmically, moving the warm air in gentle spirals down towards the clean-sheeted bed. There was a rush mat on the floor. No other furnishings were visible in the dim light.

As I stood, nervously awaiting the woman assigned to me, the curtain that served as a door moved, and a young Chinese girl entered. She was no older than I was – not beautiful, but certainly pretty, with a slim figure and small, neat hands and feet. She went, without a word, to the bed and placed a handtowel on its centre. Then she shrugged off her *cheongsam* and got on to the bed, her bottom on the towel. She beckoned to me, unsmiling, her hair like a river of jet flowing over the white pillow.

With a knot in my stomach I quickly undressed. Then I sat on the edge of the bed. She was the first woman I had ever seen without clothes on. I was not stirred to immediate arousal. I had time to reflect that there was very little difference (apart from the obvious) between our bodies. I was a slim youth, small in stature, and smooth-chested. She was delicately boned, with tiny breasts and a dry, silky skin. We were like two children. I noticed that she had shaved off all her body hair and looked entirely vulnerable, like a fragile seashell that had to be handled with extreme care.

I wanted her to like me. I wanted to tell her things: that I wouldn't hurt her; that she was the first girl I had ever been with; that I loved the texture of her skin; that her broad nose and black eyes were beautiful. I wanted us to be friends.

'What's your name?' I asked. 'Do you speak English?'

She stared at me, impassively.

'Lulu. You come to me now, please?'

She wanted to get it over with, get *me* over with, get me gone. I was depressed. I had paid twenty-five dollars for her body, yet I wanted her soul. I wanted her most priceless possession and I thought I could buy it with a handful of paper notes. I wanted her to like me. It was so important to get her to like me, to let me in, to share the secrets of her spirit with me.

I leaned towards her. She had oranges on her breath which mingled with the incense from the joss. The crisp sheet began to dampen beneath my palms as I supported my weight.

'My name is Tom,' I said, and she nodded.

'Please, you come now . . .'

The *double entendre* was lost on both of us. I lowered myself on top of her and after some fumbling, was able to enter her. After a few minutes it was over. I made no attempt to withdraw. I was disappointed. There had been no pyrotechnic display inside my head; no awesome revelations; no sudden influx of knowledge: merely an electric jolt in my loins which shuddered through my body, then relaxation and peace.

I stared down at the face, not an inch from my own, and she jerked her head aside.

'No kiss,' she said. 'Not to kiss.'

It was one of the rules. Bill had told me about the rules. I began to hate the rules.

I wanted to stay in her for a long time: feel her smooth skin against my own; share her body with her; share my body with her. The sheets were white and stiff beneath us, like those my grandmother used in her cottage at home.

But the act should have been better. I had given her my virginity and it meant nothing to her. It *was* nothing. I felt vaguely angry and it must have shown in my face, because she pushed at my chest with her thin arms.

'No hurt me,' she said.

I rolled away from her, shocked and puzzled.

'I don't want to hurt you,' I replied. 'I want . . .'

'Some men beat me – with the fist.'

Drunken louts. I was no drunk, no sadistic brute with a chip on my shoulder. There was not even a vestige of post-coital contempt, such as I have sometimes felt with other women since. I just wanted her to like me, to say to me shyly, 'Am I the first woman you have ever had? I could tell,' then hug me, possessively, as if it meant something to her.

But she was a prostitute, not the girl next door. I had paid for her body and that I had been given. I was entitled to nothing else. My rights had ceased with the jolt in my loins.

I began to get dressed as she fussed with a bowl of water on the far side of the bed. When I was ready to go, I said, 'Can I see you again? Will you see me again?'

Then she smiled – not a full smile, more a Mona Lisa stretching of the lips.

'You not butterfly? You like me for one woman?'

'Yes,' I replied, sincerely, feeling that at last I was getting somewhere. 'I just want to see you – no one else. I'm not interested in the others.'

I felt elated, quite out of proportion to the circumstances, as if I'd just asked the girl I loved to marry me and she had accepted. There was a fire in me now, burning happily. I was going to see her again. We were friends.

'You come here next week. Yes?' she said.

'What shall I say? Shall I ask for Lulu?'

'I be here,' she replied. 'You go now.'

I did as I was told. It occurred to me only later, much later, that minutes after I had left that room some boozed merchant seaman, or swaddy, belching and farting the fumes of Tiger Beer, breathing fried rice, lurched on to her delicate body and rammed her down into those starched cotton sheets with his heavy, sweaty bulk and pumped and grunted into that peach-coloured mound between her legs. Then after he was finished, another took his place. Then another. And yet another . . . The only thing that would change would be the white towel beneath her small buttocks. Some of them might be clean, wholesome men, but others would stink of dried vomit and stale alcohol – and all, all, including me, would be about as welcome to her as a bath of spiders. My poor Lulu.

In the taxi back to Changi, I could talk of nothing but Lulu, until Bill said, 'For Christ's sake, leave it out. You're a real prat sometimes.' He seemed angry at something, or someone, and stared moodily out into the dark night as the black shapes of the wayside palms flashed by us.

Before he left me for the night, he said, 'Tom, don't be a prick. They start some of these girls at thirteen – fourteen. Don't lose your head over a silly tart.'

But I refused to accept this. Lulu looked so fresh and young. I was almost tempted to dream that she had begun her work that night, and we had, unknowingly, helped each other to our first sexual union. I was full of false dreams in those days. They grew in me like flowers.

It was about 3.30 in the morning when we arrived back at Changi village. I went straight to Fred's for an egg banjo and fried rice. 'Fred' was a Chinese stall owner – one of dozens that lined the route from one end of the village to the other – and he had been given his nickname by Bill. Fred, like all the other stall owners, sold squid, eggs, rice, bread, coffee, twenty-four hours a day. They slept by their wares, amongst which there were a primus stove to cook on and a hurricane lamp to see by. They would rouse themselves from their slumbers to serve a single customer at five o'clock – or three – or two – any time. We took them completely for granted. We would arrive, singing and shouting, after a night in some bar and expect a dawn breakfast to be cooked without hesitation or a murmur of reproach. We were, completely and utterly, selfish. The kind of young men that now, in my forties, I detest with venom.

We, of course, could go back to our billets and sleep the day away, while Fred and his kind had to continue serving customers through the heat of the Singapore sun, and on into the night again.

Bill had picked out Fred's stall at random and bestowed his continual custom on the place. He had given the owner his nickname and had a sign painted at the workshops, which hung above the stall. Bill was something of a personality amongst us: a latter-day Beau Brummel, who originated trends. It was fashionable thereafter to eat at Fred's, rather than any of the other, similar stalls along the street. Fred rose in status and wealth, accordingly, though I think he was somewhat bewildered by his good fortune. I don't think he, or any of the other stall owners, really understood why young airmen queued for his food, which was no different from or superior to the rest.

It amused Bill to lift someone out of the dust and make him a local personality, at a whim. At that time, in that place, he had the power of a king. He could break Fred just as easily, by simply transferring his patronage; reduce him to one of the envious lookers-on. He had done such with a tailor; one of the many that struggled for our business. Bill was a clever, witty, good-looking, thoughtless young man, who found he could manipulate people, and did so with all the irresponsibility of a spoiled-brat monarch.

So it was to Fred's that I went, the night I lost my virginity, and I roused him from his rattan bed to cook me an egg banjo. Along the streets the hurricane lamps formed a line of light in the darkness. When the dawn came up, much later, it uncovered the beauties of a natural world of which England was but the hem of the skirt. The flared scarlet petticoats beneath a dark-green dress, decorated with emerald lizards and jewelled insects, gradually emerged from the grey. The lamps were extinguished by men with dirty, worn vests and barren faces. Faces unvisited by anything except care. Faces of prisoners serving life sentences.

The following week I visited the brothel again – and several times thereafter, until Lulu suggested that I go to a certain hut and spend my nights with her when I wished. All I had to do was pay the rent, buy the groceries and give her a little money for herself, all well within my means. I became, almost, a married man, except that I had none of the responsibilities.

Lulu was quiet, undemanding and completely devoted to my needs. I never once saw her get angry, though I often treated her with casual indifference. I took her utterly for granted, visiting her whenever I pleased and offering no explanation for long periods of absence. It may have appeared to an outside observer that she did not care, that I meant nothing to her, but I knew differently. Even a selfish young man recognises some of the signs.

In my mind's eye, I can still see her now, in the back of the tiny kitchen, her neat, economical movements ensuring that her presence caused me the least amount of irritation. I was confounded by this at the time and, to my small credit, felt a twinge of guilt.

'You're so quiet,' I said to her one day. 'And you hardly seem to move – yet you're always busy.'

'Not want to disturb you,' she replied.

Oh yes, I have lost sleep over my behaviour since, and not a minute too much. Now – now I feel a deep shame, even though I do not know that stupid youth who inhabited my body thirty years ago. But now is too late.

Once or twice I delighted Lulu by taking her to the pictures or to a dance, where she endured the baleful glares of other Chinese who did not approve of her escort. She bore them with calmness, uncomplaining. We went swimming on occasion, though for a reason unknown to me then she would stare out over the water with a wistful expression on her face and return to the hut with a sadness she could not disguise. It was after one of these trips that I discovered the baby.

She had been exhausted by her swim and was lying asleep on the bed. I remember being irritated by an insistent flying beetle that would not leave me alone and I rose from the bamboo chair on the veranda, intending to join her. Curled up, like a child, in her cotton trouser suit, she looked so peaceful I decided not to disturb her, but a wave of tenderness came over me and I could not help reaching down to stroke her cheek. She murmured something in her sleep and clutched at my hand, kissing the fingertips: something she had never done before.

I said, 'Lulu,' very softly.

She was instantly awake. She dropped my hand with a look of pain in her eyes. Then she jumped up and ran from the room. When I went to find her, she was sitting on the wooden steps to the hut, cradling a photograph, and crying.

I prised the print gently from her hand. It was of a small child, about three years of age. It suddenly dawned on me that she was not alone in the world. She had family. Why this had not occurred to me before, I don't know. Some unconscious belief that prostitutes sprang from the dust, I suppose, without connection to the rest of the human race.

'Your sister's child?' I asked, hopefully.

She lowered her head and snatched the photo from me.

'*My* baby.' She ran into the bedroom again, probably hoping that I wouldn't follow her, but I did.

I went quite pale. I could see myself in the mirror by the bed and the colour ran from my complexion, though I swear I felt nothing inside.

'Your baby? Do you know the father?'

She raised her head and looked me directly in the eyes.

'The father my husband,' she said, fiercely.

Now I did feel something. I had been sleeping with this woman for a year and I discovered that I knew nothing – absolutely nothing – about her past. I had talked about myself, but I had asked not one single question about Lulu's life. I had taken her as she was, without qualification or reference.

'Your husband,' I said, flatly.

'Yes.' The look was proud, haughty.

Slowly, I worked myself up into a state of rage. I was totally incensed by the thought that there was another man in this whore's life. Never mind all the others. Here was someone – someone she had *loved.* Perhaps she still did? The thought choked me. I could not speak, nor could I look at her. I collected my clothes, dressed and left, indulging only in the terrible, unjustified anger of a youth who had discovered that his sweetheart was a normal woman and not a pet bird. She had a husband. The thought made me sick. It did not matter that after two years I would return to Britain and leave her to whatever fate awaited her, without a twinge of remorse – as so many young men did with their girls – it mattered only that I had been fooled, duped, used. I wanted to kill her. I wanted to break every bone in her body. I was insanely jealous of this 'husband'. He had given her a baby. She had not used that infernal bowl of warm water after *he* had made love to her. I wanted to die.

I never went back to the hut again. Instead, I went on riotous evenings with Bill and his crowd, getting drunk, whoring for as little as three dollars a time in the most appalling places, running the very real risk of disease, and generally telling myself I was having a great time.

Bill congratulated me on a narrow escape.

'Let's face it,' he said, 'you were thinking of taking her back to the UK, weren't you?'

'I don't know,' I replied, dully.

'Come on, pal. I could see the signs. You almost became one of those prats that marry their whores and spend the rest of their lives regretting it.'

Would she have come with me? I thought about it often over the last six months I spent on the island and I believed I knew the answer.

One day Bill came into my billet as I was feeding my praying mantis. He staggered over to my bedside, drunk and dishevelled from a night on the town.

'Guess who I've just seen.' He grinned lopsidedly.

'Who?'

'Little Lulu-belle. She's back in the cathouse, doing her "twenny-fi' buck" turns.' He put on a mock Chinese accent for the price. 'Been there ever since you left her.' He put his arm around my shoulder and I could smell the stale sweat wafting up from his armpit. 'An' I can tell you, pal,' he said in a conspiratorial whisper, 'she's just as good as ever. Personal observation.'

I shrugged off his arm and he moved back from me on seeing what was in my eyes.

'Well, fuck you,' he said. 'Who gives a shit anyway?'

Then he walked stiffly from the room. I continued feeding the mantis.

I did see her again, before I left Singapore.

I was sitting outside Fred's one evening, talking to him. His stall was no longer fashionable and he had gone back to contending with all the others, touting for business where he could. He said something that surprised me.

I cried, 'You have a family? But you spend all your time here.'

'Not choice. Must work, or family no eat. Many people – wife, mother, sister, chil'ren – all nee' food.'

That was a funny statement from someone who ran a food stall. Suddenly I saw what kind of life he had – and all the other stall owners – sitting by his stove twenty-four hours a day in order to keep his family alive. It was while we were talking that Lulu came along the road, with a young Chinese man of about twenty.

While I had been talking to Fred, I had been putting some thoughts together. What applied to Fred must also have applied to Lulu. She had a child to feed. The mother, too, also had to eat. Work in Singapore at that time was extremely scarce. If you didn't want to starve, you did what you could. Any job – *any* job – was better than nothing.

I thought at first they were going to pass by, without stopping, but then they turned towards me. I prepared myself for the onslaught of an enraged husband, wishing to exact revenge. I prepared myself for a vindictive attack by a woman I had abandoned to the whorehouse and its ugly performances. I was very, very frightened. The week before, an airman had been stabbed to death by angry Chinese because he had insulted them.

On the far side of the street, four old men were playing mah-jong.

I could hear the clicks of the tiles and the low murmur of voices. There was a stillness in the air that seemed to me to be the precursor of violence. I was soaked with sweat. I rose from my seat as they approached.

Lulu stopped about a yard in front of me and held the man by the sleeve. She said something rapidly, in Hok Yen dialect. The young man nodded.

Then she said in English, 'Tom, this is my husband. He river-sailor – has come home. He put in jail, in Malaya, for long time. I send our money for him.'

I smiled, tentatively, and he returned the smile.

'Pleased to meet you,' I whispered, hoarsely.

Lulu said, 'He no speak English.'

She turned and again spoke Hok Yen, then for my benefit translated the words, as if she were still speaking to him, though she looked directly into my eyes.

'Mr Tom has been very kind to me.'

And then she smiled – a full-face smile.

I was stunned by the words, which had obviously been rehearsed. Kind? I had been a bastard. I had sent her back to that hole.

Then they walked away, silent with one another.

I stood there, awkwardly, as a burning sensation came to my eyes. I could not look at anyone, especially not Fred, who had heard all, seen all. I was so ashamed of the way I had treated her. *Our money*. She had called it *our* money – the money she had earned and kept until I had abandoned her. I stumbled away, hurried away, down to the beach where I could be alone.

Even now, whenever I think of that young woman, I have to find a place away from other people, in order to remember that even if she had loved me, as I believe she may have done, my unworthiness would have precluded any long-term relationship. Her capacity for self-sacrifice was beyond me and would have destroyed us, in the end, for I would not have handled it sensibly. I would have allowed her to indulge me beyond reason.

Outside my cottage, the moss grows thick on the path to the door. The winters seem to be getting longer.

# Island with the Stink of Ghosts

The Chinese jetty clans, who ruled the waterfronts along Penang's Georgetown harbour, fostered the myth that their hawkers had been responsible for its formation. It was said that chicken fat, glutinous rice, fishheads, *hokkien* noodles, prawn shells, and other waste matter, had gathered together in a stretch of still water between the currents and had formed the foundation of the floating island. Sargasso had rooted itself in the rich oils and savoury spices, on top of which gathered soil from the mainland. A rainforest had grown from its earth.

The island was about three miles off the Malaysian coast and was held precariously in place by the fronds of seaweed rooted in the ocean floor. No one, not even the ancient Wan Hooi, who ran a clan *curry mee* stall on the Larong Salamat, could remember the time when the island had not been there. Wan Hooi was the oldest hawker on Penang, but it was pointed out that he had only been around for a hundred years. The clans had been using the harbour as a waste bin for more than a thousand.

Whenever there was an onshore breeze, a sickly, perfumed odour wafted over from the island. This smell, according to both Malays and Chinese, was the stink of ghosts rotting – or to be more accurate, the odour of decaying souls. The body, when it decomposes, has a foul smell. Therefore, it seemed logical that a putrefying soul should have a sweet, cloying scent. The island was the burial ground for malefactors and murderers, whose punishment after death was for the corrupt soul to remain with the body, and rot within it.

These beliefs had little to do with religion, but came from a deeply rooted local superstition, such as is found in any region: a myth from earlier, darker minds, when reason and evidence were less important than fear.

Fishermen gave the island a wide berth, and only the old grave-digger, Lo Lim Hok, set foot upon the place.

Ralph Leeman, an Englishman in his late twenties, was one of those who witnessed the event on a hot, sultry June evening, when the island broke loose from its natural mooring. Not that there was any drama, for there was no sound and little fuss. The island simply detached itself from its anchoring reeds and began drifting down the Malacca Straits, which run between Indonesia and Malaysia. Possibly heavy rains in Thailand, to the north, had been responsible for a strong swell. This had resulted in a momentary change in the direction of the main current, the East Monsoon Drift, which put pressure on the island. That was Leeman's theory.

Leeman was on secondment to the Malaysian Harbour Authority from the British Coastal Service. Alone in the observation tower, he had been studying the erratic behaviour of a large motor launch when he suddenly became aware that the island was moving. He watched it for a few moments, as it passed a distant marker buoy.

'Good God! Stinker's on the move.'

He immediately made a call to his superior.

Sumi Pulau, the harbourmaster, arrived at the tower thirty minutes later, having fought his way through the Georgetown traffic. He studied the island through binoculars and expressed his amazement and concern. His English, like that of many educated Malays, was extremely good.

'Directly in the shipping lane. We'll have to do something about it immediately. It'll be dark soon. Got any suggestions?'

Leeman had already been considering the problem and gave his opinion.

'We could attach tugboats to it and tow it to the mainland, but given the nature of the island – the fact that it's a graveyard – I'm not sure the coastal villages would want it on their doorstep.'

Pulau nodded.

'Yes, and in any case, *I'm* not sure tugs would do it. Might take something bigger. That's a pretty sizeable piece of land out there.'

'My second thought was that we could blow it out of the water with high explosives – but I'm worried about the jetties and the stilt-houses. An explosion might create a floodwave.'

'Not to mention the fact that we would have corpses washing up on the tourist beaches . . .'

'So,' continued Leeman, eager to impress, 'I suggest we just let it float down the Straits. We put a boat in front and behind, to warn other craft of the shipping hazard. I've been judging its speed, using the marker buoys, and by my reckoning the island should reach Singapore in thirteen days. Then it can be towed into open water and disposed of . . .'

The harbourmaster looked thoughtful.

'. . . and I have a final suggestion,' said Leeman.

'Which is?'

'That we put a caretaker on the island, to place and maintain lights, fore and aft. This man could keep in radio contact with the accompanying boats and inform them of any problems. The sort of thing I envisage is the island running aground on a sandbank – which might solve all our worries – or breaking up in a storm. That sort of thing.'

Pulau scratched his head thoughtfully.

'I like it all except the caretaker. I'm not sure it's necessary to have someone actually *on* the island. It would have to be you, you know. I wouldn't get any of my men near the place. *The island with the stink of ghosts* – they would die of fright.'

'I realise that. Of course, I would volunteer. It would be an additional safety factor.'

The harbourmaster smiled at Leeman.

'You're not afraid of ghosts, I take it?'

'Not in the least.' Which was not entirely true. The thought of spending thirteen nights in a graveyard was mildly discomfiting, but only that. The physical dangers? Well, that part of it might be rewarding.

'Right,' said Pulau, suddenly becoming decisive, 'that's how we'll play it. I'll call the Minister. You get back to your lodgings and pack what you think you'll need and I'll arrange it. Tent and provisions?'

'And gaslights.'

'Of course . . . You really aren't concerned about the supernatural side of it?'

'No.'

Leeman looked at the dark mass, moving slowly through the water in the distance. Despite his disbelief, it looked eerie and forbidding. A fishing canoe, one of those traditional craft with modern outboard engines thrusting it obscenely across the water, cut away sharply from the island's path.

'What did they do – most of them? Those people buried on the island? It seems a harsh judgement on the dead,' he murmured.

'Drug runners,' replied Pulau. 'You know how we feel about them, here in Malaysia.'

A shadow crossed Leeman's mind, painfully. He remembered that drug trafficking carried a mandatory death sentence in Malaysia, for those convicted of the crime. It was, perhaps, one of the reasons why he had chosen to do his secondment in this part of the world.

'I see,' he said, quietly.

Pulau regarded him with a quizzical expression.

'Does it make any difference? To you, I mean.'

Leeman thought about his younger brother, Pete. Of course it made a difference. The cycle of thoughts which he continually had to fight, to break out of, began whirling in his head. *Not again*, he thought. *Please. Why are there so many reminders? Why can't I be left alone?*

It made a hell of a difference.

'No,' he said. 'I just wondered, that was all.'

On the way to the boarding house, in Lebuh Campbell, he told himself how much he liked it on Penang, in the Far East. He enjoyed the expatriate life, with its accompanying indulgence in a completely different culture. He was an advocate of an older way of life, with values he felt the modern world had wrongly placed aside. In the Far East, you could get closer to such values. They gave one a sense of historical continuity: a connection with the past. He could enjoy it more, if only . . . if only he could throw off the mistakes of the *immediate* past. But they clung to his mind like leeches, sucking it dry . . . He had said *sorry* many, many times, but there were no ears to hear, no one to listen . . . He had run to the Far East in order to get away from the leeches, but that had not been far enough. Here he was, running again, to a small, floating island that had detached itself from the world.

At first he was too busy to allow the sweet fragrance of the island to disturb him. He had to place the calor gas lamps at either end of the rainforest, involving a mile-long walk along the shore. Then there was the business of setting up camp (something Pete would have enjoyed): erecting the tent, unpacking provisions, starting a fire and, finally, using the radio transceiver. He reported to the accompanying craft that all was well and he was preparing to bed down for the night.

Once these duties had been accomplished, he had more time to consider his environment.

There were the usual jungle noises, that he had often heard on Penang. There were cicadas which gave out sounds like factory whistles; frogs that bellowed like megaphones; and birds that ran up and down scales as if they were taking some form of musical training.

There were also other sounds: the breeze in the palms and the rippling of water through the thick weed on which the island was based.

Then there was that *smell.*

It was by no means a disagreeable perfume and reminded him of incense, but it seemed so dense as to stain the air with its presence. Perhaps the cause lay in some unusual plant? Then again, it might have come from the thick sargasso which supported the soil and rainforest? That explanation seemed much more likely.

He took a torch and went to the edge of the island, to peer down into the shallows. There was no beach. Instead, a soil bank dropped sharply into the sea, beneath the surface of which he could see the myriad vines of sargassum, knotted together to form a mass of spongy weed. It was alive with sea creatures, mostly eels.

Leeman backed away, a little disconcerted. He was revolted, not by the creatures themselves, but by their numbers. It almost seemed as if the island were a live thing, crawling with tentacles. This, coupled with the thought that there was a great depth of ocean beneath him – a strange sensation until he managed to convince himself that the island was only a raft: a craft fashioned by nature instead of man – made him tread lightly for a while. Once he had got used to the idea that it was in effect nothing more than a platform of weed, a natural Kon Tiki, carried along by the current, he managed to keep his imagination under control.

He slept very little that first night, the smell overpowering his desire for rest. He rose, once or twice, to watch the lights drift by on the mainland, and gained some comfort from those of the accompanying craft.

When morning came, sweltering but happily blessed with bright sunlight, he was able to explore his surroundings without the intrusion of irrational fears of rotting souls. The rainforest, half a mile wide, was much like any other he had seen on Penang. It was dense, its undergrowth and canopy formed of a thousand different plants of which he knew few by name. He recognised the frangipani trees, of course, regarded by the Chinese as unlucky, and tamarind, and various types of palm. He knew there would be snakes amongst the vines, and large spiders quivering on the undersides of waxy leaves, but these did not bother him overmuch. He had sprayed the area around the tent with paraffin, which would keep any wildlife away. Pete would have been terrified of them, of course, but then Pete was not with him.

He managed to busy himself with small tasks that occupied his mind to a degree, but there was no ignoring the smell. He recalled Pulau's statement, about the graves containing the bodies of drug runners, and felt sick at heart as the guilt washed through him. He kept telling himself that he was in no way to blame. He had not known what the launches were carrying; *still* did not know. He guessed their cargo consisted of contraband of some kind, but surely not narcotics? It could have been anything. Booze? Cigarettes? But did he honestly believe that people smuggled such things into Britain any more? The real money was in heroin and cocaine. Organised crime syndicates did not bother with tobacco and alcohol. And they had been organised. Oh, yes. His payments had arrived, on the dot, every month. A plain brown envelope full of crisp banknotes. *Very* efficient, he thought bitterly. And all he had to do was turn a blind eye.

He began weeping, softly, as he stoked his fire.

'The bastards,' he said. 'The bloody, fucking bastards. They killed my baby brother . . .'

The island's peculiar cloying scent became an irritant over the next day or two. It was like a spirit in constant attendance and it bothered him a lot. He thought about the graves and wondered about their number. Were they unmarked, or were there headstones? Perhaps his tent was sited directly over a murderer's corpse, its putrefied flesh and corroding soul exuding opposing, distinctive odours? He dismissed the idea. The layer of soil was too thin near the shore. He could see the white stains of the saltwater, seeping through the grass.

He studied these white patches with loathing. They were threatening, simply because they were reminders of white powder. They demanded his attention, and once they had it, initiated that terrible cycle of thoughts which had his mind reeling. How swiftly nature turned from friend, to enemy . . .

'How long have I been here?' he asked the boat.

'Five days,' came the reply.

Another eight to go. The mosquitoes were biting well. (He preferred to think of them as biting, rather than sticking their needle mouths into his skin. That was too much like being injected, with a hypodermic . . .) It meant he had to spend time with his body, inspecting it, ministering to its minor problems.

He began doing all tasks with elaborate precision: making rituals of them, taking pains to perfect methods. Pete used to like rituals. When they were children, sharing a bedroom, he used to make fun of Pete, who would fold his clothes in just the same way, every night. It was supposed to keep away the bogeymen. Pete had liked high church, too, because of its mystical rituals. Then later – not so much later – those other rituals: the strings of powder – chasing the dragon. He should have seen all this in Pete, earlier. Done something to . . . to divert the course.

'Seven days.'

Sometimes he found himself staring at the forest that hid the graves, that breathed the scent of the dead. He discovered something which he decided no other living person had yet noticed: that shadows were not all of the same thickness. There were those that lay black and heavy, rarely moving. There were those, slightly thinner, that changed position and shape lethargically. Then there were the younger shadows, like smoky movements on the grass.

He found he had power over the shadows. Those he did not like, he removed with his machete. He gave birth to new shadows, using mats of woven palm leaves. Screens and shields were placed around the camp area, so that they cast their dark shades on the ugly white stains, neutralising them. The artist in him helped to create a territory in which the reminders were few.

Then it rained, battering down his palmthatch shields. The new, unprotected shadows drained away in rivulets.

He passed his reports at the specified times, but avoided social discourse. The reason, if he asked himself at all, was that disembodied voices from the outside world tended to emphasise his solitude, rather than provide relief from it.

He found the heat of the day extremely oppressive, and often fell asleep in his tent during the afternoon, to wake in a pool of sweat as the evening approached. Though he had plenty of drinking water, he lost so much body fluid in the airless atmosphere of the tent that he began to develop dehydration headaches.

'Nine days.'

It rained heavily for the third time since he had arrived on the island. The fire was difficult to light. He used many matches, and when he looked down at their spent forms, he saw with surprise that they made a word. He did not like the word, was angry with it, and kicked it out of understanding. After his rebellion, night and day took it on themselves to confuse him. They lost their sense of rhythm, their timing. He would lift the tent flap to find darkness where he expected light. Or the other way round. Such happenings only served to erode further his trust in the world. There were other problems. He had ceased to breathe air. There was none on the island. He breathed only the perfume that had replaced it. The fragrance was corrosive, staining him internally. He tried making masks to filter out its impurities, but there was no mesh fine enough to prevent the sickly odour from entering his lungs.

'Ten days.'

How stupid he had been! He had allowed the island to feed his guilt, keep the cycle of thoughts turning until he was physically sick, until he was so locked into himself that only a major event, like a rainstorm, could break him out. He now dismissed such ideas as weak and foolish. It was up to him to resist, not succumb, to the island's pressures. He was the master of the island. He told it this fact, in no uncertain terms.

On the twelfth night they called him, waking him from a muzzy sleep to say that the lights at the rear of the island had failed. He took a torch and trudged along the coastline, to relight the gas. On the return journey, he stumbled off the path, into the jungle, and found himself on a well-worn track. He followed it to a central clearing, where gravestones sprouted from the tall grass. The scent was overpowering here, in the glade. He turned, to leave the place quickly.

At the edge of the clearing he stumbled over an ovoid object. He shone his torch on it. It was a durian. Since arriving on the island, he had deliberately avoided eating any of its produce, though rambutan grew in abundance. The durian at his feet had split on impact with the ground and lay open. Leeman had developed a taste, almost a craving, for this addictive fruit, which the locals regarded as a delicacy. It had a sweet flavour, but highly offensive smell. Someone had once described it as like eating honey in a public toilet.

In his half-asleep state he picked up a piece of the durian and sniffed the white flesh. For a moment the perfume of the island was swamped by the foul but pleasant stink of the durian. Without thinking, he took a bite and swallowed. It tasted good.

He realised, almost instantly, what he had done. The green dragon had seduced him. He stared around him, in horror, at the graves which the roots of the durian tree must surely have penetrated, feeding there. The pressure built in his head, until he felt his skull was splitting. A numbness overcame his legs and he lost his balance, falling to the ground, where he lay trembling violently. He heard himself shouting, 'Oh, God . . .' over and over again. He had tried to ride the back of the green dragon, and had lost control. It had carried him to savage days and cruel nights, working insidiously from within him.

He crawled back to camp on his hands and knees and, once there, fell into a deep sleep. His dreams were sour.

They came for him the following morning: Singapore was in sight. He felt drugged and heavy-headed, as though he had spent some time in a smoke-filled room. Sympathetic hands helped him to the boat.

'What about the island?' he asked, as they sailed away.

'There's a dredger ready, to tow it out into open waters,' a sailor replied.

Then someone asked him, 'Are you all right? You look ill – are you sick?'

He did not feel sick, and shook his head.

'I found it hard to sleep.' They would understand that. 'I'm OK now – now that it's over. That place could send you mad – was it only thirteen days? It seemed much longer.'

'You don't look crazy.' 'The sailor smiled. 'Just exhausted.'

He tried to smile back.

'Yes – tired, that's all. I seem to have done nothing but slept, but I'm still tired. It gets to be a habit, when you're on your own.'

'I'm glad it wasn't me. I hate being lonely.'

On the journey across the water, he cleared his lungs, breathing deeply. Familiar odours were beginning to reach him, from the harbour. The smell of garbage around the sampans; of cooking from the hawker stalls; of decaying fruit. To Leeman, they were clean smells.

The cycle of thoughts, the arguments that had raged continuously in his brain, had ceased. He had reached a dreadful conclusion. He was no better than those men in the island's graves. In fact he was worse. He had been responsible, even if indirectly, for the death of his own brother. While he had been collecting payments for allowing certain launches to go unreported, past his observation tower on an English rivermouth, Pete had been dying of an overdose of heroin. He had not even known his brother was an addict: that was how much he had cared.

Not wanting to return on the boat, he booked into a hotel in Singapore town, close to the harbour. Once in his room, he undressed and threw the shirt and shorts into the waste bin. Then he showered himself, carefully, soaping his skin. He did this several times. As he shaved, his breath misted the mirror, so that his eyes were hidden from him.

Later, he went down to the bar and drank down two straight whiskies that hardly touched his throat. Although he would have preferred to keep his own company, an American began to talk to him, and he found himself responding. After several more drinks, he told the man about the ghosts of the island and the sweet stink of their souls.

'Embalming fluid,' said the American. 'Take it from me – I've smelt the stuff. It carries. Boy, does it carry. My brother-in-law was an undertaker . . .'

'I expect you're right,' said Leeman.

When he was sufficiently drunk, he went out and began to walk the streets. He needed a little more comfort than the American could offer. He wanted arms around him and a soft voice, talking nonsense. There is nothing more comforting than empty talk, when you want to keep your head clear.

He found a young woman, outside a bar, and bought her a few drinks before she took him home to bed. She chattered the whole while, even as she stripped, about her relations, about the difficulties of making ends meet, about the meanness of her landlord. He let her words wash over him, without interrupting.

Then, while they were making love, she told him that he was good. He was very, very good. He looked good, he tasted good, he *smelled* good . . .

Leeman threw her out of the bed, savagely, and screamed abuse at her. The frightened girl grabbed her sarong and ran out into the night. He dressed quickly, and left.

He walked the streets. He thought about the island's air and the fruits of its earth. It was in him, in his system. He could not scour it from him with words. It had breathed its breath into his murderer's lungs. It had tricked him into ingesting its offspring.

He found another bar and, while he was being served a drink, asked the young Chinese waiter to smell his skin. The boy hurried away, without a backward glance. Leeman stared after him bleakly, then studied the sweat on his forearm, coming through his pores.

He brought the back of his hand up to his face . . . slowly . . . convinced that time was his terrible enemy, that time was in league with corruption, leaving nothing in its wake but the faint odour of hell's flowers.

# The Thunder of the Captains

Those who have never experienced the rigid discipline of a military school cannot imagine how assiduously such establishments work to destroy individuality. There is not a single minute of the day that is not filled with gruelling physical training, base manual labour or academic study. Nor is there rest when the lights go out. The night hours might often have to be spent in preparing for an early morning inspection. Even then, someone in authority may come along and destroy the immaculate kit layout because a toothbrush is still damp, or faces the wrong way. Each item, each small or large possession, has a place in the layout, has a particular way of being folded or presented, and any deviation from this is considered a crime.

Some nightmares are formed from a state of extreme order, as well as chaos.

Just as terrible as the oppressive official requirements are the hostile attentions of the senior boys, whose brutality would not be out of place in a street gang. They choose their victims with care and destroy them with a cruelty found only in a mind disciplined beyond reason or the reach of compassion. When the lights go out in the dorms, the manufactured adolescent – a creature processed and fashioned by inflexible ritual, by rules and regulations – exercises an ungovernable will and prowls through sleeping forms, looking for the youth who is solitary, friendless and weak.

There are those who try to fight both formal and informal authority, openly, and are broken at the age of fifteen into items useless to any society except the one to which they have committed their souls. There are those who bend with the system, like malleable strips of copper, hoping that though they allow themselves to be distorted during their years at the school, they can reshape, reform themselves later. There are those who feign mental illness, or deliberately cause themselves physical harm, in order to escape. There are, of course, those whom the life suits, who have no desire to be individual. Then there are those like Jake and me, who fight in secret, fight insidiously in the dark.

There were two activities which kept us sane during our years at the school: horses and a schoolboy enthusiasm for black magic. Possibly a strange combination, but while we were out horseriding, we had the freedom of the open air, the exhilaration of animal-powered speed, and a proximity to the natural, chaotic elements of weather and nature.

Then at night, behind closed doors, we lit tinlids of rags soaked in brass cleaner and chanted incantations to unhallowed gods: to Satan, to Nahemah the princess of succubi, to Seddim, to Furfur the demon winged stag, to Ukoback the stoker of Hell's fires – but most of all, to Cimerics, the demon who rides a black horse. We studied the works of Aleister Crowley, Mathers, W. B. Yeats and others of the Order of Golden Dawn.

After our initial explorations into the art of the occult, Jake and I finally formed our own bastard religion, linking our two favourite activities. We began to pray to the spirits of dead horses. Bucephalus, Alexander's charger, Barbary, King Richard's mount, and other famous steeds. Almost from the dawn of its creation the destiny of humankind has been closely interwoven with the horse. Together we have forged civilisations out of wildernesses, have pushed back frontiers, have ploughed the land and made it fertile, have conquered wastelands and formed unions stronger than marriages.

In the dim light and foul gases of our homemade brands, we would try to conjure visions of these beasts in the unsanctified air of the laundry room, murmuring invented chants into its dark corners. Perhaps it was a trick of the mind, brought about by the atmosphere we created, but on certain occasions my heartbeat quickened to see horse-like shapes in the wispy fumes of burning rags.

We found the passage in Job, which says, 'Hast thou given the horse strength? Hast thou clothed his neck with thunder? He mocketh at fear. He swalloweth the ground with fierceness and rage. He saith among the trumpets, Ha, ha; and he smelleth the battle afar off, the thunder of the Captains, and the shouting.'

How we loved those words, would recite them backwards in an

attempt to produce this wonderful creature, Jake more enthusiastically than I, for he was the leader and I his lieutenant. No one could touch our souls, we were sure of that, for we had blackened them beyond any stains the school could overprint.

We heard the thunder of the Captains, but not from afar. We endured their shouting close to our ears and held down our heartbeats for fear of revealing fear. We were afraid of showing we were afraid. We ran ten miles in the mud and rain; scrubbed toilet pans with nail brushes; scraped, polished, washed and ironed; we oiled our weapons and slaughtered cardboard enemies; we marched and drilled; on Sundays we prayed in rigid rows, the words mechanical; we sat with poker spines in disinfected classrooms; we ate our meals to the count; we knew sudden light or instant darkness – all to the thunder of the Captains.

We did as we were told: they had our bodies and minds during daylight hours. But deep beneath the exterior show, we mocked the authorities with dark smiles, as surely as Job's horse mocked at fear. We prayed for deliverance from those who would destroy us. We prayed for the destruction of our enemies, the hated bullies, both official and otherwise.

Somehow I made it through two years at military school and then escaped on the death of my father. My mother required support at home and money was short. I had to go to work to help with the household expenses. Father had left many debts, bless him.

Jake stayed on at the school and the last I saw of him there was his wan face beneath the cropped tar-black hair, watching me through the barred gates as I walked away. He looked thin and wasted, his prominent front teeth giving him the curious paradoxical appearance of combined predacity and piteousness. For Jake there was no escape. His father was wealthy and determined to have a soldier for a son. I was sorry for him, in a general way, but I realised as I was leaving that we had never been friends in the true sense of the word. We had simply combined forces to fight a common enemy: had shared experiences, as soldiers did in the trenches, but only seeing a single side of a polyhedron. There were faces and angles to Jake which I had never been shown, because the school narrowed our viewpoints. Possibly a better way of describing my view of Jake in those days would be to say it was like looking at a folded map. One sees sections of rivers and roads, but their sources and destinations remain hidden behind sharp creases. Jake, the whole Jake, was a folded chart, and it was only years later that I was to be allowed another study of the regions and contours of the man.

Over the subsequent years my memories of the school and its horrors were obliterated from my mind, piece by piece. People speak of memories as fading, like sepia photographs under a hot sun. This is not my experience. Memories are indeed like photographs – unreliable snapshots – that are flicked in front of the mind's eye. If one wishes, one can suppress the mental hand that produces them: prevent it from showing the print. Even Jake, with his pinched, eager expression and quick gestures, was rejected. Consequently, when he came back into my life again, it was a while before I recognised him.

By the time I was thirty, my mother had joined my father. I had worked at a number of jobs and finally settled into a niche that I hoped would remain available to me for the rest of my life. I became a gamekeeper to John Setton, a gentleman farmer in the district of Rochford, in Essex. My period at military school had revealed an aptitude for marksmanship which seemed to impress my employer. I did wrestle a little with the morals of breeding birds to shoot them, but decided that there was little difference between putting a bolt into the brain of a calf, and shooting a bird. Actually, the latter had more chance of escape, since the myopic 'sportsmen' who came to Setton's shoots were mainly gin-soaked men who had never grown out of playing with guns, but whose marksmanship was questionable.

John Setton needed me, among other things, to keep out poachers. Although concentrated poaching was usually carried out by organised gangs from the city, Setton was convinced that some of our stock found its way into gypsy larders. It was not true of course – at least not to the extent John Setton believed. Gypsies are shrewd business-people, and if you are looking for a bargain, you stay clear of them, but they have no more thieves amongst them than house dwellers.

It was the gypsies that drew Jake back into my life again. They are, traditionally, horse dealers and gather in Rochford Square of a market day to trade. It was on a Thursday, in October, while I was attending the market, that I felt a lean, hard hand on my shoulder.

'It is you,' said a gaunt man, as I turned to face him. I was bewildered, and it must have shown on my features, for he added, 'Jake. Jake Dornstern.'

I felt at a loss and not a little stupid.

'Are you sure . . .' I began, but he interrupted me, saying, 'After all these years – how many? Twelve? Thirteen? Must be all of that. You lucky bastard – you escaped early, didn't you? I had two more years of . . . well, no sense in raking the coals, now that they're dead. How are you, anyway?'

By this time I had recognised him.

I shook his hand. 'Jake. Nice to meet you again. What are you doing in Rochford?'

'Buying a horse for my girlfriend. We're in London, now that the old man's gone. Yes, died last year. Left me quite a bit, which is lucky, because I'm not good for much. The only thing I've ever been good at is inheriting money. It isn't as easy as they think.' His voice had grown bitter. 'I had to *earn* it, doing all sorts of unpleasant things, like reaching the rank of captain in the army.'

'Surely, that's not so bad. The school was unpleasant, but . . .'

'Unpleasant? You have changed. Using mild words like unpleasant, for that pit of . . . Anyway, I didn't like the army either. It's their *acceptance* of you that's so hard to take. It was almost as if they had won – but I still kept fighting, the way we used to, only with more . . . well, we were just playing at it, weren't we? Just boys at a game.'

All the while he spoke to me his eyes were roaming over faces in the bustling crowd of farmers, horse dealers and market traders. I wondered then how I could have failed to recognise him. He still had that ambivalent look of the snake in a suspended moment – the second in which it's between the decision to strike or slither away. He seemed to be caught in a perfect balance between the two strong desires.

'Can you help me? Which are the gypsies?'

I nodded towards one: a short, swarthy man close by.

'Him – Henry Toupe's his name. He deals in horses, if that's what you mean.'

'I see him.'

'You'll notice the stick then? If a gypsy wishes to trade, he carries his stick that way. Do you want to speak to him?'

'In a moment.' He paused, then said, 'Where do they get their horses? They breed them, I suppose?'

'Yes. Much of the stock comes from Spain. There's a horse fair – in Andalusia – once a year. Most of our gypsies go.'

'And what do you do?' he asked, suddenly confronting me with a question more direct than polite. I was a little taken aback.

'Gamekeeping. I'm a gamekeeper.'

'Ah, yes. You always did prefer the outdoor life, didn't you?'

His tone made me defensive.

'I don't see what's wrong with that. I like to be outside, yes. It's a living.'

'You sound affronted. Are you ashamed of having an affinity with nature? Bit like a church to you, the outdoors, isn't it? Sanctified woods, sacred fields, the sepulchral heathland.'

I was beginning to get a bit annoyed with his mocking tone, but he turned his attention back to the gypsy.

'Those fellows – they have an affinity with horses. Superstitious people as well. Does that combination remind you of anything – anyone?'

'Why, those games . . .'

He turned to face me.

'Games – but I couldn't give it up, you see. Oh, you can sneer, but you escaped, damn you. I still had to face it. The bloody kit inspections, the drilling, the fucking lot . . . I still had it, up to here.' His eyes burned with a feverish anger. But then he smiled, and somehow the smile seemed more dangerous than the anger it had replaced. He said, in a pleasant tone, 'You wouldn't understand.'

I realised then what he had been telling me.

'You can't be serious. You mean, you still do all that . . . experimenting? But it was silly – come on, you're joking, aren't you?'

I thought he would immediately deny any involvement in the black arts. Instead, he just smiled – that thin, wet curvature of the mouth – and said, 'Wait here a moment, will you? I'll be back. Then we can have a pint together.'

He left me and walked across the cobbled, straw-strewn square to speak to the gypsy. I watched as Henry brought his face up to answer Jake, while Jake himself bent over, as if he were about to swallow the man. I wondered whether it would be prudent just to walk away, thinking that the bargaining would take some time anyway. I wasn't sure I wanted any more to do with a man with whom I seemed to have so little in common. He was apparently rich, and I was poor. He could afford to indulge in pastimes which I now thought dangerous, from a psychological point of view, and silly in the extreme. Such things could only be laughed at as harmless when the participant had a strong mind and retained a certain scepticism. I was not sure this was the case with Jake. As a boy he had been more vulnerable than I, and more impressionable. I could not see a great deal of change in him now.

He came back before I could make a decision.

'Made an appointment for later,' he said. 'Come on. Where's the nearest pub? What about that one, over there?' He pointed to the King's Head.

'Not my local, but it sells beer.'

'Let's to it, man.' He slapped my back and led the way, striding out in army style towards the pub.

We drank steadily, through the lunch hour, sifting through scattered incidents that I believed were better left where they had fallen several years before. Finally, I asked the question, the answer to which had been bothering me.

'What did you really want with Henry?'

Jake's eyes shone, possibly with excitement.

'Those gypsies – they know certain secrets. Our old religion. Have you ever heard of the Gytrash?'

'The Gytrash?'

'Yes. You haven't, have you? Well, it's a horse – a phantom horse. The gypsies believe in it. So do I. Don't look at me like that. It's not just hocus-pocus. It appears – look, when you see it, it's a warning that a loved one, your nearest and dearest, is going to die. When it appears, you know that death is at hand.' He swallowed more of his beer, his Adam's apple bobbing away in front of me.

He continued. 'After you left the school, I was on my own. I began to take things a bit more seriously – began to explore libraries for the right kind of books. I learned a great deal. I thought we – well, the horse is a magnificent beast, isn't it? Grace and speed, and intelligence. It's powerful, with aesthetic lines.'

'You're here to buy a horse . . .'

'No. I'm here to talk to the gypsies. I need to know certain things. Then I'll be ready.'

I studied his face in the dim light. He was surely unwell? The dusk filled the hollows of his cheeks with dark shadows. I felt disturbed, uneasy in his presence. Here was a man with an obsession. The kind of obsession that permits no barriers, nor accepts interference from moral principles. Moreover, his ideas did not make sense.

'Let me understand this correctly, Jake – you obviously want to see this – Gytrash? But if it only appears when a loved one is about to die . . .'

'*The* loved one, and it can be called.' He sounded extremely satisfied. 'Yes, it can be *called*.'

'But . . .'

'Someone has to die, yes.'

The tone was that of a man explaining a logical fact and a torpor took control of me, long enough to prevent me betraying my revulsion.

'And who do you expect that to be?' I uttered after a long while.

'In my case, a woman called Catherine.'

Since leaving military school I had lived in a placid pool of unchanging events, but somewhere in my nature revolution was waiting to erupt. I craved momentous change, which I had always hoped would come from meeting someone with whom I could fall in love. The fact that I thought this business about the Gytrash was rubbish was immaterial. Jake did not think it silly, yet he was prepared to sacrifice his Catherine to an indulgence in the black arts. He was offering someone he loved, a woman who presumably loved him, in exchange for a mystical experience. I, who would have *battled* with devils and demons to protect such a rarity as mutual love, was appalled by his callousness. He was decadent beyond words.

'You're insane,' I snapped, no longer able to keep the statement to myself. But he surprised me again.

'Don't you think that's a little trite? I expected better of you. Catherine has agreed to this. Not only that, she encourages me.'

'Then you're both mad.'

'Perhaps. It doesn't matter, does it? If we are, then nothing will happen. If not? Well, you may not understand this, but some people are willing to sacrifice all they have, for the ultimate experience.'

'And what does she get out of it?'

'For some people, life is a burden.'

My blood felt like mercury in my veins.

'Is she a cripple? In pain?'

'Not physically. She's – spiritually oppressed. And don't look as though you pity us. That's rather arrogant. We don't need it.' He glanced at his watch. 'Now I must go. My appointment.' He reached across with his hand and when I failed to take it, rested it on my shoulder for a moment.

'Perhaps we'll see each other again,' he said. His face set into a hard mask. 'I have to do this thing. You'll probably never understand.' Then he stood up and strode out of the pub, his tall, lean body stooping at the door before disappearing beyond.

I sat there for a long time, wondering how such a man had survived until now. Yet, as I reasoned, I knew how. He was a product of extremes – a combination of inflexible discipline and complete self-indulgence – which had resulted in a paradox: the rational lunatic. I did pity him, but I also envied him. He had an inner strength of conviction, a confidence, that I lacked, and I was in awe of it. Had *I* that kind of strength, I could have . . . what? Gone on a quest to find someone to share my life with me? You don't find those sort of people by searching for them. They happen in your way.

The strange thing was, until Jake had mentioned those words – *the loved one* – I had not realised just *how* lonely I had become. I was so lonely, I was not a real man at all. I was a walking effigy; a straw man. Jake had revealed to me just how empty my life was, and had been, since leaving the school. And there was someone with the very thing I needed to make me whole, and he was prepared to throw it away on something transient, an evanescence, an experience as fleeting as a puff of smoke from a burning log.

There was a sharp wind blowing from the east, which buffeted the pines that lined the road to Setton Hall. I could hear them, tossing their dark manes above me, swishing their many tails beneath the lining of the sky.

Three nights later there was an urgent knocking on my cottage door. I put down the book I was reading and rose, reluctant to open it. But the light was on and shining through the window. I had no choice.

Jake stood before me, swaying slightly and exhaling plumes of cold air. He looked intoxicated. There was an air of suppressed excitement about his demeanour. His complexion was smooth and glowing, like an infant freshly awakened from sleep.

'I saw it . . .' He stepped inside and pulled at his gloves. 'I saw it. Two days with the gypsies – then last night, out on the marshes.' He shook his head and laughed, finally managing to take off one of his gloves. 'I was *terrified.* It's one thing talking about it, but out there – it's so bleak. Just miles of dark reeds, moving to the varying pressures of the wind. Unseen hands pressing down the grasses. And desolate creeks of slick mud, shining under the starlight.

'There are birds out there you know – of course you do – but *hundreds* of them. Crouched in banks of saltwort and bladderwrack. They fly out when you disturb them. Startles you. God, this is a lonely place you've chosen to live – the Essex marshes . . .'

'Jake, look . . .'

'Let me tell you,' he insisted. 'I did it all – the incantations, the symbols, the magic rites. Once I had started, it was OK. I felt – *excited.*

That place has the perfect atmosphere. It reeks of pagan worship, old religions with pre-Christian gods. I smelled their breath on the wind. It stank of their foul odours – rank, yet charged with power.'

'The smell of rotting weed and mud,' I said, but there was no stopping him.

'I felt puny under their observations. They cluster in those marshes, you know. Primal mud is their last refuge.'

'But, Jake, *please*.'

'Finally, when I'd finished the rites, I called its name – and it came, beautiful and black, the height of three houses and eyes, white with the fires of death.

'It seemed that flying hooves struck the moon, set it spinning as a wheel of light. I was . . . was momentarily blinded . . .' He ran a hand over his face and I thought he was going to faint. I reached out for him, but he recovered and pushed me away.

'My hands . . .' He stared at them, holding them palms towards his face, one of them still incongruously gloved. 'My skin was alive with static – every hair on my body stood out. Not just a horse – the *Gytrash*.

'Then – then I became afraid. Like a coward, I turned to run, but it was there before me again, its black muscled flanks shedding flakes of light . . . each time I turned, it was there. I couldn't run. There was nowhere I could go to.'

His voice dropped a pitch now.

'This was a god-horse. It was Malech, Phlegon, Skinfaxi, all in one – its great hooves gleamed dully above me. It could have crushed me like a beetle. It was Spumador, Dhuldul, Nonios – do you see? My feelings . . .'

'Shut up!' I shouted.

The atmosphere in the room was stifling. The draught from the open door was playing havoc with my coal fire and filling the room with smoke. I could hardly breathe. I pushed past him to lean on the door-post, gulping down air as if it had miraculous medicinal powers.

When I had recovered, I said to him, 'Will you go away now, Jake. You had no invitation to come here. You know what I think – so please go away. If you'll take my advice you'll see . . .'

'I don't need your advice.' He pulled on his glove again. 'I'm going back to London – perhaps we'll see each other . . .'

'No,' I said flatly. 'I don't want to hear from you. Now if you don't mind, I wish to get back to my book.'

He shrugged. 'Well, good luck.'

Then he went out into the night, leaving me wretched and miserable. It was difficult to know which of my feelings was most dominant. I felt scorn for this man, but also pity. He had placed himself in the hands of the gypsies, and though I respected most of them, there were some who were not above trickery where big money was concerned. They had knowledge of fungi and herbs lost to the rest of us – possibly some of which were hallucinogens.

The next morning I left the cottage and made my way to Hadleigh Downs, where Henry Toupe exercised his horses. The herd were grazing on the meadow grass as I approached, and they cantered away – some thirty of them. Henry was by the trough with his black and white lurcher and, though I knew that he had seen me, he deliberately kept his eyes on some other point. My office of gamekeeper had done nothing for my popularity amongst the gypsies.

'Morning,' I said.

He replied in kind, but guardedly, his face closing down its natural geniality.

I nodded towards his herd. 'Nice horses.'

He sniffed. 'You know about horses then?'

'Used to – still do, I suppose.'

He did not reply to this, but leaned his chin on his tall stick, staring out after the playful animals, as they clustered in a corner of the field.

'The man that spoke to you about the Gytrash. He knew about horses.'

Henry nodded. 'Him?' The little man squared his chest, stretching the string that served as a button on his brown waistcoat. 'Yep, he knew about horses, all right.'

'What happened to him, Henry?' I asked bluntly.

His eyes crinkled at the corners. He may have been smiling, but it was difficult to tell. Time-set and hard, he stood like a proud rock beside the watertrough. When it seemed he was not going to answer, I said, 'Are you going to tell me?'

'He asked about summat, an' he was told. That's all.'

'Nothing else? What else did you do to him?'

'*Do* to him? Ain't no saving the lost.'

'What's that supposed to mean? Henry, the man's close to the edge – you know what *I* mean. If you've nudged him a little nearer, it'll be on your conscience.'

'Don't know as I've got one of they . . . KEE-ARR,' he yelled at his dog, which had gone looking for adventure in the hedgerow.

He walked off then, without a backward glance.

For the next two months I spent restless days at my work, fixing fences, ripping out poachers' snares and generally carrying on with my duties. At night I would sit up, staring out of the window into the darkness, wondering about the things that lay in wait out there. I would sit until I was too tired to keep my eyes open and either fall asleep in the chair or crawl away to my bed. I saw Henry several times, but we merely acknowledged each other with a nod or wave of the finger. Then, one evening, I returned to the cottage for a bite of food and found Jake sitting outside on my window bench.

His appearance destroyed any security I had salvaged since our last meeting. He had always been a thin man, but now he was emaciated, haggard and brittle-looking. He raised two red-rimmed eyes at my approach and stared at me.

'You'd better come in,' I said, unlocking the door. My hand shook as I did so. I really did not want him in my house, but had no choice.

He entered, a wraith whose clothes hung from him like curtains. It seemed that if I were to touch him, he would crumble into dust and sighs. He sat in the armchair.

'You look terrible,' I said. 'Can I help?'

'No – ' His voice was almost a whisper. 'There's nothing anyone can do. She's dead.'

My mind had difficulty in coping with this information. There were too many layers to sort through, before I could make any sense of it. Then I came to the most obvious conclusion.

'Dead? Your . . . Catherine?'

His head jerked up. 'Not Catherine. Not her. She's still alive.'

'Who then? Somebody died – you just said so.' My mind was turning over other possibilities. His mother? His sister? Who?

'I don't know her name.'

'You-don't-know . . . where's the understanding in this?'

He rubbed his hands together, in anguish it seemed, and made a dry rasping sound.

'Catherine didn't die – but somebody *did*. I've killed her. The one person that could have changed my life – the woman I could have loved above all things. Not Catherine – that wasn't love. It couldn't have been. She's still alive. The one person that counted has been murdered, by me. My selfish obsession.'

'This is ridiculous.'

'No, no, it's not.' His eyes were hot upon my own.

'Meaning what? For God's sake.'

'I called the Gytrash prematurely – that meant someone had to die.'

'Yes, yes. You told me that. A loved one . . . the closest.'

He looked away again.

'Don't you see? Can't you see what's happened? Not someone I know already – someone I haven't met. I called up the beast prematurely. Therefore, the woman who would have loved me, once we met – the woman I would have loved more than . . . Catherine is alive. It wasn't her. Couldn't have been, could it?'

My cheeks felt tight and I was light-headed. What was I to say to this man who had convinced himself that somewhere out in the world, someone had dropped dead because of his indulgence? I only knew one thing. I wanted him out of my house.

'Look, perhaps if we call Catherine? Do you have her telephone number? I'll . . .'

'I can't even put flowers on her grave. Everywhere I go, I think, did she live here? Was that her house? I look for signs of her – signs I would not even recognise if I saw them. I see other women, and wonder, was she like that? Did she have blonde hair, or brown? What colour were her eyes? Was she wise, tender, understanding, humorous? I have nothing but questions, and no answers.'

'I think you're tormenting yourself for nothing, Jake. I'll tell you what. I'll fetch Henry Toupe. We'll ask the gypsy about this thing.'

What I wanted to do was to get Henry to confess, before Jake, that the whole thing was faked. That they had given Jake some kind of drug which induced visions of a nightmare. Drugs and the power of suggestion. I *had* to get them to admit it. There was no other explanation worth a damn. Some magic mushrooms and an hypnotic voice. I bet he never even left the caravan. Now he was caught up in his own nightmare.

His sallow cheeks quivered. Bitterness replaced the sorrow in his tone.

'I know this much. I saw the Gytrash and as a consequence of that, a woman died. I killed her. You only get one chance for happiness, and I murdered mine in cold blood. Ugly, isn't it? Well, that's that . . .' He seemed to be getting more rational in his tone. '. . . I've left Catherine. Not her fault. She's still got her chance to come. So have you.'

He stood up and walked towards the door.

Suddenly the compassion flooded through me. He looked physically, as well as mentally unwell, and I stretched out a hand to stop him.

'Stay here the night, Jake? We'll talk some more in the morning. Right now, you look as though you could do with a night's rest.'

He hesitated, and then said, 'I am so tired. Maybe you're right.' He ran a hand through his dishevelled hair. There was a bleakness in his expression, but I felt we were gaining a little ground in our crawl for sanity.

'Sorry,' he said, 'to drag you into all this.'

'It's all right,' I lied. 'But let's put all these assumptions aside for a few hours, until you've rested. Then we can rationalise it all.'

He smiled, grimly.

'Yes, maybe you're right.'

'Sleep,' I said. 'You're worn down to nothing. Let's talk tomorrow.'

He nodded and I showed him to my bedroom. I left him there and went down to the sofa. I felt depressed and anxious with him under my roof. I kept turning over possibilities, undecided as to what to do. In the end it seemed proper for me to accompany him to London, where I could hand him over to Catherine. She would surely be aware of the state of his mind.

I spent an uncomfortable and restless night. When dawn came, the sparrows awoke me from a short sleep, clustering in the tree outside my window. I lay there for a few minutes observing the changing fragments of grey, caught between the crazed network of branches. I felt numb inside. What was I going to say to the man that would help him in any way? You cannot convince a man, whose whole mind has shaped itself around a negative idea, that he is wrong. I could produce nothing in the way of evidence to substantiate an argument that ran counter to his belief.

He believed he had precipitated the death of his one chance of happiness. If he could have found love, real love, with its wild energetic gestures and chaotic motion, he would have been safe. Love plays havoc with order. Love is delightful in its irrationality and its scorn of discipline. Love fashions its clocks from ill-fitting cogs of emotion and wheels of impulse.

I rose and made two coffees, taking one up to Jake.

He was gone.

I stood there, stupidly holding the hot coffee, and stared at the state of the room. It was a chilling sight. Bewilderment gradually turned into a kind of comprehension.

He had left the room in complete order. The blankets had been folded into an immaculate bedpack, squared and sharply creased, at the top of the bed. He had taken all my toilet articles and laid them out neatly, conforming to the diagrams we had followed for military inspections. My shoes were in a row at the end of the bed, lace-ends tucked tightly into the top two eyeholes. Shirts, suits, underwear, socks, ties – all were folded in the correct military manner and displayed according to regulations. Even my writing materials, pad, envelopes and pens, had been placed precisely in their correct positions on the bedside cabinet. The whole room had been dusted and straightened to a stark, clean, dull uniformity.

I knew then that nothing could save him. His determination was evident in that ugly display of regimentation and order. Whether he had done it consciously, as some kind of sign to me, or because of some inner compulsion over which he had no control, I never discovered.

The Captains had taken his soul after all.

A week later, I went to the funeral. It was a small, dismal affair attended by one or two military types, and Catherine. She and I only exchanged a few words: the guilt, whether justified or not, forced us quickly apart. Neither of us, I am sure, felt we had anything in common that was not linked by Jake – sad to say – for it might have proved something.

# Feral Moon

In those days I thought it would last forever. Of course, nothing lasts, except regret, which we nurture to keep something of the past alive inside us. When I lay my head down on this bundle of rags I call a pillow, I wonder about my bed-sharer, who works days and sleeps nights, vacating our mattress below the stairs just before I come off night shift. Do we share this eternal regret?

These are the times in which we live; a world which is shared by two distinctly separate and unequal classes, the very rich and the very poor. This is the kind of society that results from one of the worst depressions the world has ever experienced. And the responsibility, mainly, lies with the moon and its strange antics during the nineties. I used to be one and am now the other.

I still remain aware that everything I own and touch, little as it is, smells rancid (except, of course, for that faint, almost indiscernible fragrance on the pillow of late) and I detest myself and my condition. I hate my poverty, my status, with a venom that keeps the spark of a fight still alive in my brain. I want out. I want to get up there again, where I feel I belong. I want to take her with me, too, because I still love her, though we disgust each other – she without realising it is me . . .

. . . I'll run that through again, from the beginning, more completely. A songwriter knows the value of revision.

In those days I thought it would last forever. Well – why not? The songs were coming, strong and fast, and though I never had a hit in the top ten I believed that was just a matter of time. After all, I continually crept in just below the thirty slot and my work was receiving moderate but fairly widespread praise in the music columns. *Hang Ten* cut one of mine: 'Railrocker'. And Sten Stannis got to number twenty-five with my 'Peacemaker General'. It seemed inevitable to me that I was destined to follow people like John Barry, into film backing, or Mancini – those old guys that carved out a permanent career for themselves.

I had a theory then, that the capacity to develop ideas was a learned process. I couldn't accept that ideas just floated into a songwriter's head. I felt that I had undergone a sort of ideas apprenticeship in my formative years, when I sold very little and borrowed, to a certain extent. I mean *borrowed* in the sense that other songwriters, the successful ones, gave me spin-off ideas. I did not see that as plagiarism or morally wrong. I saw it as applying lateral thinking to what was going on around me. Through this apprenticeship I learned to develop my own ideas.

So – that was in the beginning. But the more you write, the more you develop that area of the brain which forms *ideas*. As time goes on, you begin to come up with original stuff and others start to collect spin-offs from the work *you* are producing. That was my theory and I stuck with it, even when it failed me. I seriously believed my dependence on others had been severed and my lyrical genius was entirely self-contained.

Janis never held with all this. She was a fan of the American poet Emerson. To him, all ideas had been there from the beginning; part of the numen of the earth. There were songs in the wind, poems in the air, right from the birth of the world. It was merely up to the gifted, the inspired, to milk them and get them down on paper. An Emersonian poet would have a mind's ear, tuned to the rhythms and tides of the earth.

'I can't accept that,' I told her. 'It means that a songwriter is just a device with the right aerial – for receiving signals. Not *me*. My songs come from *inside*, not outside.'

'Ergo, ego.' She would smile at me.

She wasn't vindictive about it. She just believed we were all cogs – part of the whole *oneness* – and that we should acknowledge our debt to the rest of the machine.

I would touch her cheek, or her arm, or her neck – anywhere, so long as I was touching her – and say, 'You just want to think you had a hand in writing my songs.' I said it to hurt her, intending the pain, because it annoyed me that she failed to recognise my independence.

'No,' she would reply, 'that's not the way it goes. Fact is,' and her dark eyes would cloud a little with a seriousness that chilled me, despite my self-assurance, 'I think *I'm* your aerial – and I don't like that kind of responsibility.'

'I need you, sweetheart – but not for that. I don't need anyone for my ideas, you included.'

'I want to think that's true.'

We were subtly cruel to each other in those days.

'Hey!' I once cried, 'I just got a surge from the rhythms of the earth – how about "the moon in June"?'

'Is that funny?'

'Don't knock it,' I said. 'Somebody once snatched that line out of the wind's repertoire. Tin Pan Alley could never have survived without it.'

'Sometimes I think you're an arrogant patronising prick.'

'And others . . .?'

'An arrogant condescending prick.'

'How long,' I persisted, 'do you think it had been floating around, waiting to be plucked out of the air? Maybe Adam sang it to Eve?'

'Or Solomon to Sheba. Come on, Dave, let's talk poetry, not trash.'

'You're the arbiter – OK, the moon in June is dead. What replaces it?'

'A feral moon – the tame one has gone wild again.'

That year the earth had been experiencing an appalling number of catastrophes; floods especially, but earth movements and eruptions too. They said it was due to a slight shift in the moon's orbit – something to do with pressures and gravitational changes – I didn't really take much interest in all the theories. Anyway, it was causing a lot of havoc and destruction, and governments were finding it hard to cope with the financial losses incurred over the disasters. The world had been plunged into a depression, which, because of my talent, I was riding very nicely. People like to be entertained while they're dying inside.

'Feral moon – hey, that's a *great* idea!' I said. 'What a title.'

I didn't write it, of course. Well, Christ, it was her idea. It was too good for me, and I was jealous of it, so I put it out of my mind and played around with other things. That was about the time it all began to go wrong for me.

Did I say I was in love with Janis in those days? I probably forgot to.

It was the same then. I never told her, either. Did I forget to tell her, or did I deliberately hold back, afraid to give too much of myself? I can't even remember that much. Convenient, isn't it, not to remember? You often read about these guys that fall from grace. They lose their jobs, if they're in business; or their fortunes, if they've inherited; or their talent, if they've got any. They fall, and their lovers leave them, right about that time. 'Bitches,' you think. 'Only hanging around the guy while the going was good.' But it's not like that. What happens is, as soon as you begin losing your grip, you start to panic and look around for someone to blame. I threw all sorts of shit at Janis, when I began slipping. It's a wonder she stayed as long as she did.

The last words she said to me, as she went through the doorway, were, 'Maybe we'll see each other again, sometime? A better time . . .', and then she was gone. Later, I clung on to those words, as if they were the truth absolute, as I looked for her face on the street, in the bars, at the theatre. It's amazing how many reminders of a person there are, once they've left you. I must have heard the name *Janis* mentioned a dozen times in as many contexts (none of them to do with *my* Janis) over the next few months. Janis Joplin records were re-issued in a blitz of publicity; switching on the TV one evening, quite by chance, I saw the last two-thirds of a political play called simply, *Janis,* about an American nun caught in a republican revolution; a European manufacturer brought out a new car they called 'The Janis' (pronounced *Yannise*, but that made no difference to my double-takes, whenever I glanced at the nameplate). It was almost as if there were a conspiracy to grind my nose into the dust. (*Love can produce paranoids too* . . . I tried a comeback with that, but the musical world called it banal). I smelled her favourite perfume in elevators, as though she had just vacated the lift the floor before I got in. (Once, I ran up two flights of stairs before I realised how foolish I was being.) Her hairstyle appeared everywhere, in just the right shade of blonde. The red scarf I had given her flashed by me in cars, on trains going in the opposite direction. Several times I half waved at a profile through a shop window, only to experience the bitter taste of disappointment even before my hand was up to my shoulder.

I tried other women. I found it was easy to be interesting to someone else, for a short time. The achievement was in remaining interesting to one woman for a lifetime and I revised my opinion on friends who had never played the field.

And all the time I was sliding down the hill, into that pit which had captured so many since the wild moon had made life a precarious business, even for those outside the disaster areas. Within two years I was flat broke, busted, with no one interested in my songs any more. The debts began to pile up around me. I couldn't even avoid being a cliché: the success story that turns sour and the hero who still tries to live the high life. I had to avoid the people from whom I had borrowed, and eventually had to skip town. I took a job, lost it, took another, until I ran out of any goodwill. For six months I joined the whisky bums and winos, and indulged in an orgy of self-pity. Finally I managed to land this job as a nightwatchman and have to stroll the grounds of a bean-canning factory during the quiet hours. By day I sleep in a shared bed in an overcrowded and crummy apartment that has not seen paint or plaster since the 1980s. I have the bed under the stairs from eight a.m. to five p.m. After that time, someone else crawls beneath the blankets. The bed is still warm from the other person's body when I get back in it the next day.

I have had different bed-sharers, I know, though I've never met any of them. The smell on the blankets and pillow has altered quite suddenly on two occasions. The pile of rags, bland and shapeless as they are, has changed too. It now seems that I share with a woman. There is a skirt and other feminine articles in the small bundle beneath the bed, next to my own belongings.

It started two weeks ago. I had difficulty in sleeping. I found myself wandering the hallway, staring at the worn floors and the cracks in the wall where the cockroaches hide. Something was bothering me, subconsciously, and I couldn't get hold of it. Each time I thought I had it, it slipped through my fingers. I thought at first it might be a startling-new original song trying to get out, but nothing found its way on to paper.

At night, while on my way to the factory, and while I was walking my beat, I kept staring up at the moon, studying its movements amongst the clouds. There were stormy skies about at that time and it gave the illusion that the moon was charging around like a mad boar amongst the dark towers of cumuli. Of course, it was the other way around; it was the clouds that were wild, but it gave me the answer to my problem. Feral moon.

I remember reading in the press in the seventies that we had given up our journeys to earth's satellite. We had tamed it, only to let it off the leash again, like a wild hawk set free, and it soon reverted to its natural state: elusive, distant, enigmatic, inscrutable. Much later it went completely out of hand and began attacking those who had dared to try to tame it.

Yesterday, instead of going straight to bed, I sat on its edge and on the back of some used envelopes I wrote the song I should have written when she was still with me. It was good. I could see that it was good. Good enough to get me back into the swim, if I was persistent enough, saw the right people, impressed them with my insistence that they at least sit down and listen for five minutes. I would have to clean myself up a little, get a haircut and shave, and brush up the fast talk, but there was a chance I could break back.

The mental irritation, if that's the right phrase, responsible for my insomnia, is still with me – but I think I know, now, where the cause lies. It is in the particular kind of warmth which lingers in the bed after the unknown sharer has vacated it for me. It is in the shape of the hollow she leaves behind. It is in the barely discernible fragrance which I believe I can smell in the pillow.

It is her. I have convinced myself it is her. I must have been aware of her just-removed form, her almost-presence, as I crept, exhausted, beneath the blankets of the bed we shared. I must have sensed that the space occupied by me had been filled by her, only an hour previously. She was there, had been there for some weeks, in the same bed. We had shared enough beds in the past (together then) for me to be disturbed by the place where she had lain not long before me. The irony of the situation – the separating factor: just an hour each day – between two ex-lovers, the intimate nature of the place we shared, was less painful, much less painful, than the knowledge of what had resulted from it. I have written *Feral Moon*, the song which will take me back into the life of ease, of public adulation, of independent arrogance, but not without a price. That price is the taste of ashes.

For it, I have had to sacrifice my belief in myself as the artist who needs no one, nothing except himself. I have had to sacrifice my idea that creativity comes entirely from within – that no other living soul can claim that they have assisted in any way. I have had to relinquish my spirit, my creative integrity, *myself*, and accept that I could not produce good material without her influence, even if it were only an imagined pillow-scent, or a blanket permeated by her body-warmth.

I have had to taste that ugly phrase that I thought would never pass my lips. *I have sold out.*

# Glory of the Seas

Abdulla Fasil had at last found a weapon with which to murder Father Matheson.

Allah wished it.

He took it from the warm waters of the lagoon with his gloved hand, careful to keep the slit away from him. Then he placed it in a jar of seawater. The creature began moving along the glass bottom.

It would have to be soon: that very evening, in fact. Yes, he gave his word before God that he would make the offering to Father Matheson after their meal together, at eight o'clock that evening.

Father Matheson was walking, head down, along the silver sands of Fedu Island in one of the Maldive atolls. It was almost sunset and the fruit bats were gliding between the palm trees, their shadows on the beach causing him to start occasionally. Father Matheson was engrossed in searching amongst the coral in the shallows for the bountiful riches of the Indian Ocean: seashells.

Fedu was encircled, like all the Maldive Islands, by a fringing reef of stony corals which hid, amongst its star and staghorn varieties, the shells which the priest was seeking. There were seven such islands, in a rough circle, containing a deep lagoon. This was Father Matheson's parish. Fedu was the largest of the seven, being four miles long by one mile wide, and visits to the smaller islands were made by *dhoni* canoe across the still, blue waters of the lagoon. As missionary posts went, it was good with respect to location and environment – a place of tranquillity and harmonious beauty – but bad in terms of Christian converts.

The islanders were a semi-pygmy race with an average height of around four feet. There were close ties to Sri Lanka in the north and the inhabitants were virtually all Moslems. The elderly Anglican priest had made only twelve converts since his arrival and two of these hardly counted since it now seemed they had joined the Christian Church because it allowed them to drink alcohol and smoke cigarettes to their hearts' content. A third member of the Father's church counted even less, in terms of conquest over Islam. She was his wife.

Still, Father Matheson did not despair. He was a stout-hearted man with a cheerful disposition and the tourists, ever-increasing in number, helped to fill the tin shack he called his church. They came all the year round, since the islands were in equatorial seas, and, human nature being what it is, people who had rarely attended services at their own churches back home in England, found themselves being persuaded to go to Father Matheson's whitewashed hut, with its simple cross adorning the roof.

He liked to think it was the islands that pulled them in: that associations with Eden and Heaven were so strong that tourists sought spiritual paradise within the tangible one loaned to them by the Maldivian Tourist Board for three weeks. However, he was aware that his gentle bullying during his walks amongst the bodies on the beach might have something to do with the half-filled church on a Sunday morning. Perhaps the truth lay closer to factors involving free time, the availability of wide-brimmed floppy white hats for women, the feeling of optimism engendered by sunshine, the total lack of worries and responsibility while on holiday, and the novelty value of a quaint missionary church overlooking a blue lagoon.

Father Matheson liked to tell people that he was a collector, of anything useless to nature or humankind. Since he had arrived at Fedu, he had spent many a glorious sunset wandering along the beach in search of seashells. The Indian Ocean has a treasure store of such objects, of myriad shapes and colours, bequeathing a legacy of beauty to the beachcombers of its coral islands. The priest believed he had become something of an expert in conchology since his arrival two years previously.

At first, he had allowed local fishermen to bring him live shells – that is, shells with living molluscs still inhabiting them – but after receiving a lecture from a visiting Buddhist friend, on the immorality of killing harmless creatures in order to possess their houses, he had made a solemn vow to collect only dead shells.

Father Matheson's walk along the beach was proving to be quite fruitful. The previous evening, there had been a storm – it was the beginning of the monsoon season – and the beach was littered with the shells of freshly dead molluscs, scoured from the reef by wild waves and thrown up on to the sands. He had already found a Strigate Auger, a small but perfect specimen, which reminded him of the spire he wanted to build for his church, once he had the money. Also in the pockets of his khaki shorts were a Triumphant Star and a Pontifical Mitre. Conchology draws many of its names from the Christian religion.

As he picked his way along the coral sands, humming, Father Matheson found himself in the shallows. Carefully, wary of coral snakes and stone fish, both deadly, he began turning over a few rocks.

A moray eel glided past his plimsolled foot. While he was keen to find shells, he did not wish to be bitten, and prepared to abandon the shallows for the safer environs of the beach.

However, like all obsessed collectors, he could not resist that final, inviting rock, and turned it over gingerly with his toe.

The hairs on the back of his neck lifted.

'Lord Almighty!' he cried out loud.

For a whole minute he stood there in a state of complete shock, his eyes transfixed to the three inches of clear water immediately north of his left foot. Simultaneously, two emotions entered his heart like small harpoons: joy – the thrill of discovery – and despair. For once in his life, he wanted to be wrong. The dilemma he had placed himself in, by lifting that stone, was painful, and the worst of it was, he knew which alternative he had to take. He had made his decision some time ago, after the talk with his Buddhist friend. He had made an oath before God.

Abdulla Fasil was a fanatical Moslem, who felt he had good reason to hate the British. Exiled from Aden during the British occupation of the Protectorate, for supposedly fomenting revolt, Fasil had travelled by dhow to the Maldives and had begun a business as a merchant, far from the shores of his birth. By the time the British left Aden, in 1967, his business network was so well established throughout the Maldives that he could not leave without incurring a heavy financial loss, and, if Fasil had a weakness, it was money. He did not *love* money, he respected it; as one who had been poor – a gamin of the backstreets – he was impressed by its power.

Ever since Father Matheson had come to the islands, again with the

the British Forces stationed on nearby Gan Island, Fasil had waited for an opportunity to get his own back on his old enemies. Matheson was a priest of the despised Christian religion, and British: a legitimate target in Fasil's *jihad*, the holy war in which Fasil was an army of one.

Like most expatriates in the Maldives, he was a conchologist, gathering shells for profit as well as for his own collection. Unlike the British priest, he took the business seriously and regarded himself as a professional, while the Father was but a rank amateur. Fasil knew the priest thought of himself as an expert, but the truth was there were some big gaps in the Englishman's knowledge. This ignorance would be the death of him, literally, that very evening.

Father Matheson writhed in frustration and let out a whimper.

'A test,' he groaned. 'I'm being tested.'

In the shallow depression where the rock had been were two gold-coloured shells nestling together like sleeping angels. Five inches long and cone-shaped, they were, as any amateur would know, *Coni Gloriamaris* – Glory of the Seas. The Glory was the rarest shell on the earth, and these two were *alive*.

'What am I going to do?' cried the priest, staring miserably at the treasure he could not possess without breaking his word to God.

Instinctively, he glanced at the tide and saw that it was on its way in. Once it covered the shallows the creatures would be on the move and would be lost to him forever. Not only must he say goodbye to a shell that would have enhanced his collection beyond his wildest dreams, but its twin could have been sold to a collector for enough money to provide the church with a spire, and more besides.

There were just seventy *Coni Gloriamaris* known to the world – often found in pairs – and now two more of the precious jewels of the ocean lay at his feet: regal shells with elegant reticulated patterns suggestive of the finest embroidery.

Arguments began to rage through his head. Tons of whelks, cockles and oysters were consumed every day, all over the globe, by clergy as well as laymen. A Glory of the Seas was no different to a whelk, was it? It was just a shellfish, coming somewhere between a jellyfish and a cod in the Chain of Being. A cow had more brains, more sense and sensitivity, more awareness, and goodness knows, he still ate beef. What if he cooked and ate the creatures? And a spire for the church. Why, that might be just the thing to attract more converts! The Maldivians were impressed by aesthetic religious artefacts: a tall, white wooden spire on the church might wean them away from the mosque, with its needle-like minaret?

Surely God would not disapprove of an action that would collect Christian souls, to the glory of His name?

Father Matheson hopped from one rock to another, as the tide began to surge over the reef and the sun dipped rapidly below the curved horizon.

It was no use. He had given his word. Such arguments were expedients: he was being tempted, as had been Our Lord Jesus Christ, in the wilderness, by the Devil.

What if, he thought, I were to take them and keep them in a tank of seawater? Then the decision could be postponed indefinitely – until they had died and become legitimate spoils.

But this, too, seemed like a betrayal, and he knew that once they were in his hands he would call them his own. He would not be strong enough to resist the forces of his instincts and enthusiasms as a collector if ever his fingers touched those golden cones, with their beautiful dog-tooth markings, shining up at him.

'Perfect,' he groaned. 'They're so perfect. If only they were chipped or blemished in some way – but they're . . . they're not. Why me?'

As the tide began to raise the level of the water above his ankles, Father Matheson spied a tourist walking along the beach. A plan formed rapidly in his mind. He would show the tourist the shells and hope that the man – an American by the look of him – would take the cones. If luck was with him the tourist would not realise the value of the find and Father Matheson could purchase one of them the next day, when they were dead.

At the last moment, he rejected his plan. He knew it was an unworthy compromise and anyway, the tourist would probably take the shells and have them made into earrings for his wife. What a sacrilege that would be.

He let the man go by, with a sad wave of his hand.

Darkness fell and the waters splashed around the Father's knees. The sea was a dangerous place, especially at night. He stepped out on to the shore and, in a melancholy mood, made his way home. God had triumphed over Satan.

The door opened and Abdulla Fasil stood before him with open arms.

'Welcome,' said the Arab. 'I have long looked forward to such a visit from my Christian brother.'

'I'm honoured to be here,' replied the Englishman, not unconscious of the irony of the situation. Fasil had spoken to him very little since they had first met two years previously, and Father Matheson had gained a strong impression of hostility from the merchant. Still, people could change, and perhaps Fasil had come to respect and accept him, now that he had made it plain that he was not just some itinerant priest who gave up at the first hurdle? Father Matheson accepted the offered hug with a natural reticence, due partly to the reserve for which his nation was famous, and partly to the personal inhibitions of an introvert.

Father Matheson cleared his throat as he was released and said, shyly, '*Salaam ali cum*.'

Fasil beamed.

'Ah, you do your homework, my friend. Peace be with you. Very gratifying – the fact that you took the trouble to learn . . .'

'Not at all. Not at all. This is your home – I must observe your customs.'

Father Matheson was shown into a spacious living room, rich with tapestries and carpets, and smelling of incense. There was a low table, set with food and drink. He was surprised to see furniture. Somehow he had expected they would be eating on the floor, sitting on cushions. But perhaps that was foolish of him?

They sat on bamboo chairs and Fasil motioned for Father Matheson to begin eating. He did so, remembering to use the correct hand, in observance of Fasil's customs.

'So,' said Fasil, 'here we are. This is your anniversary. Two years today.'

'You are very observant.'

'Not at all. As a merchant I must be aware of the calendar – of times and tides, of seasons. The markets of the world have their moods, which vary with the weather.'

'Just the same . . .' Father Matheson took a mouthful of the stew: it was hot and spicy and he tried not to show it. He felt his eyes watering. A hurricane lamp was burning fiercely just above their heads and its fumes were making the priest feel a little dizzy.

Fasil said, 'I keep note of all things which are of interest to me.' His eyes glittered in the light.

'I'm flattered you should find me of interest.'

The giddy feeling began to pass and Father Matheson began to feel more comfortable. Through the open window of the house came the sounds of treefrogs and cicadas. Around the hurricane lamp was a cloud of midges and one or two large, furry moths. These were aspects which the priest had never allowed himself to get used to. They were reminders of how rich in life these islands were. At home, people got excited if they saw a single shrew, or hedgehog, in their garden. Here, there were times when you could not step outside the front door for fear of perpetrating a massacre. After the rains, it was not unusual to see the whole island carpeted with snails and frogs. God's creatures were in abundance here, and the priest, raised in a city, found in that exciting evidence of a healthy, vigorous land.

After the meal, Fasil took him to another room, to show him an immense collection of seashells which took his breath away. There were wooden trays full of tritons, drupes, augers, olives, cowries, abalones, murexes: all neatly labelled and stacked in racks. The gloss on some of them might give rise to the belief that they had been varnished, to enhance their brilliant colours and intricate patterns, but as a collector himself, Father Matheson knew that one *never* improved the appearance of a shell artificially. The sheen was the result of a mollusc's mantle sliding back and forth over the outer surface of the shell.

'How do you clean your freshly dead?' asked the priest.

The merchant shrugged.

'I prefer not to use chemicals. It sometimes damages the shell. The natural method is always the best – bury them by an ant hill and let the ants eat them clean.'

'You have a large number here.'

Another shrug.

'But a fraction of the fifty thousand species known to us. Still, I admit. It is a good collection.'

Father Matheson picked up a Turkey Wing, a bi-valve with its distinctive halves of shell.

'Very nice,' he remarked.

'Ah, but you prefer the volutes, I am led to believe.'

'The cones – yes. I do find them more attractive than the bi-valves. Why only today, I found . . . that is, I *saw* . . .'

The Arab interrupted him.

'Later, I shall have something for you. A present. A cone that is rare in these waters – I'm sure it will make a fine addition to your collection.'

Father Matheson was taken aback.

'That's very kind of you.'

'Not at all. Now, observe these Strawberry Tops – how the scarlet flecks stand proud of the . . .'

The merchant continued to lecture, his manner becoming more agitated by the minute. Finally, he said, 'Please wait here. There is something I must fetch.' And he left Father Matheson holding a Perspective Sundial. He carefully placed the delicate shell back in its place on the tray.

Once outside, Fasil breathed deeply of the night air. He tried to concentrate on the noise – no, the *sound*, for noise implied something unpleasant – the sound of the breakers on the reef. It helped to clear his head. Despite what the British authorities in Aden had said, Fasil had not yet killed another man. For the first time in his life he wished he smoked, or chewed qāt – something that might calm his nerves. This was not as easy as he had anticipated.

Still, he had to go through with it. He had made an oath before Allah, and that was something which was unbreakable. He had to go through with it.

Reluctantly he pulled on a leather glove. Then he reached down, into a basin of seawater, extracting a live shellfish about two inches long. He held it up, in the light coming from the open doorway. It was a *Conus Geographus*, a beautiful shell with a marbled, pinkish-brown surface. It was also deadly. One of the killer cones. There were only three – the *Striatus*, the *Textile* and the rare *Geographus* – and the last was perhaps the most venomous, the most potent. The harmless-looking mollusc harboured a needle-sized harpoon containing a paralysing toxin, with which it injected small fish.

Fasil placed the creature on the ground, removed his glove and then gingerly picked up the shellfish by the back of its cone, ensuring that the opening, into which the mollusc had withdrawn, was pointing away from his flesh.

Shaking a little, the merchant went inside.

He was going to go through with his vow.

Father Matheson was studying a tray of cowries – Isabellines – when Fasil re-entered the room. Father Matheson's shaggy hair, stiff probably from the salt sea spray which drifted across the island during the monsoons, made him look like some kind of demon. Fasil swallowed hard. The adrenaline was racing around his veins.

'A gift,' he managed to say without faltering. 'I have a gift here, which you might appreciate.'

The priest looked up.

'A cone? My, that's a beauty. For me?'

'A present for my Christian friend,' said the Moslem, quickly, trying to keep the excitement out of his voice. 'Please take it.'

'Well, is it rare?' asked the other man.

Fasil knew then that his plan was succeeding. The properties of the cone were unknown to his guest.

'It is here, in the Maldives. Please, take it.'

He stretched forth his arm. An oath was an oath, although he wished now he had not been so rash, so blinded by his hatred. His enemy seemed so vulnerable: such an easy target. Too much trust. The priest had too much trust in his fellow men.

Father Matheson offered his palm; pink, soft and unprotected.

'This is extremely generous of you.'

Fasil hesitated. Had the light dimmed, or was that a trick of the mind? He could hear his own breath, labouring from his lungs. Surely the treefrogs had stopped calling? And the waves on the reef . . .? No, impossible. The frogs perhaps, but not the waves. It was the blood, pounding in his ears, blocking out all other sounds.

Suddenly, there was a swift movement, a blur before Fasil's vision. Father Matheson's hand was no longer extended. He had whipped it back to his side.

'I'm sorry,' said the priest, 'I don't want to seem impolite or ungrateful, but that creature's still alive. I can't accept it.'

'What?'

Was it possible he had been mistaken? That the priest knew of the deadly properties of the Geography Cone? However, all he could feel at this moment was a tremendous sense of relief. He had kept his word. The shellfish had been *offered*. Its rejection, though unexpected, did not mean Fasil had broken his oath.

The priest said, 'You obviously don't understand. You see, I have made a vow not to collect live shellfish. I promised – this is going to sound pompous – I promised God not to harm another one of those creatures. Seems a little immoral, though I'm not suggesting others follow my example, to kill things just for gain.'

He seemed to be struggling for words.

'This . . . this does sound pompous, doesn't it? And probably a little silly. But, there it is. Silly or not, I made a vow. Why . . .' The priest made a gesture of resignation. '. . . why, only today I discovered two *Coni Gloriamaris* in a rock pool – had to leave them there.'

Fasil carefully placed the Geography Cone on the table and stared in amazement at the priest.

'You abandoned a Glory of the Seas?'

'Two in fact. Two of the most perfect-looking beggars you're ever likely to come across. Tragic, isn't it? From a collector's point of view? But they were live, you see, and from their perspective, I imagine it wasn't such a sad thing. Pretty jolly, in fact.'

Fasil shook his head, trying to clear it of the buzzing noise. Had that mollusc speared him? No, he was just overcome. That someone should abandon a Glory of the Seas – 'two, in fact' – because of . . . He remembered his own vow and looked on the priest with new respect.

'You realise you left a fortune out there, to be taken away by the tide?'

Father Matheson sighed. 'I know, I know. I could have used the money – a new church spire – but, that's life.'

Fasil reached out and shook the priest's hand.

'You know I hated you, when you first arrived. But I want you to know that what you did out there today shows tremendous strength of character, my friend. I admire you for it.'

'Oh, come, come. You're as much a man of your word as I am.' The priest paused and then said, 'You know, after I walked away from those Glories, I thought something good was going to happen to me. One is always tempted, after such a deed, to think that the act of self-sacrifice deserves a reward. But . . .' He stopped, and smiled. '. . . that's a selfish consideration, if you like.'

'Rewards,' replied Fasil, quietly, 'are not always evident to the person to whom they are given.'

The merchant then picked up the Geography Cone and left the room with it. As he was placing it back into the bowl of seawater, he could hear the priest's voice saying, 'You're right of course. The only rewards worth having are to be found in Heaven – mine, or yours, I don't suppose it matters which . . .'

# Blood Orange

An expatriate 'gone native' was something of a cliché just after the war. Some of us just could not go home: would have found it impossible to face relatives and friends. Some of us stayed in Singapore because we were not the same people that had been sent out there. Internment had changed us drastically and we knew that we fitted into life more easily in the east than in our birthplace. Some of us, those like me, simply could not let go of the small patch of soil which had forced such dramatic changes upon our lives.

So we had stayed on, poverty ensuring that the only way we could do so was to live simply, in the most primitive conditions. It was because of our meagre pensions that we lived like the natives, not because we were ascetics or had found the secret of the Orient.

When I was released from Changi POW camp in 1945, I was twenty-four years of age. The hair on my chest had gone white and crisp. I was thin, wasted and hollow, both inside and out. I moved only two hundred yards from where I had slept for four years, to a hut in the kampong immediately outside Changi jail. There I stayed and here I will die.

One aspect of Japanese life I have adopted from my captors: a strong sense of ritual and a respect for symbolism. It is necessary to point this out, in order that I am not considered mad when I say that, every morning, I devour a child of the sun.

The earliest light of the day is filtered greenly by the canopy of palm leaves above my rattan bed. Half an hour later the sun's rays strike my face and I know it is time to rise. My bed is situated on the veranda of my hut and the first thing I see, as I search for my sandals with my feet, is a narrow, worn-earth pathway through a long arch of vegetation, at the end of which stands Changi jail.

It has of course reverted to its role as a civil, and military, prison, but it has changed little from the days when Japanese soldiers manned its pointed watchtowers. I suppose I could best describe it as looking like a Turkish fortification. It has a Middle Eastern appearance about it that is a little incongruous among the Singapore temples.

Over the pathway bats glide, seeking diurnal resting places after the night's hunting. There are insects, too, the size of hummingbirds.

Cultivated flame trees fill the morning with scarlet blossoms and there are other rich colours on the bushes that line the walk. Singapore is only just saved, by the sombre dark green of the more prolific wild palms that serve to dampen down what might otherwise be a vulgar show.

I rise from my bed and take my breakfast, which is always the same: an orange – a blood orange, if I can get it. It is a fruit that seems to be available the whole year round in these times of plenty.

I begin the ritual by peeling the object, placing the skin aside for afterwards. Then I split the flesh into segments, to destroy that appearance of a human brain. I form a line of them on the dish. I eat the segments slowly, crushing them with my toothless gums to release the lifeblood of the fruit. Finally, once all the segments have been devoured, I break the rind into small pieces and swallow them.

This morning the ritual is a painful experience – spiritually painful – and I do it because I deserve to suffer. A sense of betrayal needs sustenance to stay alive, like anything else. I feed it daily.

Daniel and I were interned together, when the Japanese overran Singapore in 1942. We were both twenty years of age and bewildered by the predicament in which we found ourselves.

For two years we had been enjoying the heady atmosphere and freedom of an exotic island, with its liberal – no, *licentious* – attitudes and its mystical culture. We had been drugged by the place, the lion city, with its temples, erotic carvings and bars full of girls. That we should confuse culture, religion and sex, and not see the pathos beneath the glitter of the night life, the sad plight of the females with whom we consorted, was barely excusable by our youth. We took things at face value, being shallow boys looking to enrich our experience of life. Of course, we looked in the wrong places, boys always do. Sensitivity is a gift of the older, more reflective man. *Sensuality* governs the young.

We were totally unprepared for the privation which was to follow such an uncontrolled existence. Of course, we told each other at the time, there was no question that we would not survive. We would see each other through. There were others who would not make it, because they could not rely on the support of a friend.

Daniel and I had been raised together from the age of four. We had attended the same schools – not very good ones – and had joined the Air Force together as mechanics at the age of eighteen. We were totally committed to one another.

It is true we quarrelled on occasion: most close friends do. Such comradeship is like a marriage, excluding the physical element. Certainly we had shared the same bed with each other, and our girlfriends, uninhibited by the presence of a friend.

Daniel was the more outgoing personality. He was not the brash extrovert who bores his listeners, but a youth with many social graces, and I was a little jealous of him at times. The ease with which he communicated with others left me feeling quite inadequate. Being the quieter, I clung to his coat-tails on social occasions, standing by his side and only injecting a remark into the conversation when there was a lull. Strangely, I was thought the cleverer, because of this, but it was essentially a cheat. Whereas Daniel was fair and lively, I was dark and moody, and in allowing him the floor most of the time, I had the leisure to form some witticism in my mind and to insert it at an appropriate point.

Daniel was always the first to praise such witticisms, always carefully placed, and would put his hand on my shoulder, saying, 'You've got to get up early to catch this lad. He's as sharp as a razor . . .'

Thus, quite wrongly, I earned the reputation for being a street intellectual; someone who said little, but when he did open his mouth, by God something smart came out.

The other area in which I was envious of Daniel was sport. He had an athletic body which he used to its best advantage. He was a brilliant swimmer, could dive to competition standard, boxed very well and was in the Far East rugby team. Those were only his major achievements: he could play most sports and games to a reasonable level. Consequently, he was very successful with girls: the two often go hand-in-hand. The daughters of older, married-accompanied servicemen sought him out at functions and dances. Strangely, he was a rotten dancer. I was much better. I had a natural feel for the rhythm and my loose-limbed frame seemed fashioned for movements put to music.

This made little difference to Daniel's standing amongst the young females. They dragged him on to the floor and insisted on trying to teach him the rudiments of dancing, and his awkward, jerky steps, instead of frustrating them, merely amused them and endeared him to them.

Daniel's quick thinking saved my life on two occasions in Singapore. Once, ignoring his advice, I swam too far out into the straits and got into difficulties in the fast currents of those dangerous waters. He coaxed and bullied me back to shore, refusing afterwards to consider his efforts to have been of any consequence. Instead of chastising me for my stupidity, he praised my stamina and endurance, saying that if *he* had had cramp in such circumstances, he could not have remained as cool and clear-headed as I had done. But it was only his presence that had prevented me from succumbing to panic: his calming influence. I had not had cramp and pure funk had caused me to struggle at a time when I should have acted rationally, thus causing myself to get caught in the mainstream of fast-flowing water.

On the second occasion, we were walking across Changi golf course, myself in the lead, when a cobra reared up not a yard in front. I froze as the snake sat, swaying its hooded head before me. I think it would have struck had not Daniel thrown his shirt over it, like a gladiator's net. We left the shirt where it was, and ran.

Daniel was shrieking with laughter, while I shook in terror at the thought of what might have happened. It was as if he had just performed some schoolboy prank. It was not nervous laughter. Danger to him was an exhilarating experience. It was *fun*. It acted on his body like breathing pure oxygen. He got high on it. His eyes would sparkle and the excitement would be apparent in his whole demeanour.

Whenever he retold this story, he maintained that I had deliberately distracted the cobra long enough for him to remove his shirt. I was the hero, not him, because my part was the more dangerous of the two.

I almost came to believe this version myself, he recounted it with such conviction, his hand on my shoulder and his pride in me evident in every word and gesture. Yet when I recalled the incident, truthfully, I remembered that he had not been wearing his shirt; he had removed it earlier to improve his tan. It had been draped over his arm when we were confronted by the snake. But Daniel was like that. He preferred to share the glory, even to the point of giving me the major role.

I hated Daniel for his selflessness, his modesty, the purity of his friendship. He turned truth into a lie which I had to live and act. I had to pretend to be this person he had made me into – brave, clever and the perfect friend.

I lived in constant dread of being exposed as a fraud, of Daniel turning to me one day and accusing me of all the falsehoods with which he had moulded me. He never did. Always his shoulders were there, ready for me to climb upon. Always his hand was willingly extended to pull me up beside him, to share in any glory. I hated him for it.

When the Japanese arrived we were ordered by our officers to parade on Changi airstrip. The first enemy soldiers I saw were riding bicycles: small, wiry men looking as if they were on their way to work at some factory. They took little notice of us, but dumped their machines before lining the route along which came one of their high-ranking officers in a staff car.

I was not afraid at that time. I certainly *had* been, before it was obvious that we were going to surrender and not have to fight to the last man to defend the island. After which, I relaxed and prepared for the inevitable. Daniel did, at one point, suggest taking a boat and trying for one of the many islands that lay south of Singapore, but I persuaded him of the futility of the scheme. The Japanese would certainly have found us.

We were herded into Changi jail, which became a prisoner-of-war camp, and we very quickly realised that our lives, henceforth, were to become one long fight against the ravages of malnutrition and disease. The Japanese guards became almost superfluous: there was nowhere to run to, even if we did escape, and the real enemy had become hunger exacerbated by dysentery. All talk centred around the stomach and bowels. Personal possessions – watches, pens, lighters – became the currency with which to buy food, and we found that this was best achieved by forming groups and pooling our resources.

I was forever on the brink of starvation and on the edge of some indefinable illness. Until you have known such unrelenting hunger and the violent misery of constantly inflamed bowels, you cannot imagine what despair the spirit suffers. It is an oppression which seems eternal. Hell could devise no worse punishment for its inmates. Around me, all the time, men died of broken spirits. They simply gave up, realising that death, whatever it was like, must be better than a life spent in constant worry about finding something to put in at one end of the body which would cause agony, later, at the other end.

It was indeed an attractive thought, that one could leave all the wretchedness behind simply by ceasing to breathe. To drift away from that detestable body and its functions, its interminable craving for nourishment, its whining, whimpering, self-pitying spirit, seemed like a sensible and blessed act.

But Daniel would not countenance surrender to the body. He insisted we fight against such considerations, our combined strength helping each other through.

'I want to live,' he said. 'And you, too. We'll prop each other up. Support each other. One of us, alone, can't make it – but together we can do it . . .'

This was a daily lecture, and indeed, such talk kept me from suicide in that humid, heavy climate that pressed down on one's soul, squeezing it dry of will and purpose.

Through guile, charm and artful manipulation, Daniel managed to get us a job, cleaning out Lieutenant Matsumara's quarters. For this work we each received extra rations, directly from our patron, though this was kept secret from the other prisoners and Captain Yakusha, the camp's Deputy Commander. It was only light, domestic housework, but it left us feeling enormously fatigued. At the end of two hours of sweeping, dusting, scrubbing and washing clothes, we would be exhausted. I complained bitterly about this fact to Daniel, quite forgetting that we were in a privileged position and receiving more than most other prisoners. Daniel rarely commented on these outbursts from me, knowing that they stemmed from something beyond that which could be put into words.

When Matsumara returned, to inspect his rooms after our cleaning sessions, Daniel would always be smiling, to show his gratitude; an attitude which seemed to please the Japanese officer. He appeared to like Daniel, though his expression never revealed such feelings, and he was fascinated by our close friendship.

He would say to us in his broken English:

'Which one you is the strong?'

Daniel would reply, 'We support each other. Our strength is in our unity.'

Once, probably one of the only times I spoke to Matsumara without being asked a direct question, I added, 'We would die for one another.'

Matsumara was impressed, but whether it was the words, or merely because I, the silent one, had uttered them, I do not know.

He said to me, slowly, 'You would die for your friend?'

'Yes. I would give my life for him, if I had to.'

His keen, Oriental-brown eyes studied me for a long time, while Daniel smiled, looking from one to the other of us, and finally, Matsumara said, 'Yes, you would.'

*I would give my life for him.* The words had not been spoken in truth, but because they had been expected of me, at some time, by my friend. I was still playing the role he had written for me, encouraged me to act. I must have been good at it, for Matsumara accepted it as fact.

Matsumara was a young officer who had recently been promoted from the ranks: a field promotion, for valour, he told us. He was in fact a fairly ignorant man – not unintelligent, but unlearned and lazy. His father was a peasant farmer, but Matsumara had distinguished himself on the field of battle and had brought himself to the notice of his superiors. He valued, above all things, courage. He was not a happy man. Most of his fellow officers were from high-born families and his lack of education was apparent – I believe he was held in scorn by his contemporaries. I was convinced he could hardly count and said to Daniel that any figure past the number of six left him confused. Why I chose this figure, I do not know, for I had no proof of it being the threshold of his mathematics, but for some reason I needed a simple encapsulating definition of his educational weakness. Whenever Daniel started defending the Japanese lieutenant, I would always fall back on my dismissive statement: 'The man's a dunce. He can't even count past six.'

Once, Daniel said, 'Does that matter?' But I was so angry with him for questioning my judgement, he never again gave me any argument. He realised, I suppose, that I was grasping at some irrational means of identifying Matsumara. In order to bring the man within my sphere of contempt, I reduced him to something smaller and more insignificant than myself. It was necessary to me that I could look down on the officer who terrified me.

Oh, yes, I was afraid of him. I did not understand the man or his culture. I thought him unpredictable and unreasonable. To me he had a lunatic's eyes and mannerisms and I could not trust his moods or rationality. No doubt he was as sane as any man caught up in a war, but I always felt insecure in his presence and worried that at any moment he might turn on me with the impulsiveness of a wild beast.

Matsumara was, like many Japanese officers, fascinated by his sword. He would be forever cleaning the blade, or honing it to a brilliant sharpness. He doted on it, lovingly, telling us as we cleaned around his desk that it was a *shinshinto* blade – a *new-new* sword – dating back only to 1860. It was a *katana*, a long sword, slung from the waist and worn with the edge upwards. He showed us the gently undulating temper line and the tight *itame* grain. There were stylised Sanskrit characters on the steel which he translated for us.

'Yamano Nagahisa: cut through two bodies.'

'Yamano Naganari: cut through three bodies.'

These were the weapon's previous owners. Matsumara often said, rather wistfully, that he had not yet had the opportunity to test the weapon's strength on a man. He wanted his own inscription on the blade. This was another reason why he terrified me. I felt that he only needed one small excuse for an execution.

The months passed and somehow Daniel and I survived. But we sank ever lower, both spiritually and physically.

Matsumara, anxious to be of active service to his Emperor, became irritable at being left in the stagnant backwater of Changi POW camp. He took out his frustration on us, sometimes beating us with a bamboo rod when the cleanliness of the hut was not up to his standard, which varied from day to day. He seemed forever dissatisfied with everyone around him, complaining about the prisoners, the guards and his fellow officers. As things went, his treatment of us was comparatively humane. Other Japanese were far more cruel in their disciplinary punishments. Then, suddenly, Matsumara found a new, subtle torture, a game, which seemed to satisfy his need to strike deeply into our spirits and helped to alleviate his bitterness.

He received a gift from his father in Japan: a box of oranges. Each day he would put three or four out in a bowl and then excuse himself while we cleaned his rooms. Just the scent of those fruits was enough to make my head reel and drive my senses crazy. I slavered over them, as I polished the desk top and touched their textured forms with aching fingers.

I dreamed about those oranges every waking and sleeping hour. They were the children of the evening sun: spherical golden objects full of goodness. One of them, just one of them, I convinced myself, could prove to be the panacea for all my bodily complaints. Rice and biscuits were sawdust in comparison to those beautiful, succulent fruits that adorned Matsumara's desk top. I was driven mad by their fragrance, by the sight of them. I tasted the juice, the flesh, in my dreams – burying my teeth in the segments, letting the amber liquid run down my chin, lapping it back into my mouth with my tongue. I tormented myself with thoughts of how I should peel the fruit, working slowly from the top. Then I should break it, first in half, then in quarters, admiring the grain, the golden threads of flesh. Then to shred my first segment, placing it between my teeth, sucking the wonderful fluid down, feeling the citric acid stinging my parched throat. My body would tingle with the electric sensation of vitamin C, as it worked its way through my torso, driving out the inflammation, the ulcerations. It would find my limbs and cure the external sores, the swellings, the constant fever. No longer would I shake and shiver, sweat and overheat, in my bed at night. The orange would wash away the malaria. The mere odour, as I pressed it to my mouth, would clear my head of the demonic ache that plagued me from morning to night, from dusk to dawn. Just a single one of those oranges held the combined secrets to perfect health of all the wizards, physicians and sorcerers, collected since the beginning of time.

Matsumara knew. Oh yes, he knew. He would watch us as we cleaned, noting when our eyes strayed to the bowl, for Daniel was just as obsessed by the fruit as I was myself.

The Japanese officer knew also how to increase the intensity of that obsession. He would pick one up, turn it over in his hand and sniff it with those wide nostrils, then rub it against his cheek. Then the ritual would start.

He would begin by peeling the object, placing the skin aside for afterwards. Then he would split the flesh into segments, forming a line of them on his dish. He would eat the segments slowly, crushing them between his lips to release the lifeblood of the fruit. It would dribble down his chin and he would wipe it back into his mouth with a stubby finger. Finally, once all the segments had been devoured, he would break the rind into small pieces and chew them, before swallowing.

The ritual was a painful experience for me – spiritually painful – and I suffered with every mouthful that he took.

Afterwards, he would give us our oatmeal biscuits – the payment for our services – knowing that they would taste like ashes in our mouths after his exhibition.

He knew the depths of his cruelty, the depravity of his actions, but when I think about it now I believe he could not help himself. He was desperately lonely – a peasant officer among aristocrats – and he wanted to be where the fighting was, out in the Pacific. He had been dumped and forgotten, and it gnawed at his spirit. Rejected by his fellow officers, out of contact with the rankers, left to rot in a prison camp, he was boiling with contained anger. He had no release valve and turned that emotion to poisonous pleasure. He needed to hurt, and we were available. I do not, now, believe he was a naturally vindictive man, but his situation produced something from the corner of his soul, blew it up, expanded it, until his spirit became a balloon full of nothing but foul gases.

Always there were only three or four oranges in the bowl. There was no way we could steal one without Matsumara knowing. The penalty for such an act would be death. So we continued to stare dumbly at the wonderful spheres and suffered the distress of watching them disappear down Matsumara's throat, one by one.

Despite Matsumara's new torture, he was as talkative as ever with Daniel. He told us, for I was always there to listen, of stories of courage amongst Japanese heroes. Daniel, in his turn, would contribute one of his own tales, and in most of these it amused him to make me the protagonist. It gave my friend a kick to see Matsumara's eyes stray to my silent form as he related some courageous incident in which I was the hero and, quite often, Daniel was the man rescued from drowning, or saved from the deadly bite of the cobra. It was in Daniel's make-up, his personality, that he could not keep a good story contained. He had to tell it, if the opportunity arose. But he was too modest to make himself the hero of the piece, even when that was the fact, so he switched the roles around.

Matsumara would look in my direction, as I swept the floor, or dusted his military reference books, and say, 'He is brave man. I see it in his eyes. I feel it in my heart. He speaks little, but his courage is strong.'

One day there were seven oranges in the bowl. Matsumara had left us alone. I stole one of the fruits.

Daniel said, 'Don't be a fool. He'll know.'

'He can't count,' I said, the hand holding the orange trembling violently. 'It'll be all right.'

Daniel protested, pleaded with me, getting angry. I stood there, strangely impervious to all his arguments. He could have taken it from me by force, but he didn't, and finally we heard Matsumara's footsteps on the front porch. I ran out of the back door and hid the fruit at the bottom of a pail, covering it with cleaning rags. I still had the bucket in my hand when I was called inside.

I went into the hut and found Matsumara confronting Daniel. The lieutenant was in a terrible rage. His face was ugly with wrath as he screamed at me to stand beside my friend. He could hardly get the words out, he was choking on his anger.

He thrust his face before Daniel's.

'Someone has eat one orange.'

Daniel said nothing. I waited and waited, my heart thumping and my legs shaking so badly they would hardly keep me upright, but no words came from the mouth of my friend. Out of the corner of my eye I could see he was white with fear and this increased my own feelings of terror. I could sense a wetness in my shorts.

'Speak!' screamed Matsumara.

But for once Daniel was silent. He stood there, in his stained khaki shorts and dirty vest, and his mouth remained tightly closed, though his eyes were still full of panic. The lieutenant sniffed his breath, then mine, and shook his head in frustration. We both had gum disease and the foul breath that went with it.

Matsumara drew his sword. Its glinting hurt my eyes as the rays of the sun from the window struck the blade. I could see the edge, brilliant in its deadly beauty, as the light seared along the honed temper line. I could not take my eyes from the weapon. It seemed to have a cold personality of its own, like a shark whose purpose blinds it to all but death.

The savage face was now before my own.

'You! Did you steal orange?'

Even now I cannot recall why I answered as I did. At the time I believe my consternation was so great that I hardly knew where I was, let alone what I was saying. It was not courage, that much is certain. It might have been that his fury filled me with dread, and like a recalcitrant schoolboy, faced by an enraged master, I wanted only to soothe, to appease the man. This is not altogether satisfactory and I only use it as an excuse in my most desperate moments of guilt, when I am overwhelmed by the horror of my betrayal of my best friend. In my more truthful moods I admit to myself that, deep down, I knew how my words would be taken. I knew that Matsumara considered me a selfless, brave man and the perfect friend. I knew that he admired such things above all other attributes in the character of a man.

I was aware that my hand still held the bucket which contained the stolen fruit. I placed it down, carefully.

'I stole the orange. I am the thief,' I said.

He stared into my features, for a long time, and then at Daniel, who remained unmoving, a slight, sickly smile forming at the corners of his mouth.

Then the lieutenant took Daniel by the hair and dragged him from the hut. I followed, stumbling down the wooden steps into the sunlight, as Daniel was forced to his knees on the hard-baked earth. My friend's head was bowed and he remained perfectly still, silent.

I saw – a dream-like scene – Matsumara raise the sword. It flashed once. There was a terrible sound. Daniel's head rolled at my feet, the neck raw and bloody.

That evening, I took the orange from its hiding place and went into a remote corner of the camp. I peeled it quickly and then broke it in half. Inside, there were red veins – blood-red veins – that ran through the raw flesh of the fruit, making it appear like an open wound.

It was a blood orange.

I stared at it in the dying light of the day. It was Daniel's head. I was holding Daniel's head in my hands.

I buried my mouth in the neck and sucked the blood from the severed veins. I remember I was crying. At least, I think I was crying. God knows, I tried hard enough. But it tasted so good. It tasted so good.